SALTED

LIFE ISN'T BETTER UNDER THE SEA

AARON
GALVIN

Aames & Abernathy Publishing

Salted

Salt Series: Book One

Copyright © 2014 by Aaron Galvin

Revised March 2016

Published by Aames & Abernathy Publishing, Chino Hills, CA USA

Edited by Annetta Ribken

You can find her at **wordwebbing.com**

Copy Edits by Jennifer Wingard **theindependentpen.com**

Cover Design by M.S. Corley, **mscorley.com**

Book Design and Layout by Valerie Bellamy, **dog-earbookdesign.com**

Small waves photo © Mibseo | Dreamstime Stock Photos & Stock Free Images

ISBN-10: 1497588073

ISBN-13: 978-1497588073

Printed in the USA

for Karen,
who has waited on this longer than anyone.

&

for Mom,
who is still holding out for the audiobook.

NO MATTER HOW BIG THE SEA MAY BE,

sometimes two ships meet.

—*Nautical Proverb*

+

to Kaden
Hope you enjoy
the read! :"

KELLEN

KELLEN WINSTEL STRODE OUT OF THE TIBER HIGH School administration office and past the school's glass trophy case. A picture of himself, seated atop a diving block at last year's Indiana state finals, caught his eye.

Kellen stopped. He looked good in that blue Speedo. The way he had tightened his muscles, the abs he trained so hard to firm up, and those pecs—no wonder the girls of Tiber High lingered around the trophy case just to stare at them. In truth, he lacked only an American flag draped over his shoulders to complete the Olympic poster boy image.

Much as he enjoyed admiring himself, it hadn't been the picture to make Kellen stop.

The pool water behind the diving block held his gaze.

He turned his head left to look at the Tiber High pool, twenty yards away. Three panes of floor-to-ceiling window glass typically allowed anyone walking by to look in. Today the overhead sliding metal gate shielded the pool from view.

All the better. Kellen left the trophy case and rounded the corner, bound for the school cafeteria. He heard the guffaws and trash talking long before he saw his friends.

Two of the football team's offensive lineman, Eddie Bennett and Ross Owens, sat at a lunch table with a scattered deck of cards in front of them. Both had a stockpile of rainbow colored candies. An even larger pile lay at the table's middle.

"I'll see your five and raise you ten," Bennett said, moving ten of his candies into the center. He cast a sidelong glance at Kellen. "Been waiting on you."

"You see him leave?"

"Nah. He didn't come my way. Might've got past Owens though. This idiot can't keep up with the game, let alone watch for Weaver too."

"Shut up," Owens growled.

"He should be in Phys. Ed.," Kellen said. "One of the office assistants looked it up for me."

"So what you're saying is—"

"He had to walk through the cafeteria to get there. How could you have missed him?"

"Sorry. Didn't see him, *Kelly.*"

Kellen clenched his fists. *Don't call me that.*

"Me neither," Owens said, studying his cards. He looked up at Bennett. "Did you say the bet's ten?"

"I raised you ten," Bennett replied. "You bet five. Five plus ten is fifteen, you freaking ogre. You need me to count it out for you too?"

Bennett reached across the table and counted out two additional groups of five.

"There! Now you have fifteen. Show me your cards."

Owens flipped them over.

"Pocket rockets?" Bennett slammed his fists on the table.

Laughing, Owens scooped up his winnings.

"Listen!" said Kellen. "We have less than thirty minutes to find that punk before next period."

"If he's in P.E., he'll have to come to the locker room sooner or later. We'll wait for him there," Bennett said.

"No. Weaver has a pass, same as me. He can roam the halls."

"Oh."

"Mell—h-s pr-bly in ma—lock—m," Owens tried to say through the wad of rainbow candy in his mouth.

"Huh?"

Owens swallowed and cleared his throat. "I said he's probably in the locker room."

Bennett straddled the bench he sat on. "Why would Weaver hide there? That's where we go to dodge class."

"It's the last place we'd look for him," said Owens.

A loud whistle echoed through the cafeteria.

"The heck was that?"

Bennett pointed to the study hall balcony above the cafeteria.

Kellen saw a reedy fifteen-year-old leaning over the open second-story ledge. The freshman insistently pointed to the gymnasium door before he ran down the steps.

"We sent Gao up there to watch while we played cards," said Bennett.

Jun Gao. Kellen frowned. Normally, Kellen would never allow a freshman around him in any circumstance, but he had yet to cross hooking up with an Asian chick off his bucket list. If letting Jun hang out convinced his older sister, Sydney, to go out sometime…

She'll come around. Kellen smirked. *Just like every other girl in Lavere County.*

"Guess you were right, Owens," Bennett said. "Now we just have to find out which locker room Wee-Wee went into!"

"Hey guys!" Jun called to them with all the excitement of a freshman being allowed to hang out with upper classmen. Half-running, half-prancing, he joined them before they turned the corner and made their way toward the locker rooms. "We going to mess Weaver up bad? What do you have planned this time, Kell?"

Kellen led the way down the hall. "He's going twelving."

Jun stopped. "You're kidding right? B-but that's just a story someone made up. You—you could kill him!"

He sounds afraid. Good. Let Weaver get a hint of what he's in for.

"Shut up, Gao," Bennett said. "Seniors can do what we want. Hey, Winst," he nudged Kellen. "What's twelving?"

Kellen didn't respond. He passed the entrance to the basketball gym on their right, then the girl's locker room on the left.

Bennett stopped at the girl's door. "Hey, Gao! Why don't you run in there and see if he's hiding."

"Why me?"

"Because the girls won't care if you see them buck naked. They know they're not your type."

Jun's face flushed red. "Funny."

"But true," Bennett said as he opened the door and disappeared inside.

"Isn't he going to at least tell the girls he's coming in?"

Owens kept walking. "Unlike you, Fresh, Bennett wants to see if there's any hotties in there. Speaking of, could you take a picture of your sister naked for me?"

"Ew," said Jun.

"Meh," Owens shrugged. "Worth a shot."

They continued on without Bennett, their sneakers echoing off the concrete floor. On any other day, Kellen would have kissed his fist and smacked the school logo—a tiger with navy stripes—as he passed. Today, even the thought of doing so escaped him.

A door slam echoed up the hall behind him.

"Maaaan, there wasn't even one girl in there!" Bennett complained as he jogged to join them.

Kellen reached the boy's locker room door and flung it open. It smacked the cinder block wall to announce his coming.

Inside, 7th grader Riley Newton jumped. A downward stream darkened the front of his pants when he saw the group coming in. He backed against the lockers.

Kellen sneered. The fact that he actually knew the twelve-year old's name disgusted him more than that the kid had peed himself. "You alone?"

Riley's eyes betrayed him. He gulped, then motioned toward the swim team's private locker area built between the showers and student lockers.

"Get him," Kellen said.

Bennett set off at once.

"Are you…are you going to hurt him?" Riley squeaked.

"I'm going to hurt you if you don't shut up," Kellen said over the sounds of scuffling and banging of lockers.

Bennett emerged a minute later, his grip firmly clasped around the back of Garrett Weaver's neck.

Kellen stared at the lanky teen dragged before him. He still remembered the day back in elementary school when the teachers gathered all the students together to explain Garrett's skin condition. Something called vitiligo.

A majority of Garrett's mocha skin looked so dark it seemed black. The other parts of skin set him apart from anyone else Kellen had ever seen. Splotchy paleness covered Garrett's ears, nose, and forehead, almost like his tan had been seared away by fire. Lighter-skinned patches streaked down his arms and legs.

Kellen didn't believe the teachers' excuses then any more than he did now. His dad had told him the real story; Garrett's mom must have slept with some black guy passing through town. *Seems to me there's nothing but no-good, cheating whores in Lavere County,* Kellen's father had said more and more of late. *That and Mexicans.*

Garrett had a Mexican mom, Kellen knew. And though she had brown skin, Kellen would never believe any child of her and Red Tom Weaver's came out as dark-skinned as Garrett.

Bennett smirked. "Look what I found."

Garrett squirmed in his grasp.

Bennett looked at Kellen expectantly.

That's right, doggy. You wait till I say go. Kellen gave his friend a curt nod.

Bennett shoved Garrett against the lockers and then to the floor. Jun winced.

Kellen scowled at the freshman. *The same thing would happen to you if it weren't for me holding these guys back.*

Garrett moaned from the floor.

"Told you to keep your mouth shut this morning, Weaver," Kellen said. "Bennett, pick him up."

Garrett crawled to his knees. "Why don't you do it yourself?"

"I don't pick up trailer trash." Kellen signaled Bennett. "Harder."

Again, Bennett threw him. This time Garrett's feet left the floor. The impact left a grooved, but noticeable dent along the locker side. He sprawled between the bench and the lockers, a thin trickle of blood seeping from his nose.

Bennett laughed. "Hey, Owens! Ever wonder if you and Weaver might be related?"

"No way," Owens said. "I'm all ebony, baby. He's just a wannabe."

Garrett spit blood from his lip. "It's a skin condition. White people can have it too, idiot."

Kellen tuned them out. The growing rivulet of blood entranced him as it slithered across the angled cement floor toward the drain in the middle of the room. Kellen swore he could hear it drip to whatever dark recesses the pipe led to if the others would just shut up.

Garrett stood. "But what if you're right, Benny? What if I am black?" He stepped forward. "That means you just committed a hate crime."

Bennett stopped laughing. "Whatever...Owens watched me do it and he didn't care."

"So because Owens is black and you *think* I am, that cancels out?"

"Is he telling the truth?" Bennett asked his friends.

Kellen stared at the blood. *It looks just like paint.*

"Well, is it or not?"

Garrett chuckled. "It's too late, Benny. Tell your mom to watch the news. Your face is going to be all over it tonight."

Bennett eyed Newton, hunched between the lockers, trying to stay as small as possible. Bennett went after him. He grabbed the younger boy by his short-sleeved gym shirt and threw him against the locker even harder than he had Garrett.

"There!" Bennett shouted. "Now you can't call it a hate crime. Newton's white. I did the same thing to both of you!"

Kellen watched the boy cry on the ground. *This isn't what you had in mind. Come on, Winst, you're better than this.*

"What's your problem, Bennett?" Garrett yelled.

"You brought him into this with that whole hate crime talk, so shut it, Weaver!" Bennett said. "Quit crying, Newton, or I'll give you a dunkie-swirl."

"What's that?" Jun asked. "Is it like when you dunk someone in the toilet and let the water swirl around?"

Bennett rolled his eyes. "Fresh, you can't just hold them there. You gotta dunk 'em back and forth." He grabbed the 7th grader's ankle and up-ended him, lifting the boy up and down as an example. "See? You have to dunk them so they get nice and wet."

"Then why don't you call it a dunkie?"

"Because it's called a dunkie-swirl! It's only a dunkie when you leave the water in the bowl. You gotta flush the toilet...to get the swirl...and then dunk him. That's how you get the dunkie-swirl, son!"

Jun shook his shaggy black hair out of his eyes. "Why not call it a swirlie-dunk then? That sounds better."

Kellen watched the 7th grader's eyes jump from one suggestion to the next in terror, his head banging against the floor over and over again.

Owens shook his head. "Naw, you should call it a swee-dunka, man. Has a nice ring to it...swee-dunka!"

"No! Give him a swirlie-dunk, Benny!"

"It's not called either of those!"

"All of you, shut up!" Kellen yelled. "We're not here for Newton. We came for Weave—"

Kellen felt like he had just been sacked. He saw the wooden bench just before his head bounced off the side. A flash of red flooded his vision. Pain struck him like being hit by a baseball bat without a helmet. Though dizzy, Kellen saw the 7th grader run out of the locker room with Jun in hot pursuit.

Weaver...Weaver tackled me...

Bennett rolled beside him, his hands covering his groin. "Racked... me..." he coughed.

Kellen rose from the floor. His head swam, and his left eyebrow felt stung by wasps. He heard sounds of a struggle in one of the bathroom stalls. His vision realigned.

Owens had restrained Garrett in a full nelson. "Kellen—you're bleeding, man."

Kellen lifted his hand to touch his skin, feeling it warm and sticky. He flicked his fingers against his jeans, and he saw the wound in the bathroom mirrors. *Going to need stitches.* He touched the wound again. Pressed on it until the sharp tingle made him wince. *Live in the pain. Use it.*

"You made me bleed, Weaver..."

Garrett struggled in Owens' arms. "Guess we're even now."

"No," said Kellen. "I still owe you for this morning."

"Why?" Garrett asked. "I think the rest of the school already knew about your mom—"

"Shut up, Weaver."

"Aw, does Kelly have mommy issues?"

Kellen's face went cold. "Don't call me that."

"Why? Does that bother you? Because I would hate to make you feel bad...*Kelly.*"

Kellen grabbed Garrett's face and screamed into it. "Don't call me that!"

"Kelly! Kelly!" Garrett yelled back. "Kell—"

Kellen punched him in the jaw. He would have done so again, but Owens stopped him.

"All right. All right, man. Chill. You got him. Let's leave it at—"

"Get out of my way!"

Owens put his arms up in a surrender pose, then looked at Garrett. "You all right, Weaver?"

Garrett worked his jaw back and forth. He glared at Kellen. "You punch like a girl...*Kelly.*"

Kellen descended on him. Grabbing the loop of Garrett's jeans with one hand and the back of his shirt with the other, Kellen hauled the taller teen to his feet with a grunt. He shoved Garrett toward the showers, kicking at his feet to keep him off balance.

"Winst," Owens shouted. "What are you doing, man?"

"Time to see if trailer trash can float."

Garrett wriggled like a worm on a hook. His feet slipped on the tile floor.

Kellen refused to let him fall. He pressed his advantage, moving Garrett toward the swim team's pool door.

Garrett fought back harder. "Owens!" his voice cracked. "You gotta help me, man! I can't swim!"

"Winst, he can't swim..."

Kellen shouldered Garrett out the door.

The smell of chlorine hung in the air and the temperature shot up ten degrees as the three teens emptied out onto the pool deck. The red- and white-checkered buoys dividing the swim lanes had been reeled in for the day. Kellen kicked off his sandals as he maneuvered to the edge.

Garrett's foot grazed the water, disturbing its calm. He trembled. "I'm sorry, man...I'm so sorry!"

Not yet you're not. Kellen hugged him with his muscular swimmer's arms and dove off the edge. The force carried both teens into the water. Kellen heard a splash before everything went mute. He embraced the familiar cold shock and opened his eyes to the swirling world of bubbles.

Garrett tussled against him.

Kellen held strong. He scissor-kicked to the surface and brought his captive with him.

Garrett coughed and gasped. "Helb! Hel—"

"Winst," Owens yelled from the pool deck. "Stop, man. This is crazy. You gotta stop!"

Kellen would not. He took a calm, deep breath, and recalled how the seniors looked at him when he had been a freshman. None believed it when he boldly asked for initiation through twelving. According to the swimmer urban legend, the idea came from U.S. Navy Seal training as a means for recruits to prove their commitment.

"Take a deep breath, Weaver," Kellen whispered in Garrett's ear. "We're going twelving."

Kellen twined his legs around Garrett's, forming a human pretzel, and let their combined weight pull them under. *I chose to go because I have what it takes.* They descended four feet. *A captain should set the example.*

It hadn't been so bad when the seniors obliged him. He had let the fear in, allowed the blackness to consume his oxygen-starved brain, safe in the knowledge his teammate would bring him back to the surface once he passed out.

Just like going to sleep and waking up again. Kellen sunk them to eight feet.

Garrett continued to writhe, his strength waning.

You get two options when you go twelving: willing or unwilling. You chose one, Weaver. I chose the other.

Garrett's remaining air bubbled upward. His body went limp.

Kellen recognized the familiar signal from all his years of life-guarding. He repositioned his arms under Garrett's pits to allow him greater pull when he pushed off the pool bottom to surface them. His feet touched the—*Rubber? When did they put a lining in the pool?*

Garrett's body convulsed.

Have to get him to the surface. Kellen crouched and kicked up.

Again, he went nowhere.

He tried anew, to the same result, and coughed up more air than he would have liked in the process.

Garrett's weight grew heavier by the second.

Kellen's lungs screamed for air. He tried to lift Garrett and failed again. *His jeans must be caught in the drain.* Kellen navigated down to Garrett's waist and legs toward his ankles. He yanked up on the pant legs.

What he saw made him scream.

The surrounding water refused to be held at bay any longer. It rushed in to flood his nostrils and throat, desiring nothing more than to fill the now vacant space in his lungs that oxygen had once occupied.

Kellen choked. His vision clouded with popping white spots. He reminded his legs to kick.

They tiredly refused.

The dark sleep came for him.

Kellen gazed upward a final time.

The blurry yellow surface lights went out, blotted by shadow.

GARRETT

WH...WHERE AM I? GARRETT OPENED HIS EYES AND
saw that he lay at the bottom of the pool.

Air!

Garrett choked. He pushed off the tiled bottom. It shot him
upward four feet.

Whoa! How did I...

He looked down.

Kellen Winstel hung like a propped marionette, suspended by
water. His chin lay dipped against his chest, and his body swayed
in the small wake Garrett had created.

He's dead...drowned himself trying to drown me.

Garrett sunk.

No. I need air!

He looked up at the blurry yellow lights above the surface.
Garrett kicked. A raw surge of power rocketed him upward. His
torso broke the surface, and he twisted midair, inhaling blessed
oxygen. He briefly saw Owens at the side of the pool.

Gravity pulled Garrett back into the pool. He looked over
his shoulder, and his body rotated with the motion. His back
slapped the water. It felt surprisingly good. He slipped head

first beneath the surface amidst the swirling blue. Again, he sunk.

No!

Garrett kicked. He descended so fast that his face smacked the bottom. Blood wisped out of his nose.

Wh-what's happening to me?

He heard splashing. Looked up.

Owens had dove in. He swam toward Kellen's body, hooked an arm around the drowned teen's midsection, took a single look at Garrett. Owens screamed.

Garrett's heart hammered against his chest. *What? Why does he look so scared?*

Owens turned his gaze skyward and pushed off the bottom, carrying Kellen with him.

Garrett kicked, zoomed through the water. In seconds he reached the slope where the shallows angled into the deep end. He turned his cheek to not smack his nose again. The rest of his body followed the move, whipping around. The self-made current tugged at his feet as it rushed past.

I don't understand. How am—

Garrett looked down. His toes seemed melted together. The tips of what remained curled downward. His shins had turned black and shiny, his calves white as fresh snow. Garrett felt like invisible magnets had been attached to his ankles, and he fought their pull to slam together. A tickle feathered its way up the inside of his legs.

"No!" Garrett tried to say. He swallowed a mouthful of water. Choked.

Garrett instinctually kicked. The move sped him up the slope.

His torso grazed the bottom, scratching him. He lifted his head and his body rose too. He bumped into a wall, careened off the side.

"*Stand up...*" said a voice from the surface.

Garrett reopened his eyes. The water seemed lighter here. Brighter. The depth could only be four or five feet at most. *The shallows. I'm in the shallows.*

"Stand up..." said the voice again.

Garrett felt the magnetic pull at his ankles. He willed them apart. Someone grabbed his hair, then wrenched his head above water.

Garrett inhaled. Chlorine stung his nostrils. He snorted the fiery sensation away, coughed for more air.

"Weaver!" said Owens. "*Stand up.*"

"I-I'm tr-trying." Garrett used his elbows to hug the pool gutter, and swung his body flush against the poolside. "Help...help me."

Owens grabbed his hand and pulled him half out of the pool. He clapped him on the back, each strike like whipping Garrett with a paddleboard.

Garrett threw up water into the gutter. He collapsed on the deck, his lower body still in the pool. The cold tile felt good against the heat pulsing through him. The pain in his chest ebbed with each new breath. "It hurts..." he said. "It hurts..."

"Sit tight, man," said Owens. "I gotta help Winst."

Garrett saw Kellen's body lain on the deck near the diving board. His flesh appeared blue and bloated. Bennett hovered over him, clapping his hands in front of Kellen's face in a poor attempt to wake him.

Garrett rolled to his back. The lights above seemed so much brighter now that he had surfaced. Groaning, he sat up. His head swum anew, and he threw up again. Righting himself, he caught sight of his feet in the water. The offsetting black and white skin gleamed beneath the mirrored surface.

Garrett shut his eyes. *This can't be real...it can't be!*

He reopened them. The offsetting skin tones trickled down his shins like streaking dyed water droplets. His hand shaking, Garrett reached down to touch the odd-colored skin before it vanished.

"Weaver!"

The voice came from the corner door. Tiber High's vice principal, Ms. Morgan, stood just inside the entryway. Today, as every other, she wore her prim and proper white button-up blouse with a black wool skirt and black leggings, almost like she hoped the old days when school marms ruled would come back into fashion.

Her back half-hunched by age, Ms. Morgan shuffled to Garrett's side. Her perfume reeked of dead lilies, and Garrett nearly threw up again as she turned one of her lazy grey eyes on him. The other drooped to the left behind her slim, half-ovaled bifocals.

"Weaver," she said. "You all right?"

"Y-yes," Garrett said, his voice hoarse. "I th-think so."

Wincing, Ms. Morgan stooped to inspect him. She tilted her head back to better see through her bottom lenses. "Yes, I think you will be. Wait here. The ambulance is coming."

"Ambulance? But I don't need an amb—"

"You're still a minor, Weaver. We're not taking any chances. Wait here."

Ms. Morgan grimaced as she stood. She placed a shaky hand on Garrett's shoulder to steady herself, then headed to the deep end.

Ambulance? Mom's not going to like that. And what if they—

Garrett glanced down at his legs. His normal skin tone had

returned again, so too had his toes. The tingling sensation had vanished also. He scooted back onto the deck, pulling them from the water, and ran his hands over his shins. Nothing about them seemed unusual.

Wh-what's happening to me?

"Move, boys," Ms. Morgan screeched.

Garrett watched her shoo both Bennett and Owens away from Kellen's body. She did not kneel gracefully, but neither did she fall. She ran her hand over his brow, leaned her ear to his chest. She came away nodding. Arching his head back, she placed one hand over the other and pumped life back into him. After a few thrusts, she coaxed the death sentence from his lungs.

Kellen became a gushing fountain. His head lolled to the side, eyelids fluttered open.

Garrett glared at him. *What did you do to me?*

LENNY

LENNY DOLAN NEVER ASKED FOR A SALTED LIFE. NO one smart ever did.

But unlike those poor wretches stolen from the surface and dragged into the depths, Lenny didn't have anything with which to compare his Salt existence. Born in the realm beneath the waves, he knew of no other life until his owner raised him up and gave him a profession.

None of Lenny's fellow catchers bothered to stir when he woke screaming from a night terror, two hours past. Each recognized the cries associated with guilt's icy stabs and the shaded memories of those they hauled back into lives of Salt slavery.

Lenny had not risked falling asleep again, opting instead for an early morning walk and the chance to study their newest locale without distraction. The Chicago skyline loomed in the backdrop as Lenny left the parking lot and headed toward his destination, the Shedd Aquarium. In the cold morning light, he made mental notes of the building's various entries and exit points.

Where would ya go, girlie? Lenny wondered.

The gentle lap of Lake Michigan called to him, promising safety and camouflage, and that too he filed away.

Where would I go?

He stopped at the balcony to watch the water and the dawn. The motivated many who ran and cycled past him with little regard that he envied such freedoms. The ability to go where and when at their choosing time.

Bmmpp. His crystal-stud earrings vibrated.

Crew's ready when you are, boss, a deep voice echoed in Lenny's mind. *Staged outside and waiting. I snagged a map for you too.*

I'm on my way. Lenny sent the thought and left the balcony. He followed a winding path to a small park where Paulo Varela, a bred-and-born product of slave owner selection, waited for him on one of the park benches.

A crayfish tattoo on Paulo's neck marked him as belonging to August "Crayfish" Collins. Its claws seemed to reach for his jaws as he yawned. Paulo wiped the last bits of sleep from his eyes. "Up early again, huh?"

Lenny snatched the Shedd Aquarium map off of Paulo's lap. "Thought ya said the crew was ready."

"We are."

"Then where are they?"

"Oscar, uh, thought it'd be best if we weren't all seen together." Paulo shifted. "You know, draw less attention. Thought you should hand out the assignments today too."

"So he's thinkin' again, huh?" Lenny sighed as he studied the map. *I'll give him something to think about.*

Paulo shrugged and stretched his arms over the bench. "Hey, boss. Since you're figuring out where to post us all up today, you think maybe you could—"

"No," said Lenny.

Paulo sat up. "Come on, Len. Just put me and her together in the same area."

"I keep tellin' ya to forget about her," Lenny said.

"You suggest a Brazilian give up on love?" Paulo sat back. Snorted. "Might as well ask me to stop breathing."

"Ya were bred-n-born in New Pearlaya," Lenny countered. "Ya neva been to Brazil."

Paulo shrugged. "Maybe not, but my mother said it's important to remember our roots so we might find our way home someday."

"Yeah? Maybe she shoulda' reminded ya of what we were sent out here to find and bring back." Lenny glanced up. "And what happens if we don't."

"Yeah, all right," said Paulo. "Buckets of blood, Len, you don't have to—"

Lenny felt Paulo nudge him.

"Here comes Ellie and the pup now."

Lenny glanced away from the map as an odd pairing approached them.

The boy, Racer, had not reached his teen years, yet his gaunt features spoke plain he had witnessed more pain in his short life than most on land ever would. He had yet to shed a boy's natural excitement, however, and he stood straighter when noticing Lenny Dolan watched him.

The other—Ellie Briceño—trudged along. As big as Paulo, she, like him, wore a dark-gold hoodie to befit her size and role. Unlike Lenny and the others, her natural human skin still fought to retain some semblance of a tan. She had lived ashore once, Lenny knew, and had not yet resided long enough beneath the waves to have her color sapped.

Lenny still hadn't figured out how long ago her surface life had been stolen, but he knew she didn't like being asked about it.

"Hey, Elle." Paulo gave her a wave.

Ellie ignored him. "So what's the plan, Lenny? You going to stick me on the bus again to play guard duty?"

Maybe I should. Teach ya to keep quiet. Lenny kept the thought to himself. He cleared his throat. "Listen up. We all know why we're here, and what needs to—"

"Are you going to quote Fenton every time we go out, boss?" Paulo asked before doing a spot-on impression of their taskmaster's voice. "Word has reached our master's ears of a proven, elusive runaway by the name of Marisa Bourgeois—"

"Knock it off, Paulie," said Lenny.

"—she is rumored uncatchable, among other things." Paulo chuckled.

"*Among other things.*" Ellie scoffed. "She's just another folk story slaves tell each other to give themselves hope, that's what she is."

Racer laughed, then failed at a similar impression. "Our wise master does not believe such claims. He has taken up wagers that any runner can be captured. You lot will prove him correct!"

"Keep it up, all of ya," Lenny said to his crew. "Rememba it when Oscar makes us go home without her and we got nothin' else to show for bein' sent out. Just like I'll rememba all of ya's were laughin' when August sends our folks to hang cause we didn't get the job done."

Their laughter turned silent.

"Now," Lenny continued. "We all know why we're here and what needs done. We find this girl, bag her, and take her back to the Salt."

"Why?" Racer asked.

Lenny glared at him. "What'd ya say?"

"I just mean, uh, you know." Racer shrugged. "I mean…we could run. We're far enough inland now…"

Lenny crossed his arms.

"I doubt they'd find us." Racer swallowed hard. "That's all I'm saying."

"What about ya pop?" Lenny asked him. "What about mine, huh? Those they kept behind?"

"Lenny, I…"

"You swore the words, pup," said Lenny. "Same as the rest of us. By the laws of New Pearlaya, should any slave not return—"

Racer refused to meet Lenny's stare.

"Say it, pup." Lenny demanded. "Say the words."

"Let my loved ones pay the price," said Racer quietly.

Cut him some slack. Paulo's voice echoed in Lenny's mind. *He's young and it's his first trip ashore.*

Lenny shot the largest among them a look, then resumed his study of the map. "Elle, ya not on the bus today. I want ya to go inside and patrol the Polar Play Zone."

"I'm on it," said Ellie, leaving immediately.

"Racer," Lenny continued. "Post up on the south terrace. Keep sharp."

"You got it, boss."

Lenny glanced up as the youngest catcher sprinted away.

"Pups, huh?" Paulo chuckled. "Makes me think of us when we were first sent catching."

We knew betta, Paulie, Lenny kept the thought.

"So where you got me today?" Paulo asked. "Maybe, say the Polar Play—"

"Ya not goin' in." Lenny folded the map and pocketed it.

"What?" Paulo stood up, looming over his smaller captain. "Why?"

"Ya wanted me to cut the pup a break. I did." Lenny stepped into Paulo's shadow. "He talked about runnin' and I didn't have ya haul him away for sayin' it."

"Len, he's not going to run."

"Nope. And ya gonna keep watch over this area to make sure."

Lenny turned toward the Shedd. The line outside had grown as a group of students, all screaming and laughing, crowded around the opening. *Gotta get inside, son.* Lenny thought of his father's teachings. *Find a place to watch.*

"I'm the strongest catcher you've got," said Paulo.

"Mmm-hmm." Lenny agreed. "And ya right outside if I need ya. Now where am I s'posed to meet Oscar?"

"He's over there." Paulo's face soured. "By the statue of a man holding a fish."

Lenny followed his point in search of their owner's son. *Could he be more obvious?*

The luxurious sheen of Oscar's pearl-white hoodie near sparkled in the sunlight as he looked on those passing by him with utter disgust.

Lenny scowled and headed over.

"About bloody time," said Oscar when Lenny arrived. "It's not wise to keep me waiting, nipperkin."

Lenny's jaw clenched, but he let Oscar's insult go. "Yeah, well I was scoutin' the place. That's what captains do."

"My father named us co-captains." Oscar sneered, then glanced at the Shedd as if weighing the truth of Lenny's words. "Next time you go out, I insist you take me along. Can't very well learn my family's stock-and-trade if I'm shut up with the crew, now can I?"

"Ya could always have Henry take ya out." Lenny jerked his head toward a couple seated not twenty yards away.

The balding white man had a grimness about him that reeked of a former taskmaster, the kind who enjoyed extended punishment rather than a quick drop.

Lenny hated him all the more for the garb he wore: a sleek grey and charcoal-spotted hooded suit, the most prized Selkie coat of all. By the look of him, he assumed Henry had killed to acquire it.

As if sensing Lenny's disdain, Henry unsheathed a black dagger from his boot. For a moment he held it aloft, staring at its blade like nothing but its deadly gleam existed. Then he picked at his fingernails with its tip.

Oscar jabbed Lenny in the shoulder. "I don't want Henry to take me. Father hired him to keep me safe. He only sent you along to teach me. Thus far, I can't say as I've learned much at all." Oscar stamped his foot and crossed his arms. "We've been at this for weeks now! How many more dead ends and cold trails must we endure before you fathom the girl might not be found at an aquarium? Or not found at all, rather."

"It's the only clue we got," said Lenny. "Fenton said she's only been seen at aquariums, and all the crews she escaped from said it seemed like she was lookin' for something at those aquariums." Lenny rubbed his head. "Anyway, we're here now. Ya ready to go or what?"

"Don't take that tone with me, slave, else I have Henry fetch me your tongue," said Oscar. "You command only so long as I allow, Lenny. Never forget that."

I'll rememba. Dolans don't forget nothin'. Lenny thought to himself. "Whateva ya say, boss, but we need to get movin'. The crowd keeps growin'."

"Very well," said Oscar. "Where would you have us go?"

Thought ya was a captain. Lenny thought. His gaze meandered between the Shedd and its patrons, the lake water, then to Henry and his slave girl.

Unlike her owner, she seemed to take great interest in her surroundings. Ebony-skinned and at least half Henry's age, her hooded suit rivaled her face for beauty. Cream in color, white bands snaked around her body; one hemmed her neckline, others wrapped around her shoulder. Another looped her waist like a belt.

Lenny watched Henry drape his arm around her shoulders, his fingers straining against her skin when she flinched at his touch.

Henry grinned at him.

Ya wanna play games, pal? Lenny's face tightened. *Let's do that.*

"I want Henry patrollin' the lake," Lenny said to Oscar. "And his girl in the cafeteria."

"Why should I allow that?" Oscar glanced between Lenny and Henry. "Henry will certainly object. He loathes parting with Chidi and—"

"Look, he's the meanest and the baddest of us all, right?" Lenny asked. "If we find this Marisa Bourgeois, my bet is she makes a run for the water to try and swim away. She does that, we let Henry know, and boom. We got her the minute she hits the lake. If not, the rest of us are on hand to swarm her."

Oscar scratched at his cheeks. "He'll want a good explanation as to why Chidi can't accompany him there…"

"She's a translator," said Lenny. "Can't do much of that in the water."

"Yes, but why send her to the cafeteria?"

Lenny chuckled. "Take a look around. These Drybacks love their food. Sooner or later, every one of them'll end up in the cafeteria. Now I dunno about you, but I heard gibberish from about fifteen languages already this mornin'. The only one of us who can tell the difference between nothin' and something in their words is Chidi."

"Fine," said Oscar. "That's all well and sorted then. But what about me?"

Play to him. Lenny's conscience urged. *Teach him a lesson.*

Lenny clucked his tongue. "Well, I dunno if ya ready or not—"

"I am," Oscar stepped forward. "I can handle anything you throw at me...*nipperkin.*"

We'll see about that.

"Fine," said Lenny. "Post up near the Dryback security station where all the guards are."

Oscar's eyes narrowed. "Why? What makes that post so all-important?"

"Slaves are stupid, right?" Lenny smiled in mirror of Oscar's immediate grin. "They wanna feel safe. Security guards, police officers - that's their job. To keep people safe."

Just like ya daddy made it all our jobs to keep ya safe, Oscar. Lenny fought down his anger and the desire to scream at his owner's son. *Ya wouldn't last a day without us.*

"I see," said Oscar. "And where will you be throughout all this?"

"Well, I was gonna watch the security station," Lenny lied. "But since ya takin' it, guess I gotta wander around and keep tabs on everyone. Takes me outta the hunt. Honestly, it should be you to—"

"No," said Oscar. "You wander. I'll take the important task. After all, this is my crew. If that runner is here, it should be me to capture her and win the glory."

Lenny fought off a grin. "Ya sure about this?"

"Go." Oscar lifted his chin.

"Aye, boss."

Lenny turned and headed for the steps of the Shedd.

Did he take the bait? Paulo asked.

Hook, line, and sinka. Lenny replied as he joined the back of the line. *That'll keep him outta our way today.*

Out of your way, you mean, said Paulo. *You sure you want me to stay outside?*

Ya gotta learn to keep ya mouth shut and ya head down, ya dumb brute. Lenny followed the line up the steps.

That's some advice coming from you, boss. Paulo chuckled. *Guess I should look at the bright side, huh? There's all this fresh air to breathe. Won't get any of that when Oscar decides he's tired of playing catcher and forces us to go back to the Salt. And hey, the sun's shining.*

Lenny squinted and shielded his eyes with his hand. *Not for long. See those clouds over there? That's rain headed this way, Paulie.*

Paulo cursed.

Lenny climbed the last of the steps and peeked around the man in front of him.

The Shedd Aquarium doors stood open.

But keep ya head up anyway. Lenny stepped inside to pay for his ticket and felt the familiar thrill of the hunt seeping into his soul. *Might be today's our lucky day.*

LENNY

HOW LONG DO WE HAVE TO KEEP WAITING BEFORE you all realize I'm right?

Lenny endured Ellie's question for what felt like the hundredth time that afternoon.

I'm with Elle, said Paulo. *We've been here all day now. Our girl's not here, boss.*

Shuddup, Paulie. Lenny sent the thought. *We got nowhere else to be.*

Yeah, well, you're not the one standing in the rain.

Lenny listened to Ellie and Racer chuckle in his mind. He had yet to hear any word from the others in his crew. Then again, Henry and Chidi had mostly kept to themselves from the start. Still, Lenny staved off a nagging feeling he had missed something as he paced around the Caribbean Reef tank, the central hub leading to all other areas of the aquarium.

Henry went to the lake without a fuss and Oscar's neva this quiet. Lenny debated as he watched a green sea turtle dive down in the tank, its rudder of a tail wiggling. *But is it that they don't care? Do they think our runna's not here, or something else?*

Lenny couldn't be sure.

It didn't help that the others continued filling his head with their own theories and debates.

All I'm saying is we don't even know what Marisa did, said Racer. *Not really.*

She ran, pup, Paulo replied. *That's enough. Back me up, Elle.*

You know where I stand, said Ellie. *But if this Marisa Bourgeois were real, and I'm not saying she is—*

But if she were…

—then it makes me wonder why so many catcher groups have been sent after her, Ellie finished.

Depends on who you ask, said Paulo. *I heard a Merrow say some highborn made her his bed slave and wants the pleasure of her company one more time before they hang her. What do you think, boss?*

Lenny looked on a moray eel, its mouth gaping open as it hid between two rocks. *I say August and a bunch of owners wanna see her caught. This girl's been on the run for a long while to hear 'em tell it.*

The eel stared ahead blankly as Lenny rounded the tank.

A runna gets away and other slaves don't see 'em brought back…

A shadow in the glass vanished when Lenny glanced up.

A teenaged girl walked away from him and the tank.

Lenny's pulse quickened.

None of the other visitors to the Shedd Aquarium saw what he did. To them it only looked a coffee-stained, raggedy hoodie some thuggish girl from the south side of Chi-town wore because she couldn't afford better.

Lenny knew different. Her scent called his attention. Salt-soaked with more than a hint of slave sweat, the kind of aroma that only came from someone who had served beneath the waves.

Marisa Bourgeois. Lenny locked his focus on her. *Gotcha.*

Whenever Marisa Bourgeois moved, he did.

She first passed a coral-filled tank. The leather-like bag at her side changed color. Brown when first Lenny saw it, and now red in mimic of its new surroundings. Its hue reverted the moment she cleared the tank. Marisa gave no indication she noticed and entered the Waters of The World exhibit where Lenny could not follow without being seen.

Yeah, said Paulo. *If nobody catches her, then it gives the rest of us ideas. Hope.*

Lenny reached to his ears. He clutched the crystal studs between his thumb and forefinger. *Mute 'em,* he thought.

Bmmpp...bmmpp...bmmpp...bmmpp... The earrings continued to vibrate, the voices silenced.

Lenny turned his attention back to the exhibit entry.

He recalled one of his father's mantras. *A catcha watches. Waits to make sure the goin's safe.*

Ahead of him, a group of inner city fourth graders made their way toward the same exhibit Marisa had entered. Lenny hustled to catch up. He joined their ranks and entered unseen. When the students paused at the new area's sudden low lighting, Lenny pressed ahead. No amount of darkness on land compared to Crayfish Cavern back home.

Lenny wove silently through the crowd, searching. He found his target in front of the octopus tank. The emanating hazy violet light made her ebony skin shine like a killer whale's backside. Lenny slunk behind a concrete pillar.

Marisa tilted her head to survey the incoming crowd.

She's careful. Lenny observed. *Watchful.*

More students came into the exhibit. They pushed and shoved

closer to the tank. "Mommy, I can't see it!" cried one of the little bleaters.

"There isn't anything in there!"

"I'm bored!"

"Look closer, sweetie!" a woman said. "It's camouflaged with the brown rocks."

Lenny shook his head. *How will they learn if ya show 'em everything?*

Several children banged their fists against the glass. One of them even dragged his snot-filled nose along the length of it. The brat didn't bother to clean the wavy green trail off either.

The octopus stayed hidden.

Lenny spied an information board, its face littered with detailed octopus habits for anyone interested enough to read them. He crept to the chrome board, careful to keep his distance, never losing sight of his target. Tucked behind it, he peered around the edge.

Marisa had filed further down the tank, away from the students.

"Why don't we all visit the sea otters next door?" A mother said. "They're fun to watch."

The suggestion sent the children racing toward their next caged victims while their guardians trailed behind like a chain gang with years left on their sentences.

They're just sea rats, lady. Lenny watched them leave. *Gnaw ya face off, sea rats.*

The air vents above him kicked on with a low thrum. A cool breeze whispered across the tiny hairs on the back of Lenny's neck. He shivered, fought against the familiar energy rush to keep it in reserve. *A catcha watches…waits.*

Bmmpp.

With the pack of children gone, the octopus emerged from hiding. Its tentacles sprawled forward, grasped at the rock wall like fingers massaging a scalp as it pulled its balloon-like body out. It promptly sank to the bottom where it morphed its body color to match the surrounding sand.

Marisa reached into her bag.

Lenny slid his right hand into his Selkie pocket. His fingers danced across the hilt of a coral dagger. *Don't do it, girlie. Not here.*

Marisa took out a spiraled notebook, then a pen that resembled bone with strange markings on the sides. Lenny recognized it for a seal tooth. Pen in hand, Marisa took notes with an occasional studious glance at the tank.

Bmmpp...bmmpp...

Shrieks of laughter echoed through the wall.

Bmmpp...bmmpp...bmmpp...bmmpp...

Quit talkin', ya idiots.

Bmmpp...bmmpp...bmmpp...bmmpp...bmmpp...bmmpp...bmmpp...bmmpp...

Lenny clutched the studs and telepathically opened his thought stream.

Len. Ellie said, her voice panicky. *Oscar's on the move.*

Lenny winced at the sudden molestation to his brain. He reopened his eyes.

Marisa Bourgeois had vanished.

Lenny burst from his position, knocking over the information board. He ran to the spot where she last stood, finding no trace of her anywhere. *She didn't just disappear!* He kicked the carpeted area near the tank's base. *Ya neva...eva...take ya eyes off the target. How many times has Pop said that?*

Len, said Ellie. *Did you hear me?*

Lenny saw movement inside the tank—an employee dropping a lidded jar inside.

The octopus sprang from the sand. It wrapped its tentacles around the bottle cap. Without warning, the eight-legged beast worked its limbs back and forth to unscrew the lid.

Lenny heard the stampede before he saw it.

"Ewww!" a girl screamed.

"Mrs. G! Come look at this thing!" the teeny monster closest to him shouted.

"Mooooom! Check it out!"

The gang of children bowled Lenny over.

He fought to stand and caught sight of a black tennis shoe just before it connected with his temple. The room spun, and he swore Marisa smiled down on him before more children crowded around. He fumbled to his knees.

*Escape—escape—*Lenny thought to his crew.

"Oh my!" a woman behind him said. "I'm sorry about that. They get so excited when they're together. Kids, right?"

Lenny shoved the children out of his way and made for the exit. The room continued to spin like he had drunk too much grog. He leaned against the wall for balance, stumbled toward the lone way into and out of the exhibit. He paused to let his eyes adjust to the brighter light and cursed himself for a fool when he saw the layout.

The lone entry point should have bottlenecked Marisa. But now, in the Shedd's central area, Lenny saw at least seven hallways she could have escaped through. Visitors crisscrossed in front of him toward other exhibits. None resembled his target.

Which way did she go? His mind raced. *Which way? Which way!*

*Len…Len…*Ellie called out. *Can you hear me?*

Lenny silenced her from his thought stream. He felt a tap on the shoulder and turned. An eight-year-old peeked at him from behind a woman's legs. Lenny assumed the runt belonged to her. Both had the same horsey face and green eyes. He took special notice of the apple-shaped sticker slapped over the woman's blouse. She had written *Mrs. G* in a stylish, cursive hand and even drawn a smiley face just below her name.

Lenny turned his attention back to Marisa's pinwheel of escape routes. *Is she blendin' with the crowd, or did she leave the grounds?*

Mrs. G coughed.

Lenny thought it sounded somewhere between clearing her throat and sneezing only she hadn't decided which. Fake. Again, he ignored her as he tried to recall every lesson his father ever taught him. *She cornered herself…*

Pop would neva do that…he'd want two exits…want to see anyone comin' for him.

Lenny took out his map. His eyes searched for an area Drybacks might congregate. *How many…what they looked like…he'd wanna blend—*

Mrs. G dug her finger into Lenny's collarbone. "Excuse me!"

"What?" he snarled.

"I'm sorry to bother you—" Mrs. G said politely, though her tone suggested otherwise. "My daughter, Jamie, has something she'd like to say to you. We'd like to consider this a teaching moment."

Jamie burrowed her face into her mother's waist.

Lenny frowned at the kid.

"Go on, pumpkin." Mrs. G nudged her daughter.

"I'm sorry my—my friends and I knocked you over," Jamie said. "It was an accident."

"Very good, dear!" Mrs. G patted her daughter on the head like she might a puppy. She turned her sights on Lenny. "Don't you have something to say *back* to Jamie?"

Lenny stared at the kid. He knew the type having grown up around Oscar. Anything this terror wanted, she would get. Didn't matter what it might be. Piece of candy, leafy sea dragon mount, this brat could have it all.

His father would have no doubt asked Mrs. G to step away from her child. Let the two adults have a teaching moment of their own.

Lenny couldn't. "Heya, kid."

"Hi," Jamie said. "Are you an elf that helps Santa?"

I'll show ya Santa's elf. Lenny pulled at the neckline of his hoodie. "Listen, I got something to tell ya. It's true I might know a couple elves. And guess what? I got something to tell 'em this year about a little girl named Jamie."

"And what might that be?" Mrs. G asked cheerily.

Prolly imaginin' her plans to share this during family dinnertime in her safe, cushy life.

"Santa keeps a list, right?" Lenny asked.

Jamie hopped several times in place. "A list of who's been naughty or nice!"

"Yeah, well, ya been a little brat this year, *pumpkin*." Lenny patted Jamie on the head. "And ya name's goin' on the naughty list... right next to mine."

The little girl's tears came like a heavy rain, and Lenny the young man ready to dance in it.

Mrs. G grabbed her daughter's hand and led the little girl away.

Lenny chuckled. "Bet she don't ask Santa 'bout no elves this year."

Then he blew Mrs. G a kiss. She had almost made him forget Marisa Bourgeois might have left the building.

CHIDI

CHIDI ETIENNE KNEW LENNY DID HER A KINDNESS by assigning her to the cafeteria. She didn't know it would trigger memories she worked so hard to suppress. It wasn't the group of eight-year-old girls, laughing at a nearby table that made her question if she had ever been so innocent. Chidi recalled she had been, long ago.

The man in his fifties seated behind the girls had been the one to bring the memories screaming back. The one watching Chidi, undressing her with his eyes the past fifteen minutes. He reminded her too much of Henry.

Chidi sneered at him so he would realize she saw him. Not that it would matter. Men like that didn't care, she knew.

She continued her search for Marisa Bourgeois. A married couple and their six-year-old with a stroller here, a pair of boys chasing each other there; Chidi dismissed them all for ordinary. She gave none a second thought until she saw the mousey man.

Seated alone, a tray of untouched fried chicken tenders in front of him, the man's beady eyes searched the room behind thin, wire-rimmed glasses. At his feet, a green canvas backpack lay propped against his chair. A grey hood with two cutout eyeholes peeked from the nearly zipped side. A Common Seal outfit, if Chidi judged the make correctly. And she had.

Chidi's brow furrowed. *Another runner? How did he take off his suit?*

"Ya dead, Cheeds," a familiar voice—one with a Boston accent—whispered and pressed something hard into her lower back.

"You shouldn't sneak up so close on someone unless you plan on killing them," Chidi said. She spun and caught her would-be assailant by the wrist.

Today, her newest captain had chosen to squeeze his chubby legs into black skinny jeans, a task made harder given the bottom of his Selkie suit also had to fit. He had tucked a checkered shirt of black and green into them. A stocking cap covered his auburn hair, despite the least bit of chill outside. She recalled his claim dressing in such a way helped him blend with Chicago's punk crowd.

Chidi could see no sense to his logic. The black hood with white circles draped down his back gave him away to anyone Salted. "Hi, Lenny. Looks like I caught you."

Lenny wrenched away and rubbed his left wrist—the one bearing the crayfish brand with the initials A.C. seared into his skin. He pulled his sleeves down when he caught her staring at it. "Dolans don't get caught, sweetheart. We don't run."

Good thing.

"Nice shirt," he said to her. "Ya don't stand out at all wearin' that ova ya suit. Real discreet."

Chidi glanced down at the off-white T-shirt she bought in the gift shop earlier that morning. It read *I ♥ my Shedd Aquarium!* across the chest with a picture of a Galápagos sea lion underneath it. "Do you really like it?"

"Whattaya think?"

Chidi smirked. *"Je mélange mieux que vous."*

"Hey!" Lenny pointed at her. "No speakin' other languages around me! I don't like not knowin' what's bein' said. How many ya speak anyhow, Cheeds?"

In truth, she had lost count. Not that she would say if she did remember. One never knew how the slightest bit of information might be recalled and used against her some later day.

Chidi shrugged innocently and resumed her watch of the mousey man.

His eyes searched the room constantly, yet he rarely turned his head. Instead, his foot quivered and tapped the chair's metal leg quickly, almost like transmitting the nervous energy into Morse code. When he wiped his forehead, she saw his sleeve come away with wet stains.

Chidi looked away before he saw her. She counted to five, then resumed her observation of him. She took note that his gaze frequented the unoccupied vending area. It had a few light panels out and a NO ENTRY sign posted. Elsewise, nothing about the room seemed remotely interesting.

Why does he keep looking over there? An escape route perhaps?

"I didn't lose her, Elle!" Lenny hissed loudly.

Chidi turned back around.

Lenny paced back and forth. His face varied between shades of red and purple.

Others in the cafeteria took notice. Several teens in the crowd even had their phones out to film the angry little man.

Uh, Lenny, she thought to him. *Might want to go thoughts on. Kind of drawing a crowd.*

Lenny took his stocking cap off and threw it. "Dolans don't lose runnas, Elle! We find 'em, bag 'em, and tag 'em! Now I dunno how they did things back in Mexico or whateva country ya came from, but keep ya eyes open. She's still here!"

Hey, Lenny, Chidi said. *Check out this guy I found. I think he might be a runner.*

Lenny immediately stopped his rant as if Chidi uttered magic words. He stood on his tiptoes to see to whom she referred. Cursing, he grasped the metal bars used to form the fast food lines. Grunting, he hoisted himself up for a better view.

Five tables up, three to the right, Chidi coached. *See him?*

"Nah, na-yeah! I got him. Ooh, whattaya think is in the bag?"

A Selkie suit, Chidi sent the thought to Lenny and kept the suddenly curious older gentleman beside her from listening in. *How about you?*

Water's wet, right? Think maybe I should go in for a better look.

Is that smart? Chidi asked. *Why not just wait to see what he does?*

'Cause that's not as much fun, Lenny said. *Don't worry, Cheeds. Things go bad, Dolans take care of their own. Stick next to me. I'll take care a ya.*

So you've said.

Males all promised the same things—protection, freedom, even love. All ended the same way. Only Henry remained.

The mousey man straightened in his chair, glanced over his shoulder again.

For a brief second, Chidi swore someone slipped into the vending area shadows. *Len, I think this guy has company.*

Maybe Marisa brought—Lenny froze.

The dark wings of fear blossomed inside Chidi. She inched toward the emergency exit, not waiting for Lenny to signal whether they should fight or flee.

Lenny reached over his head and slapped Chidi on the hip. *She's still here, Cheeds! Marisa Bourgeois is here!*

Where?

The hall entrance. She must've doubled back on me!

Chidi saw her.

Marisa had paused just inside the cafeteria. She cocked her head to the side, listening.

This doesn't feel right, Chidi thought to herself. *Why would she still be here after picking up a tail?*

Marisa yawned and chose a table near the northern terrace doors. The chair opposite her came screeching out just after she sat. She smirked at the mousey man and waved him over.

Chidi watched the man. *Don't do it.*

With a final glance back at the vending area—and another wipe of the forehead—he hastily gathered his things and scurried to join Marisa.

All right, crew, Lenny said. *I see our target, so listen up. She's meetin' with someone. Might be a second runna. Henry, keep patrollin' the lake in case she gets past us. Racer, sprint to the north terrace and gimme some eyes out there. Ellie, move ova to the Sea Otter trail and back us up. I got point. Cheeds, flank her.*

A second runner, huh? Ellie asked. *Ten anemonies says one is a forger selling fakes.*

Fakes? Racer asked.

How can you not know about fakes, pup? Ellie said. *Any slave who doesn't want to worry about running from chasers needs proof they've been freed. Otherwise, it's open season on them to be captured and resold.*

I'll take that bet, chica—

Of course you will, Paulo. Chidi thought to herself. *Anything you can do to get closer to Ellie.*

You need serious pearls to buy fakes, Paulo continued. *No way a slave has any. Well, unless he killed his owner or a Salt Child. Then they got bigger problems.*

Maybe this guy has connections, Ellie suggested.

No slave has connections like that, Paulo said.

Chidi stayed out of the conversation. She preferred to keep an eye on Marisa. *This is the Silkie no one's been able to find?* Chidi scratched her neck. She knew better than most not to judge a book by its cover, having seen would-be partners of Henry's make that same mistake countless times. Chidi refused to second-guess her gut.

Well, I'm going to find a way to buy me some fakes then, Racer said. *And once I get them, I'm gone. None of you will ever see me again!*

And what if one of us or some Merrows came looking for you? Paulo asked. *Or worse…Orcs?*

I could outrun and outswim any of them on my worst day, Racer said.

Ya can't run foreva, pup, Lenny said dryly. *Best learn that now. Save ya'self the heartache of tryin'. Ya in position yet?*

Just got here, Racer said.

Good afternoon, all. A new voice, one laced with disdain, entered their minds. *If any of you would care to see me capture this so-called uncatchable runner, come to the cafeteria. I'll have her directly.*

Lenny rolled his eyes. *Hey, Oscar—*

How dare you mock me, nipperkin, Oscar said. *You do realize I can see you.*

Chidi stiffened. She searched for Oscar's location. *This is all wrong! What's he doing here?*

Ah, yes. At least Chidi has the decent sense to look for me, Oscar said. *A bit to the left now...there!*

Chidi found him before Lenny.

Oscar Collins leaned against the southwest wall, wearing his lavish Harp Seal coat as only an untouchable could. He waved at them. *What's this, Chidi? Keeping the nipperkin happy, eh? Henry will loathe hearing of it.*

Whattaya doin' here, Oscar? Lenny asked. *Get back to ya post.*

I assume you're referring to the all-important post? Fantastic joke, Oscar said. *My father's going to love it.*

Henry. Chidi realized. *He must've told Oscar about the fake position. Young, rich, and stupid—the perfect target.*

I'll be the one catching her, Oscar said. *You're just a tracker. Congratulations. You've done your job...now stay out of my way.*

Nobody's sayin' ya not in charge, Lenny said. *But something wicked is goin' down with Marisa and that guy. Ya move in now and we could lose both of 'em. Ya fatha won't be happy with that! I'm askin' ya...wait and see what they do.*

Oscar put his hands in the Selkie pocket around his belly.

What's he playing with?

Fine, Oscar said after a long pause. *But if they don't do anything soon, I'm going in...and you will obey my orders.*

All right, Lenny said. *Racer! Ya outside the terrace yet?*

I'm here!

Gimme an—

Us, Oscar corrected. *Give us an update.*

Okay, Racer said. *Right now they're just talking. But I can't hear what they're saying. I can get closer if you wan—*

No, Lenny said quickly. *Stay there. Just keep feedin' us.*

Sure thing. Marisa just took a couple notebooks out and scooted them across the table. New guy's opening one now...Len, I...I think this guy is crying.

Slaves weep all the time, Oscar said. *And I tire of this waiting game, Lenny. How much longer?*

Crew, listen up, Lenny said, the veins in his neck pulsing. *Oscar's gonna cock this up. Everyone stay in ya positions till after he rushes her. He wants to take a runna down, let him find out they got some fight in—*

Chidi watched Oscar push off the wall and sprint for the table. He made it halfway across the cafeteria before pulling something black out of his Selkie pocket.

"He's got a gun!" a girl screamed.

Still, Oscar continued on, a malicious grin spreading across his face at the chaos he just created. Patrons cleared from tables every which way. Many screaming. Others dove to hide under tables. Chidi even saw one fool raise his phone to record the happenings.

Lenny dropped from the railing, his earrings flashing. *Paulie, get inside now! Henry and Racer stay put!*

Chidi left without waiting for Lenny to give her an order. She ran directly at Marisa. The oncoming tide of those trying to escape hampered her efforts.

Ellie, Lenny continued to bark commands. *Move west to block the hallway.*

I can't see anything out here, said Racer. *Too many Drybacks.*

Faster. Chidi urged her legs. *Take her down!*

Marisa swiveled toward her oncoming attacker. Rising from her seat, she grabbed the table with both hands and hurled it at Oscar like a Frisbee.

The table hit him square in the chest. The force of it caused his head to snap back and rebound off the granite floor. Chidi heard the cracking sound from fifty feet away, even above the ongoing screams.

At least she shut him up.

Chidi reached into her Silkie pocket for a clear, palm-sized ball. Finding the orb, she threw it down. Though soundless and odorless, the contents wafted through the room, rendering the remaining aquarium visitors unconscious. Chidi looked at the now clear path to her target.

Marisa Bourgeois remained upright. So, too, did the mousey man, cowering behind her, clutching at his canvas bag.

Chidi! Where did you get a forgetty? Racer asked.

Who cares, Lenny said as he jumped over a sprawled body and kept running. *Paulie, gimme an update.*

This place is loco, Paulo said. *The guards won't let anyone through! Everyone outside is talking about guns and making phone calls. I'll have to find a different way in. Better move, Len!*

Marisa locked eyes with Chidi and winked. Then she bounded away for the aquarium's central area.

Don't let her get away, Cheeds! Lenny said.

Chidi hurdled a table with graceful ease and trained her eyes on Marisa's backside. *Ellie! She's leaving the cafeteria!*

On my way, said Ellie. *Run her to me!*

Marisa disappeared around the corner.

Chidi slowed. She swung wide before making the same turn in the event Marisa lay in wait. The hallway before her lay empty and silent. Chidi tiptoed toward a pair of restrooms. She reasoned Marisa had to have entered one of them, but which?

"Marisa Bourgeois," Chidi said, her voice sharp. "I know you're in there. Come out!"

As jy so se, a satiny voice purred.

If you say so, Chidi's mind translated.

A violet marble rolled out of the male restroom entrance.

Squid Ball! Chidi fell to the ground just before it exploded, blanketing the area in an inky smoke. Her eyes clenched, she clapped her right hand over her mouth and nose to avoid inhaling. Chidi heard footsteps run past. She swept her left hand about in the hope of tripping Marisa. She found nothing but air. Her earrings flashed.

Ellie! She must be getting close!

Chidi crawled forward. She risked a peek. The smoke had dissipated enough for her to resume the hunt. Not far ahead, she saw a shaggy hooded figure. Chidi leapt to her feet and ran.

Marisa had slowed. She stumbled, coughing as she ran.

Her lungs are filled with ink! Chidi pushed her body harder to close the gap. She closed within five strides by the time Marisa reached the stairwell.

Hearing Chidi's footfall seemed to give Marisa new life. She took the stairs two at a time.

Three. Chidi stopped at the bottom to catch her breath. *Two...*

Marisa reached the top. She cautioned a look back.

Big mistake, sister.

Ellie stepped out of the shadows to envelope Marisa. She lifted her off the ground and smothered Marisa with forearms the size of a normal person's thighs. Ellie did not relent until Marisa passed out. "I'll carry her to the bus," she called down to Chidi. "You help Len with the other runner…"

Chidi turned to go.

"Chidi!"

"Yeah?"

"Feel free to leave Oscar behind."

The thunder of gunshots rang up the hallway, followed by an all too familiar bellow.

Chidi rushed back to the cafeteria. She rounded the corner and entered a freak show.

Lenny and the mousey man hid beneath the same table. Both fought for control of the canvas backpack. Near them, an eleven-foot long Leopard Seal bared its canines at an aquarium security guard.

The guard's gun shook in his hand as he fired it. He missed and took woeful aim again.

Don't shoot. Run!

The seal slithered its hind flippers across the waxed floor. It dove for the guard and clamped its eight pairs of teeth down on his arm. The seal shook him to the ground.

The gun skittered across the floor.

Curiously, the seal released the guard. Its grey and black-spotted skin loosened and fell away like an oversized robe.

How did he…Slaves can't do that unless—He's not a slave!

The seal reverted to human form, yet no one had been there to release him from his Salt form. The sealskin shrunk until it lay flat against a man's lean, human body. Grey and black-spotted, Chidi recognized the make. *He's a Leper.*

Her earrings flashed. *We need Henry!*

Where the Leopard Seal had been now stood a white man, over seven feet tall. Long, ratty hair streamed across his face. He took one long look around the room and saw Lenny struggling with the mousey man. He ran at them.

A personal Leper? Racer asked. *He's not messing around, that's for—*

We're not messin' around, Lenny yelled. *Get. Hen—*

With one hand, the Leper flipped the table over. He dragged Lenny out by his hood and flung him away.

Chidi saw her captain land three rows over.

Lenny scrambled to his knees and reached into his Selkie pocket. From it, she watched him pull a Dryback dagger. Small by any other standards, it resembled a broadsword in his hand. He brandished the blade and circled the opponent three times his size. *Cheeds!*

Chidi swung wide to flank the Leper.

Their opponent wheeled to face her and swiped with his yellowed fingernails whenever she drew near.

Chidi backpedaled.

The mousey man sputtered nearby.

The Leper turned passive. He ran to his wan benefactor's side and pulled him to his feet. Stroking the mousey man's face, the Leper responded in an unknown tongue.

Cheeds, what'd he say?

I—I don't know, Chidi replied. *I don't understand that language.*

The Leper shoved the mousey man toward the stairwell. He wheeled, slicing at her with a crude dagger, rusty in color, filled with porous holes, and he grinned at Chidi with blackened teeth. The tip of his blade ushered her come closer.

Just reached the bus, Ellie said. *Heard someone say S.W.A.T. is coming in. Whatever that means.*

The Leper's eyes flitted between Chidi and Lenny in debate. He settled on Chidi.

She readied to defend a blow that never came.

A blond-headed teen speared the Leper before he could attack. Both crashed over a tabletop. The assailant used the momentum to somersault away.

Racer landed on his feet. "Heard you two found a Leper."

The Leper grunted in defiance.

Racer bounced from one foot to the other. "Come on," he dared, feinting in and out of reach with lightning speed. "Time to prove Lions are better than Lepers!"

Chidi, Lenny said. *Go get Oscar. We gotta move!*

Chidi abandoned the fight and ran to Oscar's side. The table Marisa had thrown lay cracked in two on either side of him. Oscar showed no signs of bleeding, but Chidi reckoned he would have an unrelenting headache when he woke. She slapped his face to rouse him, but it had no effect. Chidi knelt and put her shoulder under his armpit. With a heaving grunt, she lifted him and struggled to stand.

Hang on, Paulo said. *I'll get him, chica.*

Chidi saw him come around the corner carrying the mousey man on his shoulders. The man's canvas pack had been trapped between his body and Paulo's, and his Selkie outfit remained inside alongside notebooks threatening to fall out. Chidi shoved them back inside.

"Found him going the other way when I was coming in," Paulo said. "Saw the sealskin and thought we might need him. Whew.

This guy's heavier than he looks," Paulo paused to catch his breath again. He pointed at Racer and the Leper. "Looks like our pup's tiring."

"Yes."

While Racer had used his speed to dodge, the Leper had conserved his energy. Though slower, Racer still danced away from the Leper's attacks.

Paulo cracked his knuckles. "Time for the big boy to step in."

"No," Chidi said. "We need to leave."

Their argument came to a halt when a blue dart struck the Leper's right thigh. He yanked it free.

Lenny aimed the tranq gun at the Leper, the same gun Oscar had used to start the panic. He took another shot. The Leper dodged it, now alerted to the new attacker.

Outnumbered, the Leper snarled. He threw the dart aside and ran for the southern exit.

Paulo started after him.

Chidi jumped in front of him, waving her arms. "No, Paulo! We need to go. Now!"

"She's right, Paulie," said Lenny. "We're outta here."

Uh, Len, Ellie's voice cut into their minds. *You're not going to like this...I see Henry. He's walking toward me right now.*

Lenny's face turned a furious shade of red. *What's he doin' outta the water?*

Dunno, ask him yourself, Ellie said. *Meantime, Henry says cops formed a perimeter at the south terrace. I saw a whole team come in the front too. You need to move.*

Paulo tossed Chidi the canvas backpack. "Time to get wet."

Chidi secured it across her back, then moved in to help steady

Paulo as he balanced the two unconscious Selkies on his shelf-like shoulders.

Ellie, get the bus to the rally point, Lenny ordered. "The rest of ya with me. We're goin' east and ova the wall! Where's Racer?"

"Here…"

Their sprinter lay flat on his back, his breath raspy and quick.

A sprinter with asthma. Wonderful.

"Cheeds," Lenny called. "Get him!"

She followed his order, much as she would have rather ran for the wall and safety of the water. Some escaping tourist had flipped the fire alarm on their way out. Chidi couldn't discern how much time had passed, but she knew it wouldn't be long before Dryback authorities stormed the area.

Chidi ran to Racer and threw his arm over her shoulder. She hauled him to his feet before he could utter any kind of thanks. Together, they limped toward the terrace.

Uh, crew, Ellie said. *I have some more news you're not going to like.*

Not now, Ellie, Lenny said.

Okay, but you might want—

Not now!

Chidi kicked the glass doors open and led Racer onto the terrace.

The weather had turned sour on them. Sunny when Chidi first entered the aquarium, it had turned to a torrential downpour. Wind whipped at her hood with no buildings to break up its force. Even so, Chidi welcomed being outdoors. She turned east for the lake and saw Lenny and Paulo paused twenty feet from the edge.

A slim figure dressed in a hooded, shaggy onesie stood before them atop the ledge.

Chidi gasped. *How did she…*

Marisa Bourgeois glanced over her shoulder. She took one look at Chidi and winked.

Buckets of blood, Lenny cursed.

Oh, good… Ellie said. *So you did find her.*

CHIDI

CHIDI TUNED OUT THE ONCOMING WAILS OF POLICE and fire sirens twinning alongside the alarms inside the Shedd Aquarium. She had eyes only for the runner prowling the veranda ledge, gazing at each of her would-be captors in turn. *How did you get away?*

"*Hoekom volg jy my?*" Marisa Bourgeois asked.

Paulo lowered both Oscar and the mousey man to the ground. His earrings flashed. *This is a fun surprise.* He gave Lenny a sideways glance. *Thought you said we had her, Len.*

Thought we did. Lenny scowled. *Cheeds, ya were there. What happened?*

I-I dunno. I would've sworn—

Marisa shook off her baggy jeans. They fell to the ground. Instead of bare legs, Marisa's hooded sweatshirt resembled a tight-fitted onesie that ran down to her ankles.

"*Hoekom volg jy my?*" Marisa asked again.

Lenny sneered. "Cheeds, ya understand what she's sayin'?"

Chidi nodded. "She asks why we're following her."

"Foreigners," Lenny muttered, his voice heavy with the accent of his Bostonian forefathers. "She knows why we're here. And tell her to use words we can all understand. I like to know what's bein' said the first time around."

Chidi translated his message.

Marisa's gaze swiveled to her. She barked a laugh and continued speaking her foreign tongue. "*Tell the nipperkin I speak in whatever language I choose. Just as I go wherever it pleases me. Can it be your captain does not recognize one who is free?*"

Chidi translated the message word for word.

Lenny spit when Chidi mentioned the word *free*. Though he said nothing, Chidi noticed both his earrings, and Paulo's, flashed throughout the exchange. Chidi also took note neither spoke to her. *They plot without me...*

Marisa studied each of the males. "*I could help them, you know... but even now they let the Salt hold its sway.*" She showed her open palm to Chidi. "*Its currents bend and break the wills of many, but I sense they have not made you forget. Let me help you find strength again.*"

Lenny's earrings flashed. *All right crew, I'm sick of this broad. Be ready. Paulie's gonna rush her on my go. If he misses and she dives in, we follow. Racer!*

The youngest of them sprang to life. *Yeah, Len?*

Ya got any speed left?

Racer shrugged free of Chidi. *I'll find some.*

Good, said Lenny. *Ya swim her down and hold on till the rest of us catch up.*

Aye, aye.

Marisa's lip curled at the sight of all the flashing earrings. "*When will you stop hunting your own kind? You send them to slavery when it could be freedom for them and yourselves!*"

Chidi translated the words with the same heated tone in which Marisa spoke.

Marisa pointed at them. "*Jy wil om my te vang, ja? Sleep my aan die Sout en verkoop my? Kom dan…kom jaag my Leonard.*"

Lenny's head snapped toward Chidi. "Did that runna say my name? How does she know my name?"

Marisa's earrings flashed, and her voice echoed in Chidi's mind. *Sê vir hom.*

Chidi took a step back. She hadn't noticed Marisa also wore the same crystal-studded earrings until now. Chidi's jaw wordlessly opened and closed. She glanced back at Marisa for the answer. *Tell him… She wants Lenny to know she's been playing with him until now.*

Marisa pointed at Lenny. *Sê vir hom!*

Chidi tried wetting her lips, but even her tongue was dry. "She knows you want to drag her back to the Salt and sell her. And she says…she says…"

"What?"

Tell it true, Chidi! "She says you—" Chidi looked at Lenny. "*You* have to chase her."

The dwarf's face flushed red. He turned to Marisa. "Why me?"

Marisa smiled at his confusion. "*Ek het van jou gehoor…en jou pa.*"

"She knows of you and your father," Chidi translated.

"*Jy is die weghol jagters,*" Marisa said.

"You and he are the runaway hunters—"

"And proud of it," Lenny interrupted. "A runna's worse than a slave. They don't care for nobody. They got whateva punishment's comin' to them."

Marisa sneered. *"Die slaaf vangers,"*

"The slave catchers," said Chidi.

Marisa donned her hood. *"Is jy seker wil hê ek moet jou prooi word?"*

"She asks if you're certain you want to hunt her?"

"I don't gotta choice," Lenny said. "It's my job."

Chidi translated Lenny's words.

Marisa's earrings flashed. Again, she spoke only to Chidi. *Daar is altyd 'n keuse.*

There is always a choice.

Marisa turned her gaze back on Lenny. *"Toe my jaag…slaaf vangers."*

Chidi hesitated. She glanced at her crewmates.

"What'd she say, Cheeds?" Lenny demanded.

"Then hunt me…" Chidi said breathlessly. "Slave catchers."

Marisa waited for Chidi to finish then giggled. The tip of her hood elongated like a descending curtain over her face. She lifted her arms outward, tilted her body, and launched off the ledge in a backward swan dive.

Chidi rushed forward with her crewmates. Her hands smacked the marbled ledge to stop her from catapulting over the side. She looked down just in time to see Marisa enter the lake, her transformation already complete.

"Go! Go! Go!" Lenny shouted.

The males donned their hoods and dove off the wall, one after the other, already shifting.

Paulo went first, the gargantuan weight of his Southern Elephant Seal body creating a plume of green lake water when he smacked the surface.

Racer entered the water with more elegance. His sleek California Sea Lion body sliced through the water with all the grace of a champion diver. He went in nose first, his long flippers flatly tapered to his sides.

Lenny reached the water last, a small, chubby Ringed Seal pup following its larger cousins on an afternoon hunt.

Chidi alone had remained atop at the terrace. *Um, boys…*

Paulie, go deep. Lenny called out orders. *Racer, find her trail.*

In their haste to follow Marisa, the others had forgotten to take the unconscious two with them. They could do without the mousey man. But Oscar…

In his current state, Oscar Collins appeared like a sweet young teenager with a good strong face and a mop of brown hair. Chidi would have known him no mere slave even without his white backed and black hooded Harp Seal coat. His lack of scars and brands gave the secret away. How her crewmates had left their owner's son behind Chidi couldn't fathom.

The veranda now cleared of voices, the mousey man peeked a look around. His face paled when he saw one of the Selkie catchers had remained behind.

Chidi gave him no opportunity to run. She sprang forward and grabbed his shirt. In one quick motion, she threw him over the edge, then grabbed Oscar by his hood and did the same to him.

She noticed movement inside the aquarium; figures dressed in black battle gear swarmed the chaotic scene the Selkie crew had left behind. One noticed her, a lone figure outside the perimeter they created. He motioned to the others.

Chidi ran for the edge. Reaching for her hood, she flew off the side of the terrace just before the S.W.A.T. team exited out onto it.

She beckoned the image of her Salt form come to mind—a female Ribbon Seal—as the Silkie hood draped over her face.

Weightless and blinded, the Silkie skin's warmth washed over her extremities as her human body morphed into seal. She tucked her broad seal head the moment she hit the E. Coli infested water of Lake Michigan. The movement catapulted her right-side up. She surfaced for air.

Nothing down here but trash, Paulo said, his voice faint.

Keep lookin', said Lenny.

Several S.W.A.T. team members pointed to the water. One yelled they had seen a girl jump.

Chidi dove before any might recognize a Ribbon Seal in an unfamiliar habitat, swimming through the green, filthy water.

She located Oscar's body six feet beneath the surface. Chidi had half-hoped the cold shock might be enough awaken his human senses. No such luck. She swam to him, nipped his black hood in her jaws.

The men on the ledge had gone by the time she resurfaced to keep Oscar from drowning. Had they not, they might have seen the mousey man flailing nearby. Though slower without his Selkie suit, it hadn't stopped him from swimming for shore.

Racer, Chidi said. *I need some help with the other runner.*

No, said Lenny. *Racer, stay put. We're findin' Bourgeois!*

But, Len—

Cheeds, we're supposed to get the girl. Not some Selkie she met with.

Maybe that runner could tell us more about her. Chidi thought to herself. *Why else would he have been meeting her?*

The mousey man had nearly reached the shore when an eight thousand pound seal surfaced behind him.

Paulo! Chidi said. *What are you doing? Lenny said to stay put.*

Paulo nipped the man's leg and dragged him into deeper water. *He told Racer to stay put. Figured I should at least catch one runner today. Come on. It's a long swim to the rally point.*

Aye, aye.

Chidi placed her foreflippers under Oscar's armpits, spooning him. To keep his head above water would mean swimming the next twenty miles on her back.

There is always a choice. Chidi recalled Marisa's words.

She snorted a stream of bubbles and resigned herself to the swim. With a swift thrust of her hind flippers, she followed Paulo's lead southeast and dragged Oscar's dead weight with her.

GARRETT

CHANGE. GARRETT PRESSED HIS FEET FLAT AGAINST the tub wall. He waited for the slightest bit of color variance in his skin tone.

Nothing.

Garrett squinted, focused so hard his head shook. *Change!*

Nothing.

Sighing, he sank back into the tub and sloshed water over the edge. He punched the side. Shampoo bottles rolled off.

A knock came at the door.

"Garrett? Honey? You all right?"

Garrett rolled his eyes. "I'm fine, Mom. Just…slipped is all."

"You sure? You don't sound okay."

"Mom, I'm fine."

"Okay, well…don't you think it's about time you got out? You've been in there for over an hour."

No way. The water would be freezing by now.

"Garrett?"

"Still here, Mom." Garrett looked at his legs and toes again. "I'll be out soon."

"Okay, well, I'm here when you do get out. If you need to talk…"

Garrett massaged his temples. "Yeah, thanks, Mom. I might."

He waited until he heard her footsteps pad away from the door. He reached over the side to check the phone, put on silent to not break his concentration. Three missed calls, twenty texts. All from Johnny Hickey and Sydney Gao asking for updates. Garrett cleared the screen of them to view the time.

6:30? Garrett dropped the phone back on his towel and dipped into the water. *Has it really already been an hour?* He flipped his hands palm-side up. *I don't even have wrinkles yet.*

He sat up. Bent to inspect his toes and the bottoms of his feet. They had no wrinkles either. *What is happening? What did Kellen do to me?*

Garrett unplugged the drain, watched the water disappear. He sat naked in the tub, waiting. He looked at his arms and legs; he saw no sign of gooseflesh, no hairs standing on end. In fact, he still felt warm.

His phone vibrated on the ground. Johnny again.

Garrett ignored it. There would come a time to talk with Johnny about all that happened that day, but not yet. Plus, Garrett wanted to prove himself an actual mutant, rather than hope his best friend accepted it as fact. Not feeling cold when staying in the bath for an extended time hardly seemed noteworthy on the chart of awesome superpowers.

He reached for his towel and dried off. *I wonder what would happen if I put ice cubes in the tub?*

Garrett pulled on his boxers and the torn up sweats his mom had begged him to throw away. He threw on an orange T-shirt from his freshman year that read Tigress Tennis in navy lettering across the chest. Below it, a tiger dressed in a mini-skirt held a tennis racket in one paw. Garrett's last name lettered the back along with MANAGER written directly beneath it.

He pocketed his phone, tossed his towel on the drying rack, and headed down the stairs. He heard his mom long before he reached the kitchen and paused at the bottom of the steps.

"You bet I'm pressing charges! Dick, he almost murdered my son," Cristina Weaver yelled into her phone as she paced the kitchen floor. "No, Garrett's not okay. I'm not okay. Those boys have picked on him long enough. It's bad enough he can't go anywhere in this town without people spreading gossip and silly rumors about him. Now he has to deal with this too?"

Garrett smiled. *Go get them, Mom. Tell that sheriff who's boss.*

Guys at school used to tell him he had the second hottest mom in Lavere County, after Jun Gao's mom of course. Garrett remembered those days when she used to take care of herself. He peeked around the corner.

She still wore her Gracin's Grille waitress uniform—brown slacks with food stains on one leg, teal and white pinstriped shirt. She had even forgotten to untie her apron. Her frazzled hair had loosed itself from the bun the Grille required her to wear. She had stuck a pencil through it to stop the full-on release.

"No, don't you give me that you'll look into it crap," she said. "I've heard it all before. I want him in jail tonight. Now."

Garrett stepped into the kitchen.

Cristina cleared her throat. "Yeah. You call me when it's done and not before."

She hung up the phone, tossed it on the counter. Wordless and crying already, she motioned him come over.

Garrett resigned himself to what felt like the thousandth hug she had given him since his release from the hospital. "Mom, I'm fine."

Cristina buried her head in his shoulder and cried harder.

Garrett patted her on the back. "Really, I am. I'm not going anywhere."

"I know," she said, her voice muffled by his shirt. "I know you're not. Just don't know what I would do if I lost you."

"You don't have to worry about that."

"I know…I know." She nodded, and let go. Wiped her tears away. "You hungry? We can order pizza."

"No. Thanks."

"No pizza?" Cristina put the back of her hand to his forehead. "Are you sure you're all right? If not, we can go back to the hospital."

"Mom…you're doing it again. The doctors said I'm fine. I didn't even need to go to the hospital in the first place. I told Ms. Morg—"

"I'm glad you did. If they had found something wrong with you…" She touched his cheek. "Don't you worry. Kellen Winstel won't be bothering you again. I already told Sheriff Hullinger we're pressing charges."

"Really?"

"You bet I am. He could have killed you."

Garrett shivered. "I don't want to talk about it."

"Okay, honey." Cristina hugged him again.

Ask her. Garrett pulled away. "Mom…did dad ever…talk to you about changing?"

Cristina's forehead wrinkled. "Changing? What do you mean, honey, change—oh." She took a seat at the table. "Changing, right. Well, your father told me once he was a late bloomer so it's only natural that—"

"Mom! I'm not talking about *puberty* changes."

"Well, how am I supposed to know, honey? You're a young man, young men go through—"

"Okay, okay," Garrett cut her off. "Can we not talk about...*that* kind of changing. Ever."

"Well, what kind of changes do you mean?"

"I-I dunno, Mom. Just, my skin...I noticed...some changes."

"Sweetie, the doctors said that can happen. It's common, even, for people with vitiligo."

Garrett thought back to the pool; how his skin color had become absolute black and white, rather than the scattered tannish splotches he had grown accustomed to. "Yeaaah. I don't think this is common."

"Did you check the forums? The doctors said if your disorder ever made you feel alone, or curious, that you should check the forums."

"Mom, I don't think—"

Cristina's phone buzzed. She glanced down at it. "Hmm. I don't recognize the number. It could be..."

"Go ahead." Garrett stood. "I'll be in my room."

"Okay." Cristina stopped him. "Honey...check the forums. Might help."

Garrett grabbed a bag of BBQ chips as he left the kitchen; heard his mom use the fake voice she had been trained to answer calls at the Grille with. He took the steps two at a time, snagged his beat-to-crap laptop from his backpack. After plopping into bed amidst a heap of dirty laundry, he booted the computer up and opened the bag of chips.

He found an old email his doctor had sent with links to various vitiligo support groups. He clicked on it, skimmed through the comments. Most threads discussed various treatments others had tried and how they had worked for a short while but the condition always returned. Some comments listed the best kinds of makeup brands for any searching to cover up the off-colored skin tones.

Garrett searched for the personal stories. He read up on bullying they had encountered, the various emotional stages that typically accompanied such treatment and odd stares from strangers.

The stories he liked best dealt with those who overcame the haters. He clicked on the *give a hug* option for a few, and marked others as helpful. Still, none made mention of their skin changing as fast as his did. Nor did any mention their disorder providing a better tolerance to cold water.

Garrett polished off the remaining chips. He crumpled the bag, threw it at the trash bin. Missed. *Of course.*

"Gare, honey?" Cristina said from behind his bedroom door. "Can I come in?"

Garrett closed his laptop. "Yeah, what's up?"

Cristina pushed the door open. "That was Sydney on the phone. She couldn't reach you on your cell so she called me instead. Wanted to know if you might like a visitor." She smirked.

"Don't do that, Mom."

"Do what?"

"Act like Sydney wants to come over because she's into me. She's probably just doing it because she's class president, or she wants me to vote her onto some prom committee or something."

"Oh, I don't think Sydney's like that." Cristina sat on the edge of his bed. "Maybe she really does want to make sure you're all right. You two have gotten awfully close since she started dropping you off after tennis practice."

"Yeah, because she feels sorry for me."

"Maybe," Cristina said. "I feel sorry for you too."

"Why?" Garrett asked.

"Because you're being silly. Honestly, just assuming a pretty girl like Sydney won't like you. You have a lot to offer you know."

"Sure I do. I have loads to offer the hottest girl in school."

"You do. You're smart, funny, handsome—"

Garrett shook his head. "You're only saying that because you're my mom."

"That's not true. Moms have eyes too you know. I see girls look at you all the time."

"Yeah, because of my skin."

Cristina grabbed him by the chin, forced him to look into her eyes. "Can you read minds?"

"No…"

"Then you don't know what people think when they look at you." She let him go. "And if you write them off as just seeing your disorder, does that make you a better person?"

"No, Mom."

Garrett's phone buzzed. He looked at the screen, dismissed it.

"Hickey again?" Cristina asked.

Garrett nodded. "He's called like ten times already."

"Maybe you should call him back. He probably just wants to know you're okay too."

"Yeah."

Garrett tossed his phone back onto his pillow but gave it a little more umph than he intended. The phone slid off the other side and knocked the picture frame on his desk over. Garrett reached for the frame and stood it back up.

The picture had been taken at the Indianapolis Zoo on Garrett's 1st grade field trip, the only one his dad ever chaperoned. The bear of a man had six-year-old Garrett wrapped around one leg, around his other, a little Chinese girl with her hair tied in ponytails. Both stood on Tom Weaver's shoes, their mouths agape in what could only be laughter.

Garrett heard sniffling behind him.

"He loved that day," she said when Garrett turned back to her. "He wished he could have done more things like that with you. He just wanted…just wanted to make a better life for you."

"I know he did, Mom."

She pulled Garrett in for hug number one thousand and one.

"Don't you go anywhere on me," she said. "Promise?"

"I promise, Mom."

She sat back, wiped her tears away. "Death has a way of making you think about all the things you should have said and done."

"I'm not dead." Garrett said.

"No, you're not." She kissed his forehead. "You call your friends back. It's not everyone who gets a second chance to tell the ones they love how they really feel."

"Okay."

Cristina kissed him again then left Garrett alone.

Garrett picked up his phone, unlocked it with the passcode. He went to favorites, his thumb paused above Sydney's name. He thought back on all that his mom had said, especially the part about the things one should have said and done.

Garrett sat up straight. He cleared the favorite numbers away and pulled up a new text instead. His fingers flew across the screen.

He read it once, twice, then hit send. Garrett sighed, slumped back into the pillows.

For the first time since early that morning, he felt normal again.

CHIDI

THE SUN HAD NEARLY SET BY THE TIME THEY reached the rally point, an empty stretch of coastline dunes just north of Chesterton, Indiana.

A lone sentinel awaited them at the beach.

Chidi felt his watchful eyes even from fifty yards out. She picked up speed on the way in, then stopped—releasing Oscar—and let her wake carry him into the shallows. She beached herself, gently bit down on his shoulder, and dragged Oscar to where the waters no longer touched him.

Chidi collapsed.

The hard and crusty lakeside sand did not easily give way like that of ocean beaches. She closed her seal eyes, listened for the sounds of gulls like she used to hear in her native Sierra Leone. She found none here, only the wind mocking her plight and the tuft of breaking sand that marked someone's approach.

Henry's fists will come. Her jaw instinctively clenched. *At least this way I might hurt his hands.*

Instead, two human fingers slipped under her upper seal lip. They tugged up, then back, and her seal head peeled away. Seconds later, she shivered without the seal's blubbery skin to warm her. She looked up.

"Thank you, Paulo," she said quietly.

He winked back then lifted Oscar's body and carried him up the beach like a shepherd boy with an injured lamb.

A small part of Chidi desired to follow him and rejoin the crew. She remained in the sand to delay the reunion with her owner.

When the sun poked through the grey skies, Chidi tilted her face upward to take in its small warmth. A moment later, the wind returned and swept loose top sand at her. Chidi heard arguing as she brushed the sand away.

Up the beach, Paulo stood between her and Henry Boucher.

Her owner wore the charcoal-spotted and grey-backed skin of a Leopard Seal. He had earned it, to hear him tell others, just as he had earned everything else in life. Chidi knew better.

She watched Henry feign ignorance to Paulo's warning. She had seen him perform the same act for countless others. And any who believed it for long wound up losing more than just their holdings and anemonies.

"You stay there," Paulo said to Henry, "and guard him."

Him being the mousey man. His once dignified, styled hair now lay flatly plastered against his forehead. He wrapped his arms around his chest, hugging himself, cowering behind raised knees.

Hope your vision isn't too bad. You lost your glasses to the lake bottom.

Henry caught her attention. His thin lips parted in a salacious grin. *"Bonjour, mon amour."*

Chidi risked turning away.

A seal with disproportionate white circles scattered across its grey back waddled onto shore. No bigger than a Labrador, its small size and sad black eyes almost made it appear it cuddly—until it clacked its jaws and growled.

Paulo hurried over as if bidden by an unheard voice. He stuck his meaty fingers in the seal's mouth, pulled up and back, and freed the dwarf of his Selkie form.

The moment he had his human tongue back, Lenny let fly a string of profanities the likes of which Chidi had sadly grown accustomed. She watched him stomp up the beach with Paulo in tow to confront Henry.

"Paulie, when I tell ya to stay in the water, whattaya do?"

"Stay in the water."

Racer, Lenny broadcast his thoughts to the entire crew. *Whattaya do when I tell ya to stay in the water?*

Twenty-five yards out into the lake, Chidi saw a California Sea Lion leap out of the water, then reenter with a noisy splash.

I, uh, stay in the water, Racer said.

Chidi would have smiled if she thought Henry wouldn't see. Racer's swim signified to her he had never done so, alone, without taskmasters to keep watch over him. He didn't seem to mind that the lake water shared neither the clearness nor depths as the oceans. Racer wouldn't leave the water until Lenny ordered him, she knew.

"So when I tell ya—" Lenny poked Henry's stomach. "That I want ya *in* the water. Whattaya think ya should do?"

"I should 'ave stayed in ze water, I suppose," Henry said coolly. "But I confess, I deed not know to whom I should leesin."

"Ya listen to me, Frenchy! I assigned ya—"

"*Oui.* You assign me to ze water, but *Monsieur* Oscar told me to take 'is post. Take 'eet up with 'im."

"Oscar told ya to move?"

Henry nodded.

"*I* make the calls here," Lenny said. "Not him."

Henry raised a defiant eyebrow. "I am only a poor, 'umble Selkie. Ze Crayfish pays me to leesin and guard 'is son."

"Well, ya not doin' a very good job, huh?" Lenny pointed to where Paulo had dropped Oscar. "Ya pup got knocked out back there. Meantime, I'm still standin' and givin' orders."

Henry shrugged. "Maybe if you paid me, I would leesin to you. Can you pay me more, leetle Lenny?"

It wouldn't matter how much someone paid you, Chidi kept the thought to herself. *Nothing will ever be enough.*

"Ya know slaves don't get paid for what we do," Lenny said. "I catch runnas 'cause I have to. Ya doin' it for the money and 'cause ya like it."

"As I said, I am only a poor, 'umble Selkie. And 'eef you cannot pay me, zen I weel 'ave to leesin to *Monsieur* Oscar."

Henry turned his back to them then. Speaking his native French, he barked at Chidi to carry Oscar's body to the bus. When she obeyed without question, he fell in beside her to whisper things that would have made her cringe before she had been Salted.

Chidi instead focused all her attention on the mammoth bus parked along the abandoned access road. Designed for transporting tourists, it rivaled the size of an eighteen-wheeler semi. A line of faded blue ran around the middle, cutting through the otherwise chipping grey paint everywhere else. Nine windows lined each side, each blacked out.

Chidi still remembered learning in school how her fellow Africans had been brought to the Americas on slave ships. Packed and stacked together, carried across the ocean in the bellies of wooden beasts.

She had not been long in her Salt life before discovering where humans stole the idea.

The bus in front of her shared the same purpose its seafaring forefathers did. Its lower half had been converted to transport captured runners and new slaves on their journey back to the Salt. Chidi estimated the bus could fit thirty upon first seeing it. Oscar had laughingly told her she lacked imagination; the holds could fit sixty-five slaves when properly stacked.

Henry rubbed his clammy fingers about her neck, massaging it as they walked.

Chidi's stomach churned.

The bus door swung outward as they approached. Ellie Briceño, an older teen slightly smaller than Paulo, sat in the driver's seat with her feet propped on the dashboard. Eating pretzels by the handful, she watched a small television hung above the rear view mirror.

"...we're coming to you live from the Shedd Aquarium, where a teenaged gunman opened fire and fled the scene. Details—"

Ellie paused it. "Lenny, they have a sketch of Oscar's description from the Drybacks who made it outside. We should get moving."

Lenny boldly stepped in front of the bus door, blocking Chidi from entering. "Where ya goin', Cheeds?"

Henry pulled her closer. "She 'eez going to ze bus as I told 'er."

"And, uh...do ya captain this merry band, Henry?"

"No." Henry stroked Chidi's cheek. "But she does what she 'eez told like a good leetle girl. Why? Because I own 'er."

"And the Crayfish owns you, so—"

"No one *owns me*!" Henry snarled. "'E only pays me—for now."

"How ya think August Collins earned the nickname Crayfish?"

Lenny asked. "Just 'cause he says he's gonna pay ya don't mean he will. And the Crayfish put me in charge."

"*Monsieur* Oscar—"

Lenny lifted a finger to his own ear. "Hmm. I don't hear much outta Oscar right now. Guess what I say goes."

Chidi prayed Lenny wouldn't ask her to translate the things her owner muttered in French. Worse, she knew Henry would have little qualm about making good on the deadly things his words promised.

"Get goin'," said Lenny. "And take Oscar with ya. After all, that's what ya were hired for, right Henry? To protect him?"

Chidi's heart raced when Henry knelt. She had seen him move quicker than most would give him credit for. His hands came far closer to the Selkie pocket in which he hid his dagger than she would have liked. The moment passed without incident, however, and Henry climbed the steps with Oscar slung over his shoulder. Both disappeared into the back.

"Lenny," said Ellie. "Did you not hear what I said? They have Oscar's description and—"

"I heard ya."

Paulo glanced at the mousey man. "What should we do with this one?"

"Ask him some questions." Lenny shuffled over. "How do ya know Marisa Bourgeois?"

The captive seemed not to have heard him. He looked a tired thing, to Chidi's mind. *Worn and beaten by the swim...or frightened we might take him back to the Salt and sell him?*

"Hey!" Lenny kicked the mousey man's shin. "What's ya name?"

"Z-Z-Zymon...G-Gorski. Please!" he whimpered. "Please. I don't know what you want, but I'll tell you anything. Only let me go!"

"How do ya know Marisa Bourgeois?"

"P-p-please, I don't know anyone by that name," Zymon said. "I need to see my family. I don't know anyone named—"

Lenny made a fist. "Gorski, I swear to the Ancients, ya lie to me one more time and I'll call Henry back out here to deal with—"

"Len, don't—"

"Shuddup, Cheeds!"

Chidi shrunk back.

"How do ya know her?" Lenny asked again.

Paulo squeezed another yelp out of Zymon before the answer came. "M—my contact told me her name was Cole...C—Colette Chaput. I never met her in person before. Please, I'm an accountant now. I've been free for ten years. Started a new family. Please...don't take me back. Don't make me a slave again."

"How did ya get ya suit off in the first place?"

"I paid a Mer—Merrow," Zymon said. "Do you want his name? I'll give it to you...only let me go—"

"We're not interested. None of us run. We don't abandon others to take our punishment."

"I have a question," Paulo said. "If you didn't wanna end up back in the Salt, why'd you keep the sealskin?"

Zymon rubbed snot from his nose. "I-I still like to swim... s-sometimes."

"So why do ya have it here, out in the open, for all to see? Why'd ya take it to that meetin'?"

Zymon's body shuddered. "To give it to the boy."

Boy? Chidi had no memory of any boy with him at the Shedd Aquarium. She looked at her crewmates.

Only Ellie seemed unbothered. "I put him in the under," she said.

Upending the bag of pretzels, she shook the crumbled remains into her wide mouth. Then she pitched the bag aside and thundered down the bus steps. "Here, Len," she tossed him a black notebook.

Lenny caught it. "What's this? What boy is he talkin' about?"

"That is a notebook. One of the few the kid carried in his pack. I think they belonged to Marisa, but I can't read most of the words. She wrote in a bunch of other languages and symbols and crap. Anyway, Marisa used the boy as her decoy. I got all the way back to the bus with him before I realized *he* wasn't a *she*." Ellie chuckled. "Looks like our runner's a smart one."

Lenny turned his hard stare on Chidi. "I saw ya chase her outta the cafeteria...which means ya were the last to see her."

He thinks I let her go. The realization hurt almost as much as the truth; that it had been her to lose sight of Marisa in the hallway.

"I was behind her the whole time..." said Chidi. "I-I never lost sight of her."

"Ya must have somewhere along the way. How else did she wind up on the ledge?"

Chidi had no answer for him.

Fortunately, Ellie did. "The kid stunk like he bathed in squid ink. Chidi choked on the stuff too when I saw her chasing him. Marisa must have used a Squid Ball, huh?"

"Yes," Chidi quietly agreed. "You can probably still smell it on me, too. Here," she extended her arm toward Lenny. "Smell."

That Lenny obliged her so fast told Chidi she had lost whatever grounds of trust the two had built thus far. "All right, Cheeds... I believe ya."

This time. Chidi finished what the skeptical captain did not say, nor need to.

While Lenny kept watch over Zymon, Paulo held the hold door open for Ellie. She reached into the blackness and dragged the captive out by his ankles. The boy winced at the sudden light.

He's from Africa...like me. Chidi knew it in her soul just by looking into his eyes. In them she saw life bursting bright and clear, even if he looked around as one lost to his surroundings. She could not recall the last time there had been such stirrings in her heart, not those of love nor passion, but kinship.

The boy's head had been shaved, most likely by Marissa to trick any of her would-be captors. He wore the same hoodie she had, a shaggy Cape Fur, and shared the same coal-colored skin as Marisa.

Lenny turned Zymon over to Paulo. "Hey, pup." He stepped toward the kid. "Ya speak any English? What's ya name, huh?"

"My name is Allambee Omondi," the boy answered without the slightest touch of fear or worry. Then he grinned at Lenny, as broad of one as any Chidi had ever seen. "Are you da one come to help me?"

Lenny scoffed. "Helpin' ya? We don't even know ya. How we supposed to help ya?"

"I don't know," Allambee said. "But Marisa told me a little magic man named Dolan could help me find my fatha."

Paulo snickered. "Know any magic, Len?"

"Shuddup, Paulie."

"How did you get here, Allambee?" Chidi asked. "Why did you come to the United States?"

Allambee blushed. "I never knew my fatha, but I am told he was a great man. My mutha say he did some bad things and dat is why he went away. One day I came home from school and found my mutha waiting for me with a girl I did not know. She told me de time to find my fatha had come, and de person beside her could help me."

"Lemme guess," said Lenny. "Marisa."

"Yes," said Allambee. "She said I must come with her because my fatha would need my help soon. She gave me a drink to help me sleep, and den I awoke in a building filled with fish. Marisa said I must wait in de washrooms while she spoke with a man who had tools that could help me."

Paulo nudged Zymon forward. "She tell you this guy could forge fakes for you?"

"I do not know him," Allambee said.

He has an honest face. She had learned to sniff out a lie in her years since being taken and heard no telltale signs in Allambee's answer.

"Forget it, Paulo," Ellie said. "He's not a Selkie. What he's wearing…it's a sweatshirt she dolled up to look like a sealskin."

"Selkie…" Zymon spit the word. "The boy doesn't even know what that word means, of what we are. My contact…Cole…she found me and said if I didn't give her the suit, sh-she would let others know wh-where to find me. Sh-she offered to buy it from me."

"So she could give it to a pup who didn't know any better?" Paulo asked. "What if she meant to Salt him with it?"

Chidi watched the ex-slave fall to his knees. Zymon trembled as he wept.

"Somebody get Henry," Lenny said. "This guy would let some pup take his place in a world chock full of monstas. Fine. I'll show him one. Henry!"

Chidi bit her tongue to keep from calling out again. *You don't know what you're asking for, Lenny.*

Henry appeared in the doorway seconds later.

"Take Zymon to the back and do what ya do best," Lenny said. "I wanna know all his secrets."

Paulo reluctantly handed his prisoner over.

"No! No!" Zymon fought as Henry drug him up the steps. "Please! Let me go home! Don't make me go back!"

"Henry!" Lenny said.

"Oui?"

"I want secrets, not a corpse. And don't cut anything off this time."

Henry frowned. "But, *monsieur*, zat 'ees ze easiest way to get secrets."

Chidi shut her ears of Zymon's begging, even as Henry dragged the older man up the steps. He closed the door to deafen the screams to come.

Paulo shook his head. "You should have let me take a go at him first, Len. Henry will—"

"Get answers fasta. Speakin' of…"

Lenny's eyes danced across the black notebook's contents. He flipped through its pages. One in the middle caught his eye. He came back to it. Studied it. His earrings flashed.

Cheeds, Lenny's voice crept inside her mind. *Henry wouldn't really cut anything off, would he?*

There's no guessing what he might or might not do. Chidi kept the thought back. *That's what makes him so dangerous.* She debated telling Lenny just that. In the end, she only shrugged.

Lenny sighed. "Paulie."

"Yeah, Cap?"

"We're gonna head out soon." He looked up. "Get the pup outta the water."

Chidi marveled how quickly the biggest and strongest amongst their crew obeyed the smallest. *He respects Lenny. They all do, even Ellie…in her own way.*

Ellie stroked her chunky cheeks as Paulo headed out. She motioned to the notebook Lenny reviewed. "Guessing you saw his name too, huh?"

Lenny raised an eyebrow. "I heard he'd been killed in the war. He's been gone, what, twenty years?"

"The Selkie Strife ended in '95…that sounds about right," Ellie said.

"Could be anotha trick," said Lenny. "The decoy act she pulled, the way she acted on the ledge…I dunno. Don't feel right. For all we know, these books are just a dummy trail. Something to keep us lookin' everywhere except the one place we should."

"I don't think so…" Chidi blurted. *What are you doing? Keep your mouth shut! If Henry heard you—*

"Why not?" Ellie asked.

Now you've done it. Chidi looked away and hoped Lenny would speak for her.

"Go on, Cheeds," he said.

Chidi licked her suddenly dry lips. "Well, the way she taunted us, she just seemed so—sure of herself. I've never seen a runner do that before. She didn't seem scared at all."

Lenny closed the notebook. "She will be next time."

"Marisa already tricked us into thinking we had her once," Chidi said. "If she had other business at the Shedd, she could have waited for us to leave and doubled back. She *wanted* us to see her out on that ledge."

She wants us to keep chasing her…why?

Lenny said nothing for a long while. Then he rubbed his fist in his eyes and yawned. "I think Cheeds is right…Marisa finished whateva she needed here. We gotta figure out which aquarium's next on the list and keep trackin'."

"That picture says the Indianapolis Zoo," Ellie hinted. "It's just a few hours south of here."

Lenny tapped the notebook. He fluttered its pages several times, almost like he hoped the pages would speak to him. "Get her fired up."

Ellie shoved the bus door open.

Chidi winced. She expected screams, but heard silence. She exhaled as the heavyset girl thundered up the bus, shaking it in her wake.

"What're they doin'?" Lenny said. "I told him to talk Racer outta the water, not get in with him!" He rolled the notebook and stuffed it in his front Selkie pocket, near his belly. "Cheeds, get this pup on the bus, will ya? He looks harmless enough."

It took Chidi a minute to realize he meant Marisa's decoy. The boy had remained quiet, sitting within the hold, alone and nearly forgotten.

The bus engine roared to life. Diesel exhaust stained the air.

Chidi coughed and stared into the fading daylight.

The colors of this sunset lacked the vibrancy of those she remembered back home. Here the skies turned purple and blue, rather than the blood red and pale oranges she grew up loving.

If I never saw blue again it wouldn't be such a bad thing. She turned her back on it and took a seat next to Allambee.

"I'm sorry they put you in there."

"It is okay," he said. "Your friend Ellie promised she would let me out soon."

Chidi didn't bother pointing out she considered none of her

crewmates as friends. *How is he smiling with everything he's been through?* She answered her own question just as fast. *He doesn't know what's happening. Doesn't know it any better than I did.*

Allambee scooted close enough for their shoulders to touch. He put his left hand in his front pocket and took out a handful of pretzels. "Look what Ellie gave me. Dey taste pretty good, but too salty for me. Would you like some?"

Tears welled behind Chidi's eyes the moment their skin rubbed against one another. *Why do you cry, stupid girl?* She willed them from falling. *It doesn't do any good. Haven't you learned that yet?* Chidi slid away from him.

Undeterred, Allambee scooted with her. "You come from Africa also, yes?"

"How can you tell?"

"I see Her light in your eyes."

Chidi vainly tried to ignore the boy who reminded her so much of home. "We'll be leaving soon."

He grinned again. "Good. I think dat I will sit with you. You are all good people, except for dat man, Henry."

Even a boy sees evil for what it is.

"They joked about him. You know, hurting that other man…" Chidi said. Her conscience immediately scolded her for the lie. He would learn better soon enough when Salted.

"I mean, Henry won't kill him, or cut anyth—"

"It is okay," said Allambee. "I have seen many worse things and am not afraid. My mutha said dat my fatha was a great warrior, and he only feared someone hurting us to get to him. I like to think dat is why he went away. But she also told me he trusted no one, and dat is no way to live."

"Trust is a hard thing to have," Chidi admitted. *Especially in the Salt.*

"My mutha said we must all learn to trust in others to find peace," Allambee paused. He reached into his pocket again and produced another handful of pretzels. He placed them in Chidi's open palm, closed her fingers around them, and held her fist with hands that felt afire.

"I think you and your friends have come to help me."

Tell him to run, Chidi—Now, while the others are distracted! "Allambee—" she started.

The boy's unwavering grin stopped her. "I see you fear Henry, like I would if my mutha had not told me to be brave for her. So I will be brave for you also, and den you will learn to run from fear no longer."

Hot tears streaked down Chidi's cheek at his convictions.

"Why do you cry?" Allambee asked.

For your innocence. Chidi wiped her tears away. *And what the Salt will do with it.*

KELLEN

"HEY, LADY," KELLEN WHISPERED TO THE WOMAN bringing him dinner. "Hey, when am I allowed out of here?"

Like the nurses, she ignored him.

Why isn't anyone talking to me?

Kellen pulled the plastic top off the tray; baked liver, carrots, and applesauce. He yacked into the bin by his bed. Kellen covered the food tray, pushed the cart away, and rubbed the rawness from his throat. He glanced up at the clock.

8:30 already? Where's Dad?

Kellen sighed. He had been in this stupid room over half the day now with no one but a couple old nurses and the food tray lady in to visit. They had even taken the phone from his room and posted a security officer outside the closed door.

Stupid. It was just a prank. Why do they need some guard to watch me?

Kellen had a fleeting image of Garrett Weaver sitting across the pool with his feet in the water. He remembered seeing Ms. Morgan, one of her lazy eyes marbling around as she yelled for him to wake up. Then the darkness had come for him again. When he awoke, he found himself in this tiny cell the hospital called a patient room.

The other image of Garrett, though, that one he remembered clear. Kellen had spent half the afternoon trying to convince himself what he saw underwater could not have been real. None of it made sense. Still, Kellen remained certain he had seen it.

He overheard a nursing code over the intercom, and the door to his room opened. Kellen recognized the portly sheriff immediately.

"Hey, Dick."

Sheriff Hullinger cocked an eyebrow at Kellen's familiar tone. He looked out the door. "Is he ready to go yet? You girls get him discharged already?"

The sheriff nodded when they gave him the okay. One of them handed him some paperwork. He scribbled a signature and gave it back. "All right, then." He looked at Kellen. "I'ma need you to come with me, Kell."

Kellen rose off the bed. "My dad ask you to pick me up or something? I thought you guys only played poker on Wednesdays."

"I'm not here to take you home, and your dad's not coming, son. I need you to turn around for me, put your hands behind your back."

Kellen laughed. "What?"

"Turn around, put your hands behind your back," the sheriff said, sterner this time.

"Is this some kind of joke?"

Sheriff Hullinger stepped forward. "Kellen Winstel, you have the right to remain silent—"

Gimme a break, Hullinger.

"Yeah, I get it." Kellen turned around. "Is my dad putting you up to this?"

The sheriff took one of Kellen's wrists in hand. "Anything you say can be used against you in a court of law."

The handcuffs clicked as they tightened flush against Kellen's skin.

Oh, Dad. You must think is real funny. "You gonna do this all day, Dick? I got it."

The sheriff tightened the final cuff. "You have the right to an attorney—"

"Yeah, yeah, yeah." Kellen popped his shoulders. He tugged at the cuffs to test the resistance. "I understand all my rights, and yada yada. Just skip to the end where you escort me out in handcuffs to embarrass me in front of everyone so my dad can get his laugh in."

Sheriff Hullinger turned Kellen to face him. His expression seemed too serious for Kellen to believe this anything but a joke. The sheriff continued reading Kellen his Miranda rights and quickly arrived at the end of his spiel. "Knowing and understanding your rights as I have explained them to you, are you willing to answer my questions without an attorney present?"

Kellen snorted. "If this were real, you know I would tell you my dad *is* my attorney. Call him to meet us at the station. I'll answer your questions there."

Sheriff Hullinger nodded. He took Kellen by the elbow and led him out of his room.

Kellen noticed the nurses look away when he made eye contact with them. It happened again when they reached the elevator and went down with a couple old farts in wheelchairs. Kellen smirked at every one of them. *Go tell this around town, folks. It'll do wonders for my image at school. Chicks dig the bad boys, haven't you heard?*

Sheriff Hullinger escorted him out of the hospital and to his parked car near the exit. He opened the rear door.

Kellen laughed and scooted in without help. "Hey, Dick. Can you play the siren on our way? I'd just love that."

Sheriff Hullinger slammed the door. A second later, he got in the driver's seat and started up the car. He did not play the siren.

Kellen leaned forward to the metal gate installed between the front and back seats. "So what'd my old man have to say, huh?"

"Sit back, inmate."

"Inmate, *whoo.*" Kellen shivered. "Sounds kinda catchy. Seriously though. What'd my dad say? He waiting on us at the station to film me getting out in handcuffs?"

Sheriff Hullinger glanced up at the rearview mirror. "I said sit back."

"Oookay." Kellen leaned back. "Whatever you say, Hullinger."

Kellen watched the town his dad forced him to live in roll by. They passed Gracin's Grille, the only real restaurant in a thirty-mile radius with food worth eating. Then the used car dealership that never made a sale but somehow stayed in business. Just the sight of them made Kellen sick with boredom.

By the time they reached the jail, his arms had begun to ache. He tried slipping his handcuffs underneath his butt, but the short links prevented it.

Sheriff Hullinger parked near the jail's side entrance marked for officers only. A minute later, he escorted Kellen through the door and down the barren hall.

Kellen felt like he just entered a tomb. "No reason to hold onto me so tight, Hullinger." He clacked his cuffs together. "Clearly I'm not going anywhere. I mean that's the point of all this, right?"

The sheriff said nothing and led him through another door marked as booking.

"Hey, Campbell," Kellen said to the officer behind the desk. "What's new?"

Like the sheriff, Campbell didn't seem his normal jokey self either. He took custody of Kellen and led him to a different room. "You have any weapons or contraband on you?"

Kellen laughed. "Oh yeah. I'm always packing heat. Never know when I might have to bust a cap in this neighborhood."

Campbell muttered a reply and continued his pat down search. Satisfied, he uncuffed Kellen, and directed him to pose for a mug shot.

Kellen cheesed throughout the process.

Campbell refused to take the bait. He next guided Kellen to a desk countertop where he took his fingerprints.

"You're taking this the whole nine yards too, huh?" said Kellen, pressing his fingertips down onto the computer pad for scanning. "Campbell, be serious with me. How much is my dad paying you guys to do this?"

"Not my place to say," Campbell said. "I need your personal information. Name, address—"

"Are you kidding?" Kellen asked. "You've known me since I could walk. We swam on the same relay team. I was a freshman, you were a senior, remember? You took me around to knock over mailboxes before you wound up a cop."

"Shut up, Winstel!" Campbell said.

"Whoa. What's your prob—"

"You're my problem." Campbell folded his arms. "What were you thinking today? Twelving?"

"What's the big deal?" Kellen asked. "It's just a little hazing. Just a prank."

"You almost drowned Garrett Weaver."

"That's the point of twelving," said Kellen. "Or don't you remember? You're the one who told me about it!"

Campbell shoved Kellen into the wall. He leaned in close enough for Kellen to notice the veins in his neck pulsing. "You keep your mouth shut about that, you hear?" Campbell seethed. "Everyone knows that's just a dumb story to scare freshman. Nobody ever took it serious until you."

Kellen sneered. "Maybe that's 'cause I'm not a pussy like the rest of you."

Campbell raised his fist.

"Do it," Kellen said. "In case you didn't notice, I'm not some little freshman anymore."

"No." Campbell lowered his fist. "But here soon you're gonna wish you could be." Campbell smoothed the creases of his shirt and tucked in the loose parts. "Take a seat."

Kellen obeyed as Campbell returned to the desk, and scribbled some notes down.

"What's that you're writing?"

"Explanation of the charges against you." Campbell tore out the paper. "You do want to know what you're being held for, don't you?"

"I know why. Daddy wants to teach me a lesson."

Campbell walked over and handed Kellen the note. "This has nothing to do with your dad. Here."

Kellen took the paper and crumpled it into a ball. He tossed it at the trashcan. He thought Campbell wanted to hit him then. Kellen would have welcomed it. Instead, Campbell grabbed him roughly by the arm and led him to a phone.

"Make your call."

"I'm not calling him," said Kellen. "I'm not giving him what he wants."

"Suit yourself." Campbell cuffed Kellen again and led him back out into the main station.

Kellen saw another pair of familiar faces waiting for him.

"Benny?"

Eddie Bennett glanced over his shoulder. He had tears in his eyes. From the look of him, Kellen guessed he had been crying awhile. Bennett opened his mouth to speak. "Winst—"

"Don't talk to him," Bennett's father said before wheeling on Kellen. "You're the reason he's in this mess. Honestly, what the devil were you boys thinking?"

"Mess?" said Kellen. "What's he talking about, Hullinger?"

The sheriff took back custody of Kellen. "You tell me."

Kellen kept his mouth shut as Bennett's father pushed his son down a different hall, bound for the main entrance.

What could have made Bennett cry like that?

Sheriff Hullinger led Kellen past the booking station, the two of them bound for another door in the back corner.

Kellen tensed. He knew where that door led. The jail had hosted a lock-in when they unveiled the new building a few years back. Kellen remembered staying overnight with a few of his friends. It had been kind of fun at the time. But even then, he felt a little too old for such things.

Now he didn't have a choice.

They walked through the door and entered the jailhouse. The room wasn't huge as far as jails went; only eight cells—four on either side of the row. The cells housed a lone inmate who looked up when he heard the approaching footsteps.

Kellen paused. "Owens?"

"Hey…" Owens's head drooped.

The sheriff tugged Kellen's arm and walked him to the cell opposite Owens. The metal door opened soundlessly on its well-greased hinges. "Turn around."

Kellen did so confidently, despite his creeping doubt something was amiss.

The sheriff unlocked his cuffs and pocketed them. Then he closed the door.

The sound couldn't have been very loud; Kellen knew that to be true. It still made him wince when the lock clicked home. Kellen looked at Owens again, then the sheriff.

"Dick..." Kellen's voice shook. "What's going on? Where is my dad? Why am I in here? Why is Owens here?"

Sheriff Hullinger fidgeted.

It's not a joke. Kellen fought down the rising bile in his throat.

"Your dad's not coming for you," said the sheriff. "Said you got yourself in this mess, you get yourself out. He wanted me to tell you that. And I think you know the reason you're here. If not, well—" The sheriff rapped a meaty knuckle against the bars. "You're gonna have plenty of time to think about it."

The sheriff turned away from Kellen's cell and went to Owens'. "All right, boy. Come on, now." He unlocked the door. "Your daddy's coming for you."

Owens didn't move.

The sheriff kicked his bunk. "Come on, boy. I said get up."

Owens looked up at Hullinger, his eyes pleading. "Can I stay here? My dad...he's going to kill me when he finds out."

"Yeah, well, you should've thought about that before, huh? Now let's go."

Owens took his time leaving, hustled along only by Sheriff Hullinger's taunts.

Kellen watched them walk up the row and exit. The sheriff closed the door and its echo shuddered up the cellblock. Kellen knew what it signified. He looked around his cell, the others down his row, even the one Owens had vacated. Emptiness.

Your dad's not coming for you...wanted me to tell you that.

The echo died off and left Kellen in complete silence.

It was just a prank. Kellen's conscience could refute the lie no longer.

He fell down hard onto the cold metal bunk. The sound it made comforted him for a moment. Then it, too, abandoned him.

LENNY

LENNY LISTENED TO THE BUS ENGINE'S HUM. HE rubbed the sleep from his eyes, and sat up. *Not goin' back. I'm done bein' afraid.*

Yawning, he spun out of his fishnet hammock, strung between the wall and bunk that Ellie occupied. In the near complete darkness, he vaguely saw she shared the bed with Allambee, their ankles shackled together in case the boy attempted escape.

Henry snored contentedly in the other bunk, his arm draped over Chidi.

The bare floor felt surprisingly warm, unlike the stone floors of Crayfish Cavern. Lenny slunk around Racer, sleeping in the aisle, and eased open the sliding door. Soundlessly, he slipped into the main cabin.

Night lingered outside the bus without the slightest trace of the coming dawn.

Lenny scowled as he passed the bathroom and captain's quarters. Oscar had seized the cramped room from the moment they began their journey. Lenny hadn't much need for its size. The principal of the matter bothered him more. He had earned rights to that room. Oscar had yet to earn anything in his life.

Blue track lights illuminated the aisle way to the front of the bus. Lenny followed them.

Paulo sat in the driver's seat, crooning to a Latin love ballad on the radio as he drove down I-65 south. He stopped upon seeing his disheveled captain.

"Nightmare again, huh? You get used to them growing up in the slums of New Pearlaya…" Paulo clucked his tongue. "My mother used to say dreams lost their power when one spoke them out loud."

"I don't wanna talk about it."

"Fine, but can you at least talk about something? I still have awhile to drive, and I've been nodding off with no one to keep me awake."

Lenny avoided the question by looking out the massive front window. The headlights illuminated nothing but endless pavement. Lenny cleared his throat. "So we're all surrounded by shadows. They—"

"Wait—" said Paulo. "I'm in the dream too?"

"Ya wanna hear about it or not?"

"I do. Keep going."

"The shadows take us one at a time. Racer's first to go. Just one second he's there, then bam! He disappears in the dark…almost like he escaped or something. The next time I see him, he's lyin' in some cornfield with his throat cut, starin' up at me like he's wonderin' what happened to him."

"Tough break for a pup."

"The rest of us make it to the water," Lenny continued. "We're swimmin' along when a weighted net pulls Ellie down."

Paulo tightened his grip on the steering wheel. His jaw clenched. "Who did it?"

Lenny shrugged. "She calls out for ya and so ya go back to help. That's when these bright streams of light lash outta the darkness."

"Jelly whips?"

Lenny nodded. "'Cept I can't see who's holdin' onto 'em. Anyhow, ya fight back."

"You bet I do."

"Ya keep 'em at bay awhile, but then one of 'em swims up from behind and...well..."

Paulo looked away from the road. "What?"

Lenny shrugged.

"I die?" Paulo's voice rose. "Why didn't you come help?"

"Too scared. Tryin' to swim away and save my own skin. Even though I know Pop would be ashamed of me and all of ya need help, I just keep goin'."

"That doesn't sound like you. So how does it end? You get away?"

Lenny shook his head. "I look back to see if anyone's followin' me. The shadow that killed ya is right on my tail...'cept now I can see teeth. Big ones, white and blood-stained, grinnin' at me."

"Nomad or Orc?"

"Couldn't tell. Always wake up just before they clamp down."

Paulo asked no more questions.

Lenny sighed. For a long while, they sat in silence with only the soft padding of pavement beneath the bus wheels to disturb it.

"Anyone else been up since I went to bed?" Lenny asked.

"Chidi. Say what you will about Henry, but he's a smart hire, if only to get her thrown in with the deal. The girl's a translating machine. Said to tell you she finished a quarter of one notebook."

"That's it? I counted four in that bag we lifted off Zymon! Did she at least find out who they belonged to?"

Paulo nodded. "She's pretty sure they're Marisa's. Figured you wouldn't be happy, but Chidi said she needs more time unless you know more languages than she does."

Lenny snorted. "What'd she do with them?"

"Table."

Lenny glanced to the darkened cabin behind them. "Flip the lights up, will ya?"

Paulo leaned forward to toggle a switch. Then he resumed his singing as the recessed cabin lights flickered on.

It had been three weeks and a day since they began their search, yet still Lenny paused to take in the opulence around him. The walls shone of polished mahogany, and the swirl of molded colors in the granite countertops resembled the stony surroundings of Crayfish Cavern. The u-shaped leather couches begged Lenny to sit on them, as did the plush chairs at the kitchen's bar.

Lenny first went to the fridge. Food, blessed food, stocked top to bottom and, unlike back home, he took what he desired. He made himself a heaping tuna sandwich and drowned it in mustard. He saw cans of a dark liquid Ellie called soda. Lenny snagged two of them and took everything to the small nook around a dining table.

There he found four different colored notebooks. Taking a bite of his sandwich, he opened the purple one first, and found a confusing collage of language.

One line written in English listed an aquarium outside Atlanta, Georgia. In the same sentence, Marisa switched to writing in a different language, but cited Genoa, Italy.

Lenny saw nothing written like any normal person might; vertical lines had instead been written in random areas while others went horizontal. Some sentences cut through others like she wanted to create a word search puzzle. Marisa had covered each page, front and back, in scribbled handwriting with hardly any space left vacant.

Lenny came across a piece of notepaper Chidi had used to translate what bits she could. Question marks sprawled over the page listing Dryback cities. He reviewed the list several times as he drank down a soda and found one area cited more than any other.

The Indianapolis Zoo...What's so special about it?

"Hey, Cap!" Paulo called back to him. "I'm going to pull over here. We're about an hour away, but I figure I'll get some rest before we go hunting."

"Fine," Lenny said.

Paulo pulled into a rest stop just outside Lafayette, Indiana. He parked alongside a slew of semis, killed the engine, and snored in his chair no more than a minute later.

Lenny polished off his sandwich and continued to review Chidi's notations.

Her second list had various aquarium measurements; the number of gallons of water per tank, chemicals used, and marine species at each location.

None of it made any real sense.

He picked another of Marisa's notebooks—one with a green cover—and flipped it open. Each page was covered in life-like and hand-drawn artwork, shaded in varying strokes of grey pencil. Lenny lingered on a portrait of a whale shark, the largest fish on the planet. White spots dotted its darker backside like an old movie theatre's marquee of lights. The next page showed a polar bear swatting one of its front paws.

Lenny pored over each breathtaking detail.

Pinnipeds outnumbered Marisa's other drawings by far; Sea

Lions with long necks and flippers, a Hooded Seal with what looked like a red balloon attached to the end of its nose, and hulking Elephant Seals with trunk-like noses. Lenny even found a drawing of a miniature, fat Ringed Seal with its mouth open.

He looks familiar. Lenny smirked. He turned to the next page. A single glance made him drop the notebook.

Marisa had captured the man's image perfectly. The portrait of Declan Dolan seemed to watch his son, even from the floor, his face set in usual sternness and his fixed stare ever watchful.

Lenny picked the notebook back up. He scoured the page for any bit of text, a date of completion, even artist initials. The portrait gave Lenny no answers, much like Declan seldom did in real life.

Lenny flipped through the other pages and notebooks with new-found energy for any other traces of his father. An hour came and went, along with the sunrise, but Lenny made no progress. Any secrets Marisa had, she kept safely hidden in the journals by a code Lenny could not hope to unravel on his own.

She had not hidden all though.

Lenny switched to the blue notebook, the only one with blank pages. The last entry held a drawing of an octopus with its tentacles sprawling forward to help explore its way down the rock face. Marisa had shaded a box above the creature. Peeking out the left side, Lenny saw a curvy bump.

He held the picture up to the light. "Hell's Bells and Buckets of Blood!" he swore. *It's me!*

The bump peeking around the box edge smacked of his facial outline. Marisa had even captured his stubby fingers gripping the placard when he had leaned out for a better view.

She knew I was there the whole time...

Lenny heard the others rousing. He tore both pictures out of their notebooks without a second thought, though he took great care in folding the picture of Declan, and placed them in his pocket. Then he grabbed a lighter before leaving the table and stormed up the aisle.

Lenny lit the picture of himself on fire the moment he stepped off the bus. He threw it on the ground, willed the paper to curl and blacken, and waited until every shred of his misstep burned away into ash. He could not burn away the memory she had seen him though.

Ya won't see me comin' next time, Bourgeois.

Lenny boarded the bus.

GARRETT

"MOM, WE TALKED ABOUT THIS..." GARRETT GAVE Cristina a final squeeze in the hope she would pick up on the signal to release him before the bus arrived.

She didn't. Not when the bus stopped at the end of their drive, not even when the crotchety old farmer-turned-bus driver, Lester Pate, honked the horn. Garrett squirmed free of her when Lester gunned the engine.

Garrett ran down the graveled drive before his mom could stop him again. The bus lurched forward the moment his stepped on.

"Bye, honey!" She called after him. "I love you!"

"Cute..." Lester said, his voice gnarled and grumpy. "I don't care if you did almost drown, Weaver. I got a schedule to keep. You see that white line there?"

Garrett saw it at the top of the landing. "You mean the one I'm supposed to stand behind while the bus is in—"

"Get behind it!"

I am behind it. Garrett debated telling him. *Just on the opposite side.*

He thought better of it when Lester slowed the bus.

If he kicks me off, Mom will take it as a sign I should've stayed home.

Garrett bit his tongue and kept moving down the aisle. The kindergartners, 1st, and 2nd graders in the front rows kept eerily quiet this morning as he passed. Even the 7th grade bully of the bus, Pete Rousey, wouldn't look at Garrett when he took the opposite seat in the last row.

Cccrrrrreeeeeaaaakkkkkk went the leather seat as Pete failed in his subtle attempt at scooching closer to the window.

"Relax, Rousey," Garrett said. "I'm not dead."

Pete flinched at hearing his name called. "I heard you were…"

"You heard wrong."

"Wh-what about Kellen Winstel? My sister said you drowned each other. She was in study hall and saw the EMTs wheel him out. She said his skin looked blue all over."

Did she tell you my legs turned black and white? Garrett stayed silent.

Pete didn't bother waiting for the bus to make its next stop before moving a few rows up.

Garrett would have chalked it up as a perk until he heard the beginnings of whispers. By the time the bus reached the elementary school drop off, he had overheard more than a few rumors. His favorite being that he must be a zombie. How else could he have survived? And as for Kellen, the elementary students logically concluded that Garrett, the newly turned undead, had eaten his corpse.

Lester eased the bus into park then yanked the lever to open the doors. "All right, hurry it up!"

The rows of K through 6th grade students emptied amidst a growing line of middle schoolers and a handful of freshman waiting outside to board. Once the last child stepped off, the older students trudged up the steps and spaced out into the newly vacated seats for more legroom.

Garrett noticed they, too, kept their distance from him. *This might work out better than I thought.*

A ruddy-faced senior of unchecked gluttony staggered on last.

Garrett grinned. He had first met Johnny Hickey in 7th grade when the two elementary schools combined. Since their peers considered them unpopular, Garrett and Johnny had naturally gravitated toward one another. It also helped that Garrett occasionally helped himself to the contents of Johnny's lunch bags. Inside those blessed totes, Johnny's mother packed doughnuts, candy bars, and sodas; solid gold since the school board had outlawed sweets and marked combating obesity as a must-fix.

Lester slammed the door closed and threw the bus in reverse.

Johnny would have stumbled down the row had his girth not held him in check between the seats. He twisted and turned through the tight aisle in a race to see if he could make it to the back before Lester arrived at the high school fifteen minutes away.

Garrett helped his friend through the last couple rows by pulling him.

Johnny fell into the seat and wiped his sweaty forehead. "Whew! Thanks, bro!"

"Heya, Hickey. I see you got my text."

"Yeah." Johnny dabbed sweat off his brow. "All right so I'm here. What's so important that you had to come back today? I'd be milking your situation like crazy!"

"Who says I'm not?"

"But…you're here…"

"Look, everyone thought I was dead—including you, right?" Garrett asked. "I mean, you wanted your mom to drive you to my house last night so you could check on me."

"Yeah, so? I don't see how—"

Garrett smirked. "Know who else wanted to come over?"

"Shut up!" Johnny leaned forward. "What'd she say?"

"I dunno. It's not like I talked to her. I told my mom I didn't want any visitors."

Johnny choked on his gum. "You told *her* not to come over? That doesn't make any sense! Why would you—"

"Johnny...the last time she saw me was right before *I almost died*," Garrett paused to let his point sink in. "*And* she's had a whole day and night now to think on all the things she should've said, the dates we could've gone on...."

Johnny's eyes lit up. "That's genius! She'll be all over you!"

Garrett's ears sang with the tune of Johnny's praises the remainder of their fifteen-minute journey to the high school. At one point, Johnny even wished aloud that he had almost been the one to drown so he could implement Garrett's newest plan.

It didn't seem long to Garrett before Lester turned off State Road 23 and into the school parking lot. Garrett enviously watched others his age milling about next to their cars. "Dude, I gotta get a car."

"Fo sho," Johnny said. "Hotties don't take you seriously if you don't have wheels."

Lester parked outside the freshman entrance and flung open the door. Unlike the younger students, he didn't bark at the teens, though he did scowl at each of them from beneath his green tractor hat.

"So last night I'm watching this show on TV, right?" Johnny raised his eyebrows skeptically. "Anyway, it's about these kids around our age who go to school in Ohio. Except their school doesn't look anything like ours. I mean it's obvious they filmed in Hollyweird."

"Yeah, so?"

"All these movies and shows about high schools got it wrong, man! Look at our school, dude. Just look at it!" Johnny's voice raised. "Does that look *anything* like a college camp—er—excuse me...*high school*...you've seen on TV? I mean, come on!"

Garrett laughed at the point well made. Whatever architect had designed Tiber High clearly lacked imagination. The school looked like a giant brick box with windows and only a dingy pole barn for bus maintenance as a separate building. No landscaping had been done to distinguish the school grounds from a prison. Not to mention the cow pastures, hayfield, and graveyard that surrounded it.

An old farming family owned the graveyard, or so the official story went. Allegedly, the family had refused to sell the land when the high school had been commissioned on account of not wishing to disturb or move the remains of those deceased. Garrett preferred a different story, one that suggested Ms. Morgan owned the graveyard. The one place she could harvest ingredients for her infamous perfume.

The two friends entered through the freshman entrance. A poorly drawn poster of a tiger greeted them just inside the doors. The phrase *Tiber Tigers are Rooooaaarsome!* had been scrawled beneath it.

"Look, Hickey, this is what the cheerleaders have been doing in their *practice* after school." Garrett chuckled. *No wonder Sydney quit.*

"Oh," Johnny whined. "Why did we get stuck with lockers upstairs?"

Garrett clapped him on the back and the two made their way up. An invisible wave silenced the normal hallway chatter when they reached the top.

"Whoa," Garrett said. "Guess nobody else expected me back so soon either."

"Looks like the P.J.s did," Johnny said. "Check out your locker."

A grey, cut out piece of cardboard in the form of a gravestone had been duct-taped to Garrett's locker with *R.I.P. Weaver* scrawled across the headstone in black.

Both of his locker neighbors sported a picture of Kellen Winstel from last year's state finals. Beside it, the word I-N-N-O-C-E-N-T had been spelled out down the locker doors in alternating orange and navy construction paper letters.

"P.J.s..." Garrett said.

Garrett assumed every high school had their collection of elitist preps and jocks. Tiber High's version preferred to spend their time in front of Garrett's locker. It seemed only natural for them to take up residence there, with Kellen Winstel as both their leader and Garrett's locker neighbor.

A typical day entailed Kellen's girlfriend-of-the-day hanging on his arm and nibbling at his ear because a magazine named it one of the *Top 10 Ways To Turn On Your Man*. Meanwhile, the remainder of the pretty and the privileged talked up how awesome it was to be them.

Today, Garrett noticed only two—Bryce Tardiff and Juan Marrero.

"Johnny..." he whispered. "Where's the other P.J.s?"

"Suspended. Eddie Bennett and Ross Owens are gone for the semester. I heard Jun Gao's only out for the week because he wasn't near the pool when Kellen threw you in. It's really because he ratted the others out though."

Garrett sniggered. "But what will they ever do without their Kelly for guidance?"

Garrett swore Bryce heard him poking fun of his fallen leader and 4x100 relay teammate. Bryce nudged his companion, pointed at Garrett.

Johnny abandoned Garrett and headed down the stairs.

Wuss. Garrett continued onward.

Marrero shoved off the lockers like he had been waiting on Garrett all morning. He stopped just shy of his nose touching Garrett's. His breath reeked of tuna from his post-workout meal.

Garrett tried to quell the fear rising in his gut. Not an easy task considering he stood toe-to-toe with the 3-peat, 185-pound state wrestling champion. It also didn't help that Garrett managed the scoreboards at wrestling meets and knew Marrero preferred to make his opponents tap out rather than pin them.

Garrett could feel the audience of peers holding their breath. In their faces he saw a pack of hyenas waiting for the pride of lions to make a sweeping kill.

Show them you're not afraid of these punks, a quiet voice inside him spoke.

Garrett wished he knew where the voice came from so he could knock it into submission. His body pled with him to run and join Johnny in the handicapped bathroom stall his friend liked to hide in during just such occasions.

"I uh...I need to get in my locker."

Marrero didn't move.

Show them, the voice said again.

Garrett looked past the wrestler in front of him. "So you're the new P.J. leader, huh, Tardiff? That didn't take long. I wonder what Kelly would say about that?"

"Finish what I started," Bryce answered.

"Hey!" A feminine teacher's voice came from the end of the hallway. "What's going on here?"

Half a second later, Mr. Tuttle pushed through the crowd and shoved his coke-bottle glasses up the bridge of his nose with pudgy fingers. "Garrett, back from the dead I see! These boys giving you any trouble?"

"Actually, Marrero here was—"

"Telling Weaver how glad we are he's alive," Bryce interrupted.

"Uh huh," Mr. Tuttle said. "Aaaaand that's why you're waiting outside his locker en masse?"

Bryce shrugged. "Just waiting on him. See we have this field trip today, and well..." he placed his arm around Garrett's shoulders. "We just wanted to make sure we saw Weaver before leaving to let him know we're happy he's okay. Right, Marrero?"

Garrett shook Bryce's arm away. Glared at him just in case Mr. Tuttle fell for the lie.

Marrero muttered something and walked away.

"Really glad you're okay, man!" Bryce said, following Marrero for the stairwell. "Hope we see you later!"

He dropped the act as soon as Mr. Tuttle wasn't looking. Sneering, he dragged his thumb across the front of his neck.

"Okay, okay, show's over people. Get to class," said Mr. Tuttle. He took out a signature yellow handkerchief from his vest pocket and sneezed into it. "Best keep a weather eye out for them, Weaver.

My nose always starts itching whenever I smell troub-a-ah-achooo!"

Mr. Tuttle turned at the last so he didn't sneeze on Garrett. Instead, he covered the stripes of a passing senior's Lady Tigers T-shirt in a thin layer of snot.

The girl's jaw hung open.

"Oh dear," Mr. Tuttle said. "Are you—"

"Ew!" she sprinted for the bathrooms down the hallway.

"As I said…" Mr. Tuttle said sheepishly. *"Trouble!"*

Garrett waited until Mr. Tuttle couldn't see, then ripped the gravestone off his locker and tossed it in the trash. The duct tape remnants left a sticky mess. Garrett opted to put them to good use. He slammed his door against the face of Kellen's. The locker door came back with half of Kellen's picture stuck to it.

"Oops," said Garrett, happily. Then he slammed it again.

Satisfied with the second result, he turned back to his own locker. Paper footballs littered the bottom. Garrett grinned. He knelt and thumbed through them, opening each with tender care.

> *Whoops! I missed you again, huh? Come*
> *talk to me when you get a chance!*
> *~Sydney~*
> *PS-History sucked today. There's a pop*
> *quiz. And before you ask…NO! I won't*
> *tell you what the questions are.*

Another read:

> *Dear Garrett,*
> *I'm going to assume you haven't found me*
> *yet because:*
> *A) You should be in choir, but instead*

you're wandering the halls dreaming up new
pranks. (BTW, I heard what you did with
the mayonnaise packets! Gross!)
B) You're hiding in the bathrooms because
you're scared of facing my wrath.
Or C) One of those jerks put you inside
your locker again and you don't want to
tell me the combination to let you out.
Come find me!☺
~Sydney~

Garrett reached for the blue, plastic art box he kept hidden behind his books. The latch popped open easily, bursting with the mass of notes already inside. He heard what sounded like a balloon popping. Garrett looked down the hallway.

Johnny slurped the lingering remains of his blue-raspberry chewing gum back into his mouth, and chomped it anew all the way to Garrett's locker.

"Thanks for bailing on me back there, Hickey," Garrett said. "And why are you in such a good mood?"

"What do you mean? How can you tell?"

"Really? You can't chew with your mouth closed on a good day and you chomp even louder when you're happy."

"I dunno," said Johnny. "Just happy you're alive, brosef."

"Dude, I told you to stop saying that. Makes you sound like a wannabe P.J."

"Right, you're totally right. I forgot they picked you to select potential members of their wannabe subsidiary."

Garrett tossed a couple more of Sydney's notes into his blue art box. "Do you even know what that word means?"

"Subsidiary? Not a clue," Johnny said. "Heard it on a detective show last night. Sounds cool, right? I might give it a whirl on you-know-who!" Johnny popped a bubble.

"Your funeral."

"What's that supposed to mean?"

Garrett sighed. "Sydney will know what subsidiary means. You'll look like an idiot."

"Oh, like your plan is so much better. She's going to care that you didn't die for like two seconds and then everything will be normal again."

What if he's right? I need a second plan.

"Oh, hey, get this," said Johnny. "So I'm watching this other show, a medical one, where the patient had some rare case like the one you have—"

"It's not *rare*, Hickey. A lot of people have vitiligo."

"Fine, whatever. *This* guy had a rare disease, disorder, whatever you want to call it. Anywho, the hot doctor wanted to give him this surgical procedure, right? Only Mc-Whatever-His-Name-Is said, 'Whoa. You can't do that because he has this new disease on top of his other, original disorder—'"

That's genius. What if the doctors discovered something like that in me yesterday?

"So then they move on to operate, right?" Johnny continued. "But some new doctor was like…'Hey, you can't do that because his blood type—'"

Could chlorine have entered my bloodstream? And it needs to have enough syllables to sound legit…Chlorinitis…no that's too easy… Chloridrone…ooh that's good. That might work. What about using two words?

Johnny leaned against Garrett's locker. "But then the doctors were like, 'Uh, yes we can, or this dude's gonna die!'"

Die? Heck yeah! They always die on TV when the doctors use more than one word to tell the patient their problem. How about chlorakitis...or something with drowning maybe? Drownemy...dronemetia... ooh, yeah I like that.

"Oh, hey," said Johnny, digging into his pockets. He took out a folded paper football. "Syd gave this to me yesterday in case I saw you. Figured you might wanna toss it in with the rest of your uh..." Johnny snorted and motioned toward Garrett's art box. "Hope chest."

Johnny handed the note over.

Garrett saw chocolate smudges stained the edges. *Of course he read it.* Garret shook his head as he took the note and unfolded it.

> *Garrett Weaver!*
> *I heard what happened yesterday and don't think because you survived means you get out of explaining what you were thinking!*

"Geesh, what is she, my mom?" Garrett asked.

"Maybe you should let her ground you," Johnny suggested with a dopey grin.

Garrett resumed his reading.

> *You had to pick a fight with them! SERIOUSLY?!?! You are in DEEP TROUBLE!! Don't think you'll slip by me tomorrow. I will find you!*
> *~Sydney~*
> *P.S. I'M GLAD YOU'RE OKAY!!!!*

"I see you got my note," said a familiar girl's voice.

Johnny choked on his gum.

Relax, Weaves. Garrett didn't turn around. He tossed the open letter into his locker and casually pushed the art box back into hiding.

"You toss all my letters away?"

"Listen, babe," said Garrett. "I toss *all* my stalkers letters away like that."

The girl laughed. "You have a stalker?"

"Stalkers…plural. I mean, sure it sounds cool and all. What guy doesn't want stalkers, right? Except this one girl…well, she has a couple things playing against her. The main one being she's Asian—"

Garrett was shoved against his locker. "Ah!"

He turned around.

The girl behind him stood a shade over five feet tall, and her thin frame belied the strength she had used to push him.

"You got a problem with Asians, Weaver?" Sydney Gao asked.

Johnny answered before Garrett could. "I don't have a problem with Asians, Syd. I love them!"

Surprised he can even talk he's chomping so hard. Garrett thought.

"All kinds!" Johnny said. "Japanese, Cambodian, Korean, oh, but Chinese…Wow!"

Garrett punched his shoulder. "Cut the crap, Hickey."

"What? I'm just telling Sydney that I think Chinese chicks, I-I mean, girls. No! *Women*…" Johnny winked. "They're my favorite."

Sydney ignored him, her focus on Garrett. But unlike the I-desperately-need-you-now look he had hoped for, Sydney gave him the I-will-kill-you look.

"Well?" she said.

"Geez, Syd, I was just kidding around."

She shook her head. "No, not that. What's the other thing?"

"The other...oh!" Garrett grinned. "I don't date hot girls."

Sydney snorted. "You don't, huh?"

"Yeah because he's gay!"

"Ugh, Johnny!" Sydney slapped him. "Do you know how stupid that makes you sound? *Because he's gay...*" She mocked. "I thought you were better than that."

"I am...I so am, Syd. You're right." Johnny hung his head. "I promise not to ever make fun of the gays again."

Sydney rolled her eyes. "Good. So, you two ready for the field trip?"

Here it is! My moment!

"I'm uh...I'm not going." Garrett turned back to his locker. "I-I didn't want to tell you guys this, but...I...look, I just can't."

Johnny stopped chomping. "What is it, dude? You forget money to get in? Because I can loan you the dough."

"My mom can get you in free since she works there," said Sydney.

Garrett tried to will tears in his eyes. They refused to come. *Come on, man! You need the tears or she won't buy it!*

Sydney took a step closer to him. "Garrett, what's wrong?"

"Nothing, it's—look, yesterday the doctor said that—" Garrett looked at his feet. "Well, she said that—"

"What? What did they say?"

Sydney's light touch on his forearm sent electrical currents racing to his neck. He felt a tear forming then turned and looked into her grey eyes.

"They said Kellen held me under too long and I had...they said I had some kind of weird reaction..." The tear rolled down his cheek. "It's called *chlorakitis dronemetia*—"

Sydney burst out laughing.

Johnny dabbed at his eyes with his shirt collar. "Dude, what's that mean? *Chlora drone—*"

Sydney bent over, laughing even harder. "It means he's full of crap!"

"I'm glad you think it's so funny," Garrett said. "It's a serious condition, Syd!"

"Whatever." She downgraded to a chuckle. "I wrote you a note yesterday about needing a good laugh. You can throw it away. That's the best joke I've heard in a long time."

"Syd, it's a serious condition!"

"Oh, okay!" she said, then gave him a wink. "I'm glad you're back to normal, Weaver."

Johnny lurched forward and hugged Garrett before Sydney could say more. "We're gonna get through this together, dude. I know I bailed on you before with the P.J.s, but—"

"Thanks, Johnny," Garrett said. *At least someone would miss me.*

"Okay, you two. We've got a field trip to go on." Sydney snorted again. "Last one on the bus has chlorakitis dronemetia."

Garrett watched her stumble away—laughing so hard she could barely stand—while he continued to console Johnny. He tried reminding himself that at least she found him funny. Besides, if he told Sydney the truth, if he had told her the first thing he saw after being pulled from the pool, she wouldn't laugh.

She'd scream.

CHIDI

CHIDI ZIPPED HER BACKPACK SHUT AND SLUNG ITS
straps round her shoulders. She looked out the bus window as Ellie
drove them into the Indianapolis Zoo parking lot. Chidi grinned
at the sight of busses lined up outside the gates. Students and
chaperones poured out of them. She tightened the straps on her
backpack. *Is today the day?*

Her crewmates readied themselves in their own ways, never guessing her intentions.

Paulo hung near the back, teaching Racer various pressure points
to coerce an aggressive runner into submission. Henry and Oscar
played a betting game of *wanfro.* The way Henry held his cards and
cast the shells suggested he would let Oscar win.

As for Lenny, he toed the line near the driver's seat, his gaze sifting
through the crowd as best Chidi could tell.

His earrings flashed. *Cheeds, whattaya think we should do with
the kid?*

She glanced down at Allambee, polishing off the last of the doughnuts they picked up in a rinky-dink town called Lavere. He smiled,
and she saw colored sprinkles in his teeth.

He's just a Dryback, she said. *Couldn't hurt any of us. Zymon is the one I'd be worried about, but he's still locked in the hold. Unless you think he'll make noise and attract attention.*

Lenny gave the slightest shake of his head. *The Crayfish sound-proofed the hold. Zymon can bang around down there and shout all he wants. Nobody's gonna hear nothin'.* Lenny turned, studied Allambee a moment. His earrings flashed. *Give him a choice. He either goes in with Zymon, or we lock him in the bunkroom. There's no windows back there but it's betta than the cold floor down below.*

Chidi pulled Allambee aside. "We're going to leave soon…you can't come with us. It could be dangerous."

"I am not afraid."

And I hope you can stay that way. She wished she could tell him that. "I know you're not. Lenny still won't allow it. *He says you can either stay in the bunkroom until we get back, or he'll make Paulo put you in the under again.*"

"Can you not stay with me?"

Henry turned his head away from the game. His icy stare fell on Allambee, then flickered to Chidi. His earrings flashed. *Give the word, my love.*

"No," she said quickly. "No, I can't stay with you, Allambee. Get in the back. Now."

Chidi felt like she just kicked a puppy.

Allambee stepped away from her and went back to the bunkroom. He turned around once inside, watched her close the door, giving him to the darkness.

I'm sorry.

Chidi clicked the lock closed.

"All right, crew," said Lenny. "Time to hunt."

Paulo and Racer crowed all the way off the bus. Even Oscar

seemed happier than usual. Thankfully, he pulled Henry away. Chidi knew her owner wouldn't have left her behind any other way.

Chidi walked up the aisle behind them. She stopped at the driver's seat. "Bad luck, you drawing the watch."

"Yeah," said Ellie. "Push comes to shove, Lenny would rather have Paulo watching his back than me. I told him so." Ellie leaned on the steering wheel. "Lotta good that did me."

"You're saying—"

"I'm saying don't screw up. I already had one knock against me because I'm a girl. Me falling for Marisa's bait and switch yesterday…that's strike two."

"But that was my fault too," said Chidi.

"The Crayfish hired you special," said Ellie. "I'm just another grunt."

Chidi pursed her lips. "I'm sure Lenny will forget it soon enough."

"Any catcher can tell you Dolans don't run. What you don't hear about is they never forget anything either. You lose their respect…" Ellie shook her head. "It's gone."

Cheeds, Lenny's voice filled her head. *Let's go already.*

Chidi hurried down the steps and joined the crew. They remained down a ways from the hundreds of students milling about the zoo's entrance. Far enough to not be overheard, but not so far to seem suspicious. *At least we won't have any trouble blending in with the crowds.*

"Hey, Henry," said Racer. "You could be our chaperone today."

Oscar and Paulo chuckled. Henry did not.

"Shuddup, pup," said Lenny. He unfolded a zoo map, and studied its layout. "All right, here's the assign—"

"Uh, excuse me, Lenny," Oscar said. "Before you overstep your bounds, know that today I insist Henry remains at my side. I'll not have another cockup like yesterday."

He's scared. Chidi fought off the grin. *Good. A little fear will do him some good.*

A blue bus stopped near the group entrance. Plastered across its side in white lettering read: ST. BLANDINA ACADEMY FOR GIRLS.

Racer and Paulo shared a look.

"We're not here to hunt Dryback girls," Lenny reminded them. "Focus."

"Come on, Len!" said Racer. "We can look for Marisa while trailing girls too."

"Oh yeah? Whattaya gonna say to one of 'em if she's interested? Come back and join me in the caverns? Maybe we can hold flippas?"

Chidi laughed.

Henry shot her a look that cut it short. His earrings flashed. *You do not smile, laugh, you do not even speak unless I allow. Have you forgotten your last lesson?*

I remember. She used her elbow to nudge the contents hiding in her backpack. The mere touch comforted her.

Lenny folded his map. "Paulie, hang near the front gates where ya can keep an eye on security and the aquarium entrance. Racer, take the walrus and polar bear exhibits. Cheeds, I want ya at the center, near the café."

"Why does she always get to stay near the food?" Racer complained.

"Ya speak any languages I dunno about?" Lenny asked. "No? That's why."

Both Racer and Paulo grumbled about the need to rotate posts more often, but they entered the zoo with little else to say.

Chidi turned to go.

Henry stopped her by digging his thumb between her shoulder blades. "She stays with me."

"Oscar wants ya with him at all times, rememba?" Lenny said. "It don't make no sense to have three of us bunched togetha when we got the whole zoo to cover."

"And what about us?" Oscar asked. "Where do you intend to place us? In the thick of action, I hope."

Lenny nodded. "I want ya both scoutin' inside the aquarium. She'll be there if she's here and got business to take care of."

"I see," said Oscar, his tone suspicious. "And where will you be?"

"In the aquariums."

Chidi cocked her head to the side. *Why would he...*

Oscar's eyes narrowed. "But you said it made no sense to have three catchers—"

"Bunched up," said Lenny. "We won't be. Oscar, Henry, the two of ya take the northwest entrance by the dolphin pavilion, I'll take the southeast. We bang around and double back the way we came when we meet in the middle."

Chidi hid her smile. *Will you fall for it, Oscar?* She watched him unfold a zoo map and study it.

Satisfied, Oscar shoved the map into Henry's chest. "Excellent. But should I discover this is another of your tricks, I'll have you and this team keel-raked upon our return. Think on that."

"I won't think on it very long 'cause I know it's a real post," Lenny said. "The most important one, so we should get movin'."

Oscar ambled away.

His bodyguard did not join him.

Lenny stepped closer to Henry. "I know ya get off on scarin' little girls, but it don't work on me. So either do something and let's have it out, or follow Oscar inside and take ya post. Either way… quit starin' at me."

Henry's thin lips parted in a cruel smile. Then he turned on his heel and followed Oscar inside.

Hey, Cheeds, Lenny thought to her. *What'd that smile of his mean?*

I…I'd rather not talk about it. If Henry ever found out I—

Geesh, girlie, I knew he had a tight leash on ya, but come on. All right, keep it to ya'self then. By the way, we get in there, circle around and keep an eye on Paulie and Racer. They hook up and talk to any girls, I want ya to play an angry girlfriend and scare 'em off.

Aye, aye.

Chidi followed him inside.

Lenny immediately broke away and headed north for the aquarium entrance.

Chidi headed west, following a path between the Commons and Forests exhibits. A group of employees had been commissioned to set up a large pavilion tent in the grassy lawn area, no doubt for children to picnic under later in the day.

She reached the outside café area in no time. Chidi removed the backpack from her shoulder and placed it on the table. Taking a seat, she turned her gaze northeast to watch visitors of the dolphin pavilion. Chidi glanced around to see if Henry had again abandoned Lenny's orders. *The last thing I need is for him to see these.*

Seeing no one, she unzipped the bag. Chidi's fingers trembled as she reached inside and took out one of Marisa's journals. *Everyone was so wrapped up in preparing they didn't see me take you, did they?*

She glossed over the purple notebook's pages. Chidi had been honest in translating the text for Lenny, but kept far more from him. Bourgeois had done more than just recount stories of those she evaded over the years; she had sketches of individual catchers, different species movement and staging patterns, strengths and weaknesses.

Marisa even claimed to have evaded the Silkstealer—a rumored boogieman known for capturing Silkies while murdering the males. None had ever seen him in the Salt, yet Marisa described seeing him on the Hard and had drawn a portrait of what she claimed was him.

Chidi shuddered at his picture, an older man wearing a black cowboy hat ringed with the seal teeth of his victims. She turned the page and discovered Marisa's list of contacts. *Were you all slaves before too?*

Names littered the back half of the notebook. Chidi assumed them aliases. She didn't recognize any, not that it concerned her. Slaves lied all the time. She had done the same when necessary. One of the columns listed what Chidi assumed to be professions, but cracking Marisa's code would take a while.

She had learned much in the few short hours Lenny had given her to translate the pages. More than enough time to recognize a treasure trove of knowledge for any slave with a desire to run. One needed only two keys to unlock its secrets: time and a vast knowledge of languages.

Chidi had the one. Now she hoped to find the time.

She tore a piece of clean paper from one of the other notebooks and searched for the profession she needed most.

A forger...I need someone to forge my fakes.

GARRETT

WHY DOES SHE ALWAYS HAVE TO SMELL SO GOOD?
Garrett collapsed the bus window. *Ugh. This is torture.*

"You hot?" Sydney asked as he sat back down.

Hot for you. Garrett shrugged. "Just like the window down."

"Weaves, come on, man," said Johnny, seated behind them. "You wanna freeze me out?"

"We're almost there, Hickey. You'll be fine."

Garrett looked out the window. A day at the zoo sounded fantastic when he had lain in bed last night. But Bryce Tardiff's threat made him nervous. He dodged bullies at school all the time. Bathrooms, unlocked doorways, bleachers—Garrett knew all the best hiding spots after years of avoiding P.J.s. He held no such advantages at the zoo.

They won't do anything with Syd around. Garrett thunked his head against the window, the cool glass soothing against his forehead. *How sad is this? My only hope is a girl will be around to keep them away. No wonder I can't score a date with her.*

"Can someone please tell me why we are going to the zoo again?" Laura Morris, the class valedictorian to-be, asked loud enough for any chaperones to overhear.

"Who cares?" others answered her.

"Yeah, it's better than being at school."

"But what can we learn?" Laura asked. "Oh, that's a tiger. This is an elephant…a toddler could tell you the difference!"

Garrett listened to his peers groan as the bus came to a stop.

Sydney patted the leather seat in front of them like drums. "We're here! Come on, Weaver."

Garrett scooted out after her. Johnny cut him off to follow Sydney up the row. He kept his head down the entire way to stare at her butt.

Garrett slapped him upside the head.

"Ow, dude! What was that for?"

"Like you don't know."

"Whatever," Johnny whispered. "Don't pretend you wouldn't do the same."

Garrett had no response for that.

Mr. Lansky waited at the bottom of the steps to hand each student a trivia sheet. "Have it filled out by the end of the day," the teacher said.

Garrett didn't bother looking over the form. He saw Sydney already scrawling answers down. He popped his elbow in her direction like an English gentleman might offer his escort. "Excuse me, my dear," he said. "Would you care to join me in a quiet stroll through yonder zoo?"

"You are such a nerd." Sydney said. She threaded her arm through the crook of his as they walked to the ticket counter with Johnny in tow.

"Preposterous," said Garrett. He sniffed the air. "Why…what is that wondrous aroma, darling?"

"Roses?" Sydney suggested.

"Nah," Johnny said in between chomps. "Probably just a rhino taking a dump."

Sydney's nose wrinkled. "Nice, Hickey."

Garrett shot Johnny a look when Sydney stepped away from them.

Johnny grinned back like breaking them up had been his plan all along. He popped a fresh piece of gum in his mouth, then chased after her. "Hey, Syd! Wait up!"

"Nope. I promised my mom I'd get tickets to see her in action at the dolphin show. You two are slowing me down."

"The dolphin show is for kids," Garrett said. "Hate to burst your bubble, Syd, but they're kinda boring."

"Uh, not when your mom is a dolphin trainer."

"Okay, fine. But they're not as cool as sharks or cheetahs or bears. That's what I want to see."

"I dunno, Weaves," said Johnny as he unfolded a zoo map. "I'm kind of excited about the show. It says here one of the dolphins can even jump through hoops."

Sydney stopped. "Look, you two fight out which exhibit we go to first. I'm getting us tickets though."

Garrett wheeled on Johnny the second she reached the counter, twenty yards away. "You're such a suck up, man!"

"Dude, it's called taking an interest in what the girl you're dating likes."

"Hickey! *You're not dating, Sydney!*"

"Neither are you!"

"Besides," said Garrett. "Girls want guys who will be honest with them—"

"Oh, you're one to talk with the whole chronakitis drone—"

"And not just fake your interests. At least that's what girls like Sydney want."

Johnny frowned. "And you know what she wants."

"Oh, I'm sorry. Did you just say Sydney drives me home after tennis practice every day and not you?"

"Schyeah," Johnny scoffed. "And now you're in the friend category, pal. Which means you're going noooowhere. That just makes you a sounding board for her to talk about the studs she really wants. Likes yours—Heeeey, Syd! You get the tickets?"

Garrett turned and saw Sydney standing behind him. *Great. No way she didn't overhear at least part of that.*

Sydney cocked an eyebrow. "Okay, they only had tickets for the afternoon show left so I'm thinking we do aquarium stuff last. Most visitors check it out first because it's right inside the entrance."

She pointed to a path on their right where a long line had already stretched around the outside portion of the Sea Lion tank.

"Sounds good to me," Garrett said. "Hickey?"

"I'm good with whatever Syd wants to do. I-I just want to make sure we hit up the dolphins before we leave. Honestly, I'd be fine if we just stayed over there all day…"

Sydney rolled her eyes. "We'll see them. Up close even. Mom said I could bring you guys down after the show if you want. All right," Sydney glanced down at her trivia sheet. "African Plains it is!"

Johnny bumped into Garrett as both followed her lead to the left pathway. "I happen to like dolphins, dude," he whispered.

"No, you don't."

"Uh, yeah, I do. They're like the coolest fish in the ocean!"

Garrett fought an urge to slap him again. "They're not fish, you dork. Dolphins are mammals. They have to come up for air. Don't you watch the Discovery Channel?"

"And they give birth to live young, just like humans do." Sydney chimed in from ten yards ahead.

Johnny scratched his head. "Oh. Well, then they're the coolest *mammals* in the ocean!"

So lame. Garrett sped up his pace to catch Sydney. "Actually, Hickey. Whales are the coolest mammals in the ocean."

"Whoa...wait a minute," said Johnny. "Whales are mammals too?"

"Yep."

"Man, I don't know what Laura was talking about. I'm learning all kinds of new stuff today!"

They wasted the rest of the morning drifting from paddock to paddock. At one stop, they watched the giraffes and antelopes graze. The next, they saw a cheetah that refused to run no matter how much Garrett begged from behind the safety of a glass barrier.

Johnny insisted on seeing the other big cats after lunch. All seemed content in their laziness. Garrett found a pride of lionesses huddled together on a large boulder. The pile of yellow fur made it hard to tell where one began and the others ended.

"Dude," Johnny said. "Twenty bucks says a tiger could take a lion in a fight."

Garrett laughed. "You're about to lose twenty dollars. No way a tiger could take the lion down."

"What about a liger?" Sydney asked.

"A wha-?"

"A liger—it's a hybrid; both lion and tiger. They're supposed to have the strengths of both its parents. Think about that!"

Sydney left her two companions to puzzle over the new variable.

"Dude, I would marry her right now," said Johnny.

"Definitely," Garrett agreed. "I mean how many girls out there are not only cool enough to weigh in on a guy debate but *trump* both our arguments?"

"There can be only one," Johnny said. "And Mrs. Sydney Hickey shall be her name."

Garrett laughed.

The afternoon brought on a surprising amount of humidity for April. The zoo employees must have sensed it too; they turned on the sprinkler park usually reserved for summer months. The trio of friends stopped for some ice cream to beat the heat. Garrett made a mental note to file away that Sydney ordered mixed coconut and caramel flavors.

Of course, that meant Johnny ordered the same thing she did.

Garrett asked for his signature strawberry and vanilla swirl. The first frigid spoonful hurt his teeth and stuck to his tongue. He didn't mind so long as he could still taste both the tart and the sweet. He had just finished his bowl when they passed the five-storied dolphin pavilion on their way back to the aquariums. The building's logo— a bottlenose dolphin—grinned down at him.

"Wait!" Sydney stopped them. She tossed her bowl in the nearest trashcan and whipped out her trusty trivia sheet. "Questions fifteen and thirty on our quiz. What type of animal does the Indianapolis Zoo specialize in housing that most other zoos do not? And, which animal's name means 'one who walks with its teeth' in Greek?"

Why is she looking at me like I'll actually know the answer? Garrett shrugged.

She pointed to a sign and, Sydney being Sydney, ran over to

read the information aloud. "Walruses are known for their tusks. In fact, the walrus family name originates from the Greek word 'Obobenidea,' which means 'one who walks with his teeth.'

While walruses don't walk with their teeth, they use their tusks like weapons during the breeding season. Only nine separate institutions in North America house walrus, with the Indianapolis Zoo being the most prestigious in terms of specializing in walrus care and reproduction. To date, there have been two walrus pups born at the zoo."

"Wow!" Johnny said. "Good eyes, Syd!"

Garrett scrawled down the answers on his trivia sheet. "Her mom works here, Hickey. She's probably seen that sign a hundred times."

Sydney stuck her tongue out at him.

Garrett walked to the edge of the paddock and looked over the side. Fifteen yards below, he saw a pair of walrus. Their wrinkled, reddish-brown skin made it easy to identify against the rocky grey surroundings.

"Doesn't she look like a big pillow?" Sydney asked, sidling up next to Garrett.

Johnny squeezed in between them. "Totally. That guy is ginormus!"

"She's a girl, Johnny," said Sydney.

"How can you tell?"

"Well, Hickey," said Garrett. "Boy walruses have a pe—"

A zoo employee cleared her throat. She pointed to a pair of children who had just walked up.

"Sorry," Garrett said. He jerked his head in Johnny's direction. "Some of us don't know the differences between boys and girls yet."

The zoo employee ambled toward them. "How's it going, Sydney?"

"Angie!"

"Hi," Angie answered. "I heard you'd be here on a field trip today. Don't you ever get sick of this place?"

"You know me," Sydney said. "Couldn't keep me out if you tried."

"I believe that. So," Angie said. "You guys want to know an easy way to tell the sex of a walrus? The females are smaller than males."

Johnny stepped up a rung on the wooden barrier to gain a clearer view at the exhibit. "If she's the small one then where is the big guy?"

"Oh, he's in there," said Angie. "Just keep watching. The others should be coming out to feed them anytime now."

Garrett joined Johnny. "I can't imagine something bigger than that walrus already in there."

"I hear that. No way something that big can stay hidden down there for so long."

Five minutes went by until another employee emerged from a poorly disguised employee entry point in the rock siding. The employee carried a tin full of clams with him and tossed a couple onto the deck.

The loud clatter of their shells instantly drew the attention of the female. She flipped to her stomach and waddled her lower half back and forth to reach the food. Sticking out her tongue, she promptly sucked the shells up.

Whoa! That's awesome.

Then Garrett saw the male emerge from the water. Twice the female's size, his head resembled an old bald man's, wrinkled and splotched a deeper shade of brown that the rest of his warty neck and body. A pair of three-feet long ivory tusks descended from his upper jaw like two icicles. The loose skin around his throat jiggled as he loosed a deep, thunderous roar that would have put the lions to shame.

"That's Brutus," said Angie. "He weighed in over twenty-five hundred pounds when we got him on the scale a few months ago."

Got him on a scale? They'd need a forklift to move that thing!

Brutus slid to the clams and shoved the female away with his head. He greedily stole any more thrown onto the deck and made loud belches in between as if telling the employee to give him more. It didn't take long for the clams to run out.

Garrett watched Brutus sniff around the now empty pail and the employee's pockets, before resigning himself to the pool. He slipped his massive girth back into the water with surprisingly little splash and vanished.

"That…was…crazy!" Johnny said.

With the show over, Garrett and his friends said their goodbyes to Angie and moved on to the aquarium exhibits. He had always thought the aquarium entrance pretty sweet, modeled to resemble a cave. As soon as the doors swooshed open, Garrett was pitched into total darkness. Air conditioning that reeked of fish blasted him in the face.

"Ugh!" Johnny said. "Somebody order anchovies?"

Garrett felt someone brush past him. *Sydney. Of course she knows the way and doesn't have to wait for her eyes to adjust.*

Garrett fumbled for the handrail then walked down the ramp and turned the corner. He found Sydney in front of a tank filled with stingrays.

The flat, fleshy creatures seemed to move effortlessly with only the slightest rippling wave on the outer rim of their bodies to suggest they did more than float. Most varied in shades of light to dark grey. A few had golden spots doppling their otherwise black hides. Still others looked brown with yellowish, flowery designs across their backs.

Garrett caught Sydney glancing at him. She smiled, and her teeth seemed to glow in the pale light. She turned back, placed her hand flat against the aquarium pane.

A brownish ray emerged from the sandy white floor like she had called it. Then it vanished to the back of the tank with a quick swish of its pointy tail. Another glided upward near Garrett's face like the ray wanted to show off its white underbelly and opposing rows of gill slits.

A little girl pressed in front of Garrett. "Look, Mommy!" she said. "That one's belly looks like a smiley face!"

"Yo, Weaves!" Johnny called. "This thing has two sets of eyes!"

"Huh?"

"I'm serious! Look at that one there." Johnny pointed to a bluish ray swimming in front of Garrett. "That one has eyes on its head, right? The one I just saw had eyes above its mouth! There it is again! Look!"

Garrett saw a ray with two small holes, opening and closing, just above its mouth.

Sydney chuckled. "I said the same thing to my mom when I was younger. I asked her if they were eyes so the ray could look down while it swam."

"Is that what they're for?"

"No. They're called nares. It's his nose. Above his mouth, just like ours."

"Cool." Garrett said. "But I know a place that's even better." He clapped Johnny on the shoulder. "Come on! Let's go pet some sharks!"

Johnny shrunk back. "Pet one?"

"It's okay, Hickey," said Sydney. "They don't bite. Even little kids do it. You'll see."

Garrett raced ahead without them. The shark pool had been his favorite part of the aquarium since he discovered it. When first he saw it, he thought it maybe a foot deep. Only after sticking his arm in did he learn it to be around three feet deep. Garrett watched the dog sharks swim. To his mind, they looked like scaled-up versions of cleaner fish that spent their lives sucking on aquarium walls.

He typically found the area packed. Today, he saw only a few people around. *Everybody's probably lining up for the dolphin show.*

He rolled up his sleeve and dunked his arm until the water reached just above his elbow.

Garrett relaxed his fingers and tried not to move them. His dad had taught him not to look down else the water would play tricks with his eyes.

A second later, something slimy and smooth grazed the back of his hand.

He looked through the glass, saw the shark swim around his hand, investigating.

Oh man, Sydney and Johnny have to see this! Garrett glanced up from the pool. He gasped. *What's Eddie Bennett doing here? I thought Johnny said he was suspended.*

Suspended or no, Eddie Bennett had just entered the jelly exhibit. Bryce Tardiff and Juan Marrero followed him in. All three split away from one another and went different directions.

Garrett pulled his arm from the tank. *Crap. They find me here, I'm a dead man.* He crouched to keep them from seeing him. *What do I do?*

He saw an emergency exit behind him, but knew that would trigger an alarm. Left would lead him back around the pool and into plain sight. A darkened doorway to his right promised entry to another area. Garrett couldn't remember what exhibit though.

Have to chance it.

He scurried through the entryway. Once he cleared the corner, Garrett saw he had entered the Galápagos Sea Lion exhibit and that he shared the exhibit with no one else. *This isn't good. I need to find some place with people.*

The clear pane in front of him stood at least fifteen feet high and sixty feet long. The water on the opposite side ran all the way up to the very tip of the ceiling, giving him perspective of the underwater surroundings.

A pair of sea lions appeared from the opposite wall, seemingly out of the rock face. They swam past the window until both disappeared where the windowpane ended. Both returned a few seconds later. They swam so close to the glass that Garrett felt like he could reach out and touch them. One of them spun around and around, putting on a show.

Garrett laughed.

"Think they're funny, do ya?" came an unfamiliar voice in the dark.

Garrett had seen enough movies to recognize a Boston accent when he heard one. It sounded angry. Almost like the person wanted a fight.

He turned, fully expecting to find a muscle-faced mob guy who doubled as an animal rights activist behind him. Instead, he saw a dwarf wearing earrings and a sweet-looking black hoodie with white circles embroidered on it.

Barely four feet tall, Garrett almost mistook the little teen for a kid. His swagger warned it would be a costly error.

The dwarf stepped into the pale light and saw Garrett plainly. His glare melted away. "Whoa-I'm…I'm sorry, okay," the dwarf fell to his knees. "I-I didn't know ya kind was out here too."

My kind? Garrett looked around the room to see if the dwarf mistook him for someone else. He saw no one. Garrett turned back around, took a step closer.

"What do you mean my kind?"

LENNY

IS HE FOOLIN' WITH ME? LIKE TO PLAY WITH HIS food before he eats it?

Lenny cautioned a glance.

"Can I help you up?" the Orc asked, extending an open hand.

Lenny warily took it and stood. *Something's not right here.*

"What did you mean by my kind?"

"Huh?" Lenny said.

"My kind. You said you didn't know my kind was out here too. What did you mean by that?"

Can he really not know?

"Garrett!"

When the Orc looked up, Lenny committed the name to memory.

An Asian girl stood in the doorway between the sea lion exhibit and the shark pool. She hurried over, joined by a fat kid who struggled to keep up with her. The girl's eyes flitted back and forth between Garrett and Lenny. Something about her smelled funny, familiar and yet not.

Lenny could make no sense of it. None of the teens wore Selkie suits or crystal-stud earrings. And unlike the Orc, the two newcomers' skin tones didn't give them away as Salt Children.

Could be Merrows. Lenny reasoned. He clutched his hidden dagger tighter. "Ya know this guy?"

"Of course we do," the girl said. "Who are you?"

"Depends on who's askin'. What's ya name, doll face?"

"Hey!" said Garrett. "You can't talk to her like that!"

Lenny grinned. *He really don't know what he is. No way an Orc would lemme talk to his girl like that.* "What's wrong? Ya girlfriend can't stand up for herself?"

"She's not my girlfriend!"

"Yeah, but ya still want her, don't ya?"

"I'm sorry," said the girl. "I don't want to seem rude—"

"*You're* not being rude, Sydney. He is!"

"Garrett, would you stop! I'm just trying to explain this is all a misunderstanding."

The fat boy shifted. "Come on, Weaver. Settle down."

"Shut up, Hickey!"

They don't even realize what they're givin' me. Lenny made mental notes of each of their names as the boys continued to argue. Both seemed to forget Lenny even stood there. *Yep. They're Drybacks.*

"Look, I got it now," Lenny said. "How 'bout we just part ways here. Sound good?"

The fat one struggled to place a piece of gum in his mouth. "It does to me."

Lenny left the punk teens behind and didn't stop until he reached the end of the exhibit. He exited the building, the beginnings of a new plan formulating in his mind.

Now outside, he saw a bottlenose dolphin logo grin down at him, almost like it could read his mind. Visitors had formed a line that stretched around the corner. Lenny crossed to the opposite side and used the taller persons like a wall to shield him.

He headed west and tried to ignore those who pointed at seeing a little person walk beside them. The children didn't bother him as much as the teens. *Don't make a scene. Keep calm.* Lenny quickened his pace.

Suddenly, his head filled with the overlapping voices of his crew.

She's here, Len! Paulo said.

I see Marisa! Chidi's voice cut in.

Where? Lenny asked, his voice calmer than he felt. *Which exhibit?*

Deserts, Paulo said.

"Whattaya doin' in the deserts?" Lenny said so loud a man in line turned to look at him. *So much for not drawin' attention, ya hothead!* Lenny kept moving. His earrings flashed. *Paulie, whattaya doin' in the deserts? She's a Silkie, not a lizard!*

Thought you only had eyes for Ellie, Racer's voice chimed in. *You were following that Brazilian girl from the academy again, weren't you?*

Never mind that, Paulo said. *I can see her, Len.*

Lenny unfolded his zoo map. He found the overturned, bowl-shaped desert logo a bit further west than the dolphin pavilion. *Good. Hold tight and keep eyes on her. Cheeds, ya anywhere near to give him backup?*

I'm already with Paulo, she answered.

Yeah, thanks for the trust in me, by the way, said Paulo. *Really appreciate you having her tail me.*

Pipe down, Paulie. I'm tryin' to think. Lenny studied the map. *Racer, where ya at?*

Almost there. Tell me where to go.

Take the exit ramp. I'll get the entry. What's the Dryback situation in there?

Empty, said Paulo. *Too hot for any sane person to hang around.*

Good, Lenny said. *Now listen up. Paulie, Cheeds, split up and work both ends of that semi-circle. If ya can't grab her, flush her out to Racer.*

What about Oscar and Henry?

Don't worry 'bout it, Lenny said. He shoved the map back in his pocket and power-walked toward the Deserts.

Find a place to hide and don't get pinned down. He repeated one of his father's mantras. Lenny spotted a lemonade vendor with a line of customers. He joined the back for a vantage point and looked through the exhibit's glass doors from afar. *All right, I'm here and waitin'. Racer, ya ready?*

Here, Racer said. *She's not getting anywhere without going through me!*

Lenny took a deep breath. *Flush her.*

Thirty seconds of silence went by.

Lenny wiped his palms on his pants. *Come on. Come on…*

What's takin' so long?

She moved into another area, Chidi said. *Paulo, over by the rattlesnakes.*

I'm standing right in front of the rattlesnakes!

No, the southwest corner…see her?

Ah, Paulo said. *Walking up now…*

Get her, Paulie. Lenny's fingers danced at his side. *Grab her and let's go home.*

Oh— Chidi said. *Paulo's down! Paulo's down!*

What? Racer said. What's going on? Cap, do we go—

Racer, stay at ya post! Lenny ordered. *Talk to me, Cheeds.*

She went through some kind of employee exit! I can—I can't get through it. Ugh! It—It's locked.

Which way?

Near the meerkat door!

Lenny pulled his map out, saw an iguana image in the bottom left corner, a rattlesnake at the top, and the meerkat image right next to—

She's goin' for the pavilion!

A side door flew open. Marisa Bourgeois bolted out, her brown Silkie hood fluttering behind her neck like a tiny cape.

Lenny gave chase.

Marisa disappeared behind a concrete inlet full of parked baby strollers and kiddy carts shaped like animals.

Don't let her get inside and blend with the crowd! Lenny ran for the front entrance to cut her off. Both came around the restroom corner at the same time. Lenny dove, caught one of her ankles. He used his momentum to roll, twisting her foot beneath him.

"Ah!" Marisa yelped.

She fell on top of him and fought back, clawing and kicking. A knee aimed at racking him connected with his upper thigh instead. She yanked his head back, near tearing his hair out.

Lenny refused to let go, elbowing her face with his other arm. He saw her feral eyes briefly, then only red when her knee connected with his groin. Lenny gasped for air and let go. His eyes stung with tears. He fuzzily saw Marisa run straight at a twenty-five foot concrete slab wall.

Marisa defied gravity. Just before it seemed she would fall, she kicked off and grabbed the top of the ledge. She pulled herself up and swung over the top.

Don't lose her, Len! Get inside!

Paulo, you okay? Racer asked. *Chidi, what happened?*

She hopped the fence!

Huh?

She hopped into the rattlesnake fence! Chidi said. *Len…Len, you there?*

Pavilion… Lenny coughed. *Get to the pavilion.*

He looked up at the wall Marisa climbed. *No way I'm gettin' ova that thing. Have to go around.* Lenny crawled to his knees. He gingerly held his groin and hobbled back to the pavilion's main entrance.

The line had died down to a few people. Lenny limped by the ticket-taker.

"Whoa, whoa," she reached out to stop him. "I need to see—"

"My friend's inside," Lenny said.

"Okay, but I need to see your ticket first."

"I lost it."

"Oh," she said. "Well, I'm sorry, you can't go in then."

"Look, lady. I told ya I lost it."

"And I'm awfully sorry about that, but I can't let you in, especially not with that attitude. Anyway, it's against regulation. We give out a set number of tickets per show, otherwise we can't fit everyone."

Lenny debated whether he could run up the steps fast enough. His groin warned against it.

"Listen, lady. I neva seen a dolphin. It's the only reason I came here today. Can't ya do me a solid and lemme in?"

"I'm sorry. Rules are rules."

Lenny decided to make a break for it.

"Aw, don't you think you could let him in, Angie?" a cutesy girl voice asked. "Everyone should see a dolphin show at least once in their life."

"Sorry, Sydney—"

Lenny glanced over his shoulder. *This crew again?*

"The park has rules," the zoo employee—Angie—finished.

An announcer's voice boomed from inside the open doors at the top of the stairwell, thanking the list of sponsors for the show.

"Oh! They're starting!" Sydney whined. "Please, Ang?"

Angie crossed her arms.

She's not gonna give in, girlie, Lenny thought to himself. *Not without a little push...*

"This has all just been a misunderstanding," Sydney shot a look at Lenny. "Right?"

Lenny reached up and slid his arm around Sydney's waist. Her back stiffened. "Don't worry about it, babe—"

Angie's eyes widened. *"Babe?"*

"Yeeeaah," Sydney said. "It's kind of a surprise."

"Oh...well...I wouldn't want to ruin that. We both know how much your mom loves surprises."

Angie looked around to see if anyone watched. She ushered the teens on.

"Thanks!" Sydney said. "I owe you one, Ang!"

Lenny gimped up the steps. He tried to hold tight on Sydney's hand. "Come on," he said. "It's all part of the act—"

"No! It's not."

Sydney shook free of his grip and took the steps two at a time.

"You could say thank you..." Garrett said.

Lenny stared at the Orc. His patchy skin begged the question of how he had drifted so far from his pod, alone, and did not know his true origins. *Don't worry 'bout him,* Lenny's conscious warned. *Get the one ya been sent to hunt first!*

"Nah…Not my nature, kid."

"You're hilarious, dude," Hickey laughed. "Weaver's just mad he didn't think of it."

"Weava?" Lenny said. "Thought his name was Garrett."

"Well, yeah," said Hickey. "Garrett Weaver."

Lenny made a mental note of the Orc's full name. "Then Weava can copy my example any time he wants." He pushed to the top of the landing where Sydney waited.

"Well?" she said expectantly.

Lenny winked at her and kept walking. "Catch ya later, doll face."

"Ugh! You're welcome!"

Lenny entered through the narrow corridor just as the announcement of zoo sponsors ceased playing. A cheesy, hip-hop beat replaced it, booming through the overhead speakers. Lenny glanced up once inside the main area. The pavilion had a domed ceiling, unlike many open-air, dolphin pavilions he had seen at other aquariums during his hunt for Marisa Bourgeois.

A musty, chemical smell hung in the air. Lenny walked between the outer complex on his right and a ten-foot-high dolphin tank wall to his left. He peeked through the pane window, saw the pool descended another twenty feet.

Other latecomers to the show ushered him to move faster.

"Hey!" he yelled over his shoulder. "Does it look like I can go any fasta? Stop pushin'!"

Ahead he saw several sections of audience bleachers. Posted signs designated 'The Splash Zone!' area closest to the tank. Lenny knew he would have a better shot of getting by the ticket-taker again without Sydney's help than finding a seat down there.

Len, where are you? Racer asked.

Pavilion.

How did you get in? The employee out here won't let me by. Chidi tried to use a different door, but it's locked. Paulo's searching for another entrance.

The final dolphin show of the day made for a packed house. Lenny scanned the crowds. *How am I supposed to find one girl in all this mess?* His earrings flashed. *Paulie, how ya doin'?*

I'll let you know when I get my hands on her.

Where are ya now?

Around back, Paulo answered. *It's the only other set of doors I see. There's some employees smoking nearby it. No way I can get in without causing a scene. I'll keep watch on it though.*

Good, Lenny said. *Cheeds?*

Waiting by the chimpanzee pens. I have the lower exit covered.

We're solid! Racer said.

We thought that twice already. Any sign of Oscar and Henry?

No, but that's a good thing, right? Racer asked.

Not when I could use anotha couple sets of eyes. Lenny thought to himself. *We'll see. Stay sharp out there.*

Safe in the knowledge his crew waited at the various exit points, Lenny ran through his options. *The Splash Zone's a no-go. I try to squeeze in there and a kid gets upset, I get tossed. Can't cut across the middle for the far end either. If she's sittin' high she'll see me walkin' by.* Lenny targeted the third tier of bleachers. *If ya can't get low, betta go high.*

An obese father dragging his equally chunky kid along passed by.

Lenny trailed him. He veered right after ascending several rows and accidentally bumped into some teens, texting on their cell phones, as he sat down. None acknowledged his existence.

The music and crowd noise died, replaced by what sounded like low thrums from a wood chipper as the dolphins called to one another.

Lenny took in the pool view.

The length of the main tank spanned the entire room, just over fifty yards long, and it had two additional, smaller, holding tanks attached to either side of it. A pair of neon orange balls and a pink hula hoop dangled twenty feet above the surface. The strings holding them in place could hardly be seen, and gave the impression magic suspended them there.

The main trainer's stage resembled a quaint New England beachside. An antiquated barn-turned-general-store, painted fire engine red with greyed shingles stood as the centerpiece. Fir trees and a two-storied blue shed neighbored either side of it with a painted backdrop of clouded skies and grey seas behind.

Far to the pool's left, Lenny saw another miniature water tower; a trainer exited another staged New England home beside it and opened the gate of the nearest holding pool.

A grey torpedo sped past the side glass windows.

Lenny only saw the last bit of its tail. *Show's startin',* he said to his crew. *Bet Marisa stays here till after. If she makes a move now she risks bein' seen. Don't get too comfortable though.*

Lenny faintly saw three more blurry shapes rush out of the holding area, one after the other. All three raced around the pool. The house lights dimmed.

Cheers erupted around from the crowd.

"Ladies and gentlemen—" a male announcer's voice echoed from the loudspeakers. "And children of all ages, at this time our trainers and dolphin friends would like to welcome you to the Indianapolis Zoo's ddddddddDOLPHIN SHOOOOOW!"

"Ya gotta be kiddin' me," Lenny said aloud.

A second wave of cheers and whistles drowned him out.

"At this time, please join me in welcoming your host for this afternoon, NAAAAATTTTTIIIEEEE GGGGGAAAOOOOO!"

The house lights brightened. Two dolphins flew out of the water completing somersaults in rhythm with one another.

A woman walked onto the staged dockside, her wetsuit black with a light blue strip down the left side. She waved at the crowd as she came to the center. "How's everyone doing today?" she asked, her voice bubbling with happiness through the overhead speakers.

The audience responded with predictable enthusiasm.

Lenny rolled his eyes.

"All right!" she said after the applause died down. "My name is Nattie Gao and I'm excited you're here! Now…who's ready to see some dolphins?"

"We are!" the crowd roared in unison.

Nattie blew her whistle and lifted her arms.

A dolphin slid onto a nearby stage and used its tail to flick water onto those sitting in the Splash Zone.

"More! More! More!" the children screamed.

"Yeah! That's what we like to hear!" Nattie cheered them on as she walked around the edge of the pool. "First, let's meet some of our friends here with us today! Let's hear it for…Mage!"

A light grey dolphin beached itself on the edge. It clicked at the audience, and shook the lower half of its body back and forth. A trainer tossed a fish into its open mouth.

"Mage is a bottlenose dolphin," Nattie explained. "He's one of the four males we have here at our aquarium! Next, we have another male...give it up for Uriah!"

A darker dolphin with light spots on its backside leapt from the water. It seemed to hang in the air before touching one of the suspended balls with its beak.

The crowd roared in approval.

"You might have already guessed it by the spots down his back," Nattie said. "Uriah is a spotted dolphin!"

These Drybacks didn't know that, Lenny thought. *They don't know nothin' about the Salt, lady.*

"Okay, girls!" Nattie said. "Time to meet our speedster...Amelia!"

A third dolphin flew from the water, this one with crisscrossing swatches of yellow and light grey down both sides of its body. Amelia performed a double somersault before reentering.

The crowd—especially the young girls—went even wilder.

"How's that for girl power?" Nattie asked. "Amelia is a common dolphin. You can tell her apart because the sides of her body look like a painted hourglass!"

All right, already. Get on with it. Lenny scanned the crowd for Marisa.

Nattie climbed the ladder at the forefront stage. She waded into the pool roughly a foot deep, and paced back and forth as she spoke.

"You can find dolphins all over the world! Like many of you out there today, dolphins make up part of a school, or pod, although it's not like the schools you go to," she added with another laugh.

Could ya sound any more fake, lady?

"Dolphins are also one of the most playful and intelligent

animals in the animal kingdom!" Nattie continued. "They have excellent hearing and eyesight, both in and out of the water, and they use echolocation to find their prey! And did you know that dolphins have also been known to protect divers and shipwrecked sailors from sharks?"

"Nooooo!" some bratty kids near Lenny said.

"Well, they do!" Nattie fake-laughed again. "The dolphins swim in a protective circle around the humans and have even been known to charge sharks at times!"

Lenny's eyes flitted to a teen girl standing up near the back of the bleachers.

She slapped a boy next to her and then sat back down, giggling.

Lenny slumped. *Where are ya, Bourgeois?*

"And now, without further ado," Nattie's voice rose dramatically. "We here at the aquarium have a special treat for all of you!"

Movement! Another girl in the stands stood, one Lenny recognized. *Doll face? What's she so excited about?*

Sydney had put her fingers in her mouth to whistle.

Lenny watched her try to pull the Orc to his feet. *What was it the fat one called him?* Lenny thought back to their earlier exchange. *Weava?*

Sydney shrugged and clapped in rhythm with the crowd.

"Okay," Nattie said. "I think she's built up enough speed. Cheer her on everyone…"

The crowd rose to their feet.

Buckets of Blood, people. Sit down! Lenny shoved to reach the aisle so he could see.

"And give a warm round of applause for our oldest dolphin… Wilda!"

The upper torso of a grandmotherly woman burst from the middle of the pool. Her silvery hair wetly fell past her bare shoulders, covering her chest. As she rose out of the water, Lenny saw her human torso merged into a sleek grey dolphin tail just beneath her bellybutton.

Lenny gasped. *What's a Merrow doin' in a Dryback pool?*

She rose toward the dangling hoop—gracefully twisting in mid-air with her arms at her sides—and floated through without touching it. As gravity beckoned her home, she elegantly raised her pale arms over her head. Her palms came together as the tips of her fingers broke the water's surface. She reentered with a teensy splash and vanished.

The crowd went wild.

Yet no one had screamed at the sight of a half-woman, half-dolphin. The annoying teens next to Lenny weren't calling or texting their friends to relay what they witnessed. Lenny continued his slow surveillance of the crowd, and found only one other person who noticed.

Weava...

GARRETT

"HICKEY! DID YOU SEE—"

"Wow! *Craziness,* man!" Johnny shouted at Garrett. "Told you dolphins rocked!"

Garrett stood. The three younger dolphins had joined Sydney's mom on the main stage, all of them arching their tails. None looked either half-human or half-dolphin.

"Hickey! Did you see her?"

"Who?"

"The lady! The old lady!"

"I can barely hear you, man!" Johnny turned back to the show.

"Look at my mom!" Sydney pointed. "Isn't she great?"

Garrett's eyes searched from one end of the pool to the next.

Sydney put her fingers in her mouth and whistled. "Yeah, Mom!"

"Oh, man, so awesome," Johnny clapped harder.

"I know!" Sydney said. "Can you believe Wilda jumped through the hoop at the end? She's getting too old for that sort of thing."

Too old? Garrett grabbed Sydney by the shoulders. "You saw her too?"

"Of course I did!"

"What did she look like?"

Sydney's forehead wrinkled. "Huh?"

"Like a dolphin going through a Hula Hoop, dude," said Johnny. "What else?"

"Neither of you saw a woman?"

"You mean Nattie?"

"I'm not talking about Sydney's mom, Hickey!" Garrett's voice cracked. "Neither of you saw a woman with a tail?"

Johnny snorted. "Dude, you're talking crazy—"

"I'm not crazy!" Garrett said, louder than he meant to. He sat down hard. "I know what I saw…an old woman with a dolphin tail! She jumped out of the water…went through the hoop…then straight back in! You guys really didn't see her?"

Sydney wouldn't look at him.

"Weaves," Johnny said. "I think swallowing all that pool water yesterday has you seeing things."

Garrett stood up. "I saw her."

"Saw what? A mermaid?" Johnny suggested. "Let me guess—scaly green fishtail, seashell bra…smoking hot redhead?"

"Wha—no," Garrett said. "She had a grey tail. And, well, I mean she looked old enough to be your grandma. I didn't see a bra."

"An old *and* topless mermaid?" Johnny's face squinched. "If this is some kind of joke, you win. Ugh. Now I'm just picturing old, saggy, granny boobs on a dolphin. Gross."

"I'm not making this up, Hickey!"

"Garrett," Sydney said. "Lower your voice…"

Most of the crowd had gone. The few waiting for the rest to clear out now led their kids away from Garrett.

She thinks I'm crazy. Garrett looked back at the pool. Every so

SALTED ∼ 157

often a dolphin would swim by the viewing panes. None of them had any parts that remotely looked human. *Maybe I am crazy.*

"Do you still want to go down and see the dolphins up close?" Sydney finally asked. "I mean…we don't have to, if…you know. If you don't want."

Johnny blew a bubble and popped it. "Heck yeah, we're going! Maybe Weaver can see this topless granny mermaid up close!"

Garrett didn't laugh. Neither did Sydney. In fact, she still wouldn't look at him directly. *Say something!*

"No, let's go," said Garrett. "I just didn't want my *chlorakitis dronemetia* to flare up again."

Lame, Weaves. So lame.

Sydney smirked. "I get it. Probably shouldn't be near a pool with those kinds of symptoms…"

"Let's go already!" Johnny hooted. He jumped from one bleacher down to the next and almost lost his balance.

Sydney leaned close to Garrett. "You sure you want to do this?"

"Definitely. Sorry about all that before. I…just don't want you to think I'm crazy."

"Crazy's what I like most about you," she said quietly. "Besides, I'm glad you're coming down. My mom is always asking about you."

"She is? What about?"

"How you're doing…why we're not dating. The usual," Sydney said. Then she winked and ran down the stairs.

"Syd!" he called after her. "What did you tell her?"

"I don't date cute boys!" she said. "Come on!"

There's that four-letter word again, Garrett thought sourly as he followed her down the bleachers. *Cute. That's what you call your brother, or your dog. Cute is a death sentence.*

Garrett saw both Sydney and Johnny reach the upper pool deck gate, both so far ahead they would never notice if he left. Garrett stepped off the last row of bleachers.

Starting to see a pattern, Weaves? She just...assumes...you'll follow her? Maybe I should just go see the sharks myself. See how cute she thinks that is.

Sydney waved for him to hurry up. She made a pouty face when he didn't immediately come.

Why do I do this to myself? Garrett jogged over.

"Hey, Garrett, this is my mom's friend, Barb," Sydney introduced him to the employee.

"He looks like trouble," Barb joked.

"Major trouble," Sydney said. "So Mom said I should swing by with a couple of friends. Is she still up there or did she go back to her office?"

Barb opened the gate to let them through. "She's up there. You can go, but keep an eye on these two."

Each of them thanked her before following Sydney's lead up onto the deck. Garrett found it slippery, and his sneakers squelched if he turned them too fast.

"This one looks like trouble..." Johnny muttered. "Ha! Why don't I look like trouble?"

"It's because you're sweet," Sydney said.

He's sweet and I'm cute. Garrett tuned out Johnny's immediate counter argument that his sweetness was a means of concealing his bad boy image. *Neither of us have a chance, Hickey.*

They crossed over a thin walkway, not much wider than a wooden plank, and headed for center stage. Nattie had just come out of the faint blue barn used to shield trainers from audience view. She carried a pair of pails overflowing with fish.

Johnny turned to Garrett upon seeing Nattie up close. *"Dude!"* he whispered. *"Sydney's mom is hot!"*

"What did you expect? I mean, look at the cow before you buy the calf, right?"

Nattie set her pails down beside one she had already brought out, and put her hands on her hips. "There's my girl!"

"Mom!" Sydney carefully walked toward her.

It's like seeing the same person at two different stages of life.

"So did you like the show, kiddo?" Nattie asked.

"Loved it!" Sydney said. "I can't believe you let Wilda out!"

"Oh, come on now. She's not *that* old! Hey…is that Garrett Weaver I see over there?" Nattie asked in the way all moms sounded when they already knew the answer. "Get over here already and give me a hug!"

Garrett obliged her. "Hi, Mrs. Gao."

"Weaver! You know I hate that! From now on you call me Nattie, or I'll have Sydney punch you!"

"Meh. She hits like a girl anyway."

Garrett moved sideways to miss Sydney's immediate swing.

"Oh ho! He knows you too well, kiddo," Nattie winked. She looked at Johnny. "Now, who's this?"

Johnny cast his usual shyness aside. "Hi, Nattie, I'm Johnny Hickey. Can I get a hug too?"

Garrett thought it would take years to dim the glow Johnny had when she actually gave him a hug.

"So you three want to feed the dolphins?" Nattie said, stepping away. She pointed to the pails she had brought out. "There's mackerel over there if you want to give them what's left, but you have to listen to Sydney. No horsing around, boys. Okay?"

"Okay," both Garrett and Johnny agreed.

"I'll be talking with Barb if you guys need anything. Come on over when you run out."

Johnny picked up a fish by its tail. His nose wrinkled, and he tried dropping it back in the pail but missed.

A small wave crashed onto the deck. The receding water carried the fish back with it, and into a dolphin's open mouth. It swallowed the meal and clacked its beak.

"Mage thinks you're funny," Sydney said.

"Did you see two what that thing just did?" Johnny yelled. "It made the wave so it could get the food!"

"You said they were smart," Garrett said.

"That wasn't smart. That was genius!"

Sydney slipped out of her shoes and socks, and placed them on the docks. "Don't stroke his ego."

"It's a dolphin, Syd," Johnny said. "You act like it knows what I'm saying."

"They know more than you might realize." Sydney undid the button on her pants and let them fall.

Garrett knew he should be a gentleman, but he couldn't bring himself to look away. Unknown to him a second before, Sydney wore a black wetsuit similar to the one her mom wore.

Stripping off her shirt and throwing her clothes in a pile near the fake rock ledge, Sydney strode to the pool's edge. The dolphin with yellowish swatches of skin appeared and swam to her side the moment she stepped into the wading area. Sydney knelt. "Hi, Amelia!"

The dolphin opened its mouth and squeaked.

Sydney kissed its nose. "You might want to take her, Johnny. Amelia's a good girl, aren't you?"

Amelia vigorously nodded her head.

"How did you get her to do that?" Johnny asked.

"She likes attention, just like us," Sydney said. She whistled, and Amelia disappeared beneath the water. "Johnny, come over here."

Johnny rolled his pant legs up, but hesitated before stepping in.

"Come on," Sydney motioned him in. "Come on, Hickey. They're not going to hurt you."

Johnny arched his neck and tried to peer further out into the pool. "I can't see them…wh-where did they all go?"

"Oh, they decided to go for ice cream," Garrett said.

Sydney shot him a disapproving look. "They'll be back in a minute. I just didn't want them to scare you." She reached into her pail and took out a mackerel. "Here, take this."

"What am I supposed to do with it?"

"Hold it out over the water."

Johnny took the fish. "But won't the—"

"Trust me. Amelia won't hurt you."

"Amelia might not," Garrett said. "But the others…"

"*Garrett!* You're not helping!" Sydney took Johnny by the hand and inched him closer to the shallows edge.

Johnny closed his eyes and extended his arm over the deeper, darker water. His arm quivered so much that the fish seemed to wiggle.

Quietly, a dolphin beak broke the water's surface and slowly rose up and down like a fishing bobber.

Garrett gasped. "Hickey…"

"What?"

"Open your eyes…"

Johnny did. "That's so awesome!"

"Right?" Sydney said. "I told you Amelia is nice. Okay, now keep your hand steady…she's going to take the fish from you."

"Out of my hand?"

"Mmm-hmm. She'll go slow though." Sydney put her left hand on Johnny's lower back and her right hand on his chest, relaxing him, then whistled.

Amelia ascended from the water. Up, up, up she rose, even to the point Garrett swore he would soon see the tip of her tail.

"Now let it go," Sydney said.

Johnny released the fish into Amelia's mouth, and she dipped beneath the surface again. "Whoa! Weaver, did you see that? I fed a dolphin! Can I do it again, Syd?"

"Sure! Hold another fish out over the edge."

While Johnny reached for another mackerel—without being disgusted this time—Sydney left them by the pool and walked behind stage. A second later, she came back out with two whistles dangling from black shoestring necklaces. She gave one to Garrett, the other to Johnny.

"Now, blow it," she said.

Johnny slipped the string over his head and put the whistle in his mouth. He thrust the fish out above the deeper water and blew his whistle.

Amelia peeked above the surface again, took the fish from his hand, and disappeared.

"See, Hickey!" Sydney said. "You've got it down!"

The dolphin with black spots appeared when Johnny performed his act a third time and tried to steal Amelia's fish.

"Uriah! No!" Sydney said. She quickly grabbed a fish from her pail and threw it far out into the pool.

Uriah shot off after it. A second later, Garrett saw a grey arc appear where the fish landed. The dolphin's tail splashed the surface and the fish Sydney threw vanished. Only a few expanding rings indicated anything had been there a moment ago. The same dolphin resurfaced back at Sydney's side, cackling.

"Think you're funny, huh, Uriah?" Sydney said.

The dolphin cackled louder and nodded.

"Okay, come over here. Johnny, you keep feeding Amelia while I take care of this rascal!"

"Syd, where should I go?" Garrett asked.

"Um…I'm not sure where Mage went. Hang on."

She blew her whistle and threw another fish to Uriah.

Garrett searched the pool to see when and where his dolphin would show.

"You don't want Mage, son," said a stately, southern voice.

Garrett turned.

The old woman sat on the edge not twenty feet from him, her dolphin tail lazily swaying in the water.

Garrett opened his mouth to yell for Sydney. His tongue refused to form the words.

"No need for that," she said. "I don't aim to hurt you."

"H-how do you—"

"Best keep your voice down. Elsewise, Miss Sydney might hear you and 'spect you gone crazy."

Now close, Garrett saw what resembled a glistening and pearl-white latex top that covered her stomach, stopped just above her breasts, and left her neckline and shoulders bare. Her human skin—pale and wrinkled—had aged, tan blotches. And from her hips down, Garrett saw a pale and slender dolphin tail no different than Amelia's.

She rested on her long, willowy arms, and used her tail to splash some water onto her stomach. A second later, she sat upright and squeegeed the water from her silvery hair. Her blue eyes twinkled.

Garrett stepped closer. "How is this possible?"

"We all are what we are," she said. "Been made such. Each and every one unique."

"You're unique. I've never seen a—"

She grinned. "A what?"

"I-I don't know," Garrett said. "I don't know what you are. You look like a lady, but—"

"Like a dolphin too."

"Ye-yes, ma'am."

She splashed more water on herself with a quick flick of her tail. "I'm a bit a both, ain't I?" she asked gaily.

"Yes…"

She laughed. "I reckon' I'm the first one you seen. Or at least the first you seen like this." She motioned to her lower body and tail.

"I'd remember seeing someone like you," Garrett said.

"Aw, come now. Maybe the others just didn't have a tail at the time."

Garrett stepped closer still. "I don't understand."

"Most don't."

Her tail began to change color. Like slipping off a pair of grey tights, her lower dolphin torso gradually morphed into pale skin. The remainder of her tail split from the top down; it changed into human legs, then calves, ankles, feet, and finished with her toes. Within moments, the dolphin tail disappeared and only an old woman sat in a one-piece bathing suit of snowy white with her feet dipped in the pool.

"Wish I had my ol' mirror, son. You look like you seen a ghost."

Garrett heard bare feet slap the surface behind him, but he couldn't look away.

Sydney walked past him and knelt to run her hand over the dolphin-lady's head. "I see you found Wilda."

"Syd, you can—"

"She can't see me," Wilda said to Garrett. "Neither can your heavyset friend. All they hear when I talk is a dolphin squeaking. All they see too."

Garrett heard a loud splash near Johnny.

Drenched and terrified, Johnny clenched a fish in his outstretched hand. One of the dolphins careened onto the ledge near him and stole it, then slipped back in the water.

"Oh, Mage!" Sydney said. "Garrett, stay here with Wilda. I'm going to save Hickey from those two."

For the first time in his life, Garrett didn't watch Sydney leave. *How is this possible?*

Wilda pointed. "Mage is laughing at your friend."

"Is Mage...like you?"

"Course he is."

Wilda's toes turned grey and rounded off together—forming the tips of a tail—and her ankles grew together. The changes moved up toward her torso like a zipper. In seconds, she had her dolphin tail back. "Any Salt Child coulda' seen me, if'n they had their eyes open, that is."

"What's a Salt Child, ma'am?"

Wilda chuckled again. "Ain't got the time to explain it to you. Wouldn't believe me if'n I told you anyhow. Don't much matter I 'spect. You gonna find out soon enough."

"How am I supposed to find out what I don't know?"

"Oh...I reckon' someone'll come to call," she said. "You'll know 'em when you see 'em. Ask if they been Salted, or if they's born a Salt Child."

"Hey, Weaver! You almost done?" Johnny yelled. "I'm all out of fish!"

"Them other type...the mean ones with Salt running through they veins...they cain't come inland. Cain't breathe the air." Wilda paused. "Less'n they figured out some ways to walk on the Hard since I been gone, that is."

"Weaver!"

Garrett did a double take from Johnny back to Wilda. "He really can't see you, can he?"

"They done forgot about our kind and all we done for 'em." Wilda looked toward the water. "I 'spect it's about time for you to move on, Garrett Weaver."

"How—how do you know my name, ma'am? And wh-what's yours?"

"Oh, I heard a lot about you. Heard Miss Sydney talk to her mama 'bout you many a night," she said playfully. "And you already know my name, if you was listenin'. Why, Miss Nattie and Miss Sydney done told you already! You remember it now, don'tcha?"

Garrett remembered. "Wilda..." he whispered. "Your name is Wilda."

She beamed a smile that made Garrett believe his heart would burst if he looked into her wizened face much longer. "Most certainly is. Don't you forget about me now! What you gonna do when someone comes to call?"

"Ask if they've been Salted, or...or if they were born a Salt Child."

"Weaver!" Johnny yelled. "Let's go, dude!"

Garrett ignored him. "Wilda…" he said. "What are you?"

"My darling child…you already know what I am."

"A…um…a…mer-mermaid," he said.

Wilda fought a fit of laughter. "Call us what you will, Mr. Weaver, but that's just what humans named us in their ol' stories. I'm a Merrow."

"A Merrow…"

Wilda grinned. "The dolphin-folk."

"Does that mean there are more of you?"

"Whole underwater cities full," she said. "But I 'spect you'll see 'em 'fore too long. They's something special in you, son. These ol' bones can feel it."

Johnny came over to join him. "Weaver! Come on, dude! We should be at the bus in a half hour!"

"Best be goin' now," Wilda majestically lifted her left hand. "It's been so nice talking with you."

Garrett raised his right hand and, realizing he lifted the wrong one, lowered it.

"We Merrows shake with our left hands," she corrected. "Lotta' things is opposite in the Salt. You gonna see soon enough."

Garrett grasped her hand. He half expected to find it cold and clammy; Wilda's hand warmed his, and her grip made him feel weak. "I-I have so many questions."

"How about I give you one more answer then? 'S about all the time you have left before your friend over there pulls you away." She released his hand.

Garrett noticed a silver ring on her forefinger with a plain, stone pebble adorning it. "What's that?"

"Oh, that ol' thing," Wilda said. She stretched out her fingers and moved them like a wave. "A special someone gave it to me so many years ago. Pretty, iddn't it?"

Garrett didn't think so. He also didn't want to lie. "Who gave it to you?"

"Now, Garrett Weaver, I said I'd give you another question and you's trying to get a second outta me."

Garrett felt a nudge in the back.

"Thought you didn't like dolphins, dude," said Johnny.

"I was wrong," Garrett said. *Please show him too.*

"He cain't see me," Wilda reminded him. "They've forgotten how."

Johnny sighed. "Let's go already! The bus is leaving soon and we still haven't seen the sharks! Plus, Nattie said it's time for them to lock up for the day."

"Okay," Garrett said. "Give me a second. I want to shake her han…fin one more time."

Johnny laughed. "You want to shake her fin? You've lost your mind, bro. Knock yourself out. I'm gonna see if I can score another hug from Nattie before we go!"

Garrett waited for him to leave before raising his left hand again. "Goodbye, Wilda…"

"Ain't saying goodbye," Wilda cheered him with another smile. Then she took his hand in hers. "What's an ol' lady like me to do if she didn't have a visit to look forward to every now and again? 'Specially from someone handsome as you."

"I'm-I'm hardly handsome," Garrett stammered. "My skin—"

"Makes you who you are," Wilda said, stroking his cheeks with the flat of her warm hand. "You are a painted beauty, my child. Don't never let no one tell you different."

Garrett looked away. "So I…I can come back?"

Wilda's smile faded. She took his hand in her and patted it. "I certainly hope so…Humans ain't the only ones who forgot what they is and where they come from. So you come back here after you seen all the wondrous things the Salt and its Children has to show you. Help remind me about all the good things I done left behind."

Then, Wilda leaned forward and kissed Garrett's cheek. Before he could react, she pushed off the rubbery floor, slid back into the pool, and vanished beneath the water.

"Whoa!" Johnny yelled from the stage. "That dolphin tried to bite you and you didn't even flinch! Hey, you all right, man? Why do you look like you're about to cry?"

Garrett searched the water for Wilda, but the last traces of growing circles where she entered had begun to fade. "I'm good."

"Cool, let's go then!"

Garrett delayed a second longer. He wiped the corners of his eyes and followed Johnny across the stage.

Sydney awaited them by the gate they had entered with fishing pails at her feet. A hose stretched across the stage. She freed the nozzle and sprayed the fish pails clean, splattering water and ice chips everywhere. She killed the stream as Garrett approached and handed his full pail to her.

"Garrett! You didn't give Wilda any?"

"I-I forgot…"

"You mean she stayed that long without giving her a fish?" Sydney asked. "Wow! Mom will be impressed. Maybe you should be a dolphin trainer!"

If I could come back here and talk with Wilda every day I would. Garrett looked out over the pool again.

"Syd, aren't you going to change?" Johnny asked.

"Sorry guys. I'm going to stay here and help Mom finish up her work. I'll see you tomorrow at school though!"

Johnny slumped. "Yeah, okay."

"So, Weaver," Sydney elbowed him. "Did we make a dolphin lover out of you?"

"Yeah," Garrett said. "Wish I could stay here with you and help out."

"Me too, but Mr. Lansky will never allow it. School permission slips and everything. By the way…don't tell him Mom let you guys come on stage. I think she forgot you guys should've signed some waiver to come up here."

"I won't say anything."

Garrett eyed the pool again.

Sydney looked at him oddly. "Well, I know you guys are leaving, but don't seem so bummed. We'll come back soon, yeah?"

"Okay. Tell your mom thanks for me…oh, and make sure Wilda gets some fish? Sorry I forgot…got caught up in being that close to a—"

"Weaver!"

"All right, Hickey! Hold on a second!"

"No worries," Sydney said. "Better hurry up. Your girlfriend would be lost without you."

"Right…"

Sydney hugged him.

Johnny stepped in to separate them when the hug lasted longer than expected. He pulled Garrett away and down the steps.

With a final wave to Sydney, the two friends exited the dolphin pavilion into a large holding area. To their left, a short hallway made of glass opened into a small room, built to give visitors a chance to see the watery world from a dolphin's point of view.

Garrett walked toward it.

"Dude! What are you doing? We have to go back to the bus," Johnny said. "But first I want to see the sharks! Come on!"

Who cares about sharks now? Garrett followed Johnny outside, doubting anything would ever again capture his attention like Wilda had.

It never crossed his mind he might be wrong.

LENNY

LENNY HUNCHED LOW IN THE SHADOWS BY THE dolphin exit doors waiting for Weaver to leave. Try as he might, he couldn't rid himself of the pesky thought the teen truly had no idea of his origins. Lenny decided to make it his business to find out. Weaver and his fat friend never saw Lenny leave his hiding spot to trail them. Always he stayed just out of sight in the event they turned around.

This is pup's play.

Lenny noticed three other teenagers also following the pair of misfits. None wore Selkie coats. He ruled out the possibility of another catching group and risked drawing close enough to listen in on their conversation.

"When should we take him, Benny?"

"I already told you! We'll follow him into the aquarium and wait till no one's around. I already scoped out the hammerhead exhibit. We'll take him in there to do it."

"What about Hickey?"

"What about him? Piggy will run back to the busses if we tell him to. Weaver's the one I want. Bryce, you two go around to the front in case he sees me and runs that way."

Lenny watched the two smaller teens break off down a separate path. The big one stayed on Weaver's trail. *Why do ya fellas wanna mess with Weava?* Lenny followed them across the lawn toward the newly built shark exhibit, and then inside.

Garrett and Hickey stopped in front of a nurse shark tank.

The big teen hung back.

Lenny cursed. If any of them looked to the right they would see him standing in the doorway. *Can't just go back outside though and risk losin 'em.* He glanced to his left and saw a bathroom. He went for it.

Lenny never heard his attacker.

The ground disappeared beneath Lenny as his captor picked him up and whipped him around, slammed his back to the wall. His feet dangled free against the concrete. "Whattaya doin', Henry?"

Henry held him there with one hand. He took out his dagger with the other, and put the tip to the corner of Lenny's eye.

Lenny winced, and heard the door lock shut.

"Lenny, Lenny, Lenny," said Oscar, coming around the corner. "I'm disappointed in you."

"Why?" he choked.

"Why?" Oscar slapped him. "My father said for us to lead this crew together, yet you've off and left Henry and I out in the cold again."

Lenny tried to ignore the sting in his cheek and keep his anger at bay. "Listen, we got other problems right now."

"*You* have problems," Oscar said. "That's twice now you've failed me. It almost begs the question if your heart is truly in this assignment."

"I got caught up."

"Aptly put," Oscar said. "You...were...caught. And of course, being the son of such a famous catcher, you know the penalty for those caught who attempt escape."

"I'm...no...runna," Lenny sputtered.

"Maybe not before. But I fear your new rank has given you a false sense of power. At least that's what I'll tell my father. Henry, wouldn't you agree that Lenny thinks too much of his captain's status?"

Henry tightened his grip. *"Oui, monsieur."*

"There, you see," said Oscar. "I even have a witness."

Need to get some help in here. Lenny pictured Paulo in his mind. His earrings flashed. *Paulie, I need—*

Henry reached for Lenny's left ear. He yanked the earring down, tearing it through Lenny's earlobe.

Lenny screamed.

Henry dropped him, put his knee on Lenny's chest. Muffled the cry of pain with his free and bloodied hand. He reached for Lenny's right ear.

"No! Wait, Henry!" said Oscar. "I want to do it!"

Oscar knelt beside him.

Lenny squirmed. He went nowhere beneath Henry's strength.

Unlike Henry, Oscar took his time. He toyed with the earring, tugging at it. Sucking his bottom lip in ecstasy each time Lenny flinched. Then he leaned low to whisper in Lenny's ear.

"Thought you could make a break for it this trip, didn't you?"

Lenny shook his head.

"No?" said Oscar. "I don't believe you."

Lenny pictured the faces of his crew. His lone earring flashed. *Help—*

Oscar ripped the earring out.

Lenny's back arched as Henry quieted the scream, his pain spasming down to his toes.

"No," said Oscar, standing and tossing the bloodied earring into the trash. He went to the sink, turned the water on, and lathered up his hands. "I think when you saw how easily Marisa escaped yesterday it put ideas in your krill-sized head."

Just keep ya mouth shut. Just stay quiet. Lenny's conscience told him. "Ya mean…yesta'day when…I saved ya?"

Oscar tore off a piece of paper towel. "You really think anyone will believe that? You think I would allow anyone to hear that?" Oscar dried his hands. "Henry."

"Oui, monsieur?"

"Show this slave why no one will ever hear that story."

Henry unsheathed his dagger.

The lack of pressure allowed Lenny to scramble out from under him. He hurried to his feet, knowing he had nowhere to go, and glanced at the dagger's black shine. "Only way ya takin' my tongue is killin' me first."

Oscar made a pouty face. "But then I would be the only captain in this crew. Why that would be…well…simply marvelous, wouldn't it? Henry." He jerked his head. "As you please."

Henry started forward.

"Wait!" said Lenny. "What if I had something ya wanted more than my tongue. More than my life."

Oscar motioned for Henry to stop.

"Ya wanna impress ya pop," said Lenny. "Prove ya got what it takes, right?"

Oscar shrugged.

What are ya doin', Len? Don't do this. Lenny saw the light dance off Henry's blade. "I can get ya something he'll want."

"My father wants Marisa Bourgeois. You remember her, don't you, Lenny? The runner you've been sent to capture, the same one who escaped you twice now?"

"Marisa Bourgeois is a slave runna, nothin' more. I found something more valuable than that...an Orcinian."

Oscar shared a look with Henry. "Are you saying there's an Orc hunting party...*here?*"

Lenny shook his head. "Just one. A calf."

"Lies," said Henry. "Orcs never allow their calves far from their side."

"This one got away somehow," Lenny said. "And there's one other thing too. I don't think he knows what he is."

Oscar scoffed. "How could he not know? Anyone Salted would recognize him by the look of his skin. Just as they recognize us by our coat designs."

Lenny nodded. "Yeah. But he didn't. I ran into him earlier, thought maybe he was part of a huntin' pod out lookin' for Bourgeois. He saw my hood plain. Even asked me where I got it. I'm tellin' ya, Oscar, he don't know nothin' about our world. We get him to go back with us..."

Henry lowered his blade. His earrings flashed. So did Oscar's.

Lenny didn't need his earrings to sense the greedy machinations working from Henry's brain to Oscar's. The young owner might not fathom the value Lenny hinted at. Henry understood it and more.

Lenny waited for their private conversation to halt. *Don't tell 'em about the old Merrow in the pool. No need for 'em to know more than they need.*

Oscar turned to Lenny. "Henry says this has never been done before. That no one's captured an Orc, to his knowledge. Let alone an impressionable calf with no knowledge of his history. Such a find—"

"Would be worth more than some slave girl ya plan on hangin'," said Lenny. "Ya pop hired Henry to protect ya 'cause Lepa's are the most dangerous kinda Selkie that anemoney can buy, right? What would he think if ya brought home an Orc to groom as a future guardian?"

Oscar simpered.

That's right. Play to his weakness. He continued. "And the thing is, this is just a calf. He's not even grown yet. When he becomes a full on Orcinian bull...what'd that be worth, Henry? Ten guardians just like ya?"

"More," said Henry.

"More?" Oscar repeated. "Henry, you can't be serious."

"'ave you ever seen an Orc in open water, leetle Crayfish?"

"Well, n-no, not exactly. Father doesn't like me venturing far from the cavern."

"Because you would not survive on your own," Henry said flatly.

Lenny suppressed a snicker. *Henry, if I didn't know ya already, I might be startin' to like ya.* The pain in his ears immediately dismissed the notion.

"Faster zan Merrows," Henry continued. "Deadlier zan Nomads, and near as powerful as ze Ancients. If ze nipperkin speaks true, zis Orc could make you rich beyond compare."

"First," Oscar pouted. "I could survive fine on my own, thank you. And second, why would someone so valuable be interested in guarding a Selkie? Even a rich one like myself?"

"Because he don't know betta," said Lenny. "Ya take someone and teach 'em something about themselves, ya own 'em for a time.

Convince him to go to the Salt, show him a world he don't know exists, teach him who he is, *what he is,* whattaya think that buys ya?"

Oscar shrugged.

"Loyalty," said Lenny. "He'll belong to ya till the end of ya days."

Oscar's grin told Lenny everything he needed to know. "Then let's go find him."

CHIDI

LENNY! RACER SAID. PAULO, WHAT JUST HAPPENED?
Why won't Lenny talk to us?

Boss, said Paulo. *Talk to me.*

Chidi cowered into a corner. *Henry,* she thought to herself. *Henry must have done it. Might even have killed Lenny.*

The zoo's exit lay just in front of her. While everyone had been hunting Marisa, Chidi used the distraction to steal away. Now if only she could will herself to walk through the gates.

A thought of Henry, stalking her to keep a watchful eye, tingled up her neck. She remembered his threat the last time she ran. *You weel never be reed of me. Don't you ever run from me, Chidi. I weel find you, and keel ze ones you run weeth.*

Her shoulders shook. Chidi touched the notebooks in her pack, took a deep breath. *Stay loose. Find a school bus, get on, and ride it out of here.*

Boss! Paulo repeated. *Buckets of blood. Ellie, get in here. Now! We might need your help.*

Ellie! Chidi had forgotten about her. *If she leaves her position she might see me!*

Chidi ducked inside the gift shop. She pretended to look at

T-shirts to give herself a better vantage point of anyone entering or leaving the zoo. A young employee behind the cash register gave her a wary look. Chidi swore he could hear her heart pounding.

Chidi, Racer, Paulo said. *Did either of you get a response from Ellie?*

No.

Me neither, Racer said. *What does that mean? Is that bad?*

I don't know. Paulo sounded frustrated. *I'm in the aquarium now, but I don't see Lenny, Oscar, or Henry.*

Chidi took three deep breaths to calm her nerves. *Henry's not there?*

None of them are! Paulo said. *Ellie...you okay? Answer me!*

Henry gone...Ellie not answering. Chidi looked out the open doorway.

A line of busses had formed behind one another like yellow train cars hooked together. *Doesn't matter. Now the crew is even more distracted. Go!*

Ellie, Paulo yelled. *Talk to me, girl. If you're there...*

What do we do? Racer asked.

Bail out. Both of ya get back to the bus right now.

Aye, aye. I'm on my way.

Me too, said Chidi, eyeing the busses each in turn. *But which one...*

She eliminated her options by those who had drivers and chaperones paying the closest attention. She found one that teens hopped on and off again with no supervision nearby. Donning her hood, Chidi casually walked out of the gift shop and toward the bus.

Someone ripped her hood down. "Going somewhere?"

Chidi whirled, grabbed her assailant by the throat.

Racer blinked in surprise. "C-calm down, Chidi...I-I was just having a bit of fun."

"What are you doing?" she hissed, releasing him.

"Same thing as you..." Racer looked to the line of busses. His earrings flashed. *Running.*

It's a trick. Chidi hid her dagger back inside her Silkie pocket. "I'm not running."

Racer pulled her away from anyone who might listen in. "Yes, you are," he said. "I've been following you since the Deserts. Marisa never hopped into the rattlesnake pit. She tripped and fell over the railing. You could have grabbed her anytime you wanted."

Chidi stiffened.

"She shouldn't have made it through that employee door before you either," said Racer. "And just now, when Paulo told us to get to the bus—"

"I was going—"

"The wrong way?" Racer shook his head. "Chidi, I know you're running. Didn't I just say that's what I want too? I'd be in just as much trouble if Oscar or Lenny saw me right now. You and me... we're the same."

"No, we're not. Even if I wanted to run, which I don't," Chidi insisted, "I don't have anyone for them to hurt if I escaped. You do. All of you do."

"My father's been preparing me for this moment all my life."

"Racer, listen to me. Your owner, August...he will kill your family if you run," Chidi said. "You know he will."

Racer's face tightened. "Maybe. But I won't be there to see it. I watched him sell my brother and sister to different buyers just because he felt like it. I'll never see them again. My parents and me...

we don't know if they're alive, or dead, or—anything. Don't you get it? My father said they can't watch that happen again. He told me if I ever had any chance to run, I should take it. That even if they killed him, he would at least die knowing one of his children ran free."

"Racer, you're not think—"

"Look at them, Chidi." Racer pointed to the groups of students horsing around. "Nothing I've seen from their world looks harder than ours. Why couldn't we fit in? It would be easier if we helped each other!"

He's lying, Chidi thought to herself. *This is some kind of trap.*

"What about Paulo?" she asked. "Ellie and Lenny? August owns them too. If you run, he'll hurt them because you got away and they didn't catch you. He'll say they helped free you."

"That's why you need to take us with you," Racer said.

"Us?"

"Me and Paulo and Ellie. They want to run too."

Chidi scoffed. "The others should know better."

"They do know better. They know we can make it! The only reason they haven't yet is because Paulo's sure he can convince Lenny to run with us!"

"You poor, naïve, pup. Lenny will never run. Hasn't he said that a hundred times? Dolans don't run. And they have his father."

Racer's blue eyes lit up. "Right, but see, that's the plan…a hostage for a hostage. Oscar for Declan."

"Are you *insane*? Your plan is to ransom your owner's son? It will never work."

"Why not?"

"Because even if August made the deal, which he won't, the second he had Oscar back he would spend a fortune hiring other crews to find you. And not just catchers like us, he'll hire Merrows, maybe even Orcs. He'll scour every reef, blue hole, and cavern to find you."

"Orcs?" Racer winced.

"Merrows and Orcs. You think your idea hasn't been thought of before? It has. Have you ever heard of the Caribbean Monks?"

"Sure, but they're all—"

"Dead," Chidi said. "Each and every one of them hunted down and killed to send a message. That's what happens to slaves who get ideas of taking down owners."

"Yeah, but that's because they took some Merrow's daughter... or was it a son?" Racer asked. "I can't remember. Anyway, we're talking about a Selkie owner! Sure he's got some power, but August isn't a Mer—"

"He has Merrow friends," Chidi said. "How do you think a former slave came into having so much anemoney and power? Why do you think Nomads don't bother him? He's protected! Henry told me. It's the only reason he took this job. He wants to find out who backs August."

Racer rolled his eyes. "Okay, fine. So what's your plan for escaping?"

"I'm not running!"

"Well, maybe not now that I caught you, but you planned to. I know you did! Take me with you," Racer said. "This is my first time around the Drybacks. I don't know what to do, or where to go. Help me!"

The sincerity in Racer's voice reminded Chidi of other slaves who had once begged the same of her. "I...I can't..." she said. "I won't."

"Why not?"

"I can't, okay! It doesn't matter why not. Y-You wouldn't be safe around me."

"That's why we need to run together," Racer said. "Running alone isn't safe. What if Henry found you? We all know he'd come after you. If the rest of us stayed together we could help."

No one helps. Chidi closed her eyes. She could still see the blood and vacant expressions of those she had run with before. "Henry would never stop hunting me."

"He would if we killed him."

Chidi covered her mouth. Racer said it with such ease, with all the confidence of one who had never known true terror. She shook her head.

"What?" Racer asked. "Why is that wrong of us to think that way? Owners can do whatever they want to us. So what? We can't get them back the same way? No! I say we send a message back. Besides, Henry has it coming. Paulo told me how he's treated you!"

"Paulo doesn't know…"

"Oh yeah?"

Racer grabbed Chidi's wrists. She fought to free herself of his grip. He forced the underside of her wrists skyward. Scores of scars lined her wrists and forearms, and the bite marks worst of all. Some ran deep; others left only light tracings.

"How'd you get those, Chidi? Huh?"

They know…they all know. Chidi flipped her hands back over. The scars on her skin anyone could see. She thanked the Ancients no one could wrestle the invisible scars out of her. Those she had buried deep.

"He's a monster, Chidi. But you don't have to worry about him anymore…I'll protect you."

Racer leaned and kissed her.

Chidi caught him by the throat. *"What are you doing?"*

"What? I thought girls wanted protect—"

"I don't need protection. You ever kiss me again and *I'll* be the monster," Chidi said, releasing him. "Get me?"

Racer stepped a few feet to her left. "Okay. Sorry."

Chidi wiped her lips with the back of her hand and spit. She looked on him again and debated what to do. Henry would kill the pup without a second thought, she knew. She turned away from him and watched several loaded busses drive off.

"Come on," she said. "We should go back to the bus before Paulo wonders where we're at."

Racer followed her into the parking lot. "But we're really going to see if he'll come with us, right? Because I'm pretty sure we'll need Paulo and Ellie to escape. Think how great it will be! With Paulo's strength, my speed, and Lenny's planning, you girls won't have to worry about anyone recapturing us!"

"Good thing," Chidi said. "I don't know what I would do without you if Zymon's guardian came after us. How did you take his Leper down again?"

Racer fake-laughed. "That's why we need Paulo too. Me and him? Unstoppable."

"So what should Ellie and I do? Be good little girls tagging along for the ride?"

"Are you kidding? We need you both too. Ellie's not as strong as Paulo, but she's pretty strong for a girl. And you know more languages than the rest of us put together. The five of us could go anywhere!"

Except near salt water.

Racer yanked her down beside a parked car.

"What—"

Racer pointed at the zoo. His earrings flashed. *We're surrounded!*

Employees barred the front gates, leaving only one open. Others brought out yellow sawhorses with the Indianapolis Zoo: Do Not Cross written in black lettering. Each employee bustled about to clear the area of visitors.

A lean and long-legged man stepped into their midst, his silhouette casting a larger shadow than the two lion statues he stood between. Chidi read the U.S. MARSHAL written in bold yellow across his navy jacket. The marshal adjusted his black cowboy hat. Even from a distance, Chidi recognized the mismatched line of white around the base of his hat.

Seal teeth!

The marshal turned in her direction.

Chidi paled. "Racer! We have to go now!"

"Why? Who is that man?"

"H-he's not a man! He's the Silkstealer!"

Racer shook his head. "That's just a story."

The Silkstealer paced around inside the barricades. The toothpick he held in his mouth danced from side to side. He removed a radio from his pocket and held it close to his mouth.

He's not alone...

Chidi watched him point at a different barred gate and speak into the radio again. A beefy zoo guard strolled over to speak with him. The Silkstealer barked at him for a solid minute. The guard cowered away.

Two more men emerged from the crowd; both wore U.S. Marshal jackets. Each took a post inside the open gate.

"Do you think they're here because of Marisa?" Racer asked.

Chidi shrugged. "Her notebooks say he's chased her before."

"The stories say no Silkie has ever escaped the Silkstealer though…"

"I don't know why you sound so worried," Chidi said. "The stories also say he only hunts girls."

"At least Silkies live to have a chance at escaping. All the stories say he kills Selkies!"

Chidi barely heard him. The bus she had planned to board pulled away from the lot. She watched it go, saw the teen's faces through the windows as it drove past, taking with it any hopes of freedom she held.

Her next breath clotted with black exhaust from the bus tailpipe. Chidi coughed and buried her nose in the neckline of her Silkie suit. She pulled Racer to his feet. "Come on, we need to get back to our bus."

GARRETT

FOR ALL JOHNNY'S TALK ABOUT HOW MUCH HE loved dolphins, he showed none of it now with sharks to look at. Garrett wished he could record his friend to prove Johnny a lying suck-up, but he had forgotten to charge his phone.

"Dude, dude, dude! Check this out!" Johnny said. "It says sharks don't have eyelids, but most have something called a ni...nictitating membrane...is that right? Whatever. Anyway, it helps protect their eyes whenever they're attacking prey! Pretty sweet, huh?"

Each informational placard only furthered Johnny's true opinion that a shark could win in a fight against a dolphin. Garrett might have agreed with him on any other day based solely on the sheer number of teeth sharks had. *I wonder what a Merrow could do to a shark?*

Johnny ran to another tank. "Aw, man! Check this one out!"

Garrett scanned a placard that read sharks had a system of pores called *ampullae of Lorenzini*. The *ampullae* allowed them to detect weak electrical signals given off by other fish and help them hunt. He paced around the rest of the exhibit, his thoughts always returning to Wilda. He eventually found Johnny at the tasseled wobbegong tank. Neither of them could find the shark anywhere inside.

Unrequested, Johnny read aloud the information card. "Whoa. It says here wobbegongs are masters of camouflage. Pretty sweet, huh?"

A few minutes later, Garrett spotted the wobbegong hunkered against a rock. Most of its body had a brownish coloring and matched the stone while the ends of its body replicated the moldish green seaweed drifting beside it.

"Whoa," Johnny said. "Look at that!"

A giant cardboard cutout of a cartoonish hammerhead shark with glasses hung overhead the exit. The hammerhead pointed toward a dark corridor with one of its fins.

"Sydney told me the great hammerhead is the only big shark the zoo has," Johnny said. "The exhibit's closed though. Pretty corny advertising, huh?"

"What do you mean?"

Johnny pointed at Garrett's feet.

Waxed into the floor, a trail of plastic hammerhead sharks swam into the darkened exhibit like fishy footprints to guide them ahead.

Johnny spit his gum into the trashcan and popped a fresh piece into his mouth. "Let's see where it goes!"

They followed the path of hammerheads down a short hallway until it diverged in two near the end. One path led to light shining through the sides of the exit door. The hammerhead path went down an unlit hall. Several black and yellow pieces of tape formed an X across the entryway, each reading: ZOO PERSONNEL ONLY.

"You know, on second thought, I-I don't know, Weaves. Maybe we should go to the bus." Johnny checked his watch. "Yeah, we need to get going. We really need to go back to the bus. It'll take us at least five minutes to walk there."

"You've been talking all day about seeing this thing," Garrett said. "Syd isn't with us to tattle, and *now* you want to go home?"

"Yeah, but what if we get caught?"

"Uh, they ask us what we're doing and tell us to leave." Garrett looked both ways for anyone who might be coming down the same hallway. Seeing no one, he ducked under the tape. "You coming?"

"I-I...My dad would kill me if I got in trouble."

"Fine," said Garrett. "Go back to the bus and I'll meet you there."

"What if Mr. Lansky asks me—"

"Tell him I went to the bathroom and I'll be right there. It's not like I'm going to take forever."

Johnny hurried away, like even listening to Garrett talk about breaking a rule might taint him.

Garrett continued into the exhibit, pausing occasionally to let his eyes adjust to the shadowy surroundings. Ahead, he saw the slightest hints of blue where the shared wall ended and opened into the exhibit. Photographs and information tidbits of great hammerheads had been hung along the walls. Garrett walked past them all without stopping to read any.

He turned the corner and gasped.

The tank sprawled before him like a movie theater screen and inside it, a fifteen-foot long shark-man. His emaciated, bare-skinned torso reminded Garrett of Aboriginal tribesman he had seen pictures of in geography class. His cheekbones looked carved from obsidian, flawed by thin scars shaped like triangles. Dreadlocks floated around him like curled black and silver snakes wrapped in brown seaweed. His eyes might as well be two pieces of coal with the slightest trace of chalk ringing his irises. Five slits on both sides of his neck fluttered open each time he exhaled, making the loose skin flutter.

Garrett shuddered. *Whatever this guy is, he's not like Wilda.* He stepped closer.

Rows of triangular teeth lined the shark-man's mouth. Each filed into a pointed tip with serrated edges down its sides. Lean muscle comprised what little meat remained on his body. Endless odd symbols, brands, and more triangle-shaped scars covered his skin.

Garrett had the morbid thought some of the scars looked like bite marks. *What could have done that to him?*

The shark-man shared the same white underside as Wilda. The similarities stopped there.

Where Garrett imagined the man's thighs should have been, a triangular shaped fin emerged, and another near where shins should be. Garrett remembered Wilda's tail splaying horizontally, the tips and sides rounded off. The shark-man's tail stood vertically, its bodylines sharp and pointed.

Garrett would have thought the shark-man dead had it not been for his tail, swaying back and forth like a pendulum.

Tick...tock...tick...tock.

Are you the one Wilda talked about? He waved.

The shark-man did not move.

Garrett waved again.

Still the shark-man would not flinch.

"Hey!" Garrett shouted nervously. "Hey, you! Shark-man!"

Maybe he can't see out. Garrett took a few steps to his right to fully see the shark-man. A dorsal fin stretched out of the middle of his back.

"Whoa..."

The shark-man twitched and whipped upside down before Garrett could back away. He plastered his face against the glass.

Garrett flinched.

The shark-man widened his black eyes. His teeth gnashed. He banged a fist against the tank and made it thud.

Oh no...why did I move? Garrett thought. *He knows I can see him now!*

The shark-man swam back and forth, like a tiger stuck in its cage. He stopped mid-swim. His back straightened and made him appear even taller and more threatening, something Garrett had not deemed possible before. Then he opened his hand, large enough to palm a watermelon. His long, bony fingers motioned for Garrett to step closer.

"No way..."

The shark-man pointed at his mouth, a trap full of dagger-like teeth. He rubbed his stomach and shook his head.

He doesn't want me to be afraid. Garrett warily looked at the tank. *That pane's thick enough to keep him in there, right?* He took a step closer.

The shark-man perked up. He motioned Garrett come forward more.

Garrett stopped a few feet away from the tank. "Were you born this way?" he asked, recalling Wilda's words. "Have you been Salted?"

The shark-man placed his left palm flat against the glass. Garrett saw traces of a rusty-colored, askew triangle seared across it, long since scabbed over.

"Well, well, well. Lookie what we have here..." a voice behind Garrett said. "We've been looking all day for you, Weaver."

Garrett turned.

Eddie Bennett and Juan Marrero stopped fifteen feet shy of the tank.

Garrett saw Bryce Tardiff hanging back to prevent his escape.

"Time to pay up for what you did to Kellen," Bennett said.

"What I did to him?" Garrett said. "He tried to *drown me*, Benny. Get your facts straight!"

Juan rushed in. He shoved Garrett against the tank, elbowed him in the ribs.

"Easy, Marrero. I want to get my shots in too!" Bennett popped his knuckles. "This one's for getting me suspended…"

Bennett punched Garrett in the gut.

He crumpled, sucking wind. Marrero lifted him back up and held him against the tank again.

Bennett punched Garrett in the nose with a right hook, then in the jaw with his left. "That's for what Owens got from his dad…"

Garrett's head lolled downward, his jaw aching. Blood flowed from both nostrils. He tasted more trickling down his throat.

Something thunked above his head.

"Whoa!" said Tardiff. "Guys, check out that shark!"

"Nobody cares about some stupid shark," said Bennett. "Pick him up again!"

Water dripped down the back of Garrett's neck.

Why is everything so wet? He wondered as Marrero lifted under his armpits again.

Garrett slumped to the floor.

"Marrero!" Bennett yelled. "Why did you drop him?"

"I-I dunno. He just got heavy all of a sudden!"

Garrett reeled. He rolled to his back.

The shark-man gazed down on him, a dark merman of death. His tail continued to sway.

Tick…tock…tick…tock. Garrett swore the shark-man grinned at him.

"Hey!" said Tardiff. "What's wrong with Weaver's leg?"

"Pick him back up, Marrero!"

The room spun in alternating black and red blurs. Bile rose in Garrett's throat.

"I-I can't…" said Marrero. "I can't lift him—"

"Why not?"

"I don't know…he's…he's too heavy!"

"He can't weigh that much!" Bennett said. "Lift him up!"

"I can't!"

"Here, move!"

Another pair of hands grabbed under Garrett's arms. Again, he did not budge.

"Wha—what's the deal—" Bennett grunted.

"I told you! He's too heavy!"

Garret's pain subsided. His eyes fluttered open. Both of his classmates continued their attempts.

Marrero's face turned purple as he tried again.

Bennett glanced downward and screamed. "Look at his leg!"

"Wh—"

"Look at his leg!"

Marrero yanked Garrett's right pant leg up. "What the…"

No…not again! The black and white skin had returned, and his legs turned smooth and hairless. He reached down to touch them. His skin felt like wet car tires. Garrett screamed. *Not again! Why is this happen—*

A *thunk* came from the tank.

"Watch out!" Tardiff yelled, pointing at the tank.

Garrett whirled to see what could make Tardiff panic.

The shark-man swam straight at them, never slowing—even when he rammed the viewing pane. *Thunk.*

The acrylic pane held. The shark-man rebounded backward, shaking his head.

"Hey! Lemme go!" Tardiff yelled.

Garrett turned with his two classmates.

A balding man in a dark grey and charcoal-spotted hooded sweatshirt held Tardiff by the back of his neck. A preppy kid in a white sweatshirt with a black hood stood beside him. Garrett didn't recognize either of them, but he remembered the dwarf standing in front of them.

All three had focused on the tank, their faces awe-struck.

"Mère de Dieu..." the chaperone said. *"Le Marteau Silencieux."*

"For once, it appears you weren't lying, Lenny," said the preppy kid. "How in a blue hole did a Nomad wind up here?"

Garrett looked back at the hammerhead tank. *They can see him too!*

"Not him, Oscar. Not the Nomad," the dwarf said. He pointed at Garrett. "*Him.* Look at his leg!"

Oscar grinned at the sight. "So it is true..."

"Wha-what's wrong with my leg?" Garrett's voice cracked.

"Ya see, Oscar? He don't know what's happenin', do ya kid?"

"What do you mean?" Garrett asked. "Why does my leg feel like rubber?"

Again the shark-man hit the pane, and once more, it held firm. The force at which he hit seemed to have dazed him. The shark-man swam to the back of the tank, slower this time, and his upper body began to change.

The grey around his waist seeped upward, similar to the way Garrett had seen Wilda's tail do. His arms vanished at his sides and turned to triangular fins. Each of his eyes drifted toward the closest ear and then jutted outward like grey fleshy telescopes on either side of his head. His nose shrunk and disappeared. In a matter of moments, the man disappeared. Only the Great Hammerhead remained. The shark swam for the viewing pane and rammed it again.

A hairline crack formed down the pane.

He's trying to break out! Garrett thought.

Marrero ran for the hallway.

The older man noticed. He flung Tardiff at Marrero.

Garrett crawled backward. *How did he...he just threw Tardiff!*

Both teens hit the wall.

"Henry!" Lenny yelled. "Whattaya doin'!"

Henry dove on top of Tardiff and Marrero, snarling and letting his fists fly at their faces until neither teen moved.

"Get away from my friends!" Bennett rushed the older man. He leapt for a tackle that would have laid most boys his age out flat.

Henry absorbed the blow.

Bennett redirected his attack. He attempted to lift Henry in a fireman's carry, a move Garrett had seen he and Marrero perform a thousand times to great success at wrestling tournaments.

Henry grabbed Bennett around the waist and upended him into the air. He grabbed the teen's chest and power-bombed him into the floor, cracking both the concrete and Bennett's spine.

Bennett's head rolled to the side at an awkward angle, his face expressionless.

He's dead. Garrett gulped. *He just killed Eddie Bennett!*

"Have ya lost ya friggin' mind, Henry?" Lenny shouted.

"Quick!" Oscar yelled. "Get him, Henry!"

Henry wiped the blood on his knuckles across his lips. He started toward Garrett.

"No! No!" Lenny tried to tackle Henry and missed. "*Talk* to him! He don't know no betta!"

Garrett hurried to his feet.

Henry grabbed him by the wrist.

Garrett remembered a self-defense trick his father had once taught him and grabbed Henry's fingers, peeling them backward.

"Ahhh!" Henry released his hold.

"*Get him, Henry!*"

Garrett took two steps.

Henry wheeled about and pounced on him again. He swung around behind and threw his long arms over Garrett's body in a hug, then tried to wrestle him to the ground. But unlike Bennett, Henry could not maneuver Garrett so easily. He growled and tried anew.

Garrett planted his feet and shoved backward.

Both careened off balance and slammed into the tank wall just as the Great Hammerhead hit the opposite side.

cccccrrrrAAAAACCCKK!

LENNY

THE ERUPTING WATER CARRIED LENNY OFF HIS FEET like a piece of driftwood caught in a raging stream. He saw the Nomad spill out before the tide of water pinned him against the wall. *Change, ya idiot! Change!*

Lenny fumbled for his hood, tucked into his flannel shirt, and spat salt water from his mouth. He yanked it free, donned it to initiate the changes. The water barriers that held his human body in check disappeared the second he turned into a seal. Lenny spun, his Ringed Seal body sliding across the slick floor like he would a patch of ice.

He saw Oscar fighting to stand, not yet grasping the idea that he could change into his Harp Seal form. He couldn't find Henry anywhere. *Where are ya, Weava?*

Lenny spotted Garrett forty feet away. The Nomad lay between them, its head and torso already reverting to human form.

Stop him, Len! Lenny swam for the pair of them.

The Nomad grabbed Weaver's leg, pulled him toward its mouth.

He's gonna kill him before he drowns. Lenny launched his seal body. He tucked his head at the last and let his skull crash against the Nomad's neck and gills. He heard a gasp and saw Weaver released.

Lenny swam to the rear and dared to hop over the Nomad's tail, then pedaled away out of reach. He used the water to slide his hind flippers around.

Weaver struggled to kick his knees above the water as he fought to reach the door marked with a neon green EXIT sign above it.

Lenny pushed off with his hind flippers and swam for it.

Weaver reached the door first. He screamed upon seeing a seal chasing him and slammed it closed.

Lenny hit the door like a battering ram. It moved an inch then shut again from Weaver's weight bracing the opposite side.

Lenny rolled to his belly. He swam for Oscar.

Free me! he said. *I need ya to free me!*

Oscar seemed confused.

Hells Bells! Why'd ya have to take my earrings? Lenny seethed. He barked with the seal's voice and snapped his teeth at Oscar's nose.

Oscar grabbed Lenny's seal lip, then yanked up and back to strip the seal head. He did not let go. Oscar jerked Lenny close the moment he freed him. "Catch him for me, Lenny. Catch him and win your freedom."

Lenny saw greed in his owner's eyes.

Oscar released him. "You heard me right. Go!"

Lenny high-kicked through the water. He reached the exit door and shoved it open.

"What should we do with the Nomad?" Oscar yelled after him.

"Let him drown!"

No skin off my back, Lenny thought to himself. *I seen how Nomads treat Selkies.*

Interspersed ceiling fixtures sprinkled trickles of light down the hallway. Lenny assumed it must be an employee service area, judging by the exposed black and grey PVC piping along the walls. He saw no sign of Weaver, but footfalls echoed far ahead of him. He ran the length of the hall until it ended with an exit door in front of him and two more long corridors stretching to either side.

Lenny sucked his teeth. *Three different ways he coulda' ran... which way did ya go?*

The left and right halls promised more darkness. Both rank of wet fur and frozen fish.

Where are ya, Weava? Lenny wondered. *No way ya hid in the dark after what ya saw.*

Lenny exited the facility. Outside, a passing family gave him an odd look and noted his dripping clothes and hair.

"Whattaya lookin' at?" Lenny asked. "Neva seen anyone wet before?"

The father ushered his wife and child down the pathway faster.

Lenny smacked himself in the forehead. *Control ya tempa! Focus!*

He surveyed the area. The possibilities of where Weaver could have gone seemed limitless. A nearby sign had a zoo map with pictures of different animals. Lenny traced his finger near the aquariums and found the YOU ARE HERE dot that placed him beside the walrus and polar bear exhibits.

Where do Drybacks teach their kids to go when they're scared, Lenny wondered. He smirked and hustled toward the zoo's security station. Through the tree line, he saw a circus tent with alternating rows of yellow and orange streaming down the top. He had seen children huddle beneath it earlier that day. Police and several men wearing navy jackets occupied it now.

Lenny stopped near the edge of the common area and hid behind a pine tree.

The family he had scared off was walking toward the exit. One of the officers waved for their attention, ran over, and had a verbal exchange with the father. The mother raised a hand to her chest and pulled her child close with the other.

Whateva they're talkin' about can't be good news, Lenny thought, watching the officer escort them through the exit.

Two men in U.S. Marshal jackets guarded the gates. Lenny put the elder one in his mid-fifties, the other, young and fresh out of whatever academy spewed out Dryback law enforcement. Lenny watched the younger marshal check the woman's stroller and purse.

Neva seen 'em check anyone out leavin' before.

The older marshal had both the father and mother turn around, then patted their upper backs. Almost like searching for something they might have hidden along their neckline.

Suits. Lenny's gut warned. *They're checkin' for Selkie suits.*

Lenny sent out a warning thought to his team before remembering he was both deaf and mute to them.

A group of teenagers approached the exit. All of them happy and joking, save one who drifted neared the back, attempting to rub his clothes dry.

Weava.

The officer who escorted the family out fast-tracked toward the group.

Weaver bumped into the girl in front of him when they came to a halt. He shrank back upon seeing the officer corner their group. So did the other teens. All of them huddled close together like a flock of sheep. The officer acted as their shepherd, herding them closer to the zoo exit.

The two marshals performed the same checks on each student as they had with the family. Both took extra time checking out Weaver and had him take off his wet T-shirt.

Lenny clenched his fists when the marshals conferred with one another. *No...*

The elder marshal spoke on a radio before allowing the group and Weaver through the gates.

Henry, ya son of a sea cook! Why'd ya have to take my earrings! I coulda' had Ellie round him up while I'm stuck in here!

Lenny turned back to the circus tent.

The police scattered in groups of twos and threes throughout the area.

Lenny left his hiding post to hunch behind a trashcan, closer to the exit.

Barricades ringed the perimeter outside the exit. Crowds of patrons stood behind them, talking to one another and pointing toward the zoo. Some shrugged at their neighbors, gossiping.

Lenny's heart pumped faster. *Have to get outta here...but how and where?*

A glint of light caught his attention. It came from a man wearing a black cowboy hat outside the front entrance. Lenny noticed the man also wore crystal-stud earrings. Alone and unafraid, he had the air of an old gunslinger awaiting his dueling partner before sunset.

And if I can see him...

The cowboy raised a radio to his mouth. A moment later, both marshals guarding the exit left their position and made their way straight for Lenny.

Lenny power-walked back the way he came. He saw the polar bear paddock ahead and cautioned a backward glance.

The marshals followed him, and both took longer strides than he.

"Hey!" the younger shouted. "Slow up a minute!"

Lenny pretended not to hear. *What do I do? What would Pop do?* Footsteps like thunderclaps drew closer behind him.

Lenny resisted the urge to look back again, to signal his chasers he knew they wanted him. Lenny passed the polar bear sign.

"Leonard Dolan!" the elder marshal yelled. "Stop!"

Lenny's blood ran cold. He turned to face them, frightened, but determined to hide it. He noticed both marshals wore crystal-studded earrings. *Looks like both of ya been Salted too, huh?*

"We want to talk to you," said the elder.

The younger already had a hand on the grip of his holstered Glock 23 handgun.

"How do ya know my name?" Lenny asked.

"Where's the rest of your crew?"

"Ya mean my class?"

The elder grinned. "If by class you mean Selkies and Silkies, then yes."

"Keys and silties?" Lenny played dumb. "What's that?"

"Where are they, Dolan? Your crew and captain."

I'm the captain. "I don't—"

"Your group is in real danger out here on the Hard," said the elder. "There's more than one crew hunting you. If any of them caught you, well, I don't think it'd be pleasant. If you gave up your captain, they may let you go free...but I doubt it."

"He's not going to tell us anything," said the younger.

"I dunno what to tell ya, believe me," Lenny said. "Ya say my crew, but—"

"Your crew consists of Oscar Collins," the elder said. "Son of slave trader August Collins, also known as Crayfish Collins. That's why you have a crayfish branded on your left wrist."

Lenny's left hand twitched. *How does he know that?*

"Others belonging to August Collins...catchers Leonard Dolan, Paulo Varela, Ellie Briceño and Racer, a sprinter slave with no surname. Also contracted, slave trader Henry Boucher and his property, Chidi Etienne," the elder rattled off the names like he had a list in hand. "And your captain...Marisa Bourgeois."

Marisa—our captain? Lenny kept his expression neutral. "How do ya know all this?"

"Where's the rest of your crewmates, Dolan?" the elder asked.

"Ya keep callin' me Dolan...My name's Lenny. Wanna tell me what they call ya, Paddy?"

"Smith. This young man beside me is Deputy Foster."

"And I'm a Nomad," Lenny called out the lies.

Smith chuckled.

Foster did not. "Tell us what we need."

"All right. Ya want my crewmates, or the captain? Ya only get one and ya gotta ask nicely."

"We'll take both, nipperkin," Foster spat. "And you're going to answer all *Deputy* Smith's questions too."

"Ooh, or ya gonna make me, right?" Lenny said. He pulled the neckline of his Selkie outfit down, revealing his chest and scars. "Ya see these? Know what they're from?"

Foster gave no reply.

"Nah, ya wouldn't," Lenny said. "Ya don't have any do ya, Fosta?

I got all these for not snitchin'. Got even more down my back. I'd show ya, but I can't get outta this sealskin by myself. 'Course ya wouldn't know why I can't do that either, would ya?"

"Quit stalling, Dolan," Smith said. "Where—"

"They left me all right! Is that what ya wanna hear? *They left me!*"

"And why would they do that?"

"I could see why," Foster said. "The nipperkin probably slowed them down."

"The son of Declan Dolan, slowing a team of catchers?" Smith scoffed. "Not likely. You and your crew are pretty far from the Salt. Who you after? And don't tell me you're running. You have the Crayfish's son with you, so I know that's not the truth. If Oscar Collins was your hostage, we'd have heard about it by now."

Ya remind me of Pop, ya know that, Smitty? Lenny thought. He studied Smith's hard, but honest, face. *Always know the answer to a question before ya ask it, don't ya?* "Ya been there…haven't ya, old timer?"

Smith rolled back his sleeves, revealed a purple conch shell with the numbers *8241969* tattooed on his left wrist. "I've been there."

"Tell us who you're after," Foster said. "Might be we could help each other."

"No one helps," Lenny replied. "If ya'd been to the Salt like the old man ya'd know that."

Smith's earrings twinkled. "All right, Dolan. Let's go. Captain says to bring you in."

"Uh huh. And who is he?"

Both marshals ignored his taunts. "We can do this one of two ways—"

"Which is that?" Lenny asked. "Ya guys lemme go and walk

away, or I take ya both down first? Don't let me fool ya...I may be little, but what I got, ya can't handle. Smitty there tell ya us Selkies are stronga than Drybacks on their best day, Fosta?"

Foster reached over his shoulder like he meant to scratch himself. He held a tanned hood when he brought his hands up. Raised the hood higher for Lenny to see, then let it fall down his back.

Aw, he's a speedsta like Racer...a Sea Lion.

Smith took out his gun and pointed it at Lenny. "What'll it be?"

Lenny flicked the sweat from his brow away. *Is this what runnas feel like?*

"He's going to run..."

Lenny watched Foster fan out, forcing him to decide which deputy to keep his eyes on.

"No, he won't. He's a Dolan," Smith said. "And Dolans are smarter than that, aren't they, Lenny?"

Foster stood within five feet of Lenny. He grinned. "Do it. *Run.* I dare you."

Runnas cry and beg.

"The old man's right," said Lenny. "I don't run. Didn't anyone tell ya, Fosta? Dolans fight!"

Lenny darted in to punch Foster in the stomach. When Foster sidestepped his attempt, Lenny slid to his left knee. He swept his right leg behind Foster's foot and drove his stocky body into the young deputy's kneecaps.

Foster fell backward.

Lenny released his hold and scrambled to the bigger man's chest. Unleashing the hatred he kept bottled up, Lenny pummeled him in a hurricane of tiny fists.

"Dolan!" Smith yelled. "Get off him. *Now!*"

Lenny would not. Each punch brought a different face to the forefront of Lenny's mind. He saw every taskmaster who'd ever beaten him. He saw August Collins, forcing him to bring runners back to their miserable lives of servitude. Foster was Lenny's guilty conscience, the part of him that even now debated whether the reward of his own freedom outweighed the cost of enslaving Weaver.

Lenny reached inside Foster's jacket. He yanked the gun from its holster, shoved the barrel under Foster's jaw, and pulled the hammer back. "Got *ya!* Now, tell ya old pal Smitty to lower his gun."

"Never…"

Lenny focused on Smith, but kept the gun pointed at Foster. "Ya gonna kill me, deputy?"

Smith trained his aim at Lenny's forehead. "If you hurt him—"

"I already hurt him!" Lenny said. "Ya keep aimin' that gun at me and I'll kill him. Drop it!"

"You won't, Dolan. You're no murderer. You're a catcher…like your father. Maybe even a runner, but—"

"I'm no runna."

Smith smirked and lowered his gun a hair. "Maybe you should be…"

"Dolans don't run!"

"Believe it or not, but I know that better than most," Smith said. "But you can't save everyone. One day you'll see that. Owners… they keep you loyal by promising to hurt the ones you leave behind. Truth is, they need our kind too much to kill us all…It's an empty threat, son."

"Nah," said Lenny. "I seen what mine does to a catcha's family when we don't come back."

"All the more reason to run then. Come with us. The man we

work for knows things. He has friends in deep places, if you take my meaning."

"Uh huh. So I let ya pal here go and come with ya. Ya take me to ya guy and he makes all my problems go away, right?"

Smith took a step forward. "Your family's known for being great catchers. Come with us and my friend will give you a job to utilize those talents of yours in a better way. Heck, those bruises you gave Foster speaks that you're capable of handling yourself. Consider it your resume."

"What if I don't wanna be a catcha no more?"

"You'll be more than that. You'll be a *releaser*," Smith said. He took another step forward. "We catch runners, then free them! Give them back what they once had and help them disappear from the Salt forever. We help them swallow the anchor."

"Yeah? So release me now." Lenny dug the barrel of the gun deeper into Foster's throat.

Smith backed off. "It's not that simple. First you have to talk to the man in charge."

"What about my Pop?" Lenny said. "Can ya friend release him too?"

"Let's go ask him together."

"Fine. Get him on ya radio. And drop ya gun, Smitty. I'm not gonna tell ya again."

Smith lowered his gun, but did not drop it. He never saw his assailant, nor did Lenny before it happened.

Paulo sprang from the tree line and batted Smith's arms downward. The gun clattered into the brush as both men tumbled to the ground.

Foster used the distraction to aim an elbow at Lenny's face.

Had Lenny been taller the blow would have broken his nose. Instead, the young deputy's arm caught the top of Lenny's head, knocking him off balance.

Lenny rolled away and back onto his feet. "Back off, Fosta!" He whipped the gun up.

The deputy stood. "You think that's my real name?"

"Not gonna matter in a second."

Foster rushed him.

Lenny trained his aim and shot Foster in the thigh. *Buckets of Blood! Someone had to hear that gunshot!*

Blood oozed from Foster's leg. He rolled on the ground, clutching at it and swearing.

Lenny stashed the gun in his pocket.

Smith grunted nearby, his face turning purple from the chokehold Paulo had him in. He gasped a final time and passed out.

"What'd ya do, kill him?" Lenny asked.

Paulo rolled Smith's limp body aside. "Me? You shot one of them."

"Neva mind that, we gotta bail. Those other cops will be here any minute."

"You want to take them with us?"

"Nah. They'll slow us down." Lenny ran toward the Commons area and Deserts exhibit. "Come on already!"

Paulo caught up quickly. He grabbed Lenny's arm and slung him around onto his broad back.

"Huh uh! No way," Lenny protested. "Ya not carryin' me!"

"Sorry, Len. You might not like it, but we're faster this way."

Lenny wrapped his arms around Paulo's neck and choked him for good measure.

"Loosen up," Paulo panted. "Unless you'd rather I carry you like a baby. Where am I going?"

"Bang a left after the monkey pens," Lenny pointed. "Go south past the pony rides and farm animals till we hit the wall."

"Up and over?"

"Aye," Lenny said.

Paulo turned left, passing the restaurants and bathrooms along the way. More than a few visitors further in all took notice of Lenny and his noble steed.

"How'd ya find me, Paulie?"

"Was on my way out…had to double back when…I saw cops… Knew something…wrong when…didn't hear back…."

"From me?"

"Ellie…"

Paulo ran by the animal farm where employees led kids around on the pony ride. Lenny had the passing thought that his ride, while bumpy, at least wasn't going around in circles.

"She didn't say anything back…" said Paulo. "Something's wrong…"

Ya tellin' me. Merrows floatin' through hoops, a Nomad in an aquarium, and anotha Selkie crew huntin' Marisa Bourgeois…why should something be wrong, Paulie?

A twenty-foot concrete wall stood before them. Paulo never slowed. "Hold on…"

Lenny clung tighter and braced for the impact.

Paulo jumped and kicked off the wall, the same way Marisa had. Grunting, he grabbed the top and pulled them over. He reached behind him on the way down, cupping Lenny's butt with his forearm in case his captain fell.

Lenny let go once they landed.

A crowd gathered near the zoo entrance amid flashing red lights. A helicopter whirred overhead. Lenny shielded the sun with his hand and saw *Channel 9* emblazoned in green along its side.

"Paulie, go blend in at the gates and find out what ya can—" Lenny looked over his shoulder.

Paulo had already turned for the bus parking lot.

"Hey, slow down!" Lenny threw his wallet of Dryback money. He landed it close enough that Paulo paused.

"What was that?"

"A clue, ya blubba' head!" Lenny picked the wallet back up. "What happens if ya get to the bus and find deputy marshals all around it?"

"Why would they—"

"'Cause they know who we are!" Lenny smacked Paulo's thigh. "They know our names and who we work for! Those two we just tuned up? They're Selkies. And the older one knows who my Pop is."

"If they're catchers—They might have Ellie!"

"*I know!*" Lenny tried to shove him. "That's what I'm tryin' to get through to ya! If we're runnin' up there, let's have a plan—"

Paulo sprinted for the parked bus.

"Paulie! We need a...aw, forget it."

Lenny followed him. Minutes later, they reached the bus. He considered the upside that Ellie had parked near the outermost edge in case the group needed to make a quick getaway. It also limited any cover Lenny and Paulo may have when running for the bus.

Paulo hunkered beside the nearest car.

Lenny proceeded toward the trunk. He crouched next to one of the wheels and peered around it.

212 — AARON GALVIN

Their bus door opened. A lean man wearing a black hooded sweatshirt tucked into torn up white jeans stepped off the bus. Shaking his ratty, unwashed hair out of his face, he glanced around the near empty lot as he dug into a bag of stolen pretzels.

The Leper from the Shedd!

Zymon Gorski descended the steps and yelled at the Leper.

"I thought we locked Zymon in the hold…" Paulo said, more to himself than to Lenny.

We did. Lenny thought, watching Zymon's seedy guardian drop the pretzels and vanish up the steps. *Someone let him out.*

KELLEN

"WINSTEL...HEY, BOY," A MAN'S HOARSE VOICE BECK-
oned from a jail cell across the row. "Come on now. Might as well
talk to me! We got nothing better to do locked up in here."

Kellen lay on his bunk, yawning. Trying to sleep the previous
night had done little good. Every time he closed his eyes, Kellen saw
Garrett Weaver's legs turn black and shiny.

He rolled on his cot, punched the cheap, flat pillow. More of the
even cheaper detergent and body odor from the cell's last occupant
seeped into his nostrils. Kellen snorted, tossed the pillow on the
floor, and lay on his back. He stared at the concrete ceiling.

He's not coming for you. Not now. Not ever. They've both left me.

"Hey, Winstel! If you ain't gonna use that pilla', toss it over to
me!"

"I'm not going to give you my pillow so stop asking, old man!"
Kellen shouted back.

One of the officers had dragged the town drunk in sometime in
the night and thrown him in a cell on the opposite side.

"Old man, huh? How old do you think I am?"

"Leave me alone, Boone."

"Guess how old I am."

"No…"

"Come on," Boone urged. "Hey! I'll bet your pilla' you cain't even come close."

Kellen glared at his obnoxious neighbor. "I'm not betting you anything. *Shut up!*"

Boone Merchant sat on his cot, a gaunt scarecrow with his knees hugged against his chest. He had rolled up his jeans like a flood might cascade into the cellblock at any minute. His head bobbed right and left, and his arms twitched of their own accord. Boone stroked his sparse, dirty beard, and patted his hands against the sides of his metal cot.

"Okay…Hey! Wanna know a secret that ain't no secret at all?" He grinned at Kellen with the five teeth he still had. "Well, come on, don't ya wanna hear my secret? I'll tell you if'n you ask nice."

"Fine. Tell me."

"You're going to look older than I do 'fore they let you out again!" Boone howled. "Heard 'em talking about it over the radio 'fore they brought me in here. They thought I was drunk again and passed out in the back of their car, but I's just playing opossum. Till I really passed out, that is. Then I weren't playing opossum. I's just drunk."

Kellen sat up. "Heard who talking? What did you hear?"

"Your daddy and the sheriff and all the rest of them ol' boys what run around together. Your dad…Marty…ah, he's a good man. Buys my drinks a lot a times. Buys 'em a lot more since that whore mom of yours ran off with that other fella. Anyhow, they's talking about you in the bar last night. 'Bout what you done to Red Tom Weaver's boy. Hey! You wanna know another secret?"

"No, I want to know what—"

"Well, most folks say he's either black, or burned, but he ain't neither one. I know what he is, but I cain't tell you," Boone shook his head. "I *cain't* tell you! No, no, no. That's tattle-telling and I promised 'em I wouldn't tell nobody secrets no more. I'm *done* telling secrets!"

He's crazy. Kellen rolled back over.

"Hey! Don't you wanna hear what they said?"

"I thought you were done telling secrets…"

"Well, this ain't no secret. Everybody likes Cristina Weaver around here, even me! She gives me the scraps after hours some nights when she's done waiting tables. And after what happened to Red Tom a couple years back, why, they don't want to see anything happen to her only boy. They're going to put you away for the long haul, son. Being sent up to the big house for attempted murder."

Kellen sat up. "Murder?"

"Mmm-hmm," Boone clapped his hands against the bars. "You heard me right! Them so-called friends of yours turned you in when they got questioned. Even went on the record saying you tried to drown the Weaver boy. Said you planned the whole kit-n-kaboodle right from the get-go! Marty said that Asian you hang around with is who turned you in. Told the sheriff you wanted to take Weaver… what'd he call it? Seven-eleven something?"

Twelving. Kellen wished he had never heard of it. He leaned over to the toilet, fighting the rising puke from his gut. "It was just a prank…" he whispered.

"Don't matter much now. You're over eighteen too, ain'tcha," Boone said. He nodded, despite the absence of Kellen's response. "Yep. That means you get tried like an adult, boy!"

How can they say attempted murder for a prank?

"Yeeeep," Boone drawled. "Going away to the big house…'less your daddy steps in."

"He won't," Kellen said with certainty.

"Hard man, huh? Hmm. My daddy was one too. Shoot, look how I turned out! Guess your momma ain't coming neither, huh? Tucked tail and ran with that other fella, huh?" Boone slapped his knee. "Golly, ain't that just like a woman? Prolly took half your daddy's money too, huh?"

Kellen put his forehead to the toilet's cool rim. *Attempted murder.*

"Prolly did—yep—she prolly did. Hey!" Boone stretched a skinny arm through the bars. "I told my secrets, now gimme that pilla'! I promised I'd shut up. I said I will, and I will. Honest Injun, I will!"

Kellen glanced over his shoulder.

Boone had pledged his left hand up. He put two fingers over his mouth, mimicked turning a key, and then pretended to throw something down the pathway between the cells.

"See! I done sealed my lips and threw away the key."

Kellen left the toilet to push his ragged pillow through the bars. He tossed it over. "There. Now shut up!"

Boone snatched it up from the floor. Hooting, he buried his nose in it, then rubbed it against his cheeks. "Oh, it's soft. Smells good too, don't it?"

"It reeks."

"Boy, you don't know stink. This here smells like purty pink flowers."

"Whatever. I gave you my pillow. Now shut up."

Boone placed his new pillow on top of the other. "I will, I will. I said I will, and I will. You might not want me to for long though. It gets awful quiet in here…oooh. That's when you start thinking!"

Kellen climbed back into his cot. *Attempted murder? I didn't mean to almost kill him.* He covered his face with his forearm.

"Yeeep," Boone crowed. "Thinking about what you done...how long you'll be here for...how much you'd take it all back if you could, but you cain't. You think too long, and you go crazy. That's what happened to me."

Kellen thought back to what he saw in the pool. *Is that what's happening? Am I going crazy?*

CHIDI

"WHY IS OUR BUS SHAKING?" RACER ASKED.

More like teeter-tottering. Chidi sprinted for the bus with Racer close behind. She bounded through the open door, and up the steps.

The mahogany walls sported gashed lines. The leather couches and chairs exploded their fluffy insides from deep slices.

"Aaaaaah!"

Chidi whirled at the cry from an overturned couch. Behind it, Paulo wrestled with an eleven-foot long Leopard Seal. Four deep and bloodied scratch marks traced his ribs down to his left thigh, mirroring the slashes throughout the bus. Paulo attempted to wrap his trunk-like legs around the seal's lower body.

The seal bucked free of him.

Paulo tried again and succeeded. He alligator-rolled the seal. The move flipped the couch like a flimsy cardboard box. The seal twisted its snake-like neck, snapping its jaws an inch from Paulo's face.

Chidi heard a gunshot from the rear of the bus. She shrunk at the sound, and saw Lenny and Zymon involved in their own battle. Zymon had the better grip on the gun. He turned the barrel toward Lenny. "Lenny, let go!" Chidi cried.

Lenny did. The move sent Zymon crashing forward into the wall. He lost the gun. Lenny scrambled to pick it up.

"No!" Racer said. He shoved past Chidi and ran at the seal.

The seal whirled to face its new opponent, hissed a warning.

Chidi used the distraction. She jumped onto the couch and swung over the bar's remains. She saw Zymon kick Lenny's face. His eyes searched for the gun.

Chidi hurtled the remains of a broken chair. Her foot caught its edge. She fell into broken glass and rolled in it. Blood streaked down her newly shredded cheek. The others did not notice; each of them still locked in their own battles. Chidi groaned as she rolled over. Blood trickled in her right eye. She faintly saw Lenny's coral dagger nearby.

Zymon had reached the gun. He picked it up.

Chidi blinked the blood away. She grabbed the dagger, climbed to her feet.

Zymon raised his aim.

Chidi leaped forward, grabbed a handful of hair, kicked him to his knees. She jerked Zymon's head back, and whipped the blade to his bare throat. "Drop it."

"Where did you come from, girl?" He sputtered.

Chidi pressed the dagger deeper. "Drop. It."

The gun clattered to the floor. Chidi kicked it to Lenny.

"Cheeds," said Lenny. "His Lepa'."

Chidi glanced over her shoulder.

The Leopard Seal had its yellowed fangs poised around Paulo's neck. Racer hung back near its tail, not daring to risk Paulo's safety.

A stalemate.

"Call your Leper off," she said to Zymon.

"Wotjek," Zymon said. Then he spoke a language Chidi did not recognize.

The Leopard Seal grunted. It did not let go.

"Cheeds, what'd he say?" Lenny asked.

"I-I don't know...I don't understand."

Zymon chuckled. "You don't speak Polski girl?" He spit blood. "I told Wotjek to kill you all if you harm me further."

Chidi tilted Zymon's head back further, looked him in the eye. "You first."

"Then your friend will die also," Zymon replied coolly.

"I don't have any friends."

"You won't let your friend die," his voice wavered.

Chidi pressed the blade so deep she thought she might cut through muscle. *"I don't have any friends."*

"If I order him to let go...you will give us our freedom, yes?"

"We work for Crayfish Collins," said Lenny, picking up the gun at his feet. "And the Crayfish don't *give* nobody nothin'."

"But you can," Zymon said. "Give us our freed—"

"We let ya go and it's our heads." Lenny sneered.

"What if I could give you freedom? I am a forger...I could give you all freedom," Zymon said. He turned his head to address Chidi. "You are their translator, yes? Tell me, did they give you the notebooks to read?"

Chidi's gaze drifted.

"Don't answer that, Cheeds!"

"Inside are the accounts," said Zymon. "The names of all we have worked to free together. You know I speak true if you have seen them. Tell your captain!"

Chidi licked her lips. "Lenny...What he says might be—"

"Stay outta of this, Cheeds!" Lenny snarled. He cocked the gun, aimed it at Zymon's head. "Last chance, Gorski…tell ya pet to back off, or join him in Fiddla's Green."

Zymon spoke some words softly.

The Leopard Seal's brown eyes flickered in its master's direction. It waited for Zymon to speak the words again. The seal released Paulo. Its long tongue lolled out like it wanted to rid the taste of its former captive.

Paulo grabbed the seal by the throat. "Where's Ellie?"

"Paulie," Lenny yelled. "Let him go."

"Not till they tell me where Ellie is!"

"She is locked in the hold," Zymon said calmly.

"Alive?"

Zymon hesitated.

Paulo shoved the Leopard Seal away, and hurried off the bus with Racer trailing after.

"Cheeds," said Lenny. "I got Gorski. Help the Lepa' outta his suit."

Chidi took the dagger away from Zymon's throat. She warily approached the Leopard Seal, kept her dagger free in case it decided to lunge. Its mouth yawned wide. Chidi tried not to focus on its teeth. Her fingers trembled as she reached for the seal's upper lip. She took hold of it quickly, and pulled up and back over its head. She stepped away the moment the changes began.

In seconds, the seal regressed into the same man she had battled at the Shedd Aquarium. Unkempt hair covered his thin face and he remained on all fours, his head bowed as he muttered.

He almost looks like he could be praying. The thought unsettled her. *To what god though?*

222 — AARON GALVIN

"Now you let us go," Zymon said.

Lenny stonewalled him. "How did he find us?"

Zymon smiled. "Tracking is but one of Wotjek's many talents."

"He didn't track ya all this way on foot," Lenny said. "Highways don't leave trails like trekkin' through the Salt and ova the reefs. Nobody smells that good."

Zymon shrugged. "Your master has a far reach and many friends, yes, but he is not the only one. Perhaps I have others friends who helped Wotjek find me. It might be possible these same friends could help you."

"Nobody helps in the Salt," said Chidi. "So why does he follow you? You own him?"

A shadow crossed Zymon's face. "I have never owned a slave. Nor do I intend to. I also have no desire to be one again. Another reason Wotjek follows me. To attend my last wishes should the need arise."

"Speak English, Gorski," said Lenny. "Whattaya mean attend—"

"The Leper will kill him," Chidi said. "I've met others with similar deals. If they're ever captured, Zymon wants Wotjek to kill him."

Zymon nodded. "That is why I am hoping you will free us and allow me to help you in exchange. I wish to live and return to my family."

Lenny kept his aim trained. "Hope all ya want. It's not happenin'."

"You needn't be frightened," said Zymon. "Your owner will never find you after I have helped you. Take this bus…take me home. I will find someone to remove your Selkie coats. A suitable place for you to hide—"

"Shuddup, Gorski."

Chidi heard a cough at the front of the bus.

Ellie ascended the stairs unassisted, despite Paulo's attempts to help her. Though matted against her sweaty forehead, her bangs could not conceal her half-closed right eye which had already turned a deep purple. The bruises had not dampened her spirit. Seeing Wotjek on his hands and knees, she rushed ahead to land a few well-placed kicks before Paulo pulled her away.

"Let go of me," she yelled. "He's mine!"

Allambee came last up the steps, his head hung low. Chidi could see no bruises on him, but he did not seem the same boy she had left behind earlier that morning. He sat in the driver's seat, gripped the steering wheel, and pretended to drive.

What did they do to you?

"Elle, ya all right?" Lenny asked.

Ellie let fly a string of curses in Spanish.

"Whateva that means," Lenny said. "Cheeds, check the Lepa's pockets."

Chidi patted Wotjek's Selkie pocket first, then his jeans. She heard a metallic jingle. "Empty it."

Wotjek rose to his full height to look down on her.

She glared back. "Empty it."

"Wotjek," said Zymon. *"Zrób jak mówi."*

Wotjek reached into his pocket and took out a set of keys. A pocket-sized silver anchor dangled from the metal ring. He gave them to Chidi.

"There. You see," Zymon said. "We can work through this without bloodshed."

Chidi twirled the anchor between her fingers. *What do these go to?*

"Paulie," said Lenny. "Get these two down in the hold. Put 'em in separate cells too. Racer, help him out."

Paulo pulled at Wotjek's hoodie. Again, he would not move.

"My friend goes nowhere without my command," said Zymon.

"Oh, I dunno about that." Lenny turned his aim on Wotjek. "I could send him to Fiddla's Green right now. Then there'd be no one here to save ya from bein' made a slave again."

Chidi didn't see the need for the threat. *Death does not frighten a man like him.* She looked at Wotjek. *What does Zymon have to hold such power over you?*

Zymon opened his arms wide. "I welcome you to shoot me as well."

When Lenny did not, Zymon lowered his arms. "Or perhaps you keep me for another reason. You must know many would delight in my capture and pay you a handsome sum. I will triple their reward."

Chidi glanced at Lenny. She knew his answer even before he spoke.

"It's not happenin'."

Zymon *tsked*. "A shame. Perhaps I should speak with someone else…" He turned his attention to Chidi. *"Unaweza kuelewa mimi?"*

Why is he talking to me?

Lenny's brow furrowed. "Whattaya doin', Gorski?"

Zymon studied Chidi's face. When she said nothing in reply, he tried a different language. *"Em pot entendre?"*

He knows I'm a translator!

Zymon continued, undeterred. *"Dívka, mluvíte česky?"*

Girl, do you speak Czech? Chidi straightened at recognizing the words.

Zymon smiled.

"Stop!" Lenny knocked Zymon to the ground. "Stop talkin' to her!"

Chidi looked from Lenny to Zymon then back again. "*Ano. Mluvím česky,*" she replied. *Yes…I speak Czech.*

"*Good,*" Zymon continued to speak in Czech. "*Do me a favor and shoot this fool. Then I will help to free you and your friends.*"

The gun wavered in Chidi's hand. "*My-my owner will come for me.*"

Zymon shook his head. "*Wotjek will handle him. Then you will be free.*"

Lenny clocked Zymon in his temple with the butt of his gun. "What's he sayin' to ya, Cheeds?"

"He-he said…he'll help free all of us."

"That all?"

No. Chidi studied Lenny's face. He had been mostly kind to her in the short time they had known one another. Far better than most other captains she had been loaned to. *But will you listen to reason?*

"Cheeds…is that all?"

"Yes," she said. "He wants to help us, but we have to free him."

Lenny frowned. "Paulie…do ya thing."

The attack came swiftly. Paulo wrapped Wotjek in a bear hug while Racer wrangled his feet.

"No!" Zymon sprung away.

Lenny fired and missed.

Zymon knocked Chidi out of his way. She slipped and fell into the glass, her head cracking off the same chair she had tried to hurdle. She saw Ellie spear Zymon to the ground.

"You like hitting women?" Ellie asked. "How about one who hits back?"

She slammed him again and again until Lenny pulled her away.

Chidi sat up. She heard Wotjek snarling and spitting as Paulo and Racer dragged him off the bus.

"No…" Zymon cried. He struggled to grasp anything solid to keep Ellie from pulling him down the aisle. His eyes found Chidi. "Destroy them, girl! You must destroy the accounts!"

Ellie pulled him down the steps.

I wouldn't dare destroy such valuable information. But why does he want them gone?

"Great. Outta bullets." Lenny threw the gun aside and turned his gaze on Chidi. "He talkin' about those books we lifted yesta'day?"

"I-I think so."

She slipped off her backpack, unzipped it, and spilled the notebooks on the now wobbly table.

Lenny flipped through them, only stopping on the illustrated pages. He glanced up at her. "Ya believe him?"

"Hard to say. There are names in there, sure. Whether he's telling the truth and they're names of other slaves he's helped free, or not…I don't know."

"Could be a list of all the slaves he owns," Lenny suggested. "Maybe even a hit list."

"Maybe."

Lenny hopped onto a broken couch. He flipped open a new notebook, studied its contents. He pointed to a hand drawn grid in the notebook's middle filled with every kind of shape Chidi had ever seen, including others she had not. All varied in size and color. "All these names and markings—what do they mean?"

"I don't know," she said. "Could be some kind of code maybe. I haven't been able to crack it yet."

Lenny rubbed his chin. "Why'd ya have 'em all in ya backpack?"

He knows I was going to run. Chidi stared back at him. "So I could study them while I ate. Try to figure out something that could help us catch Marisa. Like I told Paulo last night...it's going to take some time to translate them all."

Lenny thumbed through the rest of the notebook with an occasional pause here and there. Sighing, he tossed it aside. "Something ya wanna tell me, Cheeds?"

Why am I lying to him?

Ellie boarded the bus before Chidi could answer. "Hey, Len. Paulo wants to know—" She saw the scattered notebooks. "They are here! Which one of you had them?"

"I-I did," Chidi said meekly.

"You took them inside the zoo today?"

Chidi nodded.

Ellie laughed. She came down the aisle and hugged Chidi so tight she thought her insides might burst. "It's good you did. Those two would have been long gone before you all got back if these had been here."

"Elle, whattaya talkin' about?"

"The notebooks. That's what they were after. It's all Zymon kept asking me. *Where are the books?*" Ellie said, deepening her voice. "*I know you've got them, what did you do with them?* I told them I didn't know anything, but his Leper kept hitting me. They finally understood I really didn't know, or wasn't going to tell them. That's when they locked me and the kid down below."

Chidi glanced to the front of the bus. "Did they hit Allambee too?"

"Not that I saw. I don't think he talks much. He didn't say anything down below either."

"Ya think they planned on killin' ya after they got the books?" Lenny asked.

Ellie's chunky fingers danced on the table making quick *clip-clop, clip-clop* sounds one after the other. "Think if they wanted to kill me they'd have done it," she said finally. "And I know they didn't want the bus. Keys are still in the ignition. What made you come back, by the way?"

"Paulo," Chidi said.

Ellie chuckled. "I figured he would think something off once he didn't hear from me. That blubber-head's nothing if not predictable."

"Paulo saved your life," Racer's voice came from the front. He stood on the landing his arms draped over the front seat. "What's the plan, Len?"

Lenny rubbed his temples. "Anyone heard from Henry or Oscar yet?"

"Just tried reaching them. Must have turned their crystals off," Racer said. "Either that or they're ignoring me."

That's not like Henry, Chidi thought.

"Hey, Len," said Racer. "Where are your crystals?"

"Don't worry about it," Lenny said. "Where's Paulie?"

Racer hocked a loogie and spit out the open door. "Down by the hold. Pretty sure he's hoping our two captives try to escape so he can knock their skulls together."

"They're not goin' anywhere. Someone let Zymon out." Lenny's gaze drifted to the driver's seat. "I wanna find out who."

"Allambee couldn't have done it," Chidi said quickly. "There aren't any windows back there either so it's not like he could have climbed down."

"Chidi's right," said Ellie. "The Leper let him out. He's the one who kicked the doors in. Guy jumped on me and took my earrings before I could warn any of you. Zymon came up right behind him. I watched them let the kid out of the bedroom."

Lenny yawned and rubbed his temples. "Fine, so if the kid didn't help, how did that Lepa' find us?"

"Sounds like the question of the day," Ellie said.

Lenny glared at her. "No it's not. We got *much* bigga questions than that."

"Are you talking about the Silkstealer?" Chidi asked.

"Cheeds, I got enough problems to figure without ya joke—"

"I saw him." She found the sketch Marisa had drawn and slid the notebook across the table.

Ellie crowded over to inspect it. "Nice hat. That tooth on the end is an Elephant Seal's. And that one," she pointed to the opposite side. "That's a Sea Lion's. Geez, how many different types has this guy bumped off?"

Lenny pushed the notebook away. "It don't mean anything."

Chidi stopped the notebook from flying off the table. "But she wrote it down…"

"Oh, well, here then," Lenny picked up a pen and drew a crude stick figure. He shaded in an even worse cowboy hat. Below the figure, he wrote '*The Silkstealer*' and initialed it with the date. He held up the picture. "Tell me, Cheeds. Did ya see this man?"

Chidi's jaw clenched. "I know what I saw."

"I saw him too," Racer said. "I've never been so cold in my life. Felt like jumping in Arctic waters with no suit."

"You've never been to the Arctic," Ellie argued.

Racer stuck his tongue out at her.

"Fine," Lenny said. "Let's say it is him…what's he doing here?"

Chidi shrugged. "I saw him standing guard outside the zoo. Looked like he might be waiting on someone."

Lenny stared at the picture. "Racer, go check out the zoo entrance. Ya there to watch. No askin' around about what's happenin', no shovin' ya way up front. Just watch."

Racer disappeared down the stairwell.

Will he come back though? Chidi wondered.

Lenny picked up Marisa's picture of the Silkstealer again. "Elle, go get Oscar's phone outta the back."

Ellie raised her eyebrows as she passed Chidi and disappeared into the bunkroom. Chidi listened to her rummage around.

"Cheeds, ya sure ya saw this guy?" Lenny rubbed his thumb under his chin. "Ya'd bet ya life on it?"

Chidi studied the picture and thought back to the bus stop. Marisa had shaded the picture well, highlighting his high cheekbones and sharp nose. "It's him."

Ellie rejoined them. "Here it is. What do you want to do with it?"

"Do a search. Find me a teenager named Weava."

"That's pretty broad strokes..."

"Look, I dunno know what all ya do," Lenny said. "Ya supposed to know how to work this Dryback stuff. He's a teenager I ran into today so I'm bettin' he lives somewhere close. Look him up!"

"*Hmmpph.* Whatever you say," Ellie said. Her finger moved across the screen as she pulled up a search engine to type the name. She clicked on a social networking site and scrolled through the names with individual pictures beside them.

"There." Lenny hit the screen. "That one. Garrett Weava."

"Good thing he doesn't have any privacy settings up," Ellie said. "Okay, he's a senior at Tiber High School and he lives in Lavere,

Indiana. His birthday is January 24th, he likes women, gaming, pulling pranks, yada, yada, yada. He does *not* like reality TV, sports, and something called the P.J. club...whatever that is."

"What else?"

"He's listed a couple close friends..." Ellie scrolled through his pictures. "The fat white boy with him is named Johnny Hickey. Most of his photo albums just show the two of them making dumb faces. Aww, he's also friends with his mom, Cristina Weaver. Isn't that precious. The other close friend is some girl named Sydney Gao."

"Find his home address and the school's."

Ellie created a new search engine and cross-referenced both Garrett's name and Cristina's. She found a white page ad listing his school address: 816 N. State Road 23, Lavere, Indiana, 46071.

"Anything else, oh wise and powerful master?"

Lenny grabbed a pen and scrap piece of paper to jot down Weaver's address. "Pack those notebooks, Cheeds. Ya comin' with me."

"With you? Where we going?"

"To find Garrett Weava."

Why are we going after a teenager he ran into at the zoo? Chidi reluctantly obeyed and put the notebooks in her bag.

Ellie place a hand on Chidi's forearm. "And what's Oscar going to do when he comes back and finds you two gone? He won't believe us, Lenny!"

"Show Oscar a picture of that kid and say I went lookin' for him. Trust me, he'll approve."

"What about Marisa?" Chidi asked. "She's the one we're sup-posed to—"

"She's dodged us twice already and we got no clue where she might go next. You wanna find her, be my guest." Lenny said. "I don't wanna go back to Crayfish Cavern empty-handed."

"So what? You're going to slave a Dryback instead?" Ellie asked.

"He's not a Dryback."

"Think about what you're saying. We're catchers, not slavers!"

Lenny took Wotjek's keys off the table and twirled them by the anchor. "Come on, Cheeds."

Chidi stepped forward to follow.

Ellie again stopped her. "Lenny, if you want to leave, have at it. Chidi's not going though. Henry will flip."

"That's why she's comin' with me," Lenny said.

Ellie still would not let Chidi pass. "I don't like this."

"Ya don't have to." Lenny stormed up the aisle and out the door.

"I don't care what he says," said Ellie. "He's up to something. Racer and I will fight to keep you here if you don't want to go."

Chidi blushed. "I'll go with him. Someone has to. Besides, it *does* keep me away from Henry for a little while."

Ellie pulled Chidi close for a quick hug.

"Come on already!" Lenny yelled up the stairs.

Chidi said her goodbye and walked up the aisle. She paused by the driver's seat.

Allambee refused to look at her.

"Did they...did they hurt you?" she asked.

He shook his head.

"Cheeds!"

"I'll be back," she squeezed his arm. "I promise."

Chidi exited the bus.

Lenny stood in the middle of the parking lot. He had the keys in the air, and waved his hand around. A car alarm went off. Lenny killed it and clapped his hands.

"Come on, Cheeds. I found us a ride." He tossed her Wotjek's keys.

Chidi followed him across the parking lot to a green mini-van with a yellow Baby On Board tag stuck to the rear window. "This is what he drove?"

"It's the one that had alarms goin' off when I hit the button." Lenny looked at the car. He shrugged. "Beggas can't be choosas. Get in."

At least he tinted the windows. Chidi unlocked the van and sat in the driver's seat, her feet pushing aside a pile of fast food bags. It smelled like a bum had used it for a combination home and toilet. Covering her nose, she turned the van on and rolled down the windows.

Lenny rooted around in the glove box, finding a GPS under a layer of napkins and ketchup packets. He tossed the junk out the window. Plugging the GPS into the dash, he turned it on and input Garrett's address.

Chidi wrung her hands. "Lenny, I…well, I wanted to say thanks for—"

"Spit it out already, Cheeds."

"Thanks for looking out for me."

"I'm not," Lenny said.

Chidi recoiled. "What?"

Lenny crossed his arms. "How many times have I told ya I like to know what's bein' said the first time around? I dunno what Gorski promised ya back there, but I know ya didn't tell me half of it. Not as long as the two of ya talked for."

"Lenny, I promise it's not—"

"Save it. Maybe I did look out for ya, once. Not anymore. I brought ya 'cause I don't trust ya."

GARRETT

GARRETT PULLED AT HIS DAMP T-SHIRT.

"Decide to go for a swim after I left?" Johnny asked quietly.

"I ran through the sprinklers again before coming back," Garrett said. "Can't believe how hot it is outside."

He couldn't tell whether Johnny believed his lie or not. The image of Wilda, the iron grip of the shark-man, even the dwarf who changed into a seal and chased him—Garrett could think of nothing else. They had ridden almost the entire way back to school and Garrett still half-expected his bedside alarm to go off, waking him from what could only be a crazy dream.

"Ugh. Load, you piece of crap phone," said Mark Yono, their seat neighbor.

Johnny scooted closer to the aisle. "What's going on?"

"My mom just texted me to make sure I was okay," said Mark. "She said the shark tank at the zoo exploded! It's all over the news. Can you believe it? We were just there! Oh man, I bet it was some kind of terrorist attack!"

Laura Morris turned around in the seat in front of him. "What would terrorists want to do with Indiana?"

"Not terrorists like suicide bombers or anything," Mark said.

"Animal rights groups I mean. You know, free-the-animals-now type people."

"That doesn't make sense. Why would they blow up a shark tank? It could kill the shark!"

"Stop talking about it," said another girl from three seats up. "It scares me!"

"Yono!" said Johnny. "Turn up the volume so the rest of us can hear."

Mark flipped his phone around and held it up for everyone to see.

Garrett leaned over to watch.

Onscreen, Indy's top news anchor, Gia Perez, appeared, her natural beauty marked with appropriate seriousness for the story she relayed. The newsfeed had inserted an Indianapolis Zoo logo in the upper right hand screen beside her, and Garrett took particular notice they added a shark image with its mouth open in an attempt to make the story more terrifying.

Doesn't do it justice. He looked way scarier than that.

Mark turned up the volume.

"We're told the incident happened just under an hour ago and almost ended…*in tragedy*," Gia said in her most dramatic reporter voice. "With us live at the zoo is Jeremy Myers. Jeremy, was anyone injured, or do zoo officials have any thoughts on how the tank burst?"

The video cut away to a wide panning shot of half a dozen fire trucks and more than a few police cars. Officers stood guard behind barricades. Firemen carried hoses to and from the trucks. Then the camera showed a young reporter with slicked-back hair.

"Good afternoon, Gia," Jeremy said stoically. "I'm told no one was injured due to the exhibit having been closed for scheduled maintenance repairs. While zoo officials have not disclosed how or why the tank shattered, police have stated reason to suspect it may be due…" he paused for added effect, "to someone tampering with the tank."

Johnny fumbled at his pocket for a new pack of gum. He unwrapped it just as soon as he found it.

Give me a break, Hickey. You weren't even there.

The camera cut away again, this time to a fidgety engineer with a piece of acrylic glass, thick as a loaf of bread, on the table in front of him.

"Due to the, uh, structural integrity of these tanks, it would, uh, be almost impossible for them to fracture, let alone break. You can see by this example here," the engineer presented the acrylic piece toward camera. "The windowpanes for the tanks are extremely dense to, uh, safeguard the public and the animals. Even after extensive aging, it would take a long time and a great deal of pressure for it to break."

That or a shark-man hammering it over and over again.

The newsfeed cut back to Jeremy. "Unfortunately, we were not allowed on the premises to show the disaster I'm told lay inside. The zoo's head marine biologist, Dr. Natsuki Gao, told us the shark from the tank has been saved thanks to a team effort of zoo officials. It has since been moved to a separate holding tank for the time being."

Syd's mom saved him?

Gia returned to the screen. "Jeremy, you mentioned police officials stated they have reason to suspect the tank had been tampered with. Do they have any suspects or leads at this time?"

Garrett's stomach clenched.

"I spoke with the chief of zoo security just a few moments ago,"

Jeremy said. "He stated while they do have reason to suspect foul play, they do not have any suspects at this time."

The camera cut back to Gia. "We will, of course, be providing more updates throughout the night as this story progresses."

Gia shuffled the notes on her desk as the camera cut to a different angle. A new logo, one of a smiling little girl, replaced the terrifying shark. Like flipping a light switch, Gia turned cheerier than Sydney at a football game.

"In other news, five year old Hope Barnes is living up to her first name by giving a little hope to her community."

"Whoa! You guys, check it out," Mark shouted.

The bus had turned into the Tiber High parking lot. A brown and tan sheriff's car sat parked outside the school's entrance. Ms. Morgan stood beside it, eyeing each student through the bus windows like a warden would incoming prisoners. She saw Garrett and stopped searching.

Johnny gave another sideways glance at Garrett.

Mr. Lansky stood. "Okay everyone, off the bus and into the school."

"Why's the sheriff here again?" Mark asked.

"I don't know, Mr. Yono, but I've been asked—"

"Told, Lansky," Ms. Morgan ascended the bus steps slowly. "You've been told, not asked."

She steadied herself by gripping the front seat.

"Weaver…" she seemed to relish his name rolling off her tongue. "You're coming with me."

She doesn't know anything, dude…you didn't do anything. You've talked your way out of more than whatever she has on you.

Garrett shouldered his bag and ignored his peers as he marched to the front. He stopped shy of the yellow line when he smelled dead lilies emanating from her aged perfume.

"Where we going?"

"My office...you know the way," she said. "Hickey. You're coming too."

Garrett heard Johnny cough and choke on his gum all the way at the front of the bus. Mark Yono had to smack him on the back several times until Johnny spit it out. Johnny walked the long aisle like a man already convicted, never once daring to chance a look at his vice principal.

After exiting the bus, Ms. Morgan followed both boys into the school. Her pointy-toed shoes clip-clopped off the pavement with every step she took, reminding Garrett of the way Clydesdale hooves did during the carriage rides in downtown Indy.

"Yes, I'm still behind you, Hickey," she screeched. "Keep walking."

They entered the school and then the administration office. Sheriff Hullinger awaited them.

"Old habits die hard, eh Hullinger?" Ms. Morgan said. "That's the same chair you used to sit in when I called you into my office thirty-two years ago."

Sheriff Hullinger's face reddened. "That was a long time ago. And I'm a sheriff—"

"Call yourself what you want. To me you'll always be Dickie Hullinger, the fat boy who was made fun of all through school and became a cop so he could repay the favors," she said dryly. "Which one do you want first? Weaver prefers to dance around a bit. Hickey is like you as a teen—he'll squeal all day to not end up in detention. Now what do you want with them?"

"That's confidential," Sheriff Hullinger said in a way that

suggested he had been waiting thirty years to tell her that. "I'll take Hickey first."

"As you please," Ms. Morgan said. "Weaver, my office. After all, we want to keep your streak of visits alive, don't we?"

"Sure," Garrett said. "I'm going for the record."

"Believe it or not, you're not the most unruly student I've ever had. That record won't ever be touched," Ms. Morgan said, turning to the sheriff. "That leaves me with you two; Hickey and Dickie, my two piggies. Shall we?"

"I already told you, Ms. Morgan," the sheriff huffed. "This is confidential county business."

"This is my school. I have a right to know."

Ms. Morgan opened Principal Church's door. She had to pinch Johnny to make him walk inside. She followed him in and gave Sheriff Hullinger a rap on the arm as she passed.

"Buck up, Dickie! We don't have all day."

Sheriff Hullinger reached down to straighten his gun belt before following them in. He closed the door.

Garrett estimated it would take ten minutes for Ms. Morgan to crack Johnny, maybe less with Sheriff Hullinger in the room. *All she'll have to do is say detention and he'll fold.* Garrett could only imagine what Johnny would do if Sheriff Hullinger suggested jail.

He walked into Ms. Morgan's cold office. Tiber students had nicknamed it the mortuary. He knew the spic-and-span room by heart, but looked around to find anything to take his mind off the day's events and unpleasant thoughts of Johnny being grilled next door.

Two grey filing cabinets stood in the left corner, which Garrett thought made no sense considering she had a computer on her desk to store files electronically. He did know she locked the file cabinets though, having once snuck in to try and find his disciplinary file.

He would have pegged his vice principal a crazy cat lady, but he saw no pictures of animals or even the cheesy motivational posters most of the school's classrooms had. Ms. Morgan had only two items to signify life inside her arctic room.

A snow globe with an emperor penguin figurine inside sat atop her left file cabinet. The other, a '90s era postcard with a skier in mid-jump and a mountain of snow spray in the background.

Garrett heard the floor creak outside the office door. *That didn't take long...*

Sheriff Hullinger entered first and took the seat next to him. Ms. Morgan sat behind her desk, sizing Garrett up like an opponent before a whistle signaled the bout to begin.

"We need you to call your mother, Garrett," Hullinger said.

"Like...you want me to call my mom with you in the room?"

"Yes, Weaver. Hence the term *we*," Ms. Morgan said. "A mother would be concerned I think if her child went through what you have today, and for the second day in a row no less." She pushed her landline phone toward him. "Dial."

Garrett punched in his mom's cell number, praying she wouldn't pick up. "What if she's not there?"

"Then we'll try calling her at the diner," Hullinger said. He touched the speakerphone button. The dial tone rang several times.

"And if she's not there either?"

"Then you'll leave her a kind message informing her you'll be staying after with me today," Ms. Morgan said.

Cristina Weaver's phone went to voicemail.

"Dial the diner."

Garrett keyed in the numbers. *Great. Now the gossip-hungry waitresses will have all sorts of fresh material to feed off of…Cristina Weaver's kid is in trouble again. No new news.*

The dial tone rang. A woman using a way too cheerful and fake customer service voice answered.

"Thank you for calling Gracin's Grille, this is Geeeeeena, how may I help you?"

Garrett waited for Ms. Morgan to speak first. When she didn't, he decided she must have stopped breathing. *One more perk of the undead.*

"Hello?"

"Hey, it's Garrett."

"Oh," she dropped her act. "Well, what do you want?"

"Is my Mom there?"

"She has an eight-top right now. We're pretty busy."

At 4 p.m. on a Wednesday? Garrett thought. "Would you mind getting her? It's kind of important."

"You in trouble at school again?"

"Geena, will you just get my mom, please?"

"Oh, fine. Hold on. And for future knowledge, this line is reserved for customers."

Garrett heard a loud *clunk.* He guessed she had set the phone down on the countertop. A moment later, his mother's tired voice echoed from the receiver.

"Garrett? You there?"

"Hey, Mom."

"What's going on? Geena said you were in trouble."

"Ms. Weaver?" Ms. Morgan interrupted.

"Y-yes…hello, Ms. Morgan."

Sheriff Hullinger quickly leaned forward. "Hi there, Cristina, this is Sheriff Hullinger. Wanted to let you know I'm here too."

Ms. Morgan narrowed her eyes at Sheriff Hullinger.

He shrank back in his seat.

"Oh! H-hi, Dick," Cristina said. "Is everything okay?"

"Yes," Ms. Morgan continued. "We felt the need to inform you of a situation that occurred earlier this afternoon with your son."

"Is he okay?"

"Yes, Ms. Weaver, Garrett is fine."

"Oh, thank God," Cristina said. "Wait…did he do something wrong?"

Thanks for the support, Mom.

"Honestly, we're not sure," said Sheriff Hullinger. "Ms. Morgan and I thought it best to call and inform you of what we've heard so far. We'd also like to hear Garrett's side, with your approval of course."

"Of course," Cristina said. "What did he do?"

"Mom, I didn't do anything, I swear! I wasn't even *at* school today!"

"You skipped school?"

"No, Mom…calm down. I went on a field trip…"

"Um, Garrett. Don't parents have to sign a permission slip for their kid to go on a field trip?"

Garrett gripped the phone with both hands, wishing he could smash it to pieces on Ms. Morgan's desk. "Yes, Mom…."

"That's funny, mister. I don't remember signing anything. Why is that?"

Ms. Morgan lips parted in a wan smile.

Garrett sighed. "Because I never gave it to you."

"Uh huh…well, that's two weeks of being grounded," Cristina said. "So! Want to tell us all what happened today?"

I would love to, Mom…I talked with a Merrow named Wilda. She was great. Oh! And a shark-man broke the walls of his tank and tried to eat me. Did I forget the part about a dwarf who changed into a seal and chased me?

"Garrett…you there?"

"Yes, Mom."

"Where was this field trip to?"

"The zoo…"

"Oh my God," Cristina said. "Where you there when the shark tank exploded?"

Garrett sat up straighter. "Wh-what?"

"It was on the news. All the customers have been talking about it. A couple people said they already called the school to check on their kids. I didn't think I needed to, of course, because I didn't sign a permission slip."

Thanks, Mom. Just keep twisting that dagger.

"Garrett," Cristina said. "You okay, honey? Are you hurt?"

Yes Mom, I'm hurt. Hurt that you think I might have blown up a shark tank. Garrett looked at both Ms. Morgan and the sheriff. "No…"

"Then why is the school contacting me if you're fine? Oh, Garrett, they haven't thrown you in jail have they? Because if they have—"

"Mom! Do you honestly think I'd do something to get thrown in jail?"

"Well, I don't know," said Cristina. "You tell me. Were you involved in any of that mess at the zoo today?"

"No—"

The shark-man did it.

"Well," said Garrett. "I was at the zoo when it happened, but I didn't do anything."

"Honey," Cristina said. "If you had *anything* to do with this, now is the time to tell me."

"I didn't do anything, Mom. I swear to—"

"I believe you."

"You do?"

"Mmm-hmm. Because Garrett Lee Weaver if you're lying to me, *I'll* be on the news tonight for strangling my son. You get me, young man?"

Garrett tried not to grin. "Yeah, Mom. I get you."

"Good. Now you come home straight away and—"

"'Fraid I have to step in here," Sheriff Hullinger interrupted. "That's why I'm at the school. Seems this is all a bit more complicated than Garrett's letting you know. I got a call from a federal marshal about twenty minutes ago. Said he saw a boy wearing a Tiber High wrestling T-shirt on the security cameras. Had the name Weaver on the back. Anyhow, this marshal would like to question Garrett in person down at the station."

"Oh, Garrett—"

"Now don't get yourself all worked up, Cristina," Sheriff Hullinger cut her off again. "This here marshal just wants to show Garrett some pictures and ask a few questions is all. I can drop him back off at your house later this evening once we're finished, if you'd like."

Yeah, I'll bet you'd love that, Hullinger. You and all the other cops would kill for an excuse to stop by and flirt with my Mom, wouldn't you?

"A couple questions?" Cristina asked. "So, he's not in any kind of trouble?"

"Not that I'm aware of," Hullinger said. "Just wants to ask him if he recognizes any of the pictures. I'll be there the whole time so don't you worry your pretty self."

"All right then. And you say you'll drop him off at home after, Dick?"

"Yes, ma'am. But only if you promise to bring a piece of that apple pie you make for me to take home," Hullinger said with a laugh.

"Deal," Cristina said. "Thanks for calling and letting me know. Garrett, honey?"

"Yeah, Mom?"

"I love you."

Garrett mumbled a reply back. His mom hung up her end of the phone.

Ms. Morgan's used a single skeletal finger to hang up. "So…you *were* in the room when the tank burst. Why didn't you mention that before?"

"I—"

"Don't bother lying. Hickey already said you wanted to see the shark tank," Ms. Morgan continued. "He mentioned you were adamant about it, even when he suggested you go back to the bus like a good student ought to." She cocked an eyebrow. "What piqued your curiosity?"

Sheriff Hullinger cleared his throat. "Apologies, Ms. Morgan, but I got it from the marshal that Garrett here didn't do anything wrong. Now if you'll excuse us, we best get going. The marshal will be arriving at the station anytime now, I'd expect. Come on, Garrett."

"What's his name?" Ms. Morgan snapped.

"Pardon?"

"This marshal you're so eager to run off and impress," Ms. Morgan said. "What's his name?"

Hullinger smirked. "That's confidential…" He turned to Garrett. "All right, son, let's get outta here."

Garrett lifted his bag from the floor. He dared a glance at his vice principal before leaving, hoping to see a bit of anger, or the slightest frustration. He saw neither. Garrett followed the sheriff out of her office.

A new girl Garrett had never seen before stood near Mrs. Boyd's reception desk. She looked like she could have just stepped off a runway despite the cheesy T-shirt she wore. Across her chest, it read *I ♥ my Shedd Aquarium!* with a sea lion picture underneath it.

The girl caught Garrett staring and bashfully turned away.

"Come on, Weaver," Sheriff Hullinger said from the outer office doorway. "We ain't got all day."

The girl gave Garrett a lingering look-over, studied his face.

Great first impression on the hot new girl, Weaves. Garrett sauntered past her.

"I'm sorry, dear," Mrs. Boyd asked the new girl. "What did you say your name was again?"

"Chidi…" the girl said. "My name is Chidi."

LENNY

LENNY CURSED WHEN HE SAW THE HEAVYSET SHER-
iff lead Garrett Weaver out of school. He did remember to toss up a
silent prayer to the Ancients that he had at least picked up the trail
again, however.

Neither looked particularly happy as they got in the sheriff's
car.

Chidi, at least, had the sense to wait until the car pulled out of the
lot to exit the school. She ran for their mini-van, ignoring a group
of teens in their truck bed catcalling to her, got in the driver's side,
and waited for Lenny's order.

"Follow 'em," Lenny said.

Chidi obeyed.

They drove without speaking, much like they had the forty-five
minute drive from the zoo to Lavere. Lenny's fingers danced against
his windowpane. *Come on, Cheeds. Say something,* he thought to
himself. *Let's make an argument outta this. Least it'll make the
time go by fasta.*

She didn't.

Traveling on a two-lane state highway with barely any traffic,
it did not take Chidi long to catch up to the sheriff's car.

"Not too close." Lenny warned. "Don't wanna make 'em suspicious."

Chidi tapped the squealing brakes to drop them back two car lengths.

Ten miles later, they passed an abandoned gas station near the I-65 interstate on-ramp. Lenny noticed all the windows had been shattered out, and chains hung from the door. Several pumps hung free from their stations, left to clang against the sides at any gust of wind. The major sign had few letters remaining. Those that hadn't fallen or been stolen read: *U lead $2.05/gal.* Another read: *Dies $2.9 / al.*

Lenny made a mental note of the landmark like his father had taught him to do in new surroundings. He turned to look out Chidi's window. Her sharp eyes never left the sheriff's car.

She's a good girl. His conscience nagged. *Just scared. Ya know what it's like to be scared, don't ya?* Lenny turned back to watch the farmlands roll by. *Nothin' scares me.*

As if desiring to prove him wrong, his conscience recalled the memory of the two marshals chasing him earlier. Lenny relived their footsteps closing in on him. The hairs stood up on his arms.

Now who's lyin'?

He turned on the radio. A country crooner sang about the ex-girlfriend he needed back more than anything else in the world, including his house and dog. Lenny continued scanning until he found a station playing '80s rock-n-roll. He cranked up the volume.

Chidi winced at the onslaught to her eardrums but said nothing of it.

Five minutes later, they reached the town of Lavere.

"Slow down," Lenny ordered as they rolled by a vacated series of run-down, abandoned buildings. At first, he thought they headed for the courthouse at the center of town. He had seen the top of its greenish dome just outside the city limits. Atop it, a statue pointed its arm eastward.

The sheriff turned into the parking lot of a newer building just across the street. He parked near several navy police cars with white stripes and a man who tipped his black cowboy hat.

"The Silkstealer," Chidi said.

Their van slowed.

"Don't stop!" Lenny commanded. "Keep drivin' like normal."

Lenny scooted low in his seat as Chidi sped back up. Only after they passed the jailhouse did he raise his head to look out the passenger-side mirror.

Two men had exited either side of the SUV; one of them led Marisa Bourgeois in handcuffs. Lenny couldn't make out either man's face, but he had a sneaking suspicion he had met both already.

"Lenny…what am I supposed to do now? Where do you want me to go?"

Could the Silksteala be after Weava too?

"Drive back to that old gas station we passed earlier. Ya crystals workin'?"

"Yes."

"Tell the others to get here," Lenny said, leaning forward to turn up the radio louder. "And let Oscar know I got what he wants."

Chidi's earrings flashed. She remained quiet as they drove back through town.

Lenny kept his eyes on the steering wheel when she drove back across the interstate overpass. *If she don't wanna be taken back, all she's gotta do is drive ova the edge.*

Chidi never wavered. She did, however, fishtail the back of the van when turning into the loose gravel near the gas station. After righting it and parking, she promptly turned off the van. The quiet returned, now without even the van engine for Lenny to distract himself with.

He shifted uneasily.

Ya know this is wrong. And ya know betta than most what August will do if he gets the kid.

Chidi's earrings sparkled. She nodded to the unheard voice and turned to Lenny. "Ellie says Oscar and Henry came back not long after we left. They had to hide because of all the cops around before they could slip away. I guess Ellie told them what you wanted. They left the zoo a while ago. She says they should be here in the next twenty minutes."

"Anything else?"

Chidi nodded. "Oscar says—he says you better have found the boy or he'll have August sell you to the nearest Nomad when we go back."

"Do me a favor," Lenny said. "Ask Oscar why he's gotta be such a jerk."

Chidi chuckled. "What do you *really* want me to tell them?"

Lenny nearly laughed with her. That is, until he remembered the reason he brought her in the first place. He scowled. "Just tell him to get here quick."

"Okay..."

She coulda' shot ya any time back there with Zymon. Lenny could almost hear his father rationalize. *Just like she coulda' driven ya both off the bridge a minute ago.*

Lenny squirmed in his seat and looked out the window. *She lied to me.*

The grass had grown up through the cracks in what little black-top remained by the pumping stations. A bean field had been planted almost up to where the pavement ended.

Near the ditch line, a farmer worked on his red tractor. A younger version of the man stood nearby, watching. The farmer handed the wrench to his son, pointed where to place it on the engine. The boy jumped at the chance to help.

"I wasn't going to run, you know," Chidi said.

"Maybe ya should've."

"Maybe…Henry would come for me though."

"We all got problems."

Chidi turned in her seat. "Lenny…why are *you* such a jerk?"

Lenny sat up. "Wha-what'd ya say?"

"You said we all have problems and you're right. *We* do. We're both slaves, in case you forgot. Our owners can beat, sell, even ra—" Chidi looked away. "They can do anything they want to us. So with all we have to deal with, how in the depths can you be such a jerk when I'm trying to apologize?"

Where's this girl been the whole time? "Guess I'm a jerk, just like you're a fighta. It's who we are, Cheeds."

"I'm no fighter."

"Oh no?" Lenny barked a laugh. "Where'd that fire come from then, sparkplug? Ya got it in ya. I dunno know what all Henry's done, but ya wouldn't have made it this far if ya weren't a fighta."

Chidi looked down. "I used to be…I fought for a long time."

"My Pop says there's no such thing as used to be. Ya either are something or ya not. People don't change."

"Yes, they do," said Chidi. "I used to be naïve."

Lenny gave her a long look. "Ya not anymore."

"No...I changed. You could too, right now."

"How's that?"

"You could stop being a jerk."

Lenny smirked. "Then I wouldn't be me, sista. See? Can't change who I am. Don't got a choice."

"Daar is altyd 'n keuse..."

"Cheeds—"

"It's what Marisa said to me at the Shedd Aquarium yesterday." Chidi said quickly. "It means there is *always* a choice..."

Lenny shook his head and looked out the window. The farmer and his son had their tractor working. Both had climbed into its cab to continue their work in the field.

Could we have that, Pop? Swallow the anchor, and find a patch a land to work on in the middle of nowhere? Lenny wondered. *Far from the sea and free?*

Chidi removed her crystal-studded earrings. She handed them to Lenny. "It's Ellie. She wants to talk you."

Lenny's ear lobes screamed at the notion of putting new studs in. He took them anyway. The crystals took a second to recognize their new wearer and mold to his raw nerve endings. After they settled, he pictured Ellie in his mind and directed his thoughts to her.

Elle, it's me. Where ya at?

About five minutes away, she answered. *Len...can I ask why we're doing this? You really think this kid is a runner? I mean, why are we after him? Marisa is the one the Crayfish wants. She's the one he sent us to bring back, not some innocent kid.*

Lenny thought back on Oscar's words at the zoo. *You catch him for me, Lenny! Catch him and win your freedom!*

Oscar wants him, said Lenny.

What doesn't he want? Ellie countered. *You know it can't be for any good—*

I know what it means, Elle. Just get here already.

Lenny saw their bus turn off the exit ramp a few minutes later. It wheezed into the gas station lot. The top swayed dangerously when Ellie drove it over a gaping pothole. The doors swung open even before she could put it in park.

Oscar exited first, his white hood catching air as he leaped down the steps. Henry descended not far behind, already glowering.

Paulo and Racer followed them out. Both stayed close to the bus.

Lenny's earrings flashed as he exited the van. *Paulie, what's goin' on?*

Something you're not going to like.

Lenny didn't have time to ask anything more.

Henry ran toward him, grabbed Lenny by the suit, and shoved him against the van. "You stole my property!"

"I didn't steal nothin'," Lenny said, his hand slipping into his Selkie pocket. He fingered his hidden dagger. "Someone had to drive."

"You could 'ave 'ad one of zem drive you." Henry pointed back at the bus.

"I coulda'—" Lenny smirked. "But I didn't."

Henry punched him in the face. Then he lifted Lenny off the ground and slammed him against the van window, shattering the glass.

Lenny drew his dagger. He swiped at Henry's face before he could be slammed again.

Henry caught him by the wrist, twisted it, and forced Lenny to hold the blade at his own throat.

"Henry!" Oscar yelled. "Put...him...down!"

Henry disregarded the order. His earrings flashed. *You weel die for zis, nipperkin!*

Do that and the Crayfish will take Cheeds from ya. Compensation for his loss of property.

Henry sneered. *Maybe I would keel 'im too.*

"Henry!"

Henry wrenched Lenny's dagger away and dropped him amidst the glass. He turned to face the other crewmates. "Do you all see 'im?" He pointed at Lenny. "'*E eez your warning! Ze next time anyone takes ze girl from me zey weel die!*"

Henry threw the blade into the dirt. He strode to the passenger side, tried to open the door that Chidi fought to keep closed. Henry punched the window, yanked Chidi out by her hair. She screamed and kicked to no avail.

Lenny brushed off the glass shards stuck in his Selkie hide. A gun barrel shoved against his temple.

"Ah, ah, ah," Oscar gloated. "You're not going anywhere without my permission ever again. Where is he, Lenny?"

Lenny seethed as Henry dragged Chidi to the bus, her struggling to regain footing the entire way.

"Hey! She's not even puttin' up a fight!"

"Stop." Oscar pressed the gun barrel deeper. "Henry can do as he pleases. That's his right. She belongs to him, like you all belong to me. You do remember that, don't you, nipperkin?"

Henry grinned at Lenny from across the lot. He slapped Chidi open-handed. When she didn't get up as fast as he ordered her to, Henry slapped her again.

Lenny's fists clenched. "I rememba..."

"There's a good lad," Oscar said. "Now this business about the Orc calf...what did you say his name is again?"

"Garrett Weava."

"Weaver, yes. The crown jewel of all the gifts I mean to present my father upon our return."

Gifts? Lenny put a finger to the right side of his nose. He blew the blood seeping out of his nostril onto the pavement. "Whattaya mean gifts?"

"Ah, I almost forgot," said Oscar. "You weren't with us then, were you? It seems I'm becoming quite the catcher. Come! I'll show you."

Oscar took the gun away from Lenny's head. In his excitement, he even offered to help Lenny stand.

"Come along, come along." Oscar hustled him toward the bus. "It really is a grand surprise! My father will love it."

Lenny's stomach churned.

"You two—" Oscar motioned to Paulo and Racer. "Open it up. It's high time Lenny learned he's not the most capable catcher in this crew!"

Reluctantly, they each unlocked and lifted a hold door.

"Ellie!" Oscar called up the steps. "Be a dear and brighten the insides."

The hold lights flickered on, a thin, yellowish light that threatened to go out at any second. Oscar pushed Lenny closer that he might better see the prizes within.

Inside the first hold, Zymon Gorski and Allambee had been positioned back-against-back, both stripped to their undergarments. Each of them gagged by rope nearly too thick to fit in their mouths. Leather strippings blindfolded them, and both shivered from the heavy, iron chains binding their naked upper bodies together. Shackles looped their ankles and wrists to one another.

The middle hold contained Zymon's guardian, Wotjek. They had splayed his limbs in the form of an X; chained to anchors in the bus's steel flooring. A curved bit of metal piping secured his head and forced his left cheek down. They had let him wear his Leopard Seal coat, and, unlike the others, had not blindfolded him. They had spiked his Selkie hood just in front of his eyes; an insult to the power that lay beyond his reach.

Oscar clapped. "Now, open the last one!"

Paulo raised the final hold door.

No...

"Recognize them?" Oscar asked.

Three male teenagers lay inside. Two lay bound together like Allambee and Zymon. Neither stirred at the open hold door, but the slow rise and fall of their chests told Lenny they yet lived. The third did not. His skin had already turned a deathly hue.

"Can you believe the fools attacked us in the Nomad's exhibit? Anyhow, we couldn't very well leave them."

"Ya killed a Dryback!" Lenny said.

"Yes, and I could have right well had the other two killed if I listened to Henry's advice." said Oscar. "After all, he suggested we do the others right then and there. I thought this much cleaner. We brought the dead one along to not leave any trace we'd been there."

He paused then, and smiled at Lenny. "Hmm. It seems I've learned something from you after all, Lenny. Well done."

Lenny couldn't stop staring at the dead teen. "Whattaya gonna do with the body?"

"Dump it on the side of the road once we've left, most likely.

Ah!" Oscar clapped. "My father's going to think me exceptional! Five new slaves…the uncatchable Marisa Bourgeois—well, once I find her—and an Orcinian calf! Not bad for my first trip out of the Salt, eh?"

"Master, uh, sir," Paulo said. "Those two Drybacks came from this town. Do you think we could leave—"

Oscar sneered. "I can see threats of pain don't work on you, Paulo, else you'd remember my earlier warning. Very well. Should you make that suggestion again, I'll take the tongue and ears from your crewmates! Ellie first, I think. Is that understood?"

Paulo bowed away. "Yes, master."

"Right, then. Close up the holds." Oscar stepped onto the bus.

Lenny's earrings flashed. *Paulie, how do ya know those pups are from around here?*

Paulo reached into his Selkie pocket. From it he removed a handful of wallets; one a dark green with Velcro, another faded brown leather, a third just a money clip. The last wallet had been crafted of expensive black leather.

Paulo handed them all to Lenny. His earrings flashed. *Oscar had us check their pockets before tying them down. The fourth one is Zymon's.*

Lenny opened the posh black wallet. Inside, he found eight credit cards, and an Illinois driver's license. The name on it read: Simon Alexander Warren. Lenny tossed the wallets back over to Paulo.

A picture fluttered out of Zymon's. Racer bent down to pick it up.

"Are the lot of you deaf and dumb?" Oscar leaned out the doorway. "Close up the holds I said!"

Paulo reached for the first door.

Racer's earrings flashed. *I thought we decided not to do this.*

He'll punish Ellie if I don't. Paulo closed the door and trudged to the second hold.

Whatsamatta, pup? Lenny asked. *This job not what ya pictured when ya farmed the reefs?*

No...

Lenny nodded. *Well, get used to it. It's a hard life, so grow up.*

Paulo slammed the second door. *Len, what's wrong? Why are you so...angry? I mean, you're always grumpy, but why do you have to yell at the pup?*

Ellie stepped off the bus. Her earrings flashed. *He's mad at himself. Oscar made him a deal he knows isn't right and he's actually considering it. Said he'd give Lenny his freedom if he slaved this kid.*

Paulo crossed his arms. *That true?*

Look, Lenny said. *We've caught and hauled back hundreds of runnas before. What's one more and I get to walk away from all this?*

He's not a runner, Len, Ellie reminded him.

Lenny took a deep breath and counted to ten.

What about us? Racer asked. *If we catch him, do we all get freed?*

Paulo shook his head. *No way the Crayfish frees four catchers for one new slave.*

Ya don't know that, Lenny said. *The kid's an Orcinian. Ya know how much that could be worth?*

Ellie snorted. *Do you know how much trouble this will bring down if the wrong sort finds out? Who ever heard of an Orc being captured and sold?*

That's the point, Lenny said. *It's good business. He'll be the first to do it! And who knows? Maybe the kid is worth the price of four, maybe five, of us.*

What if it's not?

Lenny scratched his neck. *If it's not...then I'm freed and sell out to whoeva will have me catch for them. I'll save up enough anemonies and then buy all of ya.*

Paulo frowned. *That would take decades, Len.*

Ya forget who ya talkin' to? Dolans take care—

You're no Dolan, Ellie said. *You're not looking out for others. This is about you. Declan would be ashamed of you for even considering this.*

Shuddup, Elle! Ya dunno what my Pop would say!

Lenny knew the words rang hollow even as he spoke them. He hated Ellie for calling him out. Hated her being right even more.

Paulo closed the final hold. "Come on, pup," he tugged Racer's hood. "Best get moving."

Lenny trudged after them. He halted at the steps and scanned the fields a final time. The farmer and his son had disappeared far across the fields. Lenny climbed the tall steps.

Ellie closed the doors behind him. The bus lurched forward as she floored the gas pedal.

Lenny fell down the stairs. *She did that on purpose.* He reached for the handlebar to help guide him up.

Oscar waited for him at the top. "Which direction, Lenny?"

"Bang a left and follow it into town. Pass by a couple abandoned buildings and it'll be on ya right. Can't miss it."

Oscar clapped his hands together. "Best prepare yourselves! Load up on everything you need to take down an Or—er, uh, Len...what do we need to capture an Orc?"

"Get the Blue-Ringed Oc darts. Gonna need something heavy to put him down and keep him down. We gotta knock him out. It's our only shot. That cowboy—"

"The Silkstealer?"

"Whateva. He's there too," Lenny said. "I saw him standin' next to one of the SUVs. Pretty sure I saw Marisa Bourgeois with him."

"The uncatchable runner and an Orc," Oscar clapped. "I can hardly stand the excitement!"

"Paulie," Lenny continued. "Those two Selkies we got the jump on back at the zoo…I think they're the ones who came with him. Between them and the Dryback cops, we're gonna need all of us to pull this off."

Henry stepped out of the sleeping quarters with Chidi in tow. Her left eye had already swelled.

"Not all of us…Chidi and I weel be staying 'ere."

"You can't do that!" Oscar said. "You were hired to protect me!"

"I 'ave protected you for what I was 'ired for," said Henry. "Zis mission 'eez not to capture Marisa Bourgeois."

Oscar's lower jaw dropped. "But…"

"Ask him how much he wants," said Lenny.

Oscar sneered. "Is this true, Henry? You want to negotiate a higher rate?"

A smile teased the sides of Henry's mouth. "You 'unt an Orc now. Dangerous work, no?"

"Aye," Lenny answered.

"Zen I weel need paid double."

Oscar narrowed his eyes at Henry. "Done…but see to it I'm kept safe."

"You weel be safe with me, leetle Crayfish," Henry said. "But I 'ave one more condition. My Chidi does not go weeth us. She weel stay locked in ze 'old while we go. I weel not reesk losing 'er again and I weel not 'elp no matter 'ow much you offer eef you do not agree."

Oscar's earrings flashed. *What do you think, Len?*

Make the deal.

But I thought you said we needed all of us, Oscar said. *What about Chidi?*

Lenny surveyed Henry's eyes and body language. *He knows we're talkin' about him, but he's smart enough to let us finish.*

He won't budge, Lenny replied. *'Sides, if ya don't agree we'll be down two instead of one. Henry's worth two of Cheeds anyhow.*

"Done," Oscar said to Henry. "Keep in mind your first priority is to protect me. The Orc is second."

Lenny saw Chidi fidget. They exchanged a glance. Her eyes pled for aid. Lenny looked away.

Henry gave a slight bow. *"Oui, monsieur. I am your 'umble servant."*

Paulo's earrings flashed. *He'd knife Oscar right now if we had the anemonies to pay him.*

Yeah, well, we don't, said Lenny. *Get everything togetha. We're almost there.*

Paulo took Racer to the back where they stored their weapons. He opened an overhead storage bin and removed a tin with three tranquilizers filled with bluish liquid. Racer took down three of the handguns, handing over each for Paulo to load.

Lenny's earrings flashed. *Racer, pocket one of those.*

Racer slyly placed one of the guns in his Selkie pocket.

"Lenny…is this the station?" Ellie asked.

"Yeah…pull ova to that courthouse parkin' lot to let us out."

Ellie slowed the bus, swinging wide to make the turn into the courthouse lot.

"What's the plan, Lenny?" Oscar asked.

Thought you claimed to lead this group.

From his vantage point, Lenny estimated two points of entry:

the main entrance and a side door. *Goin' through the front entrance is suicide. If the Silksteala posted either of those Selkies there, they'll recognize us.*

"I'm thinkin' he'll be inside the front entrance," Lenny said. "Me, Paulie, and Racer can go through there—"

"No!" said Oscar. "Henry, Paulo, and I will take the front. You take Ellie and Racer through the side to back us up."

Lenny gave an exaggerated sigh. "Oscar...Ya don't wanna do—"

"That's the way it's going to be! I am the captain after all."

Oscar lifted his chin in the air and ushered Lenny down the steps. "Well, come on, come on. Let's not dilly-dally all night. There's an Orc to be caught." Oscar stepped off behind him. "Right. We'll lock Chidi in the under and be on our way."

Lenny turned and saw Henry lend a hand to help Chidi down the steps.

She refused to take it.

What's she doin'?

Henry grabbed her anyway and pulled her down. Though she fell forward, Henry caught her and pulled her close. "No kiss before I go, my love? Very well."

Henry kissed her cheek.

Chidi squirmed, arched her neck back, and slammed her forehead into his.

"Stupeed girl!" Henry snarled. His hand flew to her throat.

Oscar laughed. "Quite the rebel, isn't she, Henry? I can see why you fancy her so much. It's always fun to break the wild ones."

Chidi clawed at Henry's hand, fighting for the life he choked from her.

Lenny clenched the sides of his Selkie suit, and bit his bottom lip. *Don't do it. Ya a slave. And slaves do what they're told.* He closed his eyes, counted to ten, exhaled.

"We gonna go catch this Orc or what?" Lenny asked.

"Yes, let's," Oscar smirked. "Come, Henry. Release the girl. Lock her in the hold if you wish, but do it now. I want to catch this Orc and go home. I tire of this unsalted world you lot call the Hard. *Hardly* worth coming ashore I say."

Henry dropped Chidi to the ground.

Lenny watched her heave for air as Henry opened the hold door, then came back for her.

He yanked her up under the arm, dragged her limp body over. Henry threw her inside, and shackled her to the floor beside the two unconscious teens and the dead one.

"I weel return shortly…" He cooed to her. "And you weel show me 'ow much you 'ave missed me, Chidi."

Slaves do what they're told. Lenny repeated the mantra, trying to erase each of Chidi's grunts as Henry tightened her straps.

"Racer," said Lenny. "Gimme a gun."

Oscar snatched it away. "I'll take that. Give the other one to Henry. After all, we're going through the front. That's where the action will be so we'll be needing these more than you lot."

"Oscar, we need at least one of those—"

"Quiet, Lenny. I won't tell you again. This is *my* crew…*my* slaves…*my* call."

Lenny continued to fake his charade and delight Oscar. He winced when Chidi's hold door closed, and he smelled Henry's sweaty body long before the older man walked past.

Henry took the second gun. Unlike Oscar, he smartly checked to ensure it was loaded.

Oscar brandished his gun in the air. "A good captain knows how to reward those who follow him. Listen to my every command and I'll see to it you all receive an extra spot of grog upon our return home! Now, my group with me!"

Lenny's earrings flashed. *Good luck, Paulie.*

You too. Keep watch of Ellie for me.

Racer waited until Oscar had led his group across the road to draw the third tranquilizer gun. A picture stuck to its handle fluttered to the ground. He gave Lenny the gun and bent to pick up the photo.

"Racer, whattaya doin' with that?"

"I thought I'd hold onto it for Zymon. He looks happy here. Just guessed he might want something to remember his family by once we took him back to the Salt."

"Pups…" Lenny shook his head. "Give it here."

Racer handed the picture over.

The photo, bent and well worn, showed Zymon in an expensive three-piece blue pinstriped suit, his arms around two others: one, his horsey-faced wife; the other, a girl no older than seven or eight.

Little Jamie. Lenny rubbed his thumb across the image of the little girl. *Little Jamie who thought I was an elf.*

"Do you know them?" Ellie asked.

I've been a fool, Pop. Lenny pocketed the picture. He turned back to Ellie and Racer. "Follow me."

He sprinted across the street. The police station security lights began to warm and glow in the fast-approaching dusk. Lenny hunched beside the nearest cop car parked by the side entrance. His earrings flashed.

Elle, pick the lock!

She nodded and began her task. *So we're really doing this?*

Yeah…but it's not goin' down like Oscar thinks. A lot has to come togetha quick, so listen up. Lenny said. He quickly laid out his newest plan for the other two. *Ya both in?*

Ellie swung the door open. *The lock's popped…Captain Dolan.*

You know I'm in, Racer said. *Not much of a choice, really.*

There's always a choice, pup. Ya just gotta make it.

Lenny sprang up to lead the charge inside, and prayed to the Ancients he found Garrett Weaver before Oscar did.

GARRETT

A COWBOY WITH DARK SUNGLASSES CHEWED ON A toothpick outside Garrett's window.

"That there's the marshal," Sheriff Hullinger said. "David Bryant's his name. Don't embarrass me now, Weaver."

He straightened his hat and smoothed his uniform, then eased his rather large behind out of the car.

Garrett waited for the car springs to bounce back up before he exited.

"Yes, sir, brand spanking new, marshal." Hullinger pointed at the jail. "Finished her less than a year ago. Got all the newest gadgets too! Folks around here put up a fit over the cost, but with Indianapolis growing so fast, why, soon enough they'll be knocking on our door. Meantime, we'll be building up our town, readying to get swallowed up." Hullinger nodded. "Jail's the first step. What do you think?"

Bryant rapped two fingers on the back passenger window. The door opened. "These two sorry dogs are my deputies. The older one's called Smith, the younger is Foster."

Deputies? They look more like hired guns. Garrett squirmed under the older deputy's lingering gaze. He noticed a purplish bruise around Smith's neck. *Wonder how he got that?*

Whatever Smith's thinking, he kept it well hidden.

Garrett liked the look of Foster even less as the younger deputy limped around the opposite side. He led a girl in handcuffs that Garrett thought looked like the type news stations bandied about after a gangland shooting. Her hooded sweatshirt seemed coffee stained or something worse, and her chiseled features warned him she would not be one to back down from a fight.

"Who's that?" Hullinger asked.

"Why, she'd be the one who blew up the shark tank," Bryant said. He looked at Garrett. "Unless this young man knows otherwise."

"I've never seen her before in my life," Garrett said.

"That might well be…" Bryant said. "But just cause you ain't seen her don't mean she didn't see you. What's say we go inside? See this new jail your sheriff's so proud of."

"Think it might hold one more con awhile, sheriff?" Smith asked. He motioned toward the handcuffed girl.

"Don't see why not," Hullinger answered. "Like I said, we got all the newest and best stuff inside along with the best men in Lavere County to stand guard."

That's saying a lot. Garrett snorted.

The girl muttered.

Garrett couldn't understand what she said, but he knew the words had been directed at him.

Her gaze danced around his face, ears, and mouth; all the areas his skin tones differed.

"What'd she say?" Hullinger asked.

"Who knows," Smith replied. "Been sputtering all sorts of mumbo jumbo since we caught her."

"Might be that meth junk." Sheriff Hullinger assumed. "Terrible stuff. Thought we might have a problem with some of their kind around here at one time. Me and my boys here at the station—" Hullinger adjusted his gun belt. "We took care of them, if you take my meaning."

And by take care of, do you mean took a bit of their money to look the other way? Garrett had heard the rumors. No way he would say a word of that here though. The marshal and his deputies seemed to him they could be involved in darker deals than the sheriff.

Hullinger motioned for the rest to follow and led them inside. "Yep, we got us a nice, clean town here. Couldn't find a safer place in the state, I'd warrant."

Garrett half-expected to hear inmates yelling somewhere deep in the jailhouse, but the only sounds came from their shoes scuffing the waxed marble flooring. An imposing Indiana state seal glowed in the dim light of the office, and the collection of flags fluttered in the slight breeze they created as the group walked past.

Hullinger stopped at the end of the hallway. He fumbled with the keys attached to his belt loop. "Sorry about this, marshal," he said, trying a silver key in the door. "I work days and this is usually open then. Can't ever seem to find what key unlocks it."

The first key did not work, nor did the second, not even the third. After Hullinger's seventh try, and having tried both the second and third keys again, he had enough.

"Campbell?" Hullinger banged on the door, his face darkening until it resembled a beet. "You in there? Murphy? Open up!"

"Sheriff," Bryant said. "Is there someone you could radio to unlock the door? Maybe someone already inside?"

Now there's an idea. Garrett turned his head to grin at the marshal, let him know he thought the same. The marshal moved his

270 — AARON GALVIN

toothpick from one side to the other as if to reply he didn't care. Garrett faced forward again.

Hullinger snapped the radio loose from his belt and flicked it on. "This is Sheriff Hullinger! Who's on duty?"

"Yeah, sheriff," a garbled voice came back over static. "This is Murphy, over."

"Get down here and unlock the south entrance!" Hullinger paused in wait for a reply that did not come. "Murphy!"

"Uh, copy, Dick…that door's always unlocked except during a lockdown. Did you try opening it?"

Garrett had never seen Sheriff Hullinger so cowed as when he pushed down on the handle and the door swung open. He didn't bother to give an apology or even turn around.

"Dick?" the radio voice said. "Did you get it unlocked?"

Hullinger led them onwards. "Yeah, we got it! Next time follow the protocol!"

"Protocol? But, Dick, we don't have a prot—"

Hullinger flicked off his radio. He led them down the hallway past several darkened doors numbered one through five.

"This here's our conference area," he said, turning down another hall. "Down that way to your right is our officer's entrance, lockers, showers, and so forth."

Garrett glanced over his shoulder. All three men and the girl watched him rather than paying attention to Hullinger's tour. For someone used to being stared at, Garrett could tell their focus on him had nothing to do with his vitiligo disorder. The four pairs of eyes following his every move now came with a different sort of intent; one that both made Garrett feel curious and weirdly compelled to fall on his knees and beg forgiveness for whatever sin he had committed.

When they reached a gated door, Hullinger looked to the upper left corner at a security camera. He waved at it, and the gates buzzed unlocked.

Inside, a wiry officer slumped behind a desk, flipping through a magazine about firearms and occasionally watching the evening news.

"Hey, Dick, what—"

"Murphy, I need you to sign in Garrett Weaver."

The officer sat up straight in his chair when he saw Hullinger accompanied by several others. "Okay, which one's he?"

Hullinger pointed. "Him. Sign him in."

Murphy complied, typing the name into the desk computer. He gave the three marshals and the girl a curious glance. "We'll need to sign them in too, right?"

"Of course you do," Sheriff Hullinger said. "It's part of the protocol, ain't it? This here's U.S. Marshal David Bryant. These other fellas..."

"They're my deputies," Bryant said. "Smith and Foster."

Garrett's dad always told him it didn't take a liar to recognize a bad one. To his mind, the marshal gave the names up too fast for them to be true. Garrett couldn't help himself when the officer bought the line without requesting to see their IDs. "Pretty common names, don't you think?"

The marshal's lip curled. "He wanted names, I gave him some." He turned back to Officer Murphy. "Sign the girl in as Jane Doe."

Murphy typed the names in along with the time and date. "Well, hot dang! Real live marshals, here in our jail! Where you based out of?"

"The only place real marshals come from," Bryant said.

"Texas, huh?" Murphy assumed with a dumb grin. "You're a long way from home. What brings you to Indiana?"

"That's classified."

"Oh, sure. Sure. Classified, right."

Murphy's eyes wandered from Garrett to the girl, trying to work out what either could have done to deserve such a distinguished escort.

Sweat dripped from Garrett's armpits.

Hullinger slapped the desk. "Murphy, quit bugging them. We need one of the conference rooms. They locked too?"

"Yeah," Murphy answered. He pulled open a drawer from the desk. From it, he removed a long wooden plunger handle with a key dangling from the end. "Here's the key. It'll work on any of the doors."

The younger deputy laughed. "The newest and greatest stuff, huh, sheriff?"

Sheriff Hullinger snatched the key and started toward the conference rooms.

Bryant stopped him. "No need to show me the way. You gave an excellent…tour on the way in. I'm sure Garrett and I can find it on our own."

Me? Now he wants to take me in a room alone? Garrett searched the sheriff's face for help; a fool's hope and he knew it.

Hullinger had already slumped like an athlete benched before the championship game. "Oh…right. Holler if you need anything."

Bryant took the key and rod. "Sheriff, you mind showing Deputy Foster where he can lock up our young friend, Miss Doe?"

Murphy studied the girl in handcuffs. "You're going to lock her up? She don't look dangerous. Sides, you've already got her cuffed."

Bryant twirled the rod by the key. "All your officers smart as this one, Hullinger?"

Maybe you should've told Murphy not to embarrass you, Sheriff.

"Pipe down, Murphy!" Hullinger bristled. "And turn that TV back to the security cameras watching all the prisoners!"

"But we only got two prisoners."

"Flip it back!"

Murphy turned the channel to the prison cells. "All right then. You get to the cells back through that door," he pointed to the far left corner. "Then down the hallway. I'll buzz you through."

"Foster, you stay back there with her." Bryant said to the younger deputy.

"Guard duty?"

"It'll be good for you, pup."

"Pup?" Murphy's forehead wrinkled. "That some kinda new name for rookies out in Texas?"

"I've never been to Texas," said Foster. He grabbed the girl by the cuffs and led her toward the cells. "Don't plan to either."

Murphy leaned over to Hullinger. "Dick...you want me to buzz them through?"

"No, you just hold on. Now listen, marshal. This is my jail—"

"And you're welcome to have it back once we're done with it," Bryant interrupted. "Last time I checked, a federal marshal out-ranks a local sheriff from some backwoods town by a country mile." Bryant turned to Murphy. "Buzz them through."

Murphy did so in a hurry.

"Now..." said Bryant. "My good friend, Deputy Smith, he's gonna stay out here with you gentleman to answer any questions you might have." The stone-faced cowboy turned his attention to Garrett. "Shall we?"

"Sherriff," said Garrett. "I don't think—"

"Come on," said Bryant, grabbing him by the bicep. "Won't kill ya to answer a few questions, will it?"

Garrett didn't know how to respond to that. He let the marshal lead him back the way they had come, and he listened to Bryant's cowboy boots scuff the floor with each heavy stride.

Bryant unlocked the first conference room door and flipped the lights on.

Garrett looked around the mostly bare room. "Isn't there supposed to be some kind of double-sided mirror for the good guys to watch from the other side?"

"No such luck, kid. I like to keep it old school...just *mano-a-mano*."

The door slammed behind the marshal, and stole any other jokes Garrett had in mind with it.

Bryant walked to the opposite side of the table. He removed his jacket, draped it over a chair. Garrett saw the marshal had two guns holstered—one at his hip, the other hung to the opposite side near his ribs.

Bryant took out his smartphone. "Have a seat."

Garrett looked at the closed door, wondered if it had locked them in automatically.

"Nervous?"

Do I tell the truth? "Y-yes."

"Good." Bryant used his finger to scroll across the screen of his phone. "More people should feel nervous these days. Keep them all out of more trouble. You oughta count yourself lucky though."

I'm supposed to feel lucky right now? What do you do to the guys you want to feel unlucky?

Bryant noticed Garrett fidget. He put his phone down. "You and I haven't gotten off to a good start. I'm thinking I'm responsible for half that problem and you the other half. What's say we get back on the right track here?"

"S-sure," Garrett said.

"Okay. I'm United States Marshal David Bryant." He extended his left hand across the table.

Garrett put his right hand forward without thinking. "Uh... you're shaking with the wrong hand."

"Oh, right." Bryant grinned. He switched hands. "Honest mistake. I'm a lefty, ya see."

He's one of them! Garrett shook his hand. His knuckles shifted and popped as Bryant tightened his grip.

"You call yourself a man, Garrett Weaver?" the marshal asked.

"What?"

"I asked if you'd call yourself a man?"

"Y-yeah," Garrett said.

"Then shake like one."

"Huh?"

"Quit gripping my hand like you're some damned girl," Bryant said. "You ain't gonna hurt me. Put something on it, son."

"Did you just call me a girl?"

Bryant tilted his head to the side. "You shake like one."

Garrett poured all his strength into the squeeze.

"There you go," Bryant said. Then he tightened his grip so hard Garrett nearly yelped. "That's how you shake a man's hand, son. Nice to meet you, Garrett."

"You too."

Bryant held the grip a while longer before releasing him. "Now that we know each other, you wanna tell me what happened today at the zoo?"

I wouldn't like to, but it doesn't sound like I have a choice. "I went on a field trip."

Bryant frowned. "I'd prefer we don't get too smart-alecky tonight. I'll rephrase my question to get more specific and maybe you will too. Now, you were in the room when the hammerhead tank exploded, weren't you?"

"Yes."

"Any of your friends in the vicinity?"

"No," Garrett said. "My friend Johnny was with me earlier, but he left before I went in to see the exhibit."

"Johnny?"

"Johnny Hickey."

"Mmm-hmm," Bryant seemed displeased, but made a note on his phone. "So you didn't have any other friends with you today?"

"I…I don't have many friends. I was with Johnny all day," Garrett said, careful to leave Sydney's name out. "Call him and ask if you want."

"What about this," Bryant slid his phone across the table. "You telling me you decided to strike up a conversation with some strangers?"

Garrett picked up the phone. On its screen, he saw a dark photo of himself, his back against the wall. Eddie Bennett and Juan Marrero stood in front of him. In the bottom corner of the picture, a dwarf, a preppy kid, and the older chaperone appeared paused in their run at the tank.

Cameras…of course they had cameras in the exhibit! Garrett slouched.

"Now," Bryant said. "What about those friends?"

"They're not my friends," Garrett's voice rose. "Two of those guys followed me in there to beat me up. The midge, I mean the dwarf—er—I mean the little person. He's some punk that tried picking a fight with my friend."

Bryant nodded. "So you did run into them earlier in the day? What started the argument?"

"This guy," Garrett pointed at the picture of the dwarf. "He got all offended because I accidentally ran into him. I wasn't paying attention and I…well, I didn't see him there. He kind kind of stood in the shadows."

"Mmm-hmm," Bryant said. "Had you ever met any of those three before today?"

"No," Garrett said. "Look sir, I-I didn't have any differences, or problems with these guys, okay? I just went to look at the shark tank, and yes, I know I wasn't supposed to, but I didn't make the thing explode!"

"So what did?"

The shark-man, Garrett wanted to say. "You wouldn't believe me."

Bryant leaned forward. "Try me."

It doesn't take a liar to recognize a bad one. Garrett took a deep breath.

"Okay, so those jerks from my school followed me inside. They beat me up and the other three guys, the guys on your phone, they showed up…and I don't remember much after that."

"Why?"

"I…uh…I don't know," said Garrett. "Everything went fuzzy. The older guy…he tried to tackle me or…I don't know. I got angry and pushed back against him and we sorta just crashed into the tank. Then it exploded and—"

Bryant sat back, unamused. "That pane is too thick. No way the two of you could have cracked it, let alone break it. I'll ask you again, how did the tank break?"

Garrett shrugged. "Like I said. We both crashed into it, and it broke."

"No!" Bryant said. "*It's too thick!* Did you feel anything before it broke? See anything suspicious?"

"No."

"You had to," Bryant implied.

"I didn't see anything."

"There had to have been something."

"Th-there wasn't."

Bryant's questions came faster, more accusing. "Sure about that?"

"Y-yeah."

"You don't sound sure."

Garrett felt hot. "Well, I—"

"Sounds to me like you're withholding valuable information."

"But I'm not."

The marshal pursed his lips. "Go on, keep it up. See where lying gets you."

You want the truth dude. Fine. "Okay, fine…I saw a shark-man."

"A shark…*man?*" Bryant asked.

"Yeah. You wanted the truth? There it is." Garrett folded his arms. "I saw a shark-man get mad and charge the tank. He hit the glass with his forehead over and over again! That's what I saw."

Bryant sat back.

"What?" Garrett asked. "Does that not fit in with your theories? Huh? That's what I saw! Right before that other guy tackled me and the tank burst!"

Bryant's phone vibrated with an incoming text. He sighed. Cleared it.

"Who was that?" Garrett asked. "Another marshal?"

"So you never saw these three before?"

"Never."

"Did you talk to any of them after your altercation at the shark tank?"

"No," Garrett answered. "Once the tank burst we all kind of got swept away by the water."

"And you're sure you've never seen them before? Never met them anywhere?"

"How many times do I have to say it?" Garrett said. "*No.* I never met them before."

"That's funny. The girl we pulled outta our car, Jane Doe," he said. "She says you do know them. See, she was in the room at the same time. Says you seemed like a bunch of good ole' boys till the older guy got involved."

"Wait—what?" Garrett said. "I've never seen her before! She *wasn't there!*"

Bryant pulled out a new toothpick from his jacket pocket and toyed with it. "Here's the deal. I don't know if you're telling the truth or not. You seem like a slick kid to me and I don't know if you might be pulling a fast one over on me.

"Your mother has a pretty good reputation around here from the people we've talked to and, aside from you getting in trouble at school every now and again, the word around town is you're an okay kid."

Guess he didn't talk to Ms. Morgan.

"My bet is you don't know these others very well, if at all," Bryant continued. "So I'm going to give you a bit of information on who you're dealing with."

Bryant tapped his phone a few times, and then slid it across the table. "Look through those."

Garrett scrolled through the pictures.

One showed the preppy kid standing in front of a seal exhibit at another aquarium. The next showed the chaperone man with his arm draped around a young, gorgeous black girl that Garrett swore he'd seen before but couldn't quite place.

He continued scrolling through the pictures, stopping when he came across the grumpy dwarf with his arms crossed.

"Ah, so it is him…" Bryant said. "Leonard Dolan, though I hear he hates being called that. Goes by Lenny instead. That pic you're looking at, and the one after, those were taken a few weeks ago at the New England Aquarium in Boston."

Garrett scrolled to the next photo of Lenny arguing with the chaperone. "That looks familiar."

"Bit of a hot head, ain't he? His father was too, at one point, or so I've been told," Bryant said. "Anyhow, this crew has been trolling aquariums all over the states, especially those housing seals and sea lions."

"Why?"

"You tell me," Bryant said.

"What does that have to do with aquariums and seals?" Garrett asked.

Bryant leaned in his chair. He tapped the side of his head questioningly. "You don't know?"

"Why would I care about seals?" Garrett said.

He scrolled through more pictures.

Each had a combination of Lenny, the preppy kid, the chaperone, the pretty black girl, and a few others he didn't recognize. Every picture had been taken near some sort of an aquarium with seals in the background.

The last picture showed Garrett; his back to the Hammerhead tank as Lenny rushed at him. Garrett used his fingers to zoom in on the picture in the hope the camera had captured the shark-man's image. Poor lighting did not allow him to see much of anything outside the front of the tank, let alone penetrate the dark acrylic pane.

"You can see I've been tracking them awhile now," Bryant said. "I have photos of them at all kinds of aquariums across the U.S. starting in Boston and making their way southwest. They've been pretty harmless, up until yesterday afternoon in Chicago...but you already know that."

Garrett could feel the marshal watching him, waiting to pick up on any nonverbal cues he may give off. *Why am I here? What does he think I have to do with all this?* He resumed scrolling the pictures.

"I can't figure out who the ringleader is of their gang," Bryant said. "Lenny, or Oscar Collins, the one you said looks preppy. We don't know what they're after, but they've hit all the big eastern U.S. aquariums and started moving on to others. They don't move in any sort of pattern either, which is odd for a group of their kind," he added with a hint of frustration.

Their kind?

Bryant gave a long sigh. "I can't figure it out and thought you might be able to shed some light on it since ya'll know each other."

"I don't know them," Garrett repeated for the umpteenth time. "I already told you that."

"I know that's what you told me. Doesn't seem like I'm going to get much more out of you than what I already have. Lucky for me, I—"

The door rattled from someone knocking on the opposite side.

Bryant left the table to open the door. "Stupid, fat sheriff."

Garrett looked down at a picture of Lenny watching a seal swim. *Why is he smiling in this picture?*

Bryant unlocked the door. "Sheriff, I told you, I didn't want—"

Garrett heard a loud popping sound, followed by a thump.

"Everybody say night-night to the Silksteala…"

Garrett stood from his chair. He turned around.

The marshal lay still on the floor.

A heavyset girl and a blond-haired teenager stood in the front of the doorway, barring Garrett's exit. In front of them stood Lenny Dolan, a gun in his hand.

"You…" Garrett whispered.

Lenny shot him in the chest.

LENNY

THE YOUNG ORCINIAN SLUMPED TO THE FLOOR, UN-conscious betrayal in his eyes.

Lenny pocketed his tranq gun. "Let's move. Elle, get the Orc. Racer, take the Silksteala. Gotta keep movin' for this to work."

Racer knelt beside the Silkstealer's body, rolled him to his stomach, patted him down. He found a wallet, looked at the ID. "U.S. Marshal David Bryant…" Racer tossed it aside. "Guess the Silkstealer has a name."

Not for long, he won't. Lenny turned his attention to Garrett Weaver. His plan had seemed so simple when he considered Garrett just a number in an unfair equation. Now he stared that number in the face and *it* had a name. A family Lenny meant to steal him away from.

It's the right call, Len. Pop would do the same. He tried to convince himself. The lie tasted bitter. *Pop woulda' found a way to help them all.*

"Hmm…that's strange," said Racer.

"What?"

Racer tugged down on the back of the Silkstealer's jacket. "He's not Salted. No suit."

284 ~ AARON GALVIN

He's not Salted, but his two deputies are...who is this guy?

"How can he know of our world if he hasn't been Salted?" Racer asked.

"Don't have time to worry about it now," said Lenny. "We gotta get outta here before Oscar finishes his job."

Lenny heard Ellie grunt. She struggled to lift Garrett.

"Ugh," she said. "This kid sure is heavy."

"He's an Orc," said Lenny. "Just be glad ya can lift him at all. If he'd made a full change before there's no way any of us could move him."

Ellie pushed Garrett to a sitting position and wrapped her arms under his armpits. Inching her hips under her, she lifted him onto her shoulder, grunting all the way, until Garrett's upper torso hung flat against her backside. Her face turned a violent shade of red as she used the table for leverage, and struggled to her feet. She blew hot air, locked her knees. "Got him."

"Head out." said Lenny. "Racer and I'll follow with the Silksteala."

Ellie nodded, then staggered out the door.

Lenny watched her go. A whimper came from behind him. He turned. "Whatsamatta?"

"I-I don't know..." said Racer.

"Pup, ya just said outside ya wanted this."

"I know. But now...now it's real. What will happen if we...if we do this...that's real. I can't ever take it back."

Lenny grimaced. "No, ya can't. So make up ya mind 'cause right now's the only shot ya got at gettin' out."

"I-I don't know if I-I can do this..."

Lenny smacked his cheek. "Ya can. Now man up. Ya can't stay a pup foreva."

"But, L-Len…it's, it's not right—none of this is right. We're sl-slaving people."

"Lemme tell ya something. People get slaved no matta what ya want. Only question is whattaya gonna do about it? Ya gotta take care of ya'self in this world. Nobody else will. So make ya decision and make it fast."

"W-what about you."

"I'm a Dolan, pup."

Racer rubbed the snot from his nose. Sniffed back the rest. "I'll do it."

"Kay," said Lenny. "Get his arms, I'll lift his legs."

Lenny picked up the Silkstealer's feet and shuffled backward through the open door. He watched the human hammock sway back and forth as Racer pushed faster down the hall. Beads of sweat broke out across Lenny's forehead.

"Door," said Racer.

Lenny didn't stop. He backed against it, popping it open. Dusk had been overtaken by night since first they went in. Lenny thanked the Ancients for it.

"Psst! Get over here!" Ellie said, crouched behind a cop car, still holding tight to Garrett's body.

"Elle, whattaya—"

"Hurry!" She waved them over. *"Police!"*

Both catchers dropped to the ground. They crawled for the car, dragging the Silkstealer's body with them. Ellie grabbed the lapels of his jacket as they neared and helped pull the rest of the way.

Lenny thunked his head against the side door. Had they been a second later the approaching car would have bathed them in head-lights. He leaned down to look beneath the vehicle.

The officer parked next to them. Lenny assumed the window must be down else he would not have been able to overhear the radio chatter.

"*You here yet, Campbell?*"

"Just pulled in, Sheriff."

"*Well, get in here quick and double time. Something about these fellas stinks to high Hades. Got Murphy chattin' up one of them now so I could slip away. Guy gives all the right answers, but I swear there's something…fishy…about him.*"

"Copy that. On my way."

A car door slammed. Lenny heard keys jangling and the creaking of a leather belt as the officer ran inside.

Racer stood. Lenny jerked him back down. "*Stop.*" He mouthed. "*Wait.*"

They stayed that way for what felt like an hour before Lenny released the pup. His earrings vibrated. Light shone through them and reflected off the car. Lenny clapped his ears to strike it out.

Lenny, Oscar's voice echoed in his head. *We're just outside the main hall. Henry says we need backup, now. I tend to disagree, seeing as they're only Drybacks, but he remains adamant.*

Lenny thought through his plan a final time. *I'll be there,* he said to Oscar. *There's anotha cop headed ova to ya. And if ya see one Selkie in there, I'll bet his partna's around too. Wait for me.*

I don't wait for you, Oscar said. *I tell you. Get in here, now.*

Aye, aye.

Lenny turned his attention to Ellie and Racer. "We hit a snag. The two of ya gotta go without me. That means…"

"No," said Ellie solemnly. "No, it has to happen like you said. One of us…I'll take your place."

Lenny cursed. "Fine. Stick to the plan. I'll hold 'em up as long as I can."

Racer shook his head. "Lenny, I—"

"Man up." Lenny clapped him on the shoulder. "I'll see ya on the other side."

Lenny ran back into the jail before Racer could reply. Sprinting down the conference corridor, he reached to his ears to cover the flash as he spoke to his crewmates. *Paulie, tell me what ya see.*

Three Drybacks, plus the Selkie I took down. Drybacks seem antsy, especially the Sheriff. He looks ready to have a shootout. He's cursing up a storm about how it's his jail and he wants some answers.

Good, said Lenny, already hearing the sheriff's voice. *It'll keep 'em distracted.*

He reached the end of the hall and stopped at the corner. Lenny peeked around, into the processing area. The red-faced sheriff thundered on and on at the main desk, one of his officers at his side; the elder Selkie, Deputy Smith, stood behind the desk with another officer. The officers looked sternly ahead, following their sheriff's lead. Deputy Smith gave an occasional nod, but otherwise seemed unconcerned, to Lenny's mind.

You here yet, nipperkin?

Lenny sighed. *I'm here, Oscar. Tryin' to figure out what to do next.*

Why? We should rush in of course. Four of them against four of us...well...three and a half of us. But Henry more than makes up the difference for you.

Lenny surveyed the room again. He saw another door to the left corner, far behind the processing desk. *Ya back there, Bourgeois?* He wondered. *Is today the day ya get caught?* He looked at the officers. *Oscar, that desk is at least fifteen yards away from ya. Now maybe ya can get there before they draw their guns, but maybe ya can't.*

Paulo groaned. *Great…here we go again.*

What? Why is Paulo unhappy? Oscar asked. *What's your suggestion, Lenny?*

A distraction. Something to shoot at while the rest of us sneak up.

Shoot at? Oscar said. *Why not just walk in and—*

Cause that Selkie'll recognize us by our coats. The second he draws his weapon, the others will too. We might get to the first of 'em, but it's risky.

Leesin' to 'im, said Henry.

Well, Oscar scoffed. *I hardly think my father would think it prudent for me to provide the distraction, nor Henry either. We're far too valuable.*

Paulie…

I knew I didn't like where this was going…

Paulie, ya the biggest and the baddest, pal, said Lenny. *Time to give 'em a show they neva seen before.*

KELLEN

"SOMEBODY'S COMING..." BOONE SCURRIED TO PRESS his face flat against the bars.

Kellen turned in his cot. "Shut up, Boo—"

The cellblock door buzzed open.

Kellen sat up. He heard two pairs of footsteps, one heavy and the other light, proceeding down the row.

"Who's out there?" Boone shouted. "Campbell? You come to let me out? I'm s'posed to stay here for two nights more! Sheriff Hullinger hisself said I could!"

"I'm no sheriff and I'm not here to let any of you sorry S.O.B.s out," a cold voice answered. "I'm Deputy Marshal Foster and that's how you'll address me, whoever you are."

"Deputy Marshal?" Boone sounded delighted. "What's somebody like you doing in Lavere County?"

Kellen stepped to the door of his cell.

A white guy not much older than himself ambled up the row, escorting a black girl in handcuffs. Both wore strange, hooded sweatshirts, tucked into their pants. Kellen thought it odd for a marshal to dress so casually. Not to mention the young marshal wore crystal-studded earrings.

The girl laid eyes on Kellen. She immediately backed into the marshal, screaming.

Kellen stepped back. *She on crack?*

Foster glanced at Kellen, then back to the girl. "Bourgeois, calm down. What's the matter with you?"

The girl would not be calmed. She ranted in a language Kellen couldn't understand, and pointed at the deputy's gun belt. The two of them spoke to one another in the strange language; the deputy's voice calm and steady, the girl's pleading.

"Hey! You two ain't from here, huh?" Boone asked.

Kellen stepped closer to the door again, placed his hands on the bars. He watched the deputy shove the girl into an open cell. She kept her footing, despite the rough treatment, and disappeared to the furthest corner of her cell, cloaking herself in shadow. Kellen noticed she never took her gaze off of him.

"Hey, mister," Boone said. "Where you folks come from?"

The red-faced deputy slammed the girl's door closed. "Elsewhere."

Boone scratched his head. "Hmm, never heard of it. That in Indiana? Say, what's she yelling about anyway? Sheriff Hullinger don't usually let females in these cells."

Foster walked to Kellen's cell, his hand on the grip of his gun. "Sheriff Porker's not in charge right now, is he?"

"Don't know no Sheriff Porker, but Sheriff Hullinger don't let females in these cells."

Deputy Foster stopped just shy of Kellen's cell. "Who are you?"

Don't look away. Kellen glared back at Deputy Foster. "Why do you care?"

"Wouldn't say I care at all. I am curious though. Who are you to make the infamous Marisa Bourgeois over there throw such a fit?"

"You tell me," said Kellen. "I don't know her."

Deputy Foster looked Kellen up and down, studying him before he spoke. "Yeah. I don't think you do. What they put you away for?"

Don't answer that. Doesn't dad always complain about his idiot clients that opened their mouths when they shouldn't? Kellen stepped forward. "Ask my lawyer."

Deputy Foster laughed. "No need to get lawyers involved. I'll just ask your buddy over here." He glanced over his shoulder at Boone.

"He's not my buddy," said Kellen. "He's just the town drunk."

Deputy Foster grinned. "Is that right? Well, nothing wrong with drunks."

The deputy took a flask from a pocket near his stomach, opened it and took a swig.

"Say…" Boone smacked his lips with his tongue. "What you got there? Smells good."

Deputy Foster took another swig, gave a long satisfied sigh. "Oh, you wouldn't like this stuff, old timer. Nasty."

Great. Kellen watched the old man reach both his scrawny arms through the bars, clawing for the flask Foster dangled in front of him.

"Well…le—lemme try it…Cain't tell what I like if you won't lemme try it."

Foster smirked at Kellen. "You wanna tell me what you're in for yet? Or do I have to get the answer from drunkie over here?"

Kellen shrugged. "He can't tell you what he doesn't know."

"We'll see." Foster turned to Boone. "Tell you what, drunkie. I'll give you a swig if you tell me what I want to know about this guy. What's he in for?"

Boone smacked his lips again. "Cain't rightly remember now. A drink would probably help."

"Played this game before, huh?"

Foster knelt and slid the flask across the floor. It hit Boone's cell door with a light *clink.*

Kellen watched the old man fall to his knees. Boone snatched the flask up like he had found a winning lottery ticket. He upended the drink, guzzled it down, and finished with a loud belch.

"Mighty tasty, mister. Got any more?"

"Afraid not," Foster said. "Bit of Raggie's grog goes a long way though. Now, to my question...what did my new buddy do to end up in here with you?"

Kellen looked past the deputy. "Don't tell him, Boone."

The old man fumbled with the flask, cast his eyes downward. "His name's Kellen Winstel and he 'bout killed a boy close to his age."

Kellen shook his head. *It was a prank.*

"*Killed* you say?" said Deputy Foster.

Is that respect I hear in your voice, deputy?

"Yessir. Tried to drown the boy. His friends even said so."

Deputy Foster clucked his tongue. "There a lot of ways to kill a man. Drowning though...now, that's a pretty personal way of handling your business. Takes effort...control."

Kellen saw a shadow move. The girl across the row now watched him too. Her hands gripped the bars on her cell door, and her breath came ragged and quick.

Foster glanced back at her. "You hear that, Bourgeois? We have a killer amongst us. That what got you so scared?"

Marisa shook her head no.

Act tough. He thinks you're a killer? Let him. Kellen stepped all the way to his door, inches from Foster's face. "Maybe she thinks I'm in the KKK."

Foster pursed his lips. "Nah. She claims you're part of a rougher crowd than a bunch of ignorant cowards with sheets on their heads. Ever hear of the Sancul?"

"That lick...some kiney...cult, er some'n?" Boone slurred.

"Don't be rude, drunkie. Didn't anyone ever teach you not to speak 'less you're spoken to?" Foster looked at Kellen. "You ever hear of them?"

"Maybe," Kellen said. "What's it to you?"

"I thought not." Foster turned toward the girl's cell. "You're grasping in the reeds now, huh, Bourgeois? Trying to get me to buy-in on all your superstitions."

Marisa peered around Foster, squinting to see Kellen better. She closed her eyes and muttered in a language Kellen couldn't understand. Then she stopped and opened them again.

"He *is* a Surface Watcher, a Dweller of the Deep," she said ominously.

Cramps started in Kellen's calves and ran up to his thighs. He fell on his bunk. *Ah...what is happening?* Kellen massaged the pain.

Marisa continued. "And I gave you true advice. You should kill him now to save those you love and will leave behind...before he leads you to your doom."

"Before he leads me to my doom?" Foster said. "Why, he couldn't even finish the job on some kid according to drunkie over there."

Marisa leveled her eyes at the deputy. "You claim your name is Foster, but you lie," she said. "I do not. You will die tonight... Richard Caspar."

Foster's face paled.

"Yes. I know your true name. The tides sang it to me…" Marisa closed her eyes and swayed. "Among other things."

The tides sang it to her? Is this another part of your prank, Dad? Kellen tried to stand. His legs failed him. "Hey, Foster, where did you find this loony?"

Deputy Foster did not share his humor. "What other things?"

Marisa opened her green eyes. "It does not matter. You will not live to see them."

Foster slammed his palm against her cell. Kellen jumped. Marisa did not.

"You lie, girl," Foster seethed. "No one can know such things!"

Marisa did not waver. "He *is* a Sancul," she continued. "And your fate is sealed, Caspar…unless you kill him now. Before he learns of our world, before his destiny finds him."

"Twenty bucks says my destiny is going to prison, right?" Kellen jeered. "Hey, look, I'm a fortune teller too! What'd she say your name is…Casper?"

Foster wheeled on Kellen. "Don't call me that! That man doesn't exist anymore!"

"You won't soon," Marisa said.

"Stop saying that!"

"*Kill* him," she urged. "And swim the green waters in peace, knowing your actions saved others."

Goose pimples whispered up Kellen's neck.

"Hey! I don't even know you!" He shouted at Marisa. "Why do you want me dead?"

A single tear ran down Marisa's cheek. "Because of the monster you will become and the thousands who will die for it. I am sorry. The songs sometimes change, but they do not lie."

Kellen heard a *click.*

Foster had unclasped his gun holster. His hand trembled on the grip.

Whoa. What's he doing?

"How do you know all this?" Foster asked Marisa.

She bowed her head. "I am a Servant of Senchis and the Ancients."

Warmth pulsed through Kellen's legs. The pain dissipated, and he found himself able to stand again. *What just happened?*

"*Pffftt.* Nothing but Salt stories."

"And yet their songs are still sung," Marisa said. "They *sang* to me. And I listened when they told me to run. How else could I have avoided capture from so many for so long? Their songs guided me from slavery long ago, just as they led me here tonight. They will lead me out again…soon."

"Some place they led you to," Foster said. He drew his gun from its holster and pointed it at her head. "Did they sing you this song too?"

Whoa. Kellen cowered to the back of his cell.

"They led me here," said Marisa, unfazed. "Others will soon take us from this place. You will see," she nodded at Kellen. Then she turned back to Deputy Foster. "You will not."

Foster's hand trembled so much he dropped his gun. He scrambled to pick it back up.

The girl's crazy. He's crazy. Kellen tried to stay as quiet as he could. He looked over to Boone's cell in hopes the old drunk might say something to keep Foster from blowing the girl's head off. Instead, he saw Boone asleep, without snoring for a change, with Foster's flask tucked against his chest.

Kellen turned back, and saw down the barrel of Foster's handgun. He nearly wet his pants.

"Tell me what you know of the Salt," Foster demanded.

"The s-salt? I don't know anything about any salt."

"Tell me!"

What is he talking about? "Foster, listen," said Kellen. "I'm not lying. I don't—"

A bellowing roar echoed from somewhere deep in the main station, followed by gunfire in quick succession.

Foster spun to face the entrance. Bright spectrums of light shone from his earrings.

Kellen blinked. *Did his earrings...flash?*

"They have come, Caspar," Marisa said ominously. "Do what must be done."

Foster sneered as he removed a chain of keys from his pocket. He opened Marisa's door, yanked her out, and pushed her up against the cell next to Kellen's. "Bryant can decide what to do with him. Don't move."

Kellen looked at Marisa. She did not seem near as afraid now, resigned even to obey Foster's order. Kellen heard the clink of another lock popping.

Foster had opened his door. He had also trained his aim at Kellen's head. "Out! Now. And put your hands behind your back."

Kellen turned around. "Okay...just don't...don't shoot me."

Foster slapped on the metal bracelets, tightening them so deep Kellen thought he might lose circulation.

The roars came more frequent now, and Kellen swore he heard shotgun fire added to the fray.

"Bourgeois," Foster barked. "Ladies first."

Marisa stepped in front of Kellen, her head held high. She led the way down the aisle toward the jail block entrance.

Foster pushed Kellen in the direction of the noise. "Walk."

Kellen heard someone screaming. More gunfire. More roaring. He stopped. *What's happening out there...and why are we going toward it?*

A gun barrel pressed against the back of his head, and he felt a tickle in his ear as Foster leaned close to give the command.

"Move."

LENNY

THE SHOTGUN BLAST BLEW A HOLE IN THE DESK behind Lenny.

Move! Move! Move! Hunched low, he ran to a nearby cubicle. Lenny slid in and used his head to nudge away the rolling chair. He crawled beneath the desk, and sat up, leaned out to take another look.

The main processing desk had been uprooted, flipped on its side to provide cover. He saw the elder Selkie, Deputy Smith, raise his gun and point it. Lenny ducked behind the desk, tucked his head.

Gunshots ripped through the siding where he had just been and marble chips exploded off the floor.

"Ya missed me, Smitty!" Lenny yelled above the din.

More shots followed.

Hell's bells. Lenny took a deep breath. *One…two…three!*

Lenny darted out and ran for the next cubicle. Shots ricocheted around him. He dove beneath the next desk.

Paulo's roar carried throughout the room.

Lenny crawled to his knees. Through the makeshift cubicle slats, he saw an officer firing his weapon at random. The sheriff hunkered low beside him, reloading his shotgun. Lenny saw a door to their backs.

A shotgun blast eradicated one of Lenny's cubicle walls. He cringed and his earrings flashed. *I'm pinned down. There's two of 'em in front of a door marked as processin'. If any of ya can get there—*

Lenny heard a loud, long hiss followed by a man's bloodcurdling scream. He peeked through the slats again.

A slender, silvery seal with black spots and a snake-like head had surprised the sheriff and his officer.

Henry!

The sheriff wasted no time in leaving the officer behind.

"Campbell, get outta there!"

The officer reacted too slowly.

All nine hundred pounds of Henry's seal body crashed into Campbell, knocking him down. Henry hissed again, then clamped his seal jaws around Campbell's neck. With a quick, savage jerk, he ripped out Campbell's throat. Henry dropped the limp body, and hissed at the sheriff with blood-stained teeth.

No! Lenny moved forward.

Another shotgun blast cautioned him back.

The sheriff ran from the carnage, his belly bouncing like a water balloon.

Lenny heard two popping sounds and saw a pair of button-sized holes appear in the sheriff's chest. The sheriff fell dead and skidded a few feet, careening into the first desk Lenny hid behind. An expanding pond of dark crimson seeped out to surround him.

Oscar stepped from behind the processing door to see his kill. Grinning smugly, he lowered his gun. His earrings flashed. *Did you all see that? Did you all see me shoot him? And on the run too! Father will be so proud!*

"Die, you demons!"

The glass in the processing door shattered. Oscar dipped behind it.

Lenny's earrings flashed. *Henry! Earn ya keep already!*

The Leopard Seal hissed in reply, and slithered over to protect his benefactor.

Oscar! Free Henry!

Lenny saw Oscar grab hold of the seal's upper lip and pull back. The sealskin melted away.

The officer behind the desk screamed. "Demons! They're demons!" he cried, firing anew.

Henry, Lenny shouted. *Get Oscar outta here.*

"He killed Dick Hullinger," the officer behind the overturned desk said. "That boy killed the sheriff."

Lenny saw Deputy Smith try in vain to pull the officer back to safety. "Murphy, get back here, you fool!"

Murphy would not be stopped. He walked straight for the processing door, firing his gun with every step.

Henry shoved Oscar inside and closed the door.

"Die you devils!" Murphy cried. "Die!"

His gun clicked empty.

Run, ya idiot.

Henry burst out of the door, his jagged coral dagger in hand. He leapt straight at Murphy with a wicked gleam in his eyes.

Murphy screamed.

Henry thrust his blade into Murphy's chest, twisting it at the last, silencing him forever.

Lenny grimaced.

And now zere eez only one, Henry said.

"Come on then!" Smith called out from behind the safety of the desk. "Anyone can kill Drybacks, you sorry Selkie slavers! Let's see how you handle one of your own."

Smith leaned over the side and took pot shots at a row of tipped filing cabinets. The shots sparked off the sides.

Paulie, Lenny said. *Where are ya?*

You see where he's shooting? That's where I am. The old man's had me pinned down since the second he saw my ugly mug.

I'll give—

Lenny stopped. The back corner door had been opened and a shaved-headed teen tossed amongst the fray. The teen's wrists had been cuffed and he stumbled on the remnants of table, chairs, and flooring. Lenny thought his eyes looked wild, but whatever fear the teen had did not paralyze him.

The teen used his long legs to push backward and scramble inside an empty cubicle. At every lapse in the gunfire, the teen worked toward the next space, always moving closer to the exit.

At least he's no fool. Lenny thought to himself.

Lenny pictured Paulo in his mind. His earrings flashed. *Paulie. I'm gonna give ya a distraction. When I say go, get movin'.*

Aye, aye, boss.

Lenny stood, put his hands to the edges of the cubicle. *Ready... one...two...go!*

Lenny shoved away. "Hey, Smitty!"

He ran for the handcuffed teen's cubicle.

Shots sang out, always just behind him.

Lenny heard Paulo roar. He glanced over his shoulder, saw Paulo in his Salt form slop toward the main desk.

Paulo bled from several wounds, but still his tank of an Elephant

Seal body continued. He roared again and crashed into the desk, his sheer force breaking it in half.

Smith leapt clear of the debris.

No! Lenny skidded to a halt, and turned to go back.

Smith raised his gun to Paulo's seal head. "Die, you motherless—"

Lenny dove at the older Selkie's kneecaps.

"Ah!" Smith cried out. His shot went wild, his gun clattering to the floor.

Paulo shuffled over, and laid his enormous weight across Smith's body.

Lenny heard Smith suck air. "Stay down, Smitty!"

"Dolan!"

Lenny whipped around at hearing his name called. He cursed when he saw Deputy Foster in the doorway the shaved-headed teen had been kicked from. He cursed again when he saw Foster held a gun to his hostage, Marisa Bourgeois.

"I got what you're looking for," said Foster. "Now tell that piece of blubber to move!"

"Richie...no..." Smith coughed.

"Ya really gonna kill her, Fosta?" Lenny shouted back. "Go for it. I don't need her alive. We'll kill ya and then take her body back. End result's the same for us."

"I don't believe you!"

"Ya don't have to."

Keep 'im talking, nipperkin, Henry said.

Lenny saw movement from the corner of his eye; Henry inched forward while Oscar moved along a side cubicle, both of them hidden from Foster's view.

They're gonna trap him.

"Let her go, Fosta," Lenny said. "It's the only way ya walkin' outta here alive."

Lenny heard clinking metal. His gaze swept to the left. The teen convict had hopped to his feet, and his cuffs had echoed off the filing cabinet he used for support. He ran for the conference hall door.

"No!" Lenny shouted. "Stay down!"

Foster instinctually turned to see to whom Lenny spoke.

Oscar's sick laugh echoed in Lenny's mind. *And now you die.*

Lenny dropped to the floor, thinking the threat had been meant for him.

Two gunshots rang out.

Lenny saw the bullets rip through Foster's neck. His blood splattered the nearby wall like someone flicked a wet paintbrush against it.

Foster fell like a mannequin with no rod to support it. His body crumpled to the floor, his eyes still open. They lifelessly stared at the teen convict.

"No!" Deputy Smith howled, reaching.

He's dead.

Lenny half-expected Marisa to dash away, now freed from her captor. Instead, he saw her gaze hone in on the teen convict. She solemnly nodded at him, then knelt beside Foster's body and bowed her head in prayer.

The teen stood in the door as if frozen, unable to tear his eyes away from the dead marshal staring back at him.

Lenny's focus flickered between the two of them, Marisa and the teen convict. *Who are ya, pup? And why is Marisa Bourgeois so interested in ya?*

CHIDI

CHIDI WANTED TO SCREAM, TO STRUGGLE AND FIGHT her iron bonds. She did neither. Experience had taught her it would do no good and would leave her exhausted.

She could not say whether a minute or hours had passed since she had been locked away. Time itself seemed swallowed up in the blanketing dark.

Please let in a little light, she prayed. *Just a little light.*

Her left eye ached from where Henry had struck her. The pain from her throbbing forehead she welcomed. She would relish the memory of slamming her skull into his for the rest of her life. In those few seconds, she had been free of him.

She would add it to her special memories, those of home and family. Her mother singing while she fixed the fish nets, her father's baritone voice, even the joy she once felt watching dolphins skip waves off the coast before she knew the truth about them.

This trip to the Hard had brought new memories she would hold to—the knowledge in Marisa's notebooks, how she challenged them atop the Shedd Aquarium's ledge, and her graceful dive.

"There is always a choice," Chidi whispered aloud, despite the soreness in her throat.

Henry may have robbed Chidi of her innocence, her home, even ravaged her body, but he could not take away her choices. Chidi repeated it in the Afrikaans language Marisa first spoke to her, drawing strength from the words made real.

"Daar is *altyd* 'n keuse…"

Chidi tried to arch her back. Pain shot through her bound limbs. She screamed, knowing no one could hear her.

It'll all be over soon, she tried to calm herself.

Henry may help the others catch the Orcinian, but he would take her and leave once he received his payment. Then he would court her again in his own sick way, speaking endlessly about the things he would do to her upon their return to his cave. How no one could ever love her like he did.

Chidi turned her head to retch. She rubbed her cheek against the floor in an attempt to scrape off the remainder of vomit. It only succeeded in wetting the side of her face further. She turned away to blow the last bits of puke and reflected back on her newest companions to stave off any other thoughts of Henry.

She hadn't wasted time befriending Paulo or Racer. Any friendship there could not last. Ellie had been the closest thing to a female friend Chidi had made since being taken, but she still felt little kinship there.

And Lenny. Chidi wished for more time to know him better and allow him to truly know her.

She would have no chance now that Henry locked her in the under. He may bring her up a few times to lay with him, but he would not dream of letting her leave his side for long. Nor would he give her earrings back to speak with the others. He would keep her not just in the physical darkness, but deaf to the conversations she might have listened in on and enjoyed.

306 ~ AARON GALVIN

She heard a clunking near her feet and thought a rat had possibly stowed away with her. A *swoosh* came from the hold door's automatic springs. Light fought through the darkness, then she heard a clanking of keys. Hands worked feverishly at the locks on her legs.

"Who's there?" Chidi asked, her voice hoarse. *Who cares! Don't ask them any questions. They might go away!*

"It's me...Ellie!"

The shackles made a loud cracking noise and fell off, rattling when they landed on the floorboard.

"Ellie! What are you doing here?" Chidi whispered, afraid someone might overhear.

The big girl crawled inside, panting. Her hands worked up Chidi's midsection, guided their way up her arms.

"I've come to free—ah, whew, that stinks!" Ellie said. She slid her hands down to Chidi's wrists. "Here we go!"

The pressure eased as the cuffs fell off. *Is this a dream?*

"I'm here to free you," Ellie said. "We have to hurry though! Come on!"

Chidi flexed her fingers to speed the bloodflow's return. She winced when she began to feel it.

Ellie dragged her to the edge by her ankle.

Chidi filled her nostrils with the scent of fresh air. She exhaled and opened her eyes to see the night sky. *Thank you,* she offered to whomever had answered her prayers and sent Ellie.

Ellie yanked Chidi to her feet. "Come on, you have to walk. We don't have much time."

"Ellie—"

"Come on, Chidi! Do you want to be free or not?"

Ellie hunched over the Silkstealer's body. Unconscious and without his cowboy hat, he did not seem near as intimidating. Chidi thought he looked sad in unconscious sleep.

She gasped at the one lain beside the Silkstealer; the one whose skin tone marked him as an Orc.

Chidi saw past that. She saw one who would awaken far from home, enslaved to a world he could never truly come back from. "Garrett Weaver," she said, her tone hushed.

"You know," said Ellie. "I've never been this close to an Orcinian before. He's not light, I'll tell you that."

"But...what are you doing with them?"

"They're coming with us, back to the Salt—" Ellie smiled at Chidi. "You aren't."

"What?"

"Time to run, sister. Tonight. *Now.*"

"But I—I can't. Henry will come for me," Chidi gushed.

"That's why we're sending you help." Ellie whistled.

Racer hopped out of the bus, shouldering Zymon's canvas pack. "Hiya, Chidi."

"Racer, stop talking! You'll have time for that later!" Ellie said. "Help me put the Orc and Silkstealer in here."

*They're insane...*Chidi watched them work. *They've both gone mad!*

Together, Racer and Ellie lifted Garrett into the cell where Chidi had been held captive. Racer climbed inside to drag their newest prisoner under his arms. He lay Garrett's head down next to the other teens, then proceeded to shackle his wrists while Ellie fastened his ankles.

"Ugh!" Racer said. "Chidi, did you die in here or is that smell from the dead one?"

"You want to complain or be free, pup?" Ellie shouted at him. "Keep moving!"

"You're actually taking him?" Chidi asked. "Why?"

"Lenny says they have to," Racer said. "It gives us a better chance to escape."

"*Us?*"

Racer grinned. "I'm running with you."

"Not if you don't hurry," Ellie huffed. She dropped six pairs of clanking shackles inside the cell. "Here! When you're done with these, get those other chains the heavy ones—and put them on him too! I'm going to steal that SUV for you."

Racer reached for the other shackles and clasped them to Garrett's arms. "I'll put these on him, but not the chains. I should be in a hurry, remember?"

"Fine, fine, whatever! I'll put the chains on him later. Chidi, come with me!" Ellie thrust a ring of keys into her hands. "Unlock Allambee and Zymon. Don't free the Leper until I'm back, though!"

Chidi stood with the keys in hand, unable to move.

Ellie sprinted across the street for the jail's front entrance.

Meanwhile, Racer had already finished with Garrett's arms and worked to shackle the Silkstealer. "Come on, Chidi! Why aren't you moving?"

"I—I don't—I don't. Why are you both doing this?"

"Lenny told us to. Guess he's not so tough after all. Well, that or he wants to stick it to Oscar. Take your pick," Racer shrugged. "Anyway, he thinks Oscar won't waste his time chasing us down. The Crayfish will never have to know about these Drybacks that Oscar wanted to enslave. Besides, he'll be more than happy having an Orc *and* the Silkstealer to sell."

"But Racer, if you run...your father...August will kill him—"

"Did you not listen to me back at the zoo? My father told me to run if I had the chance, Chidi!" Racer's earrings flashed. "Come on. Let's get Allambee and Zymon out of those chains. Lenny says we're moving too slow."

"Lenny says—You're talking to him right now?"

"Not really. He just asks about our progress, then yells at me when I say we haven't left yet."

Racer leapt from inside the hold, then ran to another and opened its hatch.

Chidi saw Allambee and Zymon bound together. She ran to Allambee's side to help with the locks. *Which one of them did this to you?*

Racer tore Zymon's blindfold off and yanked down his gag.

"Help! Someone—"

Racer clamped a hand over Zymon's mouth. "Shut up! I'm here to free you, do you understand? I'll free you. Nod if you get me."

Chidi watched Racer's earrings light up each time he spoke. *Those are Lenny's words he's using...Lenny's telling Racer what to say right now!*

Zymon's eyes darted back and forth, his breath rapid. After a minute, he nodded.

"Good," Racer said. "You know anybody who can help take suits off?"

Zymon nodded.

"Okay then, here's the deal," Racer said in his best impression of Lenny. "I'll set you and your Leper free, but we're coming with you. We all run together. Once we get you back to Chicago, you get us out of our sealskins and into hiding. Agreed?"

Zymon nodded.

"I'm going to take my hand off your mouth. You yell again for help though and I'll leave you here for them to take back to the Salt." Racer took his hand away.

Zymon opened and closed his jaw, working out the stiffness. He looked at Chidi. *"Je to pravda?"*

"Yes, he's telling you the truth," she answered his question. "They'll free you, if you agree to help us."

"That I offer gladly," Zymon spoke English. "If you see me safely home, my friends will become yours. I swear it on my daughter's life."

Racer unlocked Zymon's shackles. "Agreed."

Bright lights bathed them.

Chidi cringed, like a startled cat, believing them caught.

Ellie killed the Silkstealer's SUV headlights. "You don't have them free yet?"

"I'm working on it!" Racer said.

"Work faster!"

Ellie ran to the two unconscious teens. She lifted them like an ox under its yoke and carried them to the vehicle. "Chidi, get the trunk open for me!"

Chidi obeyed and saw Ellie had already lain the third row down to accommodate the bodies. *Can this be? Or am I still inside the bus, locked away and dreaming?*

"Why are you doing this?" she asked.

Ellie hauled the two living teens into the back and closed the trunk. "It's the right thing to do."

"But they'll punish you."

"I've been whipped before," Ellie said. "Least this time it'll be worth it."

"What about Paulo? Lenny?"

"Paulo doesn't know," Ellie said. "He's a horrible liar. He means well, but he would give us away without meaning to."

Thunder from an incoming storm rumbled in the distance, warning them to leave.

"And Lenny?" Chidi asked.

Ellie laughed. "Lenny's fine with it, trust me. Men are always quick to follow a plan so long as it was their idea."

"Right..." Chidi agreed, trying to comprehend how this all occurred.

Ellie handed Chidi three wallets. "Here. They belong to those Drybacks. I'd drop them off somewhere soon before they wake up, not near here though."

Chidi looked back at the hold she had shared with them.

They had left the dead one on the cold slab of steel next to Garrett.

"What will you do with him?"

"Does it matter? His problems are over," Ellie said. "We have to think about ours."

Scratching and pounding echoed from inside the bus. Racer bounded out of Allambee and Zymon's cell and over to the Leper's.

Allambee climbed out. He groggily leaned against the side. Zymon stretched his back and rubbed his wrists, watching them.

Ellie scooted in front of Chidi to where Zymon could not see. "Take this too."

She shoved a tranquilizer gun in Chidi's pocket. "Lenny used the last tranq to knock out the Orc. There's no rounds left, but you can always pretend if those two try anything."

The Leper growled from his cell.

Zymon rushed to the edge of the pen. "I am here, Wotjek. Lie still my friend! They have come to free us, but we must hurry."

Ellie's earrings sparkled. She looked at the jail. "It's past time you all left."

Chidi approached Allambee. *What do I say? How do I tell him what we're doing, or even why?*

Allambee stood to greet her. "Hello, Chidi," he said. "You seem sad when you should be happy."

"I am happy...to see you again. I was afraid—"

"Because you left me?"

"Yes," Chidi said.

Allambee grinned. "And yet you have come back. Why did you fear for me?"

"Because you're still just a boy. You shouldn't have had to see these things. No one should."

"My mutha says we are all but children in de Creator's eyes. In my village, de wise men say a boy runs from fear. A man draws it close to him and takes its strength for his own," Allambee paused. "I see you are stronger now also."

"Uh...Chidi..." Racer tapped her. "We need to go."

Chidi took Allambee by the hand. "Come on. Let's go be free."

Together, they turned toward the others. Wotjek stood close to Zymon, like he thought his master's release a ruse.

Racer walked to Ellie—sitting in the hold with Garrett Weaver—and took a knee.

Chidi could not understand why. She saw Garrett's tennis shoes pointed upward, locked in place by iron fetters. *He's taking my place. Lenny's plan frees seven at the cost of one.*

Chidi knew she should be grateful, but could not fight the nagging feeling she sinned by leaving Garrett to the life she had suffered through. But when she looked back on him again, shackled where she lay not ten minutes ago, she could not bring herself to trade places with him.

"Will you tell him—"

"Tell who what?" Ellie asked.

"Him…" Chidi pointed to Garrett's body. "Tell him what he did. That we're free because of him."

"It's not like he made this decision, Chidi," Racer said.

Zymon appeared beside her. "Come. Let us leave this place before the others return and learn what has happened here."

"Please tell him, Ellie," Chidi begged.

"I can't."

"He will know someday," Zymon comforted her. "When he swims in Fiddler's Green, the Ancients will sing to him on what his sacrifice amounted to this day."

Racer stood and Chidi saw that he had shackled Ellie's legs with a long iron fetter. He picked up a second one and raised it like a baseball hat.

Ellie trembled as she rolled to her stomach. She took a crawling position, like she would if she had been hunched to fit in the narrow space while shackling Garrett.

"Al-all right…Let's get this over with."

The fetter's end swayed back and forth in Racer's nervous hands.

"What are you doing?" Chidi asked.

"It h-has to look real…" Racer's voice broke. "Oscar has to think I-I knocked her out when we brought him back."

Chidi grasped Racer's plan. "No! You can't! You could kill Ellie if you hit her in the wrong place with that thing!"

"Do it, pup," Ellie's voice cracked with fearful resolve. "Hit me."

Racer drew a deep breath. The edge of the fetter twitched.

Chidi started forward.

Zymon restrained her.

"Racer...don't..."

Tears fell down Racer's cheeks. "I have to...Oscar won't believe her if I don't!"

"Wotjek," Zymon said softly. *"To zrobić."*

Wotjek strode forward, tore the fetter from Racer's hands, and rained a blow across the back of Ellie's head.

She slumped beside Garrett.

"No!" Chidi cried. "You killed her!"

Zymon held her close. "Wotjek did a necessary thing. But he knows how to kill and when not to. He meant your friend no ill will, nor did he harm her much."

Racer touched the sides of Ellie's neck for a pulse. "She's okay. Bleeding and knocked out, but she's alive."

Zymon released Chidi. "It has to look real and for that it must hurt. Now we must go, or your friend's sacrifice will be in vain."

Wotjek slammed the hold door shut, hiding what he had done. He kept the blunt weapon as he jogged to the SUV. He got in and started the engine.

Chidi numbly stared at the closed hold.

Zymon touched Racer's ears. "My friend...how can you ever be free when others fill your head with their thoughts?"

Racer pulled the crystal studs from his ears. He threw them at the bus.

Chidi heard two light clanks when they hit the side.

"Come on, Chidi," he tugged at her. "Let's go."

I meant to have a plan this time, she thought.

Allambee lightly touched her arm, galvanizing her. "We must leave."

A gust of wind whipped at her face, seeming to whisper Henry's threat. *I weel find you, Chidi...*

She glanced back to the bus. *I never said thank you.*

"Come on, Chidi!" Racer tugged at her.

Chidi shoved him away and ran for the bus. She fell to her knees, thrust her hands in front of her, searching.

"Chidi! What—"

"Help me!" she cried. "Help me find the crystals!"

"Chidi, you're acting crazy!"

"Help me!"

Allambee hurried to her side to help.

Wotjek gunned the engine.

"They're going to leave us!" Racer said.

Where are they? Where are they? Where are they?

The loose pavement gravel cut at Chidi's hands, but she would not relent.

"Chidi! I found one!" Allambee said.

Chidi snatched the crystal from his open palm. She could have kissed him in that moment. Instead, she placed it in her ear and pictured her captain.

Lenny...Lenny, are you there?

Racer dragged her away. "Come on! You can talk in the car!"

Lenny! She said. *Lenny?*

Allambee opened the door for her.

Chidi scooted for the middle. The boys jumped in on either side of her.

Wotjek floored the gas pedal. The tires squealed, catching traction, and sped them away.

Lenny. Come on…come on…please answer. Please! Lenny!

Lil' busy right now, Cheeds, Lenny's grumpy voice filled her mind. *Did ya leave yet?*

No, I wanted to say—

What? Whatsamatta with ya? Leave already!

Chidi bit her lip. *I wanted to say thank you. Thank you for—*

Are ya kiddin' me, Lenny said. *Get rid of those crystals, quit talkin' to me, and get on the road already!*

Okay, she blushed. *Goodbye, Lenny.*

Chidi removed the earring. She reached across Allambee, rolled the window down. *See you on the other side, Lenny Dolan.* She threw it out the window. Chidi leaned back, relaxed into her seat.

"You reach him?" Racer asked.

"Yeah."

"Any last words?"

"Mmm-hmm. He yelled at me."

Racer laughed. "I'm going to miss him."

Me too.

Wotjek sped through the abandoned parts of town, and turned northbound onto I-65 headed for Chicago. The road lay empty before them.

Chidi worried more about who might follow.

I weel find you, Chidi—Henry's phantom promised. *And keel ze ones you run weeth.*

She glanced out the rear window, and saw nothing but darkness.

She turned back around, laying her head on Allambee's shoul-

der. Chidi closed her eyes, and listened to the miles toward freedom tick away beneath her. She smiled.

No...you won't.

LENNY

LENNY POINTED HIS EMPTY GUN AT THE TEEN CON-
vict. "Goin' somewhere?"

The teen glanced at the exit.

"Don't make us chase ya," Lenny said. "Believe me, ya don't
want that."

"Who—who are you people? *What* are you?"

"Neva heard of Selkies?" Lenny shook his head. "I mean whatta'
they teachin' in schools these days?"

"I saw th-that guy…" he pointed at Henry. "He-he was a seal.
How is that possible?"

"Beats me, kid. I'm just a grunt. What's ya name?"

"K-Kell…Kellen Winstel." He looked to the door again.

"Don't do it." Lenny warned. "Ya run and Henry'll come for ya.
See what he did to the last guy?"

He jerked a thumb to the dead police officer lying in a pool of
his own blood.

"Ya don't wanna be that guy. So come on."

Lenny ushered him to the middle of the room.

Kellen gave Paulo a wide berth.

Lenny's earrings flashed. *Paulie, I think the kid's scared of ya.*

The seal grunted at Kellen.

Should've let him run. Lenny cursed himself. *Now Oscar's gonna take him back. One more gift for the Crayfish.*

Oscar strolled around from behind the cubicle he had used for cover. "Did everyone see my kill?"

I saw that ya coulda' killed Marisa by shootin' at Fosta.

Paulo prodded Lenny with a soft seal kiss. Then he lowered his massive head to the ground so Lenny could release him without having to jump.

Lenny took the Elephant Seal's lip in hand and pulled up, then back.

"Whoa…" Kellen said as Paulo's changes occurred.

Lenny's earrings flashed. *Cheeds…Racer…ya leave yet?*

No response. Lenny grinned.

Oscar sauntered over to him. "What are you so happy about?"

"How good a shot ya made. Ya might make a decent catcha after all."

The lie worked.

Oscar surveyed the carnage he had helped create. He stopped when he saw Foster's body. Oscar pointed the barrel of his gun. "Is he really dead, Henry?"

"*Oui.*" Henry walked to Marisa Bourgeois. He knelt beside her, ran his hand over her head. "Don't run from me, girl."

"I have no plans to run," Marisa said to Henry. "Please, let me finish my prayer."

"Prayer?" Oscar kicked Foster's body with his foot. The dead Selkie's arm flopped to the side with a loud slap. "Who would waste a prayer on this sorry lot?"

Marisa's eyes narrowed. "Prayer cannot be wasted."

Preach it, girlie. Lenny thought as Smith fell to his knees, weeping.

"You killed my boy...you killed my Richie."

Oscar turned his aim on the elder Selkie. "Yes. Yes, I did. I'm getting the hang of this primitive Dryback weaponry, wouldn't you agree?"

"You killed my boy..."

Ya boy asked for it. Lenny thought to himself. *If he had dropped his gun like I told him...*

Oscar smirked. "I could do you in too, if you like."

Henry toyed with Foster's hood. "*Monsieur* Oscar, zis dead one 'as a nice coat. Want me to take eet? 'E weel not need it anymore."

"Yes, do. We've had quite the string of good fortune on this venture," Oscar said. "I expect we'll need all the sealskins we can find."

Henry wiped his blade on Foster's pants. He stripped the dead man down to his Selkie suit with remarkable efficiency, and rolled Foster to his stomach with ease. Then he shoved his dagger into the neckline.

Lenny didn't look away from the spouting blood. *Even a cuke-head like him deserves betta than this.*

Henry shoved the dagger deeper, stopping the flow. He made a sawing motion, grunting with each back and forth, and worked the blade down Foster's backside.

Prayer cannot be wasted, huh? Lenny closed his eyes, and recalled the one he had heard his father mutter over the corpses of former slaves. *Go now, brotha. And swim Fiddla's Green. Don't dive below, to the depths unseen.*

He reopened his eyes. Foster remained dead. *Well, what'd ya expect?*

Smith seemed to have aged twenty years from the man who

threatened Lenny at the zoo. He leaned on Paulo for support as Henry did his work.

"Don't take his coat," Smith pled. *"Please.* He can't swim in Fiddler's Green without it."

"There's no such place," Oscar said. "Once you die, that's it, old chap."

Paulo's earrings flashed. *What should we do with him, boss?*

Ya know what Oscar's gonna do with him, said Lenny. *He'll be comin' with us. Just like the rest of 'em.* Lenny saw Oscar eyeing Kellen and knew his prediction was true.

"Are you an officer?" Oscar asked the teen.

"No, I-I was locked up. In the back."

"A prisoner! Ooh, I do like that," Oscar said. "On what charges, pray tell?"

"M-murder," Kellen said. "I k-killed a kid."

Lies. Lenny had grown up amidst murderers and thieves. The teen in front of him might have the makings of one, someday. He had the look.

Oscar let the barrel of his gun bounce up and down in a threatening way. "Tell me, how did you ever manage to escape your cell?"

Kellen nodded in Foster's direction, but he would not look at the body. "He let me out when we heard the gunshots...said he needed backup. That he'd let me go if I helped him."

Lenny's earrings flashed. *Kid's a quick study, huh, Paulie? Gotta give him that.*

Might not be a good thing.

Lenny surveyed his crewmates' faces. *It will be where he's goin'.*

Oscar dropped the gun to his side. "Out of the frying pan and into the fire then, eh, Kellen? You know...I could help free you—

if you're willing to hear my proposition, of course. Seeing as you did me a favor, why, it's only fair I should help you in return."

"I did?"

"Why yes! You distracted our dearly departed Selkie here," Oscar pointed at Foster. "Thus leaving our dangerous friend Miss Marisa Bourgeois alive and well."

Is she dangerous? Lenny weighed the assessment. She had escaped him twice now. And both times had the drop on him. Even now, he knew she could have attempted escape after Foster's murder. *She's dangerous.* He decided. *And something more. But what?*

"In fact," Oscar continued. "She is the very reason we're here. We're sort of like…officers of the law. She's escaped and we've come to bring her back. Those men we killed, they wanted to stop us. But you're missing my point. My friends and I…we can all transform into seals! Wouldn't you like to possess that sort of power?"

Lenny noted how Kellen's gaze seemed to linger on Henry's hood.

"You mean I-I could change too?"

"Oh, yes," Oscar said. "Come with us, Kellen, and I'll open your eyes to a new world of possibilities! You'll have a nice, new Selkie suit to swim the open ocean, and experience a life you never could here."

A slave life. And those open waters have a way of closin' in real fast.

"So I-I could change into a seal?" Kellen asked again, bolder this time.

"Of course," said Oscar. "And besides it's not much a choice, is it? I mean…we could let you go on your merry way of course. Oh, you will have one slight problem. We'll be off soon and with all these corpses left behind, why, I would assume it wouldn't take long before other authorities surmise who murdered these poor fellows. Given that their prisoner wanted for murder has fled, that is."

"But the dead guy," Kellen looked at Foster's body again and away just as quickly. "H-he said they were federal marshals."

"Lies, all lies," Oscar said. "Lenny, where is our dreaded Silkstealer?"

"Racer and Ellie took him and the Orc to the bus."

"Ugh. I'll be happy to bid that dreadful vehicle a fond farewell soon enough." Oscar turned back to Kellen. "Were there any other prisoners with you, by chance?"

"Our town drunk. He's—"

"Henry, collect Kellen's cellmate," Oscar said. "We'll meet you at the bus!"

Paulo's earrings flashed. *And we just enslaved two more Drybacks.*

Yeah. Lenny chewed his tongue until it bled. *Yeah we did.*

Henry finished his work, folded the bloody Sea Lion coat, and tucked it under his arm. He left Foster's naked body to rot.

Lenny wished he had something to cover it with.

"And you, my dear Marisa…" Oscar glowed, taking her by the arm. "So glad to meet you in person. I'm Oscar Col-"

"I know who you are," she said. "And what you want."

"Oh, but I want a lot of things, love."

"You want *one* thing," Marisa said.

Oscar leered at her. "Of course. And right now, that thing is you. Won't you—"

"I already told your manservant I would."

"Willing, eh?" Oscar said, his tone marked with surprise. "Marisa Bourgeois, the uncatchable runner, caught by Oscar Collins. Has a nice ring to it, wouldn't you agree?"

"Did you catch me?"

Lenny smirked. *I think this could be love, sweetheart.*

"You're here and I have you. That makes you mine," Oscar said. He motioned toward the front entrance. "Right this way, darling."

Oscar turned to lead her away. He came face-to-face with Smith.

Tears streamed down the father's cheeks, but not of sadness.

Lenny recognized them as hatred made liquid.

"You killed my Richie…"

"Yes, I'd thought we'd established that," Oscar said. "Paulo, escort him to the bus."

Paulo's earrings flashed. *Give me a reason to end all this, Len.*

Lenny's flashed back in reply. *Ya girlfriend's waitin' for us at the bus and ya Ma is back at Crayfish Cavern. They're dead, along with me and Pop, if we try to run and cock it up.*

"All right," Paulo said to Smith. "Come on."

Smith shrugged Paulo's hand away. He walked over to Foster, knelt to stroke his son's hair. With a gentle touch, he closed Foster's eyes. Then he bent forward and kissed his forehead. Smith stood, wiping his nose. He walked away without a second glance.

"Pathetic," Oscar said. He took Marisa by the arm and faced Kellen. "Well? Will you be joining us?"

"I have to decide now?"

"I'll tell you what, take a few moments, then join us at our bus across the street. Have your decision made by then. Deal?"

"O-okay…" Kellen said, his gaze falling on Foster's face again.

"There's the spirit!" Oscar said. His earrings flashed. *Lenny, no matter his decision, he comes with us.*

Because ya had me fooled. Lenny followed them out of the jail, his stomach churning. *I free a couple and he finds a few more to slave. Great plan, cuke-head.*

The temperature outside had risen with the thunderstorm. Still, Lenny thought the rain falling around him a comforting relief from the sweltering heat inside the jail. He watched Paulo lead Smith to the bus side and open the hatch.

Forgive me, Paulie...

The lights inside the hold flickered on, illuminating Ellie's prostrate body. A deathly mask of crimson streaked down her brow, yet the slow rise and fall of her great backside spoke that the true lifeblood remained in her.

"Ellie," Paulo screamed. "Who did this to you?"

I did. It should've been me layin' in blood and Ellie gone free with the rest.

"What in a blue hole is he on about?" Oscar asked.

Paulo abandoned Smith. He shoved up the bus steps, returned a moment later with a ring of keys. He climbed inside next to Ellie— a considerable chore for someone of his size—and feverishly worked at opening the locks.

Time to play my part.

Lenny rushed in. "Paulie! What's goin' on?"

"Look what they did to her..."

"Who?"

"Ellie!"

"What happened?" Lenny asked. "Is she all right? Is she dead?"

The last bit of iron fell off her. Paulo lifted Ellie gently, holding her head in the crook of his elbow. "Come back to me."

"Paulo," Ellie said weakly. "Paulo—"

He stroked her hair. "I'm here. Who did this to you?"

"I—I don't—"

"Who?" Paulo demanded.

Lenny heard a different hold door bang open.

"No…" Oscar said.

Then another.

"Lenny!" Oscar stormed to the hold three of his catchers shared. "Where are the others?"

"Huh?"

Oscar's face turned feral. "Where are they?"

Far from here I hope. Lenny climbed out of the hold. "Whattaya talkin' about Oscar?"

"Racer…" Ellie winced. "Racer…h-hit me…"

Paulo punched the bus side, denting it. "I'll kill him! I'll *kill* him!"

"You tell me where they've gone, Lenny," Oscar seethed. "You tell me right this instant."

"I dunno know what ya talkin' about. Both the Orc and the Silksteala are right here." Lenny pointed to both bodies.

Oscar stamped his foot. He slammed one of the empty hold doors. "The Orc is the most valuable! Why would they leave him behind?"

"How should I know?" Lenny shrugged. "I was inside with the rest of ya."

"You expect me to believe that this—this breakout just magically happened on its own?" Oscar paced back and forth. He stopped suddenly and turned back to the jail, hearing someone approach.

Henry hastened across the street. In his arms he carried the body of a slumped old man.

Oscar wheeled on Lenny. "This is your fault! And you're going to pay for it in blood!"

Lenny climbed out of the hold. "My fault? If I had been with 'em the whole time this wouldn't have happened! We'd already bagged the Orc and the Silksteala and were on our way out when ya called *me* to back ya up, rememba?"

Henry scanned the scene. He dropped his prisoner on the black-top, arriving at the conclusion of what had occurred far sooner than Oscar.

"Where 'eez she?"

"Who?"

Henry grabbed Lenny by the collar. *"Where 'eez she?"* his spittle flew in Lenny's face. "Where 'eez my Chidi?"

"I dunno!"

Paulo erupted out of the hold and tackled Henry. The two wres-tled for control.

Henry grabbed Paulo by the hair, pounded his skull into the ground. He only released him to unsheathe his dagger. Henry whipped the tip of the blade to Paulo's throat. "Where 'eez she, Lenny? Tell me or I cut 'is throat!"

"You'll do no such thing!" Oscar yelled. "Paulo is too value—"

"Shut up, leetle fool," Henry said.

Oscar's jaw dropped. "What did you call me?"

Henry never took his gaze off Lenny. "Where 'eez she?"

Lenny's face turned to ice. "Guess she turned runna. Which means every second ya stay here she gets furtha away."

Henry lifted his nose to the sky. He took a deep breath. "I weel find 'er Lenny. And after she tells me you 'elped 'er...zen I weel find you."

"Ya know where I'll be," Lenny said.

Henry took one more sniff of air. Like catching a scent, he ran for the police station.

"Henry! Where are you going?" Oscar called after him. "Henry!"

An engine revved and blue and red lights lit up the night sky. A police siren wailed. The stolen cruiser sped toward the highway.

Lenny watched Henry drive away with a sort of grim satisfaction. *Good luck, Cheeds.*

"*You!*" Oscar pointed at him. "You did this. I know it!"

"Ya think I'd put my skin on the line for a bunch of Drybacks and a pup?"

Paulo dabbed the blood from the back of Ellie's head. "No way. Lenny would never do that. Not for anyone."

"I'll bet you didn't believe Racer would ever do such a thing either," Oscar said. "Look where that landed your girlfriend!"

"Find him and put him in front of me," Paulo said. "See if I don't strangle him."

"Excellent," Oscar said. "It just so happens I agree. We'll follow Henry—"

"Ya think that's smart?" Lenny asked.

"What's that you Dolans say so often? You look after your own…" Oscar said. "It seems to me that Racer *nearly killed* one of your own. Wouldn't you like to have justice for that?"

"I would," Lenny agreed. "But they'll be time for that later. Ya forget what we got sleepin' down here? Hmm? Well, he's not gonna be sleepin' for long. Used up the last of the tranqs, rememba?"

"So that's why they left the Orc," Paulo said. "If he wakes up and realizes he can change—"

"He could rip the hold apart," Lenny finished.

"Oh, well, *bloody fantastic.*" Oscar pouted. "You're saying we either hunt them down and risk losing the Orc or we go home now?"

"Can't see any other way." Lenny ran his hands through his hair. "And we'll have to drive through the night to make it by mornin'."

Oscar cursed.

"It's not so bad," said Lenny. "Henry's after the others. We got Bourgeois and a couple more to boot. I think ya fatha's gonna be pretty happy."

"He might be, but I am not," Oscar leaned in close, whispering to Lenny. "I know you had something to do with this. And when I prove it…you'll pay."

"Whateva ya say, Oscar. Now can we get outta here before the Orc wakes up and we lose him too?"

"Yes," Oscar said. "And since you're so concerned about the Orc tearing the hold apart, let's show him the courtesy one of his kind should warrant. Paulo, unchain him. Ellie, can you walk yet?"

"Y-yes."

"Excellent," Oscar said. "Carry him aboard and lay him in my captain's quarters. Such a prize deserves better than being locked in a place we store common slaves. This way, he'll awaken on a soft bed to all the niceties I can provide him. After all, I want him happy before I gift him to my father. And when you've finished, I'll want a warm meal directly."

Ellie nodded. With Paulo's help, they unlocked Garrett and dragged him to the steps. Paulo carried Garrett. Ellie staggered behind him.

Lenny looked at Smith and the man Henry had dropped. "And whatta we doin' with Bourgeois and this lot?"

"Put them in the under, of course," Oscar said.

Smith's earrings flashed. *Don't worry about me running, Dolan. I know where this road leads. I won't go rogue…not till I avenge my son.*

Smith picked Kellen's unconscious cellmate off the ground and loaded him into the hold. He climbed inside and looked back at them. "You want to shackle me or not?"

There's a first, Lenny thought, unsure whether he should be impressed or wary. He walked over to shackle him in personally.

Smith's earrings flashed again. *See you in the Salt.*

Lenny removed Smith's earrings and pocketed them. Then he chained both men down and closed the first of the three hold doors.

"And now you, my lady," Oscar said to Marisa. "Will you go willingly to your cell?"

Marisa shrugged his arm away and walked toward the bus.

She could escape anytime she wants. Lenny thought as she entered the second cell, much too confident for his liking.

Marisa shackled her own legs and lay back, allowing him to ensure the bonds snapped closed. He bound her arms and neck with the iron fetters for extra measure.

Lenny climbed out and closed the hold door, locking it. He looked at the third, the one with the dead Dryback. "What do we do with him?"

"Leave it here for all I care," Oscar said, then entered the bus.

Lenny pulled the already rigid corpse out of the hold where it fell like a piece of lumber. He left the door open to air it out.

Paulo descended the steps. He saw what Lenny had done and came to close the door. "We really going to leave him here? Out in the open?"

"No," Lenny said. "Take him inside the jail. Use the side entrance and make sure to knock the handle off. Light a fire after ya drop him. Make sure it's big."

"A fire? That'll trigger an alarm and the firemen will—"

"They'll come and bring any other cops with 'em," Lenny explained. "Draws their focus here. The fire should keep 'em busy awhile and then they'll have to figure out how it all happened. All that time helps us get furtha away."

Paulo picked up the body and ran across the street.

Lenny watched him go. He reminded himself that he should be elated. He had fulfilled Oscar's wishes by successfully capturing Garrett Weaver *and* Marisa Bourgeois. Not to mention the rumored Silkstealer. Freedom awaited him upon their safe return.

Alone for once, Lenny closed his eyes and tilted his head back, letting the rain drizzle on his face to wash away his guilt. He stayed that way for a long while, refusing to open them until he heard footsteps running back across the street. *Whattaya doin' here, kid?*

"I've made my decision," said Kellen. "I'm coming with you."

Lenny glanced up at the tinted bus windows, wondering if Oscar had already seen Kellen. "Ya don't wanna do that. What ya should do is run. Get out—"

"And go where?" Kellen said. "Your buddy is right. Where am I going to go? If what Boone said was true, they're going to send me to prison for attempted murder."

"I dunno anything—"

"You think I should go back to my jail cell and wait for others to come?" Kellen asked. "What do I tell them happened? Hmm? Think they'll believe me that someone turned into a seal and killed Sheriff Hullinger? Or some kid shot Murphy? And what about the fire?"

Lenny looked across the street. The beginnings of smoke trickled out of the jail windows and doorways.

"Tell 'em whateva ya want." Lenny tried to keep his voice low so Oscar wouldn't hear. "This life isn't what ya think it is."

"It can't be worse than here," Kellen said.

"Things can always be worse," said Lenny.

Kellen shook his head. "My parents hate me. My mom abandoned me. And my dad...He wouldn't even talk to me on the phone."

"Well, boo-frickin'-hoo. We all got problems."

"Kellen!" Oscar stepped off the bus. "Made your decision, have you?"

"I think so. This place we're going...is it far away from here?"

Oscar grinned. "Leagues away."

"That's what I want."

"Wonderful." Oscar clapped Kellen on the shoulder and led him toward the front of the bus. He stopped just shy of the doorway and the third hold opening.

"Now. Before we go...I'll ask you one last time. You should be happy with your decision, after all. Are you certain in your want to come with us?"

"I want to go," Kellen said firmly.

"As you wish."

Oscar shoved him into the hold.

Kellen slid to the back on the remains of Ellie's blood. He clanged against the side.

Lenny saw him spin to look out the door, his blue eyes wide.

"No!"

I tried to warn ya.

Oscar slammed the door closed, locked it. He smoothed his hair back. "Did you hear that, Len? Kellen asked to be Salted!"

"Nobody smart asks to be Salted," Lenny said.

"Well, who ever accused slaves of being smart?" Oscar clapped his hands together, then stretched. "Ah. I do love this profession.

Right then, order Paulo to hustle along, won't you? I want to set off for home."

"Aye," said Lenny.

He didn't bother watching Oscar reboard.

A captain's gotta have all the answers, Lenny reflected on his father's teachings. Lenny didn't feel like he had any answers right now. As he stared at the closed hold doors, he wondered if anyone ever truly did.

We did the right thing, Ellie's voice echoed in his mind.

Lenny looked up at the bus windows. He couldn't see her through the tinted glass, but he felt her presence behind them, watching him.

You did the right thing, she said. *Your father will be proud.*

Lenny wished he had her certainty. His earrings flashed. *Pop's not gonna find out. No one can know what we did tonight.*

I know what you did. What you risked by doing it. Chidi, Racer... they know it too. Seven people escaped slavery tonight because of you.

Yeah, said Lenny. *And it only took slavin' six others to do it.*

I realize you Dolans aren't known for your optimism, said Ellie. *But try to think on the good things...at least one good thing.*

What's that?

There's a little girl somewhere in Chicago that will see her dad again because of you, said Ellie. *She'll never know Zymon was almost stolen from her forever. She won't have to grow up wondering why he never came back. She won't wonder if it was something she did wrong. Or what she would say or do if she had just one more chance to be in his arms again.*

Lenny turned away; not wishing Ellie to see her words moved him. He saw smoke seeping out the jail windows, and heard the side door clang open as Paulo exited. Lenny's earrings flashed. *Hustle up, Paulie. Gotta move out before more Drybacks get here.*

Lenny used the back of his hand to wipe away the last vestiges of tears as Paulo came near.

"Time to go home, boss?" Paulo asked.

"Yeah." Lenny cleared his throat. "Time to go home."

Paulo headed up the bus steps.

Lenny turned to follow. He watched Paulo take the driver's seat, heard him start up the engine.

Ellie stepped into the light at the top of the stairs. She had wrapped her head wound in a cloth bandage, but the bandage had not covered her earrings. They flashed. *Not everyone is as lucky as that little girl. Not everyone has a Dolan looking out for them.*

Lenny stepped aboard, felt the whoosh of the doors closing behind him.

Sometimes that has to be enough, Ellie finished.

And for at least that moment in Lenny Dolan's life, it was.

APPENDIX

SELKIES

LENNY DOLAN, slave catcher captain, *Ringed Seal,*
+ his crew:
  - ELLIE BRICEÑO, slave catcher brute, *Southern Elephant Seal,*
  - OSCAR COLLINS, heir to Crayfish Cavern, *Harp Seal,*
  - PAULO VARELA, slave catcher brute, *Southern Elephant Seal,*
  - RACER, slave catcher speedster, *California Sea Lion,*
+ his father:
  - DECLAN DOLAN, former slave catcher, *Ringed Seal,*
+ his owner:
  - AUGUST "CRAYFISH" COLLINS, slave trader and owner, *Harp Seal.*

HENRY BOUCHER, owner and freelance slave catcher, *Leopard Seal,*
+ his property:
  - CHIDI ETIENNE, linguist, *Ribbon Seal.*

MARISA BOURGEOIS, runaway slave, *Cape Fur Seal.*

ZYMON GORSKI, runaway slave, *Common Seal,*
+ his guardian:
  - WOTJEK, also known as THE LEPER, *Leopard Seal.*

LAVERE COUNTY RESIDENTS

GARRETT WEAVER, high school senior,
+ his mother:
  ▲ CRISTINA WEAVER, waitress at Gracin's Grille,
+ his friend:
  ▲ JOHNNY HICKEY, high school senior.

KELLEN WINSTEL, high school senior,
+ his friends:
  ▲ BRYCE TARDIFF, high school senior and swim teammate,
  ▲ EDDIE BENNETT, high school senior and fottball player,
  ▲ JUAN MARRERO, high school senior and wrestler,
+ his cellmate:
  ▲ BOONE MERCHANT, town drunk.

SYDNEY GAO, high school senior and friend of GARRETT WEAVER,
+ her family:
  ▲ Nattie Gao, dolphin trainer at the Indianapolis Zoo,
  ▲ Jun Gao, high school freshman and friend of KELLEN WINSTEL.

MS. MORGAN, Assistant Principal of Tiber High School

SHERIFF DICK HULLINGER
+ his staff:
  ▲ OFFICER CAMPBELL, former swim teammate of KELLEN WINSTEL,
  ▲ OFFICER MURPHY.

NON-RESIDENTS

ALLAMBEE OMONDI, Kenyan teenager and one-time ward of MARISA BOURGEOIS.

DAVID BRYANT, U.S. Marshal, rumored SILKSTEALER

ACKNOWLEDGEMENTS

I began this journey in early winter 2009. Even then my darling wife told me I should pour all my focus into writing this story rather than chase other pursuits. This book and the Salt universe would not exist were it not for her constant nudging. Love ya, K.

For my Little Miss, let this book be an example you can accomplish anything if you knuckle down, never give up, and listen to your mother.

To Annetta Ribken, the editing goddess come down from Olympus, you made my ramblings cohesive and understandable, went beyond the call of duty to guide a fellow wildling, and kept me in stitches all the way. If I have any success with *Salted*, much and more of that is due you.

For Gene, Jon, Sarah, Samantha, and my kid sister, Whit, thank you for being my first readers. Thank you also to Tyler and my Blue Box Betas for their invaluable insight.

Mike Corley, you proved every bit the legend I knew you would be. Thank you for the fantastic cover! Thanks also to Valerie Bellamy, the design wizard, who made me gasp when I saw her transformation of my work into an actual book. For Jennifer Wingard, whose love of the nautical world and attentiveness to detail I could not have done without.

For my parents, siblings, and the countless family and friends who have followed my crazy antics all this way, my thanks for your continued patience and support, or for faking it at least. I remain none the wiser if it's all been just an act.

To the indie authors who blazed this path ahead of me, my sincerest thanks for having the courage to write of your successes and, more importantly, missteps that we newcomers might benefit from your experiences.

And last but never least, to you, dear reader.

ABOUT THE AUTHOR

Aaron Galvin cut his chops writing and performing stand-up comedy routines at age thirteen. His early works paid off years later when he co-wrote and executive produced the award-winning indie feature film, *Wedding Bells & Shotgun Shells*. Aaron has since penned two YA series and a middle grade novel.

He is also an accomplished actor. Aaron has worked in everything from Hollywood blockbusters, (Christopher Nolan's *The Dark Knight*, and Clint Eastwood's *Flags of Our Fathers*), to starring in dozens of indie films and commercials.

Aaron is a native Hoosier and a graduate of Ball State University. He currently lives in Southern California with his family.

For more information, please visit his website:

www.aarongalvin.com

Now, here's a sample chapter of the next book in

AARON GALVIN'S

SALT SERIES

TAKEN WITH A
GRAIN OF SALT

the sequel to

SALTED

GARRETT

"HELLO?" GARRETT ASKED THE LINGERING DARKness. The scent of chlorine clouded his nose. He had a vague suspicion he knew this area well.

He reached around, felt the cool grooves of painted cinderblocks laid atop one another. He slid his hand up the wall face, but could not find its end. With naught else to guide him, Garrett walked forward. Each step put gingerly forward as if it might be his last.

An invisible, icy finger grazed down Garrett's backside as he fumbled in the darkness. Its touch hastened him to keep moving.

There's nothing there...nothing at all.

The finger would not be dismissed so easily. It former light touch now seemed to push him onward.

In minutes, his cinderblock guide changed into a smooth door. He glanced down. Saw a thin tracing of light where its base stopped an inch from the tiled floor.

A cold breeze flowed from beneath it.

Gaaaaarrrrrreeeettttt...the breeze whispered. Or was it the darkness behind him?

Garrett could not tell. He ripped the door open. Heat smacked him in the face. Garrett welcomed it, rather than the cold black he came from.

He stepped out the door, and recognized where he was.

The pool...I'm at school.

The still water seemed a crystal-clear mirror, dyed hazy green by the underwater lights embedded in the sides of the pool.

A bench creaked in the student bleachers above him.

Garrett jumped back. The locker room did not budge.

"H-hello?" his voice echoed throughout the empty room.

The darkness gave no reply.

Garrett tried the door again. *Who would lock me out? Why?*

He heard three padded steps behind him, then a splash.

Garrett whipped around.

The diving board bounced up and down so heavily it had left the rails. *THONK! THonk! Thonk! Thonk! Thonk!* It went, until finally settling.

Garrett saw expanding ringlets in the water. Something had disturbed its stillness.

Garrett could not help himself. He stepped forwards, stopping with a few feet to spare before reaching the pool's edge.

Something swam at the bottom. Its tan half halted. The gray swayed side-to-side.

Garrett stepped closer. His bare toes gripped the pool's tiled edge. He felt a sharp prick in his foot. A trickle of blood dripped into the ledge. A few drops fell into the pool.

Garrett watched his blood stain the water. *No...*He knelt and tried to scoop his defilement out with cupped hands.

"Wouldn't do that..." a raspy voice came from the pool.

Garrett glanced up.

A thick-bodied and bare-chested man bobbed in the middle of the pool. His unblinking, greenish-gold eyes leered at Garrett.

Garrett backed away from the edge. "Who are you?"

The man smirked. "Call me...*Ishmael.*"

"What are you doing here?"

"I'm the one who came to call," Ishmael mocked Wilda's southern voice. His face grew serious. "I'm here for *you*...to take you home."

Ishmael seemed to effortlessly glide towards Garrett, yet he did not use his arms to paddle and remained upright.

Garrett backed away as the stranger neared.

"Why do you flee?" Ishmael opened his palm to Garrett as he reached the pool's edge. "Don't you want to come home with me, Garrett?"

"Wh-where's home?"

"Oh, look at you! You're shivering." Ishmael said sympathetically. "You'll feel warmer if you jump in."

"No..." Garrett took another step back. "It will be colder in the water."

"*Will it?* Come with me," Ishmael insisted, motioning towards the middle of the pool. "I'll show you such things as you couldn't begin to dream about. You can bring anything you want. *Take* whatever you want."

"I-I don't know," Garrett stammered, backing away until he reached the locker-room door. He turned from Ishmael and fumbled with the handle, praying for it to open.

"Bring *anyone* you want..." Ishmael said quietly.

Garrett heard a giggle. He turned back to the pool. "Sydney?"

Like Ishmael, she seemed to bob effortlessly in the water. Her grey eyes beckoned him closer. "Garrett, come with us," she said. "Come with me...and we'll play."

Garrett took an unconscious step forward. "I want to, but...I-I don't know..."

"He doesn't want to come with me," Sydney pouted to Ishmael. "I told you he didn't want me."

Sydney sobbed.

Ishmael wrapped his arm around her. "You shouldn't deny a lady what she wants, Garrett," he said coldly. "Don't you desire her? Don't you wish to be with her?"

"Y-yes, but—"

"Then come with us."

"No," said Garrett. "This isn't real. It can't be real. I'm dreaming. You're just a dream."

"Am I?" Ishmael asked. His lips parted in a cruel smile, revealing pointed teeth. "Let's ask her..."

Ishmael brushed Sydney's hair aside and kissed her neck. He worked down to her shoulder, his eyes open and focused on Garrett. Ishmael stopped at Sydney's shoulder blade. He lifted his lips from her pale skin.

Then he bit her.

Sydney's body went rigid. Her arms flailed as she clawed for Ishmael's face, screaming.

"No!" Garrett howled. He ran towards the pool, yet halted at the edge.

Ishmael shook his head back and forth, ravaging Sydney's shoulder. Her blood gushed, streaked the water crimson as she writhed and convulsed beneath his bite.

"Please stop!" Garrett begged. "I'll come with you! Just don't hurt her anymore!"

Ishmael released his hold.

Sydney splashed into the water face first.

"You *will* come with me Garrett Weaver," said Ishmael. "One way or another."

"Yes! I'll come with you! I'll go with you, only please let her go!"

"No. You had your chance. Now I want both of you…" Ishmael looked past Garrett, up into the stands.

Garrett turned.

Someone sat in the student bleachers; their feet propped on the navy guardrail, their face cloaked in darkness.

"Take him," Ishmael commanded.

The figure leaned forward into the light. Poked his head through the rails.

"Kellen?" Garrett said. "What are you doing—"

"Take him!" Ishmael snarled.

Kellen stood robotically, his face blank. He turned away from Garrett, and walked towards the stairwell. Then he disappeared from view.

Garrett heard a faint *slap, slap, slap* followed by a swishing noise, like something dragging after each slap.

From around the corner, a seal with a black backside and a silvery, dark-spotted underbelly waddled onto the deck. The seal tilted its head quizzically at Garrett as if studying him.

Garrett heard a splash. He spun around.

Ishmael had vanished.

Sydney's lifeless body remained—floating face down in the middle of the pool. The water had become unclear and choppy, splashing over the edge. The tip of a triangular fin broke from the water near her face, its sharp edge pronounced high above the surface. The fin circled her.

"Sydney!" Garrett cried out.

Come in, come in, Ishmael's voice echoed in Garrett's mind. *In where it's nice and warm.*

The fin bumped into Sydney, rolling her onto her back. Her eyes fluttered open. She coughed.

"Sydney!"

Sydney sat up in the water upon hearing her name called. "Wha—Garrett...what happened?" she asked.

The fin passed in front of her.

Sydney gasped. "Garrett! *Help* me!"

You will come with me, Garrett Weaver, Ishmael promised. *One way or another.*

The fin nudged Sydney, prompted her to scream again. "Help me!"

Garrett stared into the red water. His body shook. "I-I can't..."

You can, said Ishmael. *Come into the water.*

Garrett would not. "Please," he cried. "I can't...I can't..."

Very well. Take him, seadog.

A low growl came from behind Garrett. He turned and saw the snarling, open mouth of the seal before it lunged at him. The seal's weight easily toppled Garrett into the pool.

Ishmael's dark laughter invaded his mind.

He lied, Garrett thought as the cold encased him. His breath caught in his throat. He felt a nip at his feet as the seal hooked its teeth around Garrett's belt loop and dragged him downwards. Down, down, down, Garrett went, his mind ticking off the marks numbering the pool depth.

Five feet…eight…ten…twelve…twelving!

Garrett looked upwards. He saw only darkness above and the greenish haze below.

The seal entered his halo of light. It watched him with sad black eyes.

I'm drowning. Garrett closed his eyes.

You're not, said a grandfatherly voice.

Garrett opened his eyes. Saw no one. Not even the seal. *Who said that?*

Me.

You sound…

Ancient? The voice chuckled. *I like your voice too, young one, though in truth you're still finding it. Do not trouble yourself with Ishmael for now. A liar he may be, but the water is warm…isn't it?*

Garrett felt sudden warmth in his toes that crawled up his body. He ceased fearing the water. His brain no longer panicked. And the water did feel warmer. *What's happening to me?*

Open your eyes, said the voice.

Garrett obeyed.

The stain of red no longer tainted the water. He saw no darkness here. No boundaries in this overpowering watery world. No edges for him to cling to. Garrett saw only an endless sea of blue, beckoning him to explore and revel in it.

Is this heaven?

This is your home, the voice said.

Garrett searched for the voice's source. He could not locate it.

Are you ready to come back?

Yes, Garrett thought. He slowly ascended towards the surface. *Are you the one Wilda spoke of?*

I am, the voice said, already fading. *Remember the wonder you felt when first meeting her—*

The water felt warmer the faster Garrett rose. The light brightened.

Cast away your fear of the scorned ones—

Garrett closed in on the surface. *Twelve...ten...eight...*

Keep the memories of those you love safe within you.

Six...four...

Follow the one who turns his heart to stone, the voice said, barely above a whisper. *Help him to see—*

Four...two...one...

And follow your heart home.

Garrett opened his eyes.